D0464735

KINGDOM

OF

ICE & BONE

Criswell, Jill,
Kingdom of ice & bone/
2020.
33305249021282
cu   09/23/20

KINGDOM

OF

ICE & BONE

JILL CRISWELL

**BLACK
STONE**
PUBLISHING

Copyright © 2020 by Jill Criswell
Published in 2020 by Blackstone Publishing
Cover and book design by K. Jones
Map illustration by Amy Craig

All rights reserved. This book or any portion
thereof may not be reproduced or used in any manner
whatsoever without the express written permission
of the publisher except for the use of brief quotations
in a book review.

The characters and events in this book are fictitious.
Any similarity to real persons, living or dead, is coincidental
and not intended by the author.

Printed in the United States of America

First edition: 2020
ISBN 978-1-982556-28-0
Young Adult Fiction / Fantasy / General

1 3 5 7 9 10 8 6 4 2

CIP data for this book is available
from the Library of Congress

Blackstone Publishing
31 Mistletoe Rd.
Ashland, OR 97520

www.BlackstonePublishing.com

For Katla Sahara, who is a force of nature

Upon her death, blessed Aillira found no peace,
for her soul was condemned to the bowels of the Halls of Suffering,
where the god of death reigned.
In rage and envy, Gwylor did rend Aillira's soul
and thus did the serpent-goddess, the eater of souls, devour the pieces.
From his black prison, Veronis screamed for his beloved,
the sound swallowed by the infinite dark.

—The Forbidden Scriptures

PART ONE
CLAN OF THE FORSAKEN

PROLOGUE

The grass was mossy and green beneath his boots, the air smelling of soil and rain. With the spring snows mostly melted, the vast lava field teemed with life. He crept with his brother through the sprawling maze of rock, so tall he couldn't see over the top. Silently, they watched and listened for signs of game hiding among the crevices.

A rustle made them both turn their heads. His brother raised his bow, following the sound until the hare appeared. The boy let the arrow fly and it sailed through the air, piercing the creature through its neck. "Did you see that, Aldrik?"

"That shot was beneath you," Aldrik said. "You could have struck it in the head."

Reyker's face fell. It was easy to diminish the boy, to make him question his abilities. Aldrik knew it was cruel, but someone had to push him. Katrin, the boy's mother, was far too soft on him, and their father let Reyker think too highly of his small accomplishments. Reyker's other weakness—his desperate desire to please his older brother, to make him proud—was a whetstone Aldrik used to sharpen the boy's focus, to hone his strength like a blade.

"Let's find another, then," Reyker said, retrieving his arrow and picking up the hare by its hind legs. "I'll strike the next one straight through the eye."

As they made their way between two long sections of rock that rose up like a tunnel from the earth, a new sound came from behind them—the crunch of feet on the ground, the shuffle of bodies. The noises of something stalking closer, but these were boots, not the paws or hooves of game.

Aldrik drew his sword. "Announce yourselves or be slain!"

Laughter answered. Above the rock wall he saw the telltale flash of steel. "We are the wolves at your door, lordlings," a booming voice said. "It is you who shall be slain."

"Aldrik?" Reyker whispered. "Who are they?"

"Enemies." Aldrik and Reyker's father was lord of the lands of Vaknavangur, and he served Jarl Gudmund, a powerful overlord who claimed to be a child of All-God Sjaf's loins rather than simply one of the god's many distant descendants. Vaknavangur was surrounded by tribes who disputed Gudmund's claim as king of the Streamlands. "Your sword, Reyker. Now."

The boy drew his sword with trembling hands.

Aldrik grabbed his arm and shook him. "You are a rival lord's son. They won't hesitate to gut you. Remember your training. Kill them before they kill you. No mercy."

"No mercy." The boy steadied his hands on the hilt.

Eight armed men clambered over the rocks and leaped down, circling them. One was huge with a misshapen nose—a brawny ogre.

"Your father was warned to stay out of Jarl Eldjarn's affairs," the ogre said. "Yet he sent men to aid the campaign against Eldjarn on behalf of Gudmund the Pretender. He should've listened. Perhaps he finally will, when we send him his sons' heads."

The warriors closed in on Aldrik.

Aldrik sliced his sword through three of them before the men had even begun to swing their weapons. But the ogre was faster than the others, and Aldrik had to duck under the arc the hulking man's axe made.

"I've got the snake-eyed bastard," the ogre said to his comrades. "Get the boy."

Three warriors stepped toward Reyker, and something fluttered in Aldrik's chest, a rancid taste rising from his belly. *Is this what fear feels like?* He ignored it, bringing his sword up to meet the ogre's axe. The blow sent vibrations up his arm. The axe's blade hovered just above his head.

"Is it true your harlot mother was a *volva*?" the ogre asked. "Is that why you have eyes like a demon?"

"True enough." Aldrik smiled. These men had no idea the danger they'd walked into, the secret strength he possessed because of his witch mother. Aldrik shoved, and the giant stumbled into the wall of rock behind him.

Aldrik glanced at Reyker. The boy had blocked the strike of one warrior's axe, but he was merely defending himself. He did not take the opening the man left, did not let loose the killing blow Aldrik knew he was capable of delivering.

"Fight, Reyker! Kill them!"

The boy did not listen.

The ogre launched himself at Aldrik once more, and their weapons locked. "After I gut you, I'm going to eat your demon heart and gain your half-breed powers. Then I'll send the rest of you to Ildja in pieces."

Aldrik dropped his guard, baiting his opponent, and the ogre rushed forward, crashing his axe into Aldrik's stomach. Pain shot through his nerves, and it was a struggle to stay on his feet. The ogre came closer, grinning. "You've overlooked one thing," Aldrik said.

The pain was worth it for the look on the ogre's face as he watched the bleeding hole in Aldrik's belly close, the skin knitting itself back together.

"My mother was blessed by Ildja. As was I."

Aldrik thrust his sword below the ogre's ribs and sliced sideways, eviscerating him. The ogre hit his knees, holding his intestines as they spilled out into his hands.

"No witch's mutt, are you?" the ogre mumbled—his dying words, as he toppled sideways into a puddle of blood.

Aldrik made quick work of cutting down two of the warriors who'd gone after Reyker. The third—who wore a torque of braided gold that marked him as a keeper of the god shrines, a warrior priest who killed only in the name of the gods—had dropped his sword and backed away.

Aldrik kept an eye on the priest as he grabbed Reyker and searched his wounds, ensuring none were life-threatening. Then he shook the boy so hard his teeth clacked together. "Why didn't you kill them?"

"I couldn't," the boy said. "I couldn't."

"Gud-mund," the priest gasped, staring at Aldrik. "You are the god-man I've heard whispers about, not your overlord. Only flesh born of the serpent-goddess herself can evade death."

A beat of silence passed before Aldrik scoffed. "There is no god-man, you fool. That's a yarn spun by weak jarls desperately clinging to power they did not earn."

The priest kneeled. "I've witnessed it with my own eyes. You are the one we have searched for. I pledge my fealty to you, son of Ildja."

Something shifted inside of Aldrik, tumblers sliding gears into place, unlocking a door he didn't want to open.

It wasn't true. It couldn't be true.

He'd heard the prophecies of a god-man, progeny of Ildja, the eater of souls. But he was not that man. He had a mother, a *volva* from one of the covens in the Haunted Isles. She had died giving birth to him—that was what his father had told him.

The priest kept babbling. "All my life, I've waited for a child of the gods to exalt our nation, to conquer the world in the name of the Ice Gods. You are meant to lead us."

To lead Iseneld into war. To become a plague upon the earth. To thirst for bloodshed and hunger for power, bring the world to its knees. That was what the prophecy said of the god-man.

Aldrik had never been a good person—goodness was arbitrary, and too often used as a kinder label for weakness—but neither had he strove to be a villain.

"I'm not a monster," Aldrik said. He'd been saying it to the villagers of Vaknavangur since his father brought him there, screaming it at anyone who stared too long at his eyes or called him cursed beneath their breath. But to them, he would always be Lord Lagor's witch-born, serpent-eyed bastard. A stain on the lord's reputation.

A foil to Lagor's trueborn son, the golden-haired, blue-eyed heir. A boy who smiled freely, fought honorably, offered to help anyone who needed it. A gods-damned storybook hero shaped into flesh.

Innocent.

Breakable.

"You will free us," the warrior priest said. "You will reign supreme."

The priest needed to be silenced. For some reason, Aldrik could not lift his sword. His mind and body were numb. *I'm not a monster.*

"Reyker," Aldrik rasped. "Kill him."

The boy stood frozen, his sword still raised. "Aldrik? He's not a threat."

"Please," the priest said, dropping his axe at Aldrik's feet, raising his arms in supplication. "Allow me to serve you, god-man."

"I cannot listen to this!" Aldrik pressed his hands to his ears. He had killed many men in the eighteen years he'd been alive, would gladly kill many more, but an unarmed priest worshipping him? "Reyker, he's lying. And he'll go on telling his lie, and others will listen. I'll be hunted. Do this for me. You must."

Reyker's hands began to shake again. "Are you certain he's lying?"

No. Aldrik wasn't certain of anything anymore. "We can't let him go. He'll tell people what he saw. The overlords will find out. They'll come for me. Or Father will send me away. Do you want me to go away?"

Reyker shook his head. "But, Aldrik—"

"You must protect your family. You must protect me. Help me, brother." Aldrik's voice cracked on the last word, one he so rarely spoke. He'd never been a good brother—Aldrik had purposely broken Reyker's toys; pursued every girl of age who the boy held childish fantasies of courting; scolded Reyker, barked at him like a warlord, the way their father had always treated Aldrik—but that word, that label of their bond in blood, was something Reyker treasured. It was attention, validation.

Manipulation.

"Why would you hide, god-man?" the warrior priest asked. "You will be celebrated as our savior. We will announce your existence to all of Isen—"

Reyker's pupils swelled to black circles, engulfing the blue of his irises. With brutal efficiency no earthly boy possessed, Reyker drove his sword through the priest's chest.

Aldrik released a breath—a gasp, a sigh—as he watched the priest's blood spill across the earth. Reyker was weak when it came to those he cared for, and the boy had done for Aldrik what he would not do for himself. Just as Aldrik had predicted.

Until that very moment, Aldrik hadn't known that his brother was god-touched. No wonder the boy was so nauseatingly noble. It was a thing Aldrik would remember, a thing he could use again.

I will break you, Reyker, Aldrik thought, *so no one else can.*

The blackness of Reyker's pupils receded and the boy's eyes widened in horror, as if his body had acted without his mind's permission. The priest slumped forward, and Reyker's sword went with him.

"I am damned," Reyker said as he pulled his sword free.

Aldrik put a hand on his brother's shoulder. "Now you are a man."

It was Reyker's first kill. The boy was only nine, years younger than Aldrik had been when he'd taken his first life. Reyker swiped at his eyes and stared silently at the dead priest, all emotion leaching from his face. The boy was as blank and pale as a slab of marble.

He did not speak the entire walk back to the village.

When they returned, late and spattered with blood, their father was waiting. He rushed to his younger son, but Reyker would not answer him, would not even look at him. The boy stared off at some distant point, as if he could see something the rest of them could not. Their father's fear turned to suspicion. "What did you do, Aldrik?"

Lagor, lord of Vaknavangur, was a man whose presence demanded respect. He was tall and muscular, handsome according to the whispers of the village women. An honest and fair lord, though one you did not want to cross, according to the men. To Aldrik, he'd always felt like a stranger. Indeed, Lagor had been a stranger that day when he appeared in the Haunted Isles—looking wary and not at all like it was his own choice—and took five-year-old Aldrik away from the coven that had raised him since he was born. His mother's coven. Or so he'd thought.

"What did *you* do, Father?" Aldrik asked. "Did you lie to me about my mother? Have you been lying to me since I was a boy?"

Katrin ran from the house, wrapping her arms around Reyker. Even at his mother's pleas, the boy would not wake from his stupor.

"Tell him, Lagor," Katrin said, looking at her husband, then at Aldrik. She had always been kinder to him than his own father, but she had never quite accepted him. She did not approve of the influence Lagor's bastard held over her son. "Aldrik deserves to know what he is."

What. Not who.

Aldrik glared at them, his father and the woman who'd been the closest thing to a mother he'd known after he was taken from the *volvur's* island—his family, though they'd never treated him as such. After Katrin ushered Reyker into the cottage, Aldrik turned on Lagor. "Ildja is my mother. I am the child of the serpent goddess."

He knew it was true as he said it aloud.

Lagor bowed his head. "Ildja came to me after a battle between rival jarls in the Highlands. We must have displeased the goddess because she rained fire down on all of us. Every man fell. I was badly burned, but I stayed on my feet with my sword out, calling her name. When Ildja appeared, I thought I was dead. But she took me to her home and healed me. She kept me there, and we had a brief affair before I returned to Vaknavangur. My time with her felt like a fever dream and I dismissed it. Then she came to me again years later and told me about you. She told me where to find you, so I brought you home."

The seething hate that had roiled inside Aldrik as long as he could remember flared. The feeling that he was not like anyone else in his family, his village, his country, had isolated him, made him question his sanity. This knowledge of his true origins could have granted Aldrik peace, or at least acceptance of his own peculiarities, yet his father had kept it secret, allowing Aldrik to suffer.

"This is not my home," Aldrik said. "It never was."

"It could've been." Lagor regarded Aldrik with his stony gaze. "But there's too much of her in you. Even as a boy, you were quick to anger. You hurt the other children when they only wanted to play. You hurt your brother."

Aldrik hadn't understood his own strength at first, and even after he did, he hadn't always held back. He'd sent the other village boys home with bruises and broken bones, his brother included. Some were accidents. Some were not. He should have been repentant for the harm he'd caused.

He wasn't. "Poor Reyker. Wouldn't want your precious heir to be damaged."

Lagor stood up straighter, shifting his body in front of the cottage door. "Reyker has always been loyal to you. No matter what you've done to him, he has always loved you."

Aldrik's hands squeezed into fists. "Curse his loyalty. Curse his love. I don't need him, or any of you. Where do I find my mother?"

"She lives in the belly of the Mountain of Fire, in the center of Iseneld."

Aldrik headed for the stables.

He was on the outskirts of his father's lands when he heard another horse coming up fast behind him. Aldrik didn't glance back, but he let his horse slow to a canter.

Reyker's mount, already lathered and spent, pulled abreast of Aldrik's. The boy hadn't stopped to saddle his horse or even to pull on a coat. "Father told me you are leaving to join Gudmund's army," Reyker said. "I want to come with you."

"No." Aldrik saw no point in correcting his father's lie. "Go home."

"Don't leave, Aldrik. Not without me."

It hit Aldrik again, that feeling he'd had when the warriors had attacked Reyker—a gut-deep revulsion at the thought of the boy coming to harm by any hand besides his own. Lagor was right. Reyker was the only one who had ever looked past Aldrik's unearthly eyes and cold demeanor and saw someone worth admiring. Some part of Aldrik enjoyed the boy's admiration.

No more.

"What use is a sniveling brat in a war between men? You are worse than useless. You are a liability. A cursed priest killer. Why would I take you along?"

Reyker jerked back like a chastened dog. "Because I—I killed him for you. Because we are brothers."

"In name only." A dog. That was what Reyker looked like—a beaten pup, begging its abusive master for attention. "There is no place in my world for weak little lordlings. You are nothing to me."

Aldrik kicked his horse hard and it surged ahead, leaving Vaknavangur in its dust. He was bound for the bright fire that burned in the heart of the island, for a mother who would welcome him and make him the strongest warrior alive, a destiny greater than he'd ever dreamed.

Maybe the prophecy was wrong. Maybe he could become a legend and lead his country without transforming into a monster. And if he could not, well . . . being a monster was a small price to pay for glory, for kinfolk who shared his blood and his mien and didn't expect virtue where there was none.

He did not look back, but he felt Reyker's eyes on him, watching him until he was out of sight.

CHAPTER 1

LIRA

"I love you."

It was a whisper, a breath, caressing my skin like a breeze. The whisper became a kiss. I closed my eyes and leaned into it, into him, his chest pressing against my spine, his arms encircling me. His mouth started at my ear, wandering leisurely down my neck.

I sighed, my bones turning to liquid. "Do you think you'll ever get tired of saying it?"

"Perhaps in a thousand years." He took hold of my chin, turning my head so he could reach my lips with his own. They were warm and soft.

For a moment, I'd thought they might be cold. I wasn't sure why.

I pulled back. "I don't think I'll ever get tired of hearing it."

"Then I'll say it a thousand more times." And he did, his voice deep and quiet, like a placid river meandering through a canyon. He undressed me slowly, trailing kisses up and down my body, repeating those three lovely words in both our languages.

Then it was my turn to undress him, to pour those words over every inch of him, to unleash that promise of devotion into the wind, where it would be carried across the world. The next time I said it, for perhaps the thousandth time, he pulled me against him, his fingers tangling in my hair as mine dug into his back. He said the words with me—a breathless moan that became a roar, and he followed it with my name, a battle cry telling all who heard it how we belonged to each other, that nothing could come between us.

It was a dire warning to any who dared try.

We lay beside each other on a bed of clovers, and I hummed a tune under my breath—an old sea ballad. His body was a warm mass of muscle and flesh. Solid. Unwavering. His chest rose and fell beneath my cheek with each breath he took.

Because he *was* breathing—his lungs filling with air, not water.

No, he did not drown. That's what happened to the woman's lover in the sea ballad, when his ship sank in a storm. That man was not Reyker.

I was getting confused. I stopped humming.

We'd been talking for hours, sharing stories about our families, our childhoods. Confessing our deepest hopes and fears and desires. No matter how much of ourselves we bared, no matter how much I learned about him, I always wanted more.

"What will you do when you go back to Iseneld?" I did not add *after you kill Draki*, but it hung in the air between us, regardless. Above us crimson branches stretched out like gnarled arms. Aillira's thorntree, the one she'd planted in honor of Veronis. It seemed to be watching us, listening to every word.

Reyker smiled sadly, staring into the distance. "I want to go back to Vaknavangur." The village where he was born. The village Reyker would have become lord over had Draki not destroyed it, executing every last man. "To rebuild and restore it to what it once was. To find the survivors who were forced to flee and help them return to their own lands. They deserve to have a true home. I want to give that to them. I want to look after my people, to be the kind of leader my parents believed I could be. After everything I've seen, and done, and survived . . . it can't all have been for nothing. I must be alive for a reason. I have to do something that matters."

My mind snagged on the word *alive*.

Yes, Reyker was alive. How could he not be?

"My kindhearted wolf." I took his hand, trailing his fingers over the flame-shaped scar on my wrist, relishing the familiar tingle it sent through the mark.

"My brave deer." He brought my hand to his lips, placing a kiss on the *skoldar*. "If I did rebuild Vaknavangur, would you come with me?"

"For how long?"

"Forever. Or as long as you'll have me. I know it's a lot to ask of you—to leave your island, your home."

A flood of heat spread through me. Reyker had chosen me, not just as a lover, but as the person he wanted to share his life with. I could have pressed my palm to his chest to peer into his soul, so familiar to me now, but I worried over what I might find. What if it was shredded? What if it was empty?

Why would I think such things?

I looked back at him. He was still waiting for my answer. "I'll come with you if you promise every day will be like this one."

He plucked a handful of moonflowers from the cluster surrounding the thorntree's trunk. "Every day, I will give you whatever your heart desires." He tore the blooms from the moonflowers and shook a spray of petals from his fist so they drifted over me. "I'll shower you with roses."

"You know those aren't roses."

"*Shh.* Don't ruin it." He dumped the rest of the petals in my face. "I'll stay up each night writing odes to commemorate your overwhelming beauty and sharp wit, and I'll serenade you with them as you wake each morning."

"If you're going to serenade me, I'm definitely not going." I shook the petals off and put my hands over my ears. "Your singing sounds like a sick gull."

"It sounds like a drunken gull. There's a difference."

"Both squawk like they're trying to make the sky fall."

"Yes, but at least the drunken gull is enjoying himself." He pulled me against him. "Fine. No singing. How about I stay up each night making *you* sing." His teeth grazed the curve where my neck and shoulder met.

I ran my hands across his chest, down his stomach, brushing my fingertips against the sliver of skin just above where he most wanted my hands to be, smiling as his body tensed, as his pulse galloped.

His pulse. It was beating—not silent, not static.

A strange thought to have.

"What's wrong?" he asked.

"Nothing. It's just . . . You're right here with me, but it feels like you're far away." I noticed the tightness in his jaw, the downward curl of his mouth. "You feel it, too, don't you? That something's wrong."

"I *am* right here," he said, lacing our fingers together. "I told you, I will never let anything take you away from me."

"But what if you can't stop it?" And then another worry crept over me, one I dared not voice: *What if it's already happened?*

"I was dead before I met you," he said.

Dead. The word was like a blade sliding into my chest. No—not my chest. His. I closed my eyes and saw a gleaming scythe, a gush of blood.

My eyes snapped open. "Don't say that."

"It's true." He pressed our joined hands against his thundering heart. "The man who washed up on that beach in Stony Harbor was a corpse. But you found me. You brought me back to life. I am yours, Lira, and nothing will keep me from you—not oceans, or time, or the gods themselves."

A breeze drifted across the valley, tousling our hair, scattering the moonflower petals, and making the thorntree's branches creak. Beyond the branches, the sky overhead was an endless, perfect blue.

Too perfect. Colors only looked like this inside souls.

Or dreams.

I sat up with a start. "Is this real?"

"It is. It must be." Reyker sounded as panicked as I felt.

Of course this was real. Why wouldn't it be? What was the nagging fear, digging like thorns into the back of my mind, that something irrevocable had occurred? That everything was already broken?

"Reyker," I whispered.

His name echoed across the valley, bouncing off the stone ruins, turning into a terrified scream. A grief-stricken sob.

A memory.

He froze, his eyes widening. "Lira?"

My name became a ripple of sound, stretching into an anguished cry.

We stared at each other.

In the distance, a rumble shook the earth. Around us, the valley began to crack apart. The ruins dissolved into the ether.

Understanding swept over us. The cold cruelty of it left me shivering.

"No." I clung to him, as if I could hold on tight enough to keep him from being torn away. He did the same, and I knew then that the dream was not a fantasy. This *was* Reyker. I'd found him somehow, in the other-worlds. Or he had found me.

But it could not last.

The ground shuddered. A howling wind ripped at us. The moonflower petals eddied around us like a ghostly whirlwind until they were sucked out into the growing void.

"I love you," he whispered fiercely, his forehead pressed to mine. There was sorrow in his gaze, but not a trace of doubt as he said, "No matter what it takes, no matter where you go, I will find you again."

A moment later, my arms were empty, holding on to nothing.

CHAPTER 2

LIRA

I woke with a gasp, tangled in my blanket, cold sweat trickling down my neck, the smooth walls of a cave surrounding me. The floor was crowded with pallets, each one topped with the sleeping bodies of nomads. A few paces away, my brother grunted in his sleep, one arm slung across his face, the other resting on the hilt of his short sword.

Truth seeped in slowly. Painfully.

I am in the Green Desert with Garreth.

Stony Harbor has fallen.

Reyker is dead.

Pushing past the ache in my chest, I reached for my sword. Beside it were two large rats, watching me with glassy eyes.

This had been happening more and more often—animals being drawn to me, sensing the blood of Veronis, the god of all creatures, inside me. "Get away," I hissed, shooing the rodents.

Strapping on my sword, I crossed the cave on quiet feet. As I passed the nomad guards standing outside the cave's entrance, they edged back. They knew what I was. A soul-reader, a Daughter of Aillira. And now the vessel of the Fallen Ones—the girl who carried the blood of imprisoned gods in her veins.

Outside, the sky was black and clouded, hiding every star. I trudged up the grassy knoll that concealed part of the cave—the nomads' temporary base as Garreth and Zabelle debated what to do next, where to go now that Ghost Village had been destroyed—and stared at the rolling hills stretching as far as I could see in every direction.

Should I take Wraith and leave again? Or would Garreth ride after me as he had before, threatening and begging until I returned with him?

It had been a week since Stony Harbor was invaded. Since Draki chased me through the forest and I'd leaped from the northern bluffs rather than become his captive. I was only alive because a vengeful god had willed it, thinking I could free him.

I held my hand out, staring at the veins crisscrossing beneath my skin. I could hear the scrape of blood pushing through my body. I could *taste* it—the tang of earth and iron mixed with something ancient, like tendrils of an ageless sentience on my tongue. If I closed my eyes and concentrated, I could hear the rustle of a blade of grass a half league away, taste the dew collecting on its edges. I heard my brother snoring in the cave below, tasted the leather and steel of the armor he wore even while he slept.

I didn't know what sort of power now resided in me. There was my heightened senses. And the trail of rats and birds that often followed me, the impression that I was connected to every creature in Glasnith. But beyond that? I had no way of knowing. Veronis had not spoken inside my head since telling me to sing underwater so the Brine Beasts would come, though I'd been listening for his voice, waiting.

Patience had never been a strength of mine. It was why I'd stolen off last night, heading for Stony Harbor. To search for Ishleen. To help any survivors escape.

To kill Draki.

I'd not realized how foolish my plan was until Garreth caught me and talked me out of it. But that didn't mean I wouldn't try again. The alternative was endless, useless waiting. And thinking. And dreaming.

Of Reyker.

Though she moved with stealth, I heard Zabelle coming long before I saw her walking nimbly up the hill. She sat down next to me, stretching her legs out in front of her.

"I don't need a keeper, Zabelle."

"I am not offering." She pulled a flask from her long coat and drank deeply, then held it out to me. "I have enough trouble looking after my own people."

Accepting the flask, I took a swig to match Zabelle's and instantly regretted it. The foul liquid tasted like sulfur and burned going down. I wiped my whiskey-numbed lips on my sleeve. Zabelle's sleeve, actually; she'd lent me some of her clothing—trousers that were so long I had to roll the cuffs up, a flowing tunic that I cinched at the waist with a belt, and soft hunting boots. The wardrobe suited me well enough that I'd sworn off dresses indefinitely.

"Let me tell you a story," Zabelle said. "When I was a small girl living with my mother in an Aukian brothel, she used to send me out to beg on the streets while she worked. I was so ashamed of her for being a whore, ashamed of myself for being a beggar and a whore's daughter. But when I told her so, Mama would say this to me: 'In this life, we cannot control what gifts we are given. We can only use them as best we can. So keep your head bowed and your hands open, and no matter what someone gives, smile at them like you are grateful, because even the smallest bit of coin puts bread in our bellies so we may survive one more day.'"

My life had not been easy, but I sometimes forgot how privileged it had been compared to others. "You're telling me to appreciate everything I have—my brother, my abilities, being alive when so many are dead—and do the best I can with those gifts."

"I am telling you to be glad you are not a starving beggar living in an Aukian brothel."

A laugh burst from my chest. How long had it been since I'd laughed? Zabelle laughed with me, and we passed the flask back and forth once more.

"I'm sorry about Mago," I said. "He seemed like a good man." The exiled mercenary had been captured by Dragonmen and flayed alive by a Daughter of Aillira with a gift for torture.

"He was," Zabelle agreed, her expression softening. "He would be grateful to you for getting Eathalin away from those monsters. We are all grateful."

"Don't be. Not until we find her." When I'd last seen Eathalin—

another Daughter of Aillira, a gifted spell-caster—she'd been boarding a boat bound for Selkie's Quay. I wasn't sure if she'd made it. Garreth had sent scouts to find out, but they had yet to return.

"We will. Nomads don't abandon our people." There was weight to her words, an unspoken invitation. I wasn't a nomad, but I could be. Like Garreth, I could join a new clan to replace the one I'd lost.

"Garreth assumes I'll stay with him, but I'm not sure I belong with the nomads. I don't even know who I am anymore. All I know is I want vengeance for my clan." On my backstabbing uncle. On the tyrant warlord.

"When I feel as you do," Zabelle said, "I find that whiskey helps. So does a good fight. Or seducing a spirited man or woman into my bed."

The thought of someone other than Reyker in my bed—someone else's hands on me, someone else's mouth on mine—made me ill. "Is that what Garreth is to you?" I asked.

Zabelle's eyes narrowed. She started to say something, but I shushed her as sounds drifted toward me from across the hills. Clomping. Wheezing. A horse and its rider, a league or so away. I tasted the salt of sweat, the tang of iron. Blood. There was something familiar to it. I knew this person.

"Someone's coming." I was already on my feet, hurrying to where the nomads' horses had been corralled, Zabelle following close behind.

"Friend or enemy?" She didn't ask how I knew, simply accepting that I did.

"I can't tell until we get closer." The horses had all turned, every pair of dark eyes trained on me. There was a bubbling in my blood, a spike of energy. The herd moved aside as Wraith trod through their midst and stopped in front of me, waiting, as if I'd called aloud to him.

We mounted our horses and led them to the cave's mouth so Zabelle could warn the guards. "Should we wake the prince?" one of them asked.

I answered before Zabelle could, shaking my head. "Let him sleep."

With nothing but a thought from me, Wraith headed into the hills. Zabelle's horse caught up quickly. "Garreth will be angry," Zabelle said.

"I don't need my brother hovering about everywhere I go. Besides, you and I can handle whoever is out there." I flashed her a grin. "Perhaps a good fight awaits us."

We beckoned our horses to run faster, closing in on the lone rider.

I smelled the reek of his injuries, heard the pain in his ragged breaths, and they struck open a memory from years ago: Garreth instructing Rhys and me as we swung practice swords in the training yard, showing us how a real sword fight looked as he challenged a fellow warrior-in-training and they circled each other in an impressive display of swordsmanship. The match ended with both of them panting, bearing scratches, and I'd held a cloth to a cut on the warrior's cheek—the same warrior barreling toward us now. I could see him, slumped awkwardly in his saddle, his brown hair mussed, blood splashed across his armor.

"Quinlan!" Before I could snag his horse's reins, it stopped in its tracks, staring at me as the rats had.

"Lira?" Quinlan lifted his head. "I—I thought you were dead." A smile crept across his face, and then he teetered sideways. I threw my arms around his waist, trying to hold him up, shouting for Zabelle. Together, we settled him back onto his horse.

"Looks like a nasty wound in his side," Zabelle said, pointing at the red stain pooling beneath his left arm.

"What happened, Quinlan? Who did this to you?"

He blinked heavily, as if he'd just remembered something. "They're coming," he said, throwing a frightened glance over his shoulder.

I'd been too focused on Quinlan to notice, but now I heard them—shouts and pounding hooves. I smelled them—their lathered mounts, the dirt and sweat of their skin, and the heavy stench of their battle lust. There were three of them. I didn't know these men, but I knew where their loyalties lay. I knew whose orders they followed blindly.

I drew my sword. Zabelle nocked an arrow, pulling her bowstring tight.

The Dragonmen crested the hill that had blocked them from view. They saw us and howled, the victory song of predators cornering prey. The three invaders spurred their horses, rushing toward us, carrying murder in their eyes.

CHAPTER 3

LIRA

The Dragonmen's battle song echoed across the hills. Zabelle released her arrow and it slammed through one invader's throat.

Their howl became a roar as the dead invader fell from his horse. The other two charged at us, long yellow braids streaming behind them.

Zabelle let another arrow fly, but the invader she'd aimed at dodged. They were nearly upon us. Zabelle put down her bow and reached for her spear. Quinlan's sword was in his hand, though I doubted he had the strength to swing it.

"I've got the one on the right," Zabelle said. "The other's life is yours to take, Lira."

I squeezed the hilt of my sword, my own battle song rising in my blood. "His life belongs to his gods," I said, "but his death will belong to me."

No matter how much I had trained at swords with my brothers, I'd always insisted that I was no warrior. But whatever power lay in the Fallen Ones' blood had seeped into my muscles, into my bones. I felt stronger. Faster. Deadlier.

The invader's sword was a massive, shining star slicing the air near my neck. My sword was a paltry bit of stardust by comparison, but it was more than enough. Wraith shifted out of the way, and as the invader's arm swung to the side with his momentum, I shoved my blade between his exposed ribs. The hilt slipped from my hands, stuck in the screaming Dragonman's side.

The gods did not speak inside my head, yet I felt them there, eyes opening from slumber, waiting to see what I would do with the strength they had given me.

Grabbing the knife sheathed to my thigh, I leaped from Wraith onto the injured invader's horse. I gripped the Dragonman by his long blond hair, wrenched his head back, and jammed the blade through his throat. Blood sprayed in a bright burst of red.

I released the Dragonman's hair and his body thumped to the ground.

The energy housed inside me sparked with approval, sending embers of wicked warmth through my veins. I sensed Veronis's amusement.

Quinlan was hunched over his saddle, clutching his horse's mane. "How in Gwylor's name did you do that, Lira?"

"Divine inspiration." I hopped down from the horse and stalked to where Zabelle had the third Dragonman on his knees, her spear pointed at his neck. "A prisoner?" I asked.

"He might know something useful to the prince," Zabelle said.

I used my belt to bind the Dragonman's wrists together. "You're coming with us, Westlander," I told him in Iseneldish. "Behave, or the pretty warrior with the spear will make you wish you had."

We made our way back to the camp, Zabelle pushing our snarling captive along with the tip of her spear while I rode beside Quinlan, making sure he stayed upright on his horse. At the cave, there was a crowd awaiting us. Standing at the front was Garreth, a scowl forming deep lines across his features, but his anger ebbed as he recognized Quinlan. He ran to help his friend down from the horse, calling for healers.

Quinlan was unconscious by the time they laid him on a pallet. The healers went to work, cutting open his leather armor and tunic, examining the gash across his ribs.

"How bad is it?" Garreth asked.

"The wound is deep, but not lethal," the eldest healer said. "We'll clean and stitch it and watch him for signs of infection."

At her assurance, I released the breath I'd been holding.

"This man is a brave warrior, and he is like a brother to me," Garreth said. He winced at the word *brother*, and I knew he was thinking of Rhys, missing the only true brother he'd ever had. "Make sure he wants for nothing. Give him the same care you would give me."

Garreth beckoned to me, and I followed him outside the cave, away from the camp. As soon as we were alone, he said, "What the devils were you doing, riding off to meet enemy soldiers, just the two of you? You know better. So does Zabelle."

"Don't blame Zabelle. It's my fault. I thought it was a single rider."

"Why would you think that?"

"I heard him coming from across the hills. Quinlan, I mean. But not the Dragonmen. I only heard them when—" My mouth snapped shut as I saw how Garreth was looking at me. Like I might be losing my mind.

"How could you have heard such things from so far away?"

"You know what they did to me." The mystic. The Fallen Ones. "I'm different now."

Garreth scratched at his scruff-covered jaw. He'd always kept his beard neatly trimmed, but out here he left it unkempt. It made him appear wild, like he belonged with the nomads.

He did belong with them, I reminded myself. He was their prince.

Resentment welled in me, sudden and sharp: *Why didn't you come for me, Garreth? Why did you leave me in Stony Harbor, instead of bringing me to Ghost Village, to be at your side?*

"You don't look different to me," Garreth said.

It was a lie. I'd only glanced at myself once in the last week, as I washed in the makeshift privy that had been erected adjacent to the camp. Splashing water from a pail, I'd noticed my reflection wavering along the surface. The water revealed someone far older than her seventeen years. My face had lost its softness, shadows clinging to the sharpened angles of the bones beneath. Where an innocent girl used to live, I'd found a hardened woman staring back.

Garreth and I arrived at an outcrop near the camp, where Zabelle and several other nomads were securing the prisoner. "He can't be coaxed into confessing anything," Garreth said. "The Frozen Sun beasts are hard and heartless."

Heartless beast. He wasn't speaking of Reyker, yet I couldn't help but bristle. I put a hand on my brother's arm. "Let me question him. Maybe I can reach him."

Not only because I spoke the invader's language, but because I understood his training, his culture. Thanks to Reyker, I knew my enemy well.

The Dragonman appeared to be in his midtwenties and looked just like his brethren—tall, muscled, with long yellow hair. He growled and snapped at the nomads, calling them foul names even though they couldn't understand him. He grinned when I stepped forward. "I know you. You're the bitch the lordling tried to hide from the Dragon." He scanned the faces around him. "Where is the traitor? Does he need his wench to do his fighting for him?"

The question caught me off guard.

The invader read my expression and grinned. "Dead, is he? Pity. I hoped I'd get a chance to sink my axe into his skull."

"This axe?" I took the axe from Zabelle, held it up beneath the invader's nose, and spit on the blade. A grave insult, disrespecting a Dragonman's weapon. They believed the Ice Gods blessed every blade, and each man was as possessive of his own weapons as he was of a lover.

The invader thrashed against the ropes binding him. "You filthy little—"

"What is your name, Dragonman? Tell me, or I'll have the others piss on your precious axe." I started to hand it to Garreth.

"Andrithur," he said through gritted teeth.

"An-dree-thur," I repeated, and the invader glowered at my clumsy accent. "I'm Lira."

"I don't care."

"Where will Draki strike next? What is he planning?"

Andrithur laughed. "Do your worst to my axe. Do your worst to me. Even if the warlord wouldn't kill me for it, I would tell you nothing. Your island is overrun with spineless dogs. I will die smiling, knowing you'll all end up skewered upon Ildja's fangs, suffering at the whims of the serpent goddess and her Destroyers for eternity."

I switched back to Glasnithian. "This will take time. Give me a week, then perhaps—"

Garreth shook his head. "It cannot wait. We're heading south soon, and we must ensure there won't be Dragonmen waiting to ambush us. You don't need his permission to get answers."

Read his soul. It wasn't an order, though it might as well have been. Like our father and our clan, Garreth wasn't above using my gift—using *me*—to get what he wanted. But I wanted vengeance, a way to stop Draki, a way to hurt him. I wasn't above using my gift to get what I wanted either.

"I'm going to put my hand over your heart," I told Andrithur. "And you're going to be still and let me do it."

"Trying to seduce me, wench? That might have worked on the lordling fool, but I have higher standards than most Dragonmen. I'd sooner mount a dead horse than touch a Green Isle whore."

I smacked my palm into his chest.

My mind was open. Andrithur's protests, Garreth's threats, the shuffling of nomads, every footfall of human or beast—it all faded.

Everything was quiet, just for an instant. And then a tidal wave swept over me.

My senses were inflamed, every bit of Andrithur's essence—memories, emotions, sensations—slamming into me. Where I usually waded through someone else's consciousness, here I was instantly sucked under. I wasn't reading his soul, I was being pummeled by it, suffocating in it. His love and pain and fears and lies shredded me apart.

I tried to scream, but I had no mouth. Tried to cover my ears against the roar, tried to pull my palm away from his chest, but I had no body.

Too much. It was too much. My mind was coming undone.

So was his. We were both weapons, slicing at each other. As the Dragonman's soul flayed me, I ripped and tore through it like cobwebs. I'd seen this before, when I touched the soul of a Dragonman I'd stabbed. I'd felt his soul die. That's what was happening. I was killing Andrithur from within.

Just as suddenly as it started, the crushing sensations ended, the darkness lightened. I was back in my body, my hand outstretched in front of me, the space between it and the Dragonman growing. Garreth's arm was around my waist, hauling me backward.

Andrithur was screaming, a glowing red shape burned into his chest: a handprint. My palm was bright as a blacksmith's forge—a tiny, blazing sun.

Garreth let go of me. "What is it, Lira? What happened?"

Soul-reading was an ability bestowed by the True Gods, but the Fallen Ones' powers coursed through me now too. I was a paradox, with gifts from antithetical forces. "I think the fallen gods' power changed how my ability works. I couldn't control it."

I felt as if some invisible weight was pressing down on me, realizing what it meant if I was right.

"My gift. It's broken."

CHAPTER 4

REYKER

The dream washed over him, cresting waves of pleasure that dumped him into a trough of pain. She was alive. She was dead.

Where are you, Lira?

The black river woke before he did, already screaming inside him, boiling his blood, leading his hands to his weapons. He was on his feet, sword raised, before he remembered where he was: the Tangled Forest, on the northern tip of Glasnith.

Three Dragonmen entered the thicket he'd bedded down in. "Little lordling," one of them said. "The warlord requests your presence in Dragon Harbor."

Dragon Harbor. Because Stony Harbor was gone, its homes and people burned to ashes and bones.

Reyker flexed his fingers around the sword's hilt. The knuckles he'd broken, punching them against Draki's invincible face, throbbed dully. "I'll show you where the warlord can stick his request."

The men edged closer, lifting their axes and swords. "It would be better for you to come with us. If you force the Dragon to hunt you himself, you'll pay for it."

"All of you will pay. Everyone who stepped foot in her village. Anyone responsible for its destruction."

He'd killed every other warrior Draki had sent after him over the past days, leaving a trail of bodies like bread crumbs to follow through the trees. He would add these men to his count. It wasn't enough to sate him, not even close, but it would ease the ache in his chest for a short while.

Again, the black river hissed. *Let me out again.*

So he did.

He felt her here still, in these lands. Not as she was before, not a bright spark in a sea of darkness. Now she was part of the darkness. Tainted. Angry. As if her spirit clung to all the wrongs done to her and to Glasnith, demanding vengeance.

I will grant it, he told her. *To my last breath.*

Lira's horse was waiting for him, its dewy-eyed gaze eerily observant. The mare bowed her head and Reyker pulled himself onto her back. He nudged the horse and it galloped deeper into the forest, just as it did yesterday, and the day before that. Reyker had searched, over and over, for the Grove of the Fallen Ones. He'd scoured every inch of this forest and found nothing, as if it were hiding from him.

The same way he'd searched for her body at the foot of the bluffs, waiting until the tide was low and the sea was calm, diving from the boat he'd stolen. Swimming so deep his lungs burned and the dark water threatened to crush him. Yet there had been no trace of her.

"You will show yourself, Veronis." He pressed his hand to Lira's medallion, resting against his chest. "I will not stop until you answer me."

This time, someone—the island, the grove, the gods—finally responded. The sounds of life in the forest tapered off into an unsettling hush. Green trees were replaced by ones ripe with decay. A land of death rose around him.

"Gods aflame," he said. Beneath him, his horse's mane fell out in clumps. The flesh on the mare's bones began to rot.

"Sword of the Ice Gods." The voice was brittle, like a branch snapping in half. "I know what you seek, but you are too late."

The girl was balding, only a few brown curls hanging from her scalp. Her creamy skin was pocked with black, molding spots. She stared up at him with burned-out holes where her eyes should have been, but there was an eye watching him from the wrist she held up, another in the center of her throat. A lump grew atop her bare foot, the skin splitting open, and a third eye sprouted. It winked at Reyker.

The rotting horse stopped in front of the rotting girl, and she placed her hands on its muzzle. "You were touched by this place as well, noble mare," she murmured. "You sense what others cannot. You will serve your new master well, if he bothers to listen."

There was something impossibly familiar about this girl.

"Ishleen?" Reyker said.

The girl cocked her head. "Oh. That was my name once, I suppose. Now I am only the mystic. The last one died, and there must always be a keeper of the portal. The loch called to me after I fled into the forest. It offered me shelter and a purpose. I could not refuse."

The filthy loch burbled. It reeked of old blood and decaying meat, sacrifices left to the gods in exchange for favors. This was where Lira had brought him when he was dying, where she'd bled into the loch as an offering, to save him. Where he planned to do the same. "I wish to speak with the Fallen Ones."

"There is nothing left for you here. The Fallen Ones have gone silent. When I arrived, they showed themselves to me, revealing all I needed to know." She tapped her empty eye sockets. "They speak only to their vessel now."

"No." This was his last hope—that he might bargain with the gods to bring Lira back, or at least to see her one last time outside of his dreams, to tell her he would come for her after Draki was dead and their countries were safe. "Please. I came to give an offering. Can I find this vessel? Will the gods answer me through it?"

Three eyes blinked at him in tandem. "The vessel has a destiny. So do you. Your path leads you to the Dragon. To make up for what you could not save by saving what you can."

Reyker shook his head, puzzling over the words. "You mean the ones who didn't escape Stony Harbor. And the other *magiskas*, the Daughters of Aillira Draki captured."

He glanced down at himself, at the blood of Dragonmen staining his clothes, dead because they'd tried to drag him back to the warlord. How was he supposed to go willingly? How could he stand to be in the Dragon's presence? Every time he looked at Draki, he saw his mother bleeding out on a stone floor. Now he would also see Lira leaping to her death.

"It's what she would want you to do, is it not?" Ishleen smiled, revealing a glimpse of the girl she'd been before the grove's plague fell upon her.

The horse craned its neck to peer at Reyker, vertebrae peeking beneath the mare's mouldering coat. Agreement clear in her keen gaze.

"Yes." Reyker sighed. "It is."

CHAPTER 5

LIRA

Quinlan slept through most of the next day. Sitting across from where he lay, I watched the healers change his bandage, the wound already healing nicely. When he woke that evening, I leaped to his side, and he gave me a tired grin. "Fancy meeting you here."

"How are you feeling?"

Quinlan touched his side and winced. "Like you beat me with a practice sword after I passed out. You didn't, did you?"

"Tempting, but no." I moved to pour him some of the special herb tea the healers had brewed. "Here. This will help with the pain."

He drank, his lips puckering. "Uck. That is vile."

"How were you injured, Quinlan? Why did you come to the desert?"

He stared into the greenish liquid in the mug. "Houndsford was sacked. We saw the smoke coming from Stony Harbor, and we were strapping on our armor, ready to ride to your clan's aid, when they slipped into the village. Mercenaries. Dragonmen. They were cutting men down before we realized they were among us."

I saw my own pain reflected in Quinlan's face.

"Some of us managed to escape. We got separated when a group of Dragonmen attacked us near the Silverspires. I took a sword to the ribs.

There was nothing I could do but run for the Green Desert and hope . . ." His eyes met mine. "I can't believe you're here. Thank the gods you got away."

Yes. Thank them for infecting me, for keeping me alive and away from Draki so they could use me for their own ends.

Quinlan set his hand on top of mine. "You were all I could think of when I was running for my life. That I had to get to Garreth and tell him what happened, so we could save you."

I pulled my hand away. His comfort, his affection, was too much to bear when the only touch I wanted to feel was Reyker's. Careless words rushed from that pit of despair inside me. "I don't need to be saved. I survived on my own."

Hurt flashed in Quinlan's eyes. "I know you're not weak, but that doesn't mean I don't fear for you. You're my friend, Lira."

It was unfair of me to snap at him, to let my misery turn into callousness. *I've not been myself lately*, I started to say. No, that was an understatement. *I am a wreck, I am drowning, I need to be saved from myself.* But I couldn't say those things, not to anyone.

There was a clamor behind me as Garreth entered the cave and rushed over. "Quinlan. Gods, what a fright you gave us."

"You two should talk," I said. Garreth would need to know all the details of the attack on Houndsford, things I wasn't sure I wanted to hear.

And with Garreth occupied, I had somewhere else to be.

Outside the cave, tents and makeshift shelters stretched into the distance. While I was still in Stony Harbor, Garreth had been riding across Glasnith, visiting refugees from sacked villages, offering the dispossessed a new clan. Promising that with their help, he would raise an army that could banish the Dragon and his minions from our lands. Only a few refugees had accepted then, but over the last weeks, more had trickled in every day—from Stalwart Bay, Ballygriff, and Taloorah, villages that had been turned into graveyards. They had lost faith in their traditional clans. They had put their faith in Garreth's promise.

They were ghosts, in need of a prince.

I headed to where several nomad women were making flatbread—one rolling the dough, another cooking them over the open flame, a third stacking the warm bread into piles. Ignoring their clucks of annoyance, I plucked a few slices from a pile and made my way up the hill.

Andrithur was tied to a stake. Two guards were on duty, and they sat by a small fire, watching him from a few paces away. The Dragonman snarled as I crouched in front of him. "Get away from me, witch."

My handprint was scorched into his skin, swirls of pink and red and black. I jerked my chin at the burn. "I didn't mean to do that."

"Perhaps I won't mean it when I snap your neck. Will that make it easier to bear?"

I took a bite of bread. "You must be hungry. Would you like some?"

"Keep your rotten food. I will tell you nothing." He turned his head away, but I saw the gleam in his eye. The invader hadn't eaten in days. Under his breath he murmured, "I am Sjaf's disciple, servant of Iseneld, a blade to be wielded for the glory of my gods and homeland."

The Dragonmen's code. Reyker had taught it to me.

I knew the fierce pride and undying loyalty Draki inspired in his men. I also knew the brutal ways he corralled them when they didn't follow his orders. I knew the threats he made, the fear he used to bind the Dragonmen to his will. I had to be the opposite of that. I had to be the brave deer who earned the trust of a wolf by appealing to the kindness in his heart.

"Eat." I waved the bread in his face. "I'm not going to let you starve."

"I told you, I don't want it. Probably poisoned anyway."

"I'll let the birds have it, then." I drew my arm back as if to throw it, calling his bluff.

"Fine," he huffed. "I'll eat your garbage if you'll stop yammering and leave me alone." I held the bread out so he could take a bite. "It's overdone."

"Take it up with the cook. Andrithur, why do you hate my people so much?"

"Because you're weak, pathetic dogs," he said around a mouthful of bread.

"Not too weak to capture you."

"The brown-skinned woman captured me. She's not one of you. She's a true warrior. I'd take her back to Iseneld if I didn't already have—" He stopped.

"If you didn't already have what? A woman? A wife?" He answered with a scowl. "You must miss her. And the rest of your family."

I'd built trust between myself and Reyker by telling him of my mother's death. Maybe I could reach this invader in a similar way.

"Let me tell you why I should hate your people," I began.

As he ate, I told him about the first invasion of Stony Harbor, about Rhys, and how he died defending me. I didn't look at Andrithur until I'd finished. "Fighting and dying to protect those you love is the opposite of weak. I don't hate you, Andrithur. I hate that you brought war to these lands. I hate that you kill my people. But I believe your people and mine are not so different. That one day there could be peace between us."

"You're a fool."

"Perhaps. But I found a good man among your kind. I have hope that he wasn't the only one. I owe it to him to try and help his people understand, to try and find others who are as honorable as he was. I'll bring you more food in the morning, but next time, it's your turn to talk." I stood, heading back toward the cave.

"Witch-girl."

I paused.

"I see why he chose you. Your lordling bastard. You're as stupid as he was."

"Aye." I smiled at the Dragonman, taking his words as an offering given in empathy, whether they were meant that way or not. "I am."

It took days, but slowly, hesitantly, Andrithur began to speak.

Never of Draki or the Dragonmen, but of Iseneld. His home. His family. He still snarled and cursed me, but he ate everything I brought him, and there was a change in him—a desire to live, so that he might see his wife and daughter again.

Garreth didn't ask me what the invader said, knowing I'd share information if I had it. My brother was busy planning the nomads' exodus across the desert, sending scouts ahead in search of secure places to set up a new camp, dispatching envoys to meet with the clans of Glasnith and propose alliances.

"They'll refuse," I told Quinlan, because Garreth wouldn't listen when

I tried to tell him. "The clans see the nomads as foreigners like the ones invading their shores, exiles with no loyalty."

"Maybe." Quinlan's injury hadn't hindered him long. He was back on his feet, acting like his old self, full of bad jokes and easy smiles. He'd be well enough to ride soon. "But the desert is no longer safe. Garreth has to try."

Through the mouth of the cave, I watched my brother stalk from warriors to cooks, blacksmiths to seamstresses, ensuring there was enough food, weapons, and tents for the upcoming journey. Though it wasn't the clan he was born to, it was clear he felt responsible for their safety. Their future.

"Rest, Quinlan. I'll be back later."

"Off to see Andrithur?" There was a hint of jealousy in his tone.

I knew what Quinlan saw, what all the nomads saw—a girl known for bedding invaders, who spent more time with her enemy than her own kind. They didn't understand that being with Andrithur made me feel closer to Reyker, that speaking of Iseneld with another Dragonman helped keep him alive in my memory.

"Rest," I said again. I didn't owe Quinlan, or anyone else, an explanation.

When I got to the stake Andrithur was always tied to, there were no guards, no invader, nothing but cut lengths of rope. No one in camp was distressed, as they would be if the prisoner had escaped. I closed my eyes, concentrating, and over the drone of insects, the swish of wind, came sounds that made my stomach clench.

The pounding of fists against flesh. The moans of a man in pain.

Garreth called my name, but I ran for the horses. Jumping onto Wraith, I headed toward the noises coming from the other side of a hill, a short distance from the camp.

Andrithur was on the ground, bleeding. One of his eyes was swollen shut, and the fingers of his right hand were bent at odd angles. Four nomad warriors surrounded him.

I slid off Wraith's back and unsheathed my sword. "Get away from him."

"Lira!" Garreth rode up behind us, dismounting, moving between me and the other warriors. "Put down your sword."

My sword stayed where it was. "You ordered this? How could you?"

"We need him to tell us what he knows. This is what we do to enemies. This is what they do to us, and worse. Remember what happened to Rhys."

"Of course I remember." The sword trembled in my hand. "Rhys died in my arms, not yours. But Andrithur is not Draki."

"He's not Reyker either."

"Don't." Hearing Reyker spoken of so casually was like a kick to the gut. "You know nothing about Reyker. You know nothing about Andrithur, or any of the warriors of Iseneld."

"I know the only way to get information from a savage is to treat him like a savage." Garreth nodded at the nomads. "Keep at him until he tells us something useful."

Distantly, I heard the flapping of wings, the shiver of wind sliding through feathers. "No one touches Andrithur again," I said, stepping forward.

"Lira. Go back to the camp or, gods help me, I'll have you tied up next to the invader."

His words struck a painful chord deep within me, dredging up memories of being locked inside Torin's manor. The scars on my back prickled. "Try it."

The flapping grew louder, and a din of squawks and caws drew our attention upward, to the birds circling above us. Black crows. Tiny sparrows. Vultures. All of them flying together, in chaotic formations, as if we were a carcass they hungered to pick apart.

A buzzing filled my head. It sounded like an unspoken question, repeating, beating as rhythmically as wings—*Yes, yes, yes?*

The men looked from the birds to me.

I'd called these birds, as I'd once called the lammergeiers, the forest demons, the Brine Beasts. But those times I'd done it at Veronis's insistence, when my life was at risk, and only by speaking in the old language. This time I'd brought them on my own, unintentionally, without saying a word.

The flock hovered, their flaps and shrieks impatient. Soldiers, awaiting their orders. I could use them to stop Garreth and the others, to hurt them. I was heady with power, with rage, enough to frighten me. Enough to startle me back to my senses.

"Go," I told the birds. They dispersed, scattering through the sky, gone as quickly as they'd appeared. I met Garreth's wary gaze. "Fetch a healer. Take your men with you."

My brother balked. "I'm not leaving you—"

"With an unarmed man your warriors just beat half to death? Worry less about my safety, Garreth, and more about your own conscience."

"This is not who you are, sister."

"It's who I've become." Though I didn't say it, it hung there between us—this was who I turned into after the invasion, after the Culling. After Garreth left me in Stony Harbor, at the mercy of Torin and Madoc. "You don't know me so well as you think, Garreth. Not anymore."

For a moment, I could tell Garreth considered springing at me, wresting the sword from my hands. Wraith pulled his lips back from his teeth, hissing at Garreth, whom he'd belonged to since he was a foal. It was clear where the stallion's loyalties now lay, and this, more than anything else, seemed to shake Garreth. He led the nomads away.

I knelt beside Andrithur, helping him sit up.

"Is it your turn to torture me, witch?" The bite had gone out of his tone. He sounded weary, accepting of death.

No, Andrithur was not Reyker. But there was honor in him. I'd seen it. I couldn't stand by and watch another Iseneldish warrior be so cruelly abused.

I whistled for a horse. We were a ways from camp, but I knew one would come. "I'm going to give you a horse, and you're going to head for the coast, steal a boat, and sail home."

Andrithur laughed, and blood oozed from his split lips. "Draki will kill me if I desert."

"I will kill you if you don't."

A bay horse trotted over the hill. With effort, Andrithur hauled himself onto its back, and I handed him the knife sheathed to my thigh, the one Garreth had given me years ago.

The Westlander stared at the knife. "Why would you help me?" he asked.

It was hard to look at him, hunched over, bruised and bloody, blue eyes regarding me through strands of gold hair. "What your people have done to mine is wrong. What my people do to yours in return is also wrong. Those who lead our armies will never admit this. It's up to us, the soldiers and warriors, to show mercy. To remind our clans, our tribes, that winning a war isn't worth losing our souls."

Andrithur shook his head. "A witch and a fool. I will tell my people about you, though I doubt they will believe it."

"Farewell, Andrithur. You are a Dragonman no more."

He considered this, thinking, debating. Nodding. "As you say, witch. A Dragonman no more."

Andrithur spurred the horse, and I watched him go, until the invader disappeared over the hills.

One life saved. One mind changed.

It wasn't much, but it was something.

CHAPTER 6

LIRA

The nomad host crossed the moorlands by horse and cart and on foot. Heading toward the Boglands to build a new camp on land as harsh as the Green Desert, though not nearly as vast. The mercenary Bog Men had abandoned their settlements at promises from the Dragon of more fruitful places to call home. Places like Houndsford and Stony Harbor, according to Garreth's scouts. Since the mercenaries had taken our villages, Garreth aimed to take theirs.

Until the groups spread across the desert converged, I hadn't realized how many nomads there were. Hundreds, perhaps even a thousand. More than any single clan on Glasnith, and that number grew each day, thanks to the Dragonmen's attacks and the spreading rumors that Garreth was not only a prince but a prophet, the only one capable of standing up to the Dragon.

Stories, like those from the scriptures. Only as real as the faith people put into them.

The nomad warriors kept to the outer edges, surrounding those who were too young or old or ill to fight if Dragonmen attacked. Garreth had wanted Quinlan and me in the center of the group, but we'd both defied him to ride in the rear.

I turned to look at Quinlan. "How long do you think it will take Garreth to forgive me?"

My brother had calmed some, but he still refused to look at me. We'd had quite a row after he discovered I'd set Andrithur free. It worsened when Garreth and a handful of warriors tried to go after the invader, and I'd kept their horses still as stones.

"Not long," Quinlan said. "You are his clan. His kin."

Maybe. But Garreth had an army of nomads following him across the desert who believed him to be their savior. I had no one except him and Quinlan.

Wraith nipped at my foot, as if to remind me I had him too. I felt the hum of the stallion's energy, just as I sensed it in all the horses, the birds above, the catamounts and coywolves hiding in the rocks, every creature that haunted the desert. Hundreds of heartbeats. A well of hungers. Their souls brushed mine like ribbons waving in a breeze.

That night, we stopped to rest near a stream, and nomads crowded around the cookfires, talking and eating. I sat down next to Quinlan, picking at my bowl of lentils.

Garreth and Zabelle stood away from the rest of us, their heads bent close as they spoke. They were a study in contrasts. Zabelle was long and lean, while Garreth was broad muscle. Zabelle's skin was rich copper to Garreth's sun-crisped beige, her hair coal black to his rusty brown, her eyes golden topaz and his like spilled whiskey. Garreth had told me how Zabelle found him wandering in the Green Desert after he'd been exiled, woozy from blood loss, delirious with fever from the festering wound where our father sliced off his warrior-mark. She'd saved his hand, overruling the nomad healers who'd wanted to amputate it. In turn, he'd helped her save her people, a thing she could have done herself were she not a foreigner and a woman in a land that undervalued both.

To some, the two of them might have looked like a prince and his commander, planning and strategizing, but I'd witnessed how Garreth and Zabelle found each other's gaze from across the camp. The air seemed to crackle when they were together, the heavy hush that came when two dominant forces were about to collide.

Gods, is that what Reyker and I are like when we're together? The thought drifted into my mind, falling like a lash as the loss of him cut through me.

From where the horses were hobbled next to the stream, Wraith whickered, sensing my agitation across the distance.

Quinlan leaned toward me. "Do you want to move closer so we can hear them better?" He gestured across the fire, where one of the nomads from Savanna was telling a story about being chased by lions, waving his arms through the air. The others listened, laughing. Among them, I spotted Brayen. The Skerrian boy who'd shot the poisoned arrow that nearly killed Reyker. The reason I'd gone to the Grove of the Fallen Ones and given them a taste of my blood.

Rage swept over me in a torrent, dousing everything in its wake.

The horses gave my anger voice, all of them shrieking and rearing, fighting their hobbles. Garreth and Zabelle drew their weapons, as did every warrior, and the rest of the nomads fell quiet, everyone searching the night for threats.

Dark amusement sliced along the edge of my mind, but it wasn't my own. It was the cacophony of an ancient god's mirth.

⸻

The nomads slept wherever they found room, with their weapons beside them. I volunteered to be on the first watch.

I wandered farther from the group than I should have, needing a moment alone. What I'd done—tonight, agitating the horses, and days ago, when I'd nearly commanded birds to attack Garreth and his men— had frightened me, and I sensed I'd only skimmed the surface of my powers. If I lost control, could I call a dangerous creature without meaning to? Could I influence it to harm someone, if the desire was conflicted, as it was with Brayen?

"I don't want these gifts," I said, hoping the Fallen Ones were listening. "Take them away. I'm not going to help you."

Something fluttered from beneath my sleeve. It glistened like a snow-flake, but it felt like silk in my hand. I held it up to the moonlight, even though I already knew what it was. A moonflower petal. Like the ones Reyker had showered over me in my dream.

When I glanced up, Reyker was standing in front of me.

My knees buckled.

It wasn't him. It *couldn't* be him.

He looked just as he had the night we'd celebrated the Birth of Summer in Ghost Village—small braids wound through his hair, deerskin trousers and jerkin. His eyes were bright, full of joy. Full of life.

"Reyker?"

He smiled at me, and I fell apart.

I choked on a sob, wanting so badly to believe the lie. To ignore the small things, like how my *skoldar* was silent, when it should've tingled from the nearness of him. Or how I knew that if this was truly Reyker, he wouldn't just stand there—he would already have pulled me to him, held me close, whispered my name. Those were intangible differences, so I latched onto one that was solid, indisputable.

"You aren't him." I forced myself to look away from that beautiful, deceptive face. "That jerkin was ruined. He was shot with an arrow while he was wearing it. It was covered in his blood. I had to cut it off him."

He didn't move. He kept standing there, flashing that glorious smile.

"Who are you?" I unsheathed my sword. "You dishonor his memory with this cruel trick. He isn't here to make you pay for it, but I am."

LIRA.

The god's voice echoed through my head. The sword fell from my hand.

Was he looking out at me through Reyker's eyes, as he had that day in Ghost Village when I had played the part of his beloved Aillira? Was that why he'd chosen to show me a vision of Reyker from that precise moment in time?

YOU WILL FREE US.

"I won't. Leave me alone."

The thing that was not Reyker stepped forward and stroked my cheek. I tried to resist leaning into him, but I couldn't. It wasn't him, but it was his face, his body. Maybe I could pretend, just for a moment—

Not-Reyker struck me with the back of his hand. The blow slammed me to the ground.

I stared at him, shock and betrayal rippling through me, but this thing was only an illusion, a disguise. Reyker would never have hurt me.

YOU WILL RESTORE WHAT WE LOST.

Veronis wanted me to free him and his brethren, to reunite him with Aillira, his lost mortal lover. Apparently, he was willing to do whatever necessary to force me to do his bidding. My temper got the better of me.

"Break yourself out of prison. I'm not beholden to you."

OH, BUT YOU ARE.

Not-Reyker straddled me.

"Get off." I shoved at his chest, but he didn't budge. Before I could scream, he clamped a hand over my mouth.

WE CAN TAKE AWAY EVERY MEMORY YOU HAVE OF HIM. WE CAN REPLACE THEM WITH NIGHTMARES.

Not-Reyker tore at the buttons on my trousers.

When I dove into the loch in the Grove of the Fallen Ones, I'd felt Veronis's power, how dark and twisted he'd become after spending eons locked in a cage, but I'd still not expected him to be as vicious as the god of death. That was the point of the Forbidden Scriptures—to show that Gwylor was the villain and Veronis the hero.

Maybe that was a lie too.

This thing that wore my dead lover's skin was going to ravish me, and Veronis would make me believe it was Reyker.

But I still had the upper hand.

Do this and you lose your only chance at freedom, I said in my mind, knowing he heard. *I won't help you. You'll rot down there. You'll never see Aillira again.*

Not-Reyker released my mouth but kept me pinned. The life I'd seen in his eyes was gone. He took my hand and pressed my palm to his chest.

There was no soul inside this replica of Reyker. What I saw when I fell into him was a series of images that I knew weren't memories. These were predictions: Draki, burning village after village on Glasnith. Every Daughter of Aillira, hunted down, enslaved. A mass execution, like the one in Vaknavangur, but I recognized the prisoners being beheaded. Zabelle.

Quinlan. Garreth. All while I stood at Draki's side like a prize, watching it happen—my eyes unfocused, my mind torn away.

OUR PRISON DRAINS US. GWYLOR AND ILDJA FEED OFF OUR SIPHONED POWER, AND THEY USE IT TO AID THE SERPENT GODDESS'S HALF-IMMORTAL SON. AS LONG AS THEY REIGN AND WE REMAIN TRAPPED, THE DRAGON WILL BE INVINCIBLE.

My hand dropped, and the images dissolved.

It was divination, not truth. Not yet. But it seemed the likeliest end to all this. If I refused Veronis, I was gambling with my brother's life. With the freedom of every Daughter of Aillira. With the fate of my country.

"What must I do?"

GO TO HER TEMPLE. FIND THE KEY.

Her temple—Aillira's Temple, that had been sacked by Draki and his Dragonmen. "What key?"

THE KEY OF THE SOUL-EATER. THE KEY OF DAMNATION.

The serpent-goddess Ildja, keeper of the Mist, where she tortured and devoured the souls of the damned. She was Gwylor's sister. Draki's mother. "What do I do with the key?"

TAKE IT TO THE MOUNTAIN OF FIRE, IN THE CENTER OF THE FROZEN SUN. BURY IT IN THE HEART OF ILDJA. DO NOT LET HER TAKE THE KEY FROM YOU OR ALL WILL BE LOST.

Iseneld—of course that's where I had to go. To Reyker's homeland . . . without him. To Draki's kingdom, where the Dragon would be even stronger than he was on Glasnith.

To fight his mother. A goddess.

I didn't bother asking any of the hundred questions I had about what powers I possessed and how to control them, how I would free the gods, what would happen to me after I did. Veronis would give me no answers, and there was something else I wanted far more. "I'll do as you ask, on one condition."

WE DO NOT TAKE ORDERS FROM VESSELS.

"Consider it a humble request. After I restore what you've lost, you return the favor. I want him back." I squeezed the moonflower petal in my fist. "In this world, in the flesh, if possible. If not, then in the otherworlds. When I die, you send me to him, wherever he is." Even if it was in the Mist, to be devoured by Ildja—I'd rather be tortured by his side than spend eternity without him. "Agree, and I'll put up no more resistance to your commands."

Silence. I waited, breath held.

WE WILL CONSIDER IT.

Not-Reyker vanished. Veronis spoke no more.

I buried my head in my hands. There was a glowing ember floating in the cold puddle of darkness inside me, and I curled around that hope, nursing it, clinging to it. Beneath the fading moonlight, my knees drawn against my chest, I whispered the same thing over and over, as if the more I said it, the truer it became.

"I will find him. I will find him. I will find him."

CHAPTER 7

REYKER

It was morning when Reyker rode into the ruins of Stony Harbor, crossing beneath Draki's flag—a jagged-armed star the color of blood against a blue backdrop. The Star of the Dragon. The warlord marked his territory the same way he marked the gifted women he enslaved.

The fires had burned out days ago, but the scent of smoke and charred flesh still hung in the air. A peculiar mix of satisfaction and sorrow welled in Reyker at the sight. This was what Torin, Madoc, and all who followed them deserved. But Lira, Ishleen, Quinlan—they weren't like the others. There was no way to pick out the innocent from the guilty. All suffered equally. His time fighting alongside the Dragonmen had taught him this.

Around him, yawning men rose from their beds, some sleeping in the open, others emerging from simple shelters of cloth and wood, some alone, some with the village thralls at their sides. Some were Dragonmen, and others were Glasnithian mercenaries—traitors to their own countrymen.

Heads turned toward Reyker as he passed. There were whistles, shouts, jeers. He ignored them, guiding his horse to the largest shelter in the center of the village.

Draki knew he was here, as he always did.

The warlord pushed through the pelt covering the shelter's opening, dressed only in trousers, his exposed tattoos quivering like living creatures as he made a show of rolling his shoulders and stretching his neck, a knife-edged smile spread across his face. "The Sword of the Dragon returns. Did you miss me, Reyker?"

"I've come to make a deal." Reyker dismounted and stood before the Dragon. "I'll join you. I'll be your Sword." The pledge was like broken glass, tearing him to pieces as it left his mouth. "But for each raid, for each kill, you let some of your captives go, unharmed."

He thought he'd escaped this. When he'd washed ashore in Stony Harbor all those months ago, and everyone believed him dead, he had thought he could start over. Live a different life. Be a different man. Now here he was, back where he'd started, aiding the monster who'd killed and conquered everything he loved.

"Oh, we're bargaining now? Hmm." Draki called over his shoulder, and two half-nude women slipped past the pelt and joined him, wrapping their arms around him. They were young, lovely. Terrified. "I killed the weak men of this village. Those left alive have never been freer. They stay because they desire it. They desire us."

The only desire Reyker could see in these women was to stay alive, even if it meant bedding the warriors who murdered their kin.

"I saved the best of the women for you," Draki said.

A hand touched Reyker's arm. His pulse stumbled as he looked at the girl beside him and realized why Draki had chosen her. Her features were different: She was a little too short, her eyes more the color of moss than grass, her hair more like fire than wine. But the resemblance was striking.

"I love you," the girl said, leaning toward him.

Reyker pulled away, but the girl continued to profess her undying love, rubbing against him until he pinned her arms as gently as he could. Her gaze was unfocused. She squirmed in his grip, mewling as if it pained her to be close to him without pawing at him. Reyker glared at Draki. "Stop this! Return the girl's mind to her."

"I will, after you fulfill your end of the bargain. I've appointed an overlord to stay here, since I must leave soon to check on Dragon Bay—"

"Stalwart Bay."

"—and in the meantime, you will sack Selkie's Quay for me, and declare it Dragon's Quay, so I will control the two biggest ports in northern Glasnith. When you are done, choose someone to stay on as overlord and then join me in Dragon Bay, where we will plan our return to Iseneld."

Reyker stilled. "What?"

"There has been news of attacks from the Fjull Uprorsmund on my holdings back home. You'll travel there ahead of me to eliminate the rebels, so they do not spoil my triumphant return as high jarl of Iseneld and emperor of the Eastern Isles."

The Fjull Uprorsmund—the Mountain Renegades. The same warriors Reyker had planned to seek alliances with when he'd sailed toward Iseneld on behalf of Torin and the Sons of Stone, before he took a scythe to the chest and was left in the freezing sea to die. Draki wanted him to hunt them down and take them out, to make Reyker his Sword once more, slicing through anyone who opposed him, securing Draki's standing as high jarl. No longer just a warlord, but *king* of the entire island.

In spite of all this, that one word stuck in his head, beating like a drum: *Iseneld.*

Home.

The fist clenched around Reyker's heart loosened a fraction, before constricting again. He had to stay on Glasnith to protect Lira's people, to shield them as much as he could from the unrest Draki had sown, the Dragonmen's destruction that would continue even after their leader left. He owed her that.

"I love you, Reyker," the girl in his arms said, kissing every part of him she could reach. "I belong to you, and you to me."

He wanted to scream, to shake sense into the girl, to punch Draki's grinning mouth so hard his fist came out the back of the warlord's skull.

"I will win you Selkie's Quay, and you will release every survivor from Stony Harbor."

Draki pretended to deliberate. "They are yours. I've had my fill of them, and this island is full of maidens who yearn for the touch of a real man." He disentangled himself from the two women attached to him like frightened barnacles, shoving them at Reyker. "You are his possessions now, my pretty ones."

"It's all right," Reyker told them in Glasnithian. "I will keep you safe."

They stared at him. He was just another Dragonman, splattered with blood, his arms locked around a panicked girl. Of course they would trust nothing he said. He jerked his head, and the women followed him reluctantly.

Draki called after him. "Welcome back, brother."

CHAPTER 8

LIRA

Taloorah was abandoned. After what happened to the temple, superstition that the gods had cursed the village had spread, keeping people away. Even the Dragonmen.

We weren't far from the Boglands, and the nomads less suited for long travel needed to rest. It took little prodding for me to convince Garreth to stop here. Aillira's Temple was the holiest place on our island, and he wanted to see what the warlord and his Dragonmen had done to it as much as I did.

With no Daughters of Aillira left to conceal the temple, we saw it clearly: an area as large as the rest of the village, surrounded by stone walls. Our horses carried us beneath the archway, through a broken gate, into the courtyard. A dense quiet lingered here. It was the silence after someone took their final breath, the stillness after a failing heart contracted for the last time.

Sliding from Wraith's back, I walked across the grass, taking it all in. I'd witnessed Draki's attack on the temple in a vision, but I hadn't seen the aftermath. The library, the dormitories and lecture halls, the sanctuary with its spired towers—whether by Draki's own hand or by an earth-shifter under his control, every building had been reduced to a pile of rocks.

I climbed over stones to reach the sacred thorntree at the center of the temple. The oldest and largest tree in all of Glasnith, planted by Aillira in memory of her lost, beloved Veronis. In another realm, frozen in time, Reyker and I had pledged our love to each other beneath this tree. Here in this realm, it was poisoned by Draki's magic, and lay on its side like a felled giant.

My gift was fractured, but I had to try. Pressing my palm to the trunk, I opened myself to the tree's essence.

The images crashed into me: Temple guards and priestesses sliced open by Dragonmen's blades; the Daughters of Aillira, tied up and forced to kneel; Draki's stiletto cutting into them, one by one, ensnaring their minds. Screams filled my ears. I experienced every fall of sword and axe, every wound, every ounce of terror, all at once.

It ended as Garreth pulled me backward, holding on to me as I thrashed and howled, until the memories dissipated.

"We can't let them get away with this," I said when I could finally speak.

"We won't."

My handprint glowed bright red on the thorntree's trunk. I glanced around at the temple wreckage, wondering how I'd ever find a goddess's key here, especially when I had no idea what it looked like. Garreth was already trying to lead me away, but I snatched my arm from his grip.

"This place has been fouled," he said. "We shouldn't stay."

"I can't leave yet." I moved toward the rubble of the sanctuary. Maybe if I touched every stone, one would tell me where the key was. I reached my palm out, but Garreth moved between me and the rubble. "I have to do as the gods ask, Garreth, or they'll never let me be."

"For how long?"

"Until the end." Until I freed Veronis from his prison and Aillira from the otherworlds, and the gods released me. "I'm part of this. The wars between Gwylor and the Fallen Ones, between the clans of Glasnith and Iseneld."

"No. This is not your war, and I'm not Torin. I won't let you wind up like Rhys."

So this was how it would be. Garreth and I loved each other as much as any brother and sister could, but we'd spent most of our lives at odds— Garreth watching over me, training me to defend myself, but never giving me space to use that training. He'd never understood me, never believed in me. Not like Rhys had.

"You're right," I said. "You aren't Torin. You are not my chieftain, my commander, or my father. I'm under no obligation to obey you."

Garreth opened his mouth to yell, then caught himself, glancing toward the audience of nomads just beyond the ruins. He was still out of sorts over the news his envoys had brought days ago—some of the clans had accepted the offer of an alliance, but most had refused. Out of fear, these clans had already pledged allegiances to the self-proclaimed high king of Glasnith. Our traitor uncle, Madoc.

My brother's shoulders dropped in resignation. "You have two days to find whatever it is you're looking for, and then we head into the Boglands. All of us."

Garreth could think whatever he wanted. The nomads were his people, not mine, and I wasn't leaving until I found the key.

Once he was gone, I pressed my palm to the first stone.

———◈———

By the time the sun set, my head pounded, my ears rang, and I'd watched the sacking of Aillira's Temple hundreds of times, through hundreds of stones. The stones were less overwhelming to read than any living being— they didn't have souls exactly, just imprints left by all the souls that had surrounded them—and with practice, I'd learned to pull myself out of the memories, but it still felt like I was being ripped apart.

I'd come to realize it wasn't my gift that was broken. My abilities were stronger than ever—I didn't observe the destruction, I lived it, the crushing heat of the fires, the stench of sweat and tears and blood. It was more like my gifts were warring with one another, trying to break *me*.

Other memories slipped through the stones too—they had witnessed much and they held stories of every god-gifted girl who'd passed through the temple's halls. These glimpses of their lives were threads connecting me to the Daughters of Aillira, past and present. Though they were strangers, they were still my sisters.

Quinlan came looking for me and convinced me to take a break. He sat down, passing me a hunk of bread and a wedge of cheese, filling me in on the latest argument between Garreth and Zabelle. My brother was still bent on resettling in the Boglands, but Zabelle wanted to stay in Taloorah. "She makes a good case," he said. "The land is good. We can repair the walls, rebuild the cottages. Make it a home."

A home. We. I'd been thinking of Quinlan as an outsider among my brother's people, like me, but I was wrong. He was on his way to being fully nomad. And I was still a temporary trespasser.

"No luck finding the key?" Quinlan asked.

"None." After a few more bites, I put my food down and went back to the wall. "You should go. I have to keep searching." The sooner I found the key, the sooner I could move on to other things: freeing the Daughters of Aillira, killing Draki, bringing Reyker back.

Quinlan followed. "I could help you look."

"You don't know what you're looking for. I don't even know what I'm looking for." Quinlan kept talking, but I was stuck on that notion—*What am I looking for?*

I thought I kept seeing the destruction of the temple because it was the strongest imprint on the thorntree and the stones, but what if it was because that was the memory I expected to find? The other memories from the temple had only surfaced when my concentration slipped. And I hadn't been able to isolate a single image inside Andrithur's soul because I didn't know him, didn't know what to look for, and the intensity of my newly enhanced gift made it difficult to focus. If I expected the memory I needed, if I wielded my gift instead of letting it wield me . . .

"Show me the key," I said, pressing my hand to a stone.

A young woman rushes into the tower, her violet hair flowing around her. The head priestess is waiting.

"Do you have it, Iona?" the priestess asks her.

Iona pulls a box carved of black rock from beneath her cloak. "Brought on a ship that just arrived from the Frozen Sun." She opens the lid.

Inside is a dagger forged of what appears to be pure crystal, glowing bluish-white as the sunlight streaming through the window hits it.

"The key," Iona says. "Gwylor left it with his sister Ildja to guard. The serpent-goddess gave it to her mortal lover years ago as a token of her affection, and he gifted it to us. All he asked in return was a potion from our healers to save his new bride. She took ill on their wedding night—likely a curse from Ildja."

The priestess takes the box from Iona. "It's just as the Forbidden Scriptures described. The key must be kept safe until the time comes to use it. We'll protect its whereabouts with our lives."

"Where will you hide it?"

"Where none would think to find it, where none would see anything amiss." She runs her finger over the crystal blade. "In a place born of the pain it caused."

Iona and the priestess turn to the window, their gazes drawn to the same place: Aillira's thorntree.

My hand fell to my side and I sank to the ground.

The woman working with the head priestess, who brought the key to Veronis's prison here to Aillira's Temple. The woman, Iona . . .

. . . was my mother.

I knew Mother was from Taloorah, that she must have visited the temple on occasion, but the priestess seemed to know her well. Was it possible she was a Daughter of Aillira? What did she have to do with the Fallen Ones and the key?

The key!

Quinlan called my name, trying to help me to my feet. I pulled away from him and ran to the corpse of the thorntree, picking a branch and running my fingers over every long white thorn, searching for one that didn't belong. When I finished that branch, I moved to the next, ignoring the pinch of needles jabbing into my skin, the blood coating my fingertips.

Behind me Quinlan was talking, but I pushed the noise to the corner of my mind, closing my eyes, focusing all my senses on the thorntree.

My fingers traced another needle. "No." Then another. "No." Then . . .

This one was different. Smoother. Warmer, like something simmered beneath its shell. I felt the phantom of my mother's touch upon it. I felt the burn of a goddess's wrath.

I dug at the bark around it, first with a knife, then with my nails, until I'd loosened the bark enough to pull the crystal needle free. As I held it, it lengthened from a needle to a blade, a hilt forming at its base. A dagger.

The soul-eater's key.

I kept my mind shut, afraid of what I might see if I opened myself to the key's memories, but its power slithered over me, hissing at what it found—the lingering essence of the gods it had trapped. Inside my veins, the gods hissed back.

"What is that?" Quinlan asked.

"Salvation," I answered. For the Fallen Ones. For Glasnith.

For Reyker, wherever his soul had gone.

CHAPTER 9

LIRA

It was barely past dawn the next day when a band of heavily armed riders was spotted heading across the plains to Taloorah. Bog Men, their clothing and skin streaked with mud. Kelpies, dressed in armor etched like fish scales. Ravenous, their heads shaved and painted with red stripes. Warriors from the mercenary tribes.

The nomad infantry formed lines on the outskirts of the village, with Zabelle commanding on horseback from the front. I waited with Garreth in the rear cavalry lines. It chafed my brother not to be at the head of his army, but this was what he'd agreed to after quarreling with Zabelle.

From the ranks of mercenary riders, a man rode forward. Brown hair and eyes, medium build—ordinary, but for the malice in his expression and the crown on his head.

Madoc. Unappointed, alleged king of Glasnith.

"Nephew," he called, searching the crowd. "A word, if you please. Stone to Stone."

Garreth motioned for me to stay in the back, hidden from view. Madoc assumed I'd burned to death in the cells he had set fire to. Better to keep it that way.

The nomads parted to let Garreth through. Zabelle joined him, his steadfast protector, and a large Kelpie was glued to Madoc's side as well. They met in the center of the field: the false king and the Ghost Prince.

I squinted across the distance until my acute vision kicked in, tugged at my ear until it obeyed and let me listen from afar.

"What's your business here, Madoc?" Garreth asked.

"Lovely to see you alive again, and only slightly maimed." Madoc's eyes fixed on the vambrace and gauntlet on Garreth's right hand. "My business is this is *my* kingdom, yet there are rumors of another man calling himself royalty and amassing an army."

"I'm not pretending to be royal. My people know who I am and named me their prince as a term of endearment, not an imperial title. Glasnith is no kingdom. It's a land of chiefdoms, and always will be. Those of us in Taloorah are merely forming our own clan to defend ourselves, which we have every right to do, especially considering how the other clans have denied us aid and alliances."

"Alliances." Madoc grinned. "Tricky things, those. You must know I made one with the mercenary clans of the south, and they, in turn, allied with the Dragon."

I glanced among the mercenaries. How could they follow Madoc? What had he promised them?

A Bog Man among them shifted restlessly. There was something strange about his eyes—for an instant, it seemed like spider legs were crawling out of his pupils, then they were gone, and I wasn't certain I'd seen anything at all.

"Do I know that you betrayed our family's clan, its warriors, and your own kin? That you sent my father and his men to their deaths?" Garreth's hand twitched, no doubt aching to reach for his sword. "Yes. I'm aware."

"I came here as a courtesy to you, my brother's eldest and only living spawn, to warn you to disband this pathetic tribe of stragglers before you force your king's hand. Heed my command, or there will be a reckoning."

Garreth leaned forward. "Oh, there will be a reckoning. On that you can bet. But not today. Keep pouring lies into the ears of the clan leaders. When it catches up to you, I'll be there, waiting. Until then, stay out of Taloorah. This village is mine."

As one, Garreth and Zabelle turned their horses and rode away.

Madoc tapped one finger against his chin, an odd gesture. No—a signal. I caught movement from one of the mercenaries behind Madoc. The fidgeting Bog Man raised his bow and nocked a venom-tipped arrow, aiming it at my brother's back. My mind reached for the horses. The assassin's mount tossed its rider a half-second too late—he'd loosed his arrow, and it sailed straight for Garreth. But I'd already sent Garreth's horse dancing out of the way.

The arrow passed within an inch of Garreth's shoulder.

A second arrow flew, this time from Zabelle's bow. It struck the assassin through the neck. She trained her next arrow on Madoc.

The false king's mercenaries raised their weapons in a tide of silver.

Garreth's eyes traveled over the rival army, then over his own, assessing the possibilities, the gains and losses. The cost of killing Madoc. It could be done, but not without bloodshed on both sides. And if Garreth let Zabelle take her shot, she would be the first to die.

The Prince of Ghosts raised his hands. "A rogue assassin, acting alone," Garreth declared. "The threat is ended. There's no need for further retribution. We shall leave the body to your disposal and return to our village."

Madoc inclined his head. "As you say, nephew. Until we next meet, Gwylor keep you."

Zabelle lowered her bow. The prince and the false king dared to turn their backs to each other, but their guards rode sideways in their saddles, ready to protect their leaders.

The nomad army parted once more to let Garreth and Zabelle through. As he got closer, I noticed the tremble in my brother's muscles, the lack of color in his skin. It was his birthright to be a commander, to lead warriors, but this was the first time the balance of hundreds of lives had been on his shoulders.

As his horse passed mine, Garreth touched my arm, whispering, "Thank you."

The power Veronis gave me had saved my brother. If I could keep those I cared about safe, I would embrace these gifts. And hope I could keep them under control.

That night, I lay awake in the tent I'd set up inside the temple ruins. A sanctuary where I could feel close to my lost sisters. A place where no one heard me cry out when I woke from dreams of Reyker.

Or when I screamed against the claws scratching at my mind—the Dragon, searching for me. Always searching.

The crystal dagger I wore at my hip, hidden under my clothes, vibrated with power. Impatient, just as I was. I had to find a ship and a crew that could get me to Iseneld—a feat that took resources I lacked, especially when the port I'd need to sail from belonged to the warlord. And there were many unfinished tasks left in Glasnith, most importantly to save the Daughters of Aillira. My loyalties were torn, indecision cleaving me in half.

I drifted toward slumber, feeling Draki waiting for me on the other side. I sank deeper, and he dug his hooks into my consciousness, picking away at my defenses. There was only one way to make him stop. It would put everyone around me in danger.

I did it anyway.

On the cusp between awareness and sleep, I let him in.

"Little warrior."

Draki looks just as he did the last time I saw him, on the bluffs—silver hair flowing, eyes glowing golden. The sharp definition of bone and muscle visible across his face, his body, give him the mien of a weapon—elegant, lethal. He stands on an unfamiliar shore, waves lapping at his feet, not the least bit surprised to see me.

I float a few paces in front of him. The landscape around me is as blank as unmarked parchment, as if something—likely the gods in my blood—is concealing every trace of my whereabouts.

"You knew I wasn't dead, didn't you?" I say. "You've known this whole time."

He steps closer. "I told you, you are not so easy to kill. Did you truly think I would let you leap off a cliff to your death?"

"You let me jump?"

He flashes his teeth—a beautiful, savage smile. "There were distractions. Interruptions. I want you all to myself, and I will accept nothing less. That is why I have left you alone to wallow in the remains of your namesake's temple. But I believe we have waited long enough."

He knows where I am, yet he hasn't come for me. This is another game, one only he knows the rules to.

"I'm going to kill you for what you did to Aillira's Temple and Stony Harbor."

His eyes sparkle with merriment. Serpent eyes, inherited from his mother. "You are going to try, and I shall enjoy every moment."

"Where are the Daughters of Aillira you took? I want them released." Though I've met few of the other god-gifted women, we are bonded. We are kin. I will fight for them.

I will kill for them.

Draki's laughter chills me. "The magiskas stay with me. They are mine, as you are. I do have a gift for you, though—someone you thought lost. Someone you might like returned."

"Who?"

He tilts his head. "If you want him, you must retrieve him."

"Where are you?"

"Dragon Bay." He crooks a finger at me. "Come get me, little warrior."

CHAPTER 10

REYKER

He stared at the fortress, rising like a stone reef out of the wild waves surrounding it. Mere weeks ago, he'd been dragged to the fortress in Selkie's Quay at the end of a chain, tortured inside its walls. Now it was up to him to breach it.

The villagers had gotten word that the Dragonmen were coming, and had abandoned their cottages, retreating to the fortress. Reyker needed to get the Dragonmen across the mad currents and past the archers waiting on the rooftop turrets. He rubbed a hand over his face, knowing what he had to do.

"I need your help," he told the two Daughters of Aillira. A tide-teller and a fire-sweeper, the one Draki had forced to believe she was in love with Reyker.

The tide-teller cowered from him. The fire-sweeper spit on his boots. Just like Lira would have.

Reyker pushed the thought away. He'd pressed Draki into freeing the magiskas' minds, but Reyker still needed them. Draki wouldn't free the rest of the captives from Stony Harbor until Reyker succeeded. He'd explained the deal he made to the Daughters of Aillira, but they didn't believe him. Why should they?

Coaxing wouldn't work. He'd have to threaten them. He'd have to use the weaker girl against the stronger one, a tactic he'd learned from the warlord.

Reyker pressed a blade to the tide-teller's throat. "You'll lead us safely through the current." He looked at the fire-sweeper. "And you'll burn up any arrows shot at us before they land, or I'll kill your friend."

She spit on his boots again, but her eyes dimmed.

He didn't have the energy to hate himself.

The Selkies had taken most of the boats to the fortress and burned any left behind. Reyker had sent Dragonmen to find something to ferry them across the water, and they came back with three sad, leaking vessels. Reyker sat in the bow of the first boat, beside the tide-teller, shouting orders to the Dragonmen rowing based on the direction of the girl's pointing finger.

The boats rocked madly, but the tide-teller's legs were steady as steel, born for this. When they were in range, the Selkie archers lit their arrows on fire and shot them into the sky. The Dragonmen lifted their shields in precaution, but the fire-sweeper raised her arms, and with a wave of her hand, the fire on the arrows swelled and turned each projectile to ash before fizzling out, nothing but harmless embers raining down.

The archers realized what she was. The next volley of arrows had no flames, but Reyker had brought a torch in anticipation, and the girl took it, moving her hand over it. A mist of fire spread above their heads, burning up most of the arrows. A few slipped past, slamming into the boat, and Reyker pushed the girls behind him, under his shield.

Sudden pain clawed up his side. Flames curled from the fire-sweeper's fingers where they clasped the hem of his tunic—stupid of him not to expect her to try to kill him the first chance she got. He nearly dropped the shield as more arrows fell. At the next lull, he shoved the girls onto their bellies and set the shield on top of them before draping himself over the side of the boat and smothering the flames in the sea.

The vessel made its way to the foot of the islet. More archers awaited them, but the Dragonmen's arrows thinned their ranks. Then Reyker and the other Dragonmen were on the stairs, swords and axes out, cutting their way through one Selkie warrior after another, until they were at the doors to the fortress. A small army stood before them.

Reyker closed his eyes. He didn't want to do this. *A Dragonman no more*—that's what he'd promised himself, what he'd promised Lira.

But Lira was dead.

When he opened his eyes, he saw Draki's face on every warrior.

He lifted his sword. He screamed, pouring out his grief and fury, and the Dragonmen screamed with him. They rushed forward, crashing into the Selkies, and then he heard nothing but the black river's call: *Again. More. All.*

Dragonmen tossed the dead over the side of the fortress, until the sea around the islet was red, corpses bumping against the rocks in a macabre dance. They'd surrendered, at the end, but Reyker had been too lost in his battle-madness to stop the Dragonmen from stabbing half the warriors who'd kneeled before them.

As the blood dried on his weapons, he went to the side of the fortress that faced land, the rolled-up flag beneath his arm. He wanted to burn it. Instead, he unfurled it so it fell down the stone wall: the Star of the Dragon.

The Selkies were no more. This was Dragon's Quay now.

He kept the magiskas with him as he oversaw the march of the few surviving warriors down to the dungeons, and as he searched the fortress for any Selkies who might have fled during the battle. Entering a storage room, he noticed a strange shimmer, like light playing over water—there, then gone. One step, and the air became heavy, resistant. One step, and an empty room was suddenly full of women and children. They gasped, shying back.

Reyker spotted a familiar face among them. Eathalin, the nomad spell-caster he'd met in the Green Desert, another Daughter of Aillira. Her eyes met his, widening in shock, and he shook his head, pressing a finger to his lips.

"Stay here," he told them, keeping his voice low. "I will come for you once it's safe."

Later that night, the Dragonmen drank and celebrated and passed out. Reyker killed those on guard duty, throwing their bodies over the fortress walls to join the Selkies. He cleared a path to the narrow jetty where several boats were moored, and helped the villagers scramble into them. He sent the other two magiskas away with the villagers, the tide-teller leading them past the maelstrom, the fire-sweeper lighting their way with a flame in her palm. Eathalin lifted a hand in farewell as the boats drifted out of sight, and Reyker returned the gesture.

This wasn't his island, these weren't his gods, but he prayed for their safety, to whomever was listening. He prayed to Lira to forgive him.

CHAPTER 11

LIRA

I found my brother alone in what had once been Taloorah's great hall, leaning over a table covered in maps, looking so much like our father that it startled me for a moment.

"What's our next move?" I asked, the question tasting sour on my lips, because whatever Garreth had planned, I'd be gone before it came about.

Garreth glanced up. I half expected him to leave me in the dark, as Torin always had, but he beckoned me closer. "We could hole up here in Taloorah and hope Madoc was bluffing. Wait for the mercenaries and Dragonmen to turn on one another. That's what Zabelle wants."

"Or?"

He jabbed his finger at several villages on the map, to the north and south of Taloorah. "Or we could march to the gates of the clans that refused us and show them they made a terrible mistake. Convince them to ally with us. Declare war. All the remaining clans of Glasnith against Madoc, the Dragonmen, and the mercenaries."

"Can we win that war?"

"Doubtful. But at least we wouldn't be giving up."

I sat on the edge of the table. "Sounds like the prince and his commander are at odds."

His mouth quirked, an almost-grin. "The commander is ready to strangle her prince for trying to lead her people into a war she wants no part of."

"But they're your people too. No matter what we do, Madoc and the Dragonmen will never let us stay here in peace. They'll come for us eventually." The scouts Garreth sent out periodically had brought back news of more villages destroyed across Glasnith. Even Selkie's Quay, with all its defenses, had just fallen to a garrison of Dragonmen.

"Mago's death hit Zabelle hard. She doesn't want to lose more nomads."

"She doesn't want to lose you," I said. Garreth looked away, his face flushed. "She's not the only one."

"You aren't going to lose me, Lira."

Yes, I was. Just not the way he thought.

Garreth dropped into the chair behind him. "I'm sorry I haven't had more time for you. The ordeals you've suffered . . . I wish I could do more to help you through what's happened. As soon as everything settles down, I promise I'll be a better brother."

"You're doing the best you can." I put my hand over his. "You always have."

He held my wrist as I started to pull away. "I was going to come for you, after I was exiled. I thought you'd be safer in Stony Harbor than in the middle of the desert with only me to protect you. I kept waiting to have enough nomad warriors, enough fortification in the camps. Losing Rhys . . . I couldn't handle that happening again. I didn't want to take any chances. And, stupid as it sounds after what Torin did to us during the Culling, I never thought he'd hurt you—his devoted, god-gifted daughter. But I was wrong. I'm sorry."

I'd been so angry, so confused, worried Garreth had abandoned me for his new family of nomads, I'd not stopped to think of the situation from his perspective. He'd always valued my safety over my happiness. I didn't agree, but I understood.

"We've both made mistakes. I forgive yours, as I hope you'll forgive mine." I leaned down and kissed the top of his head—a thing I'd done often to Rhys, but rarely to Garreth. I fled the room before he noticed the tears I was struggling to hold in, before he grew suspicious and found a way to talk me out of what I had to do.

It was just as well Quinlan had gone with several nomads to escort any survivors back from Selkie's Quay. I didn't know if I could handle another goodbye.

Back at my tent, I packed up my supplies and called Wraith to me. I tried to sneak away, but Zabelle was waiting as I rode to the broken gates. The warrior's features were pinched with disapproval. "Nothing I say will stop you. I am only here to see you off."

"You'll take cake care of my brother?" There was so much more I didn't say: *He needs you. He won't understand why I had to go. If I don't make it back, he'll never forgive himself.*

"I will watch over my prince," Zabelle said. "You take care of yourself."

I nodded, taking a last look at the temple ruins. When I was ready, I whispered into Wraith's mind and he broke into a gallop, leaving Taloorah, the nomads, and the last of my family behind.

It was less than a day's ride from Taloorah to Stalwart Bay, an easy trek over green fields and hills. I kept an eye out for Dragonmen, spotting Draki's scouts with my heightened vision, avoiding them before they spotted me. I was halfway to my destination when I sensed a horse coming up fast through the fields behind me, its rider's identity announced by the sound of his breath, the scent of his skin.

I slowed so he could catch up. "You're going to reopen your wound, riding that hard," I said once his horse was beside mine.

Quinlan smirked. "That would be unfortunate, considering I'm in the presence of the worst seamstress in Glasnith."

"How many survivors from Selkie's Quay?"

"Nearly fifty. Eathalin and the other women you saved in Stony Harbor were among them, safe and sound."

I released a sigh. "How did you find me?"

"A scout saw the warlord ride into Stalwart Bay yesterday. When I found out you'd left, I took a wild guess that's where you were heading. I promised Garreth I'd find you and keep you out of trouble."

"How angry is he?" I asked.

"On a scale of one to ten? Eleven. But he's more worried than anything. He and Zabelle were arguing when I left because he wants to gather our forces and march on Stalwart Bay. A show of strength to convince the remaining clans to ally with the nomads."

I turned to look over my shoulder across the hills, as if I could see all the way to Taloorah. Garreth would win that argument—he'd convince Zabelle. But what then? "The Dragonmen could slaughter them."

"Our army can't fight like the invaders, but we have as many men as they do. All we need is a little luck to swing the odds in our favor. I'm assuming you have a plan to get into Stalwart Bay. Whatever you're up to, let me help." He grinned like we were children planning a prank on our tutors rather than two warriors up against a demigod and his garrison of frost giants.

"You're going to have to break your promise to Garreth," I said. "Trouble's exactly what we're in for."

I told him my plan. He didn't like it, but there was no other way in that I could see.

We rode on in silence. Quinlan glanced at me, starting to speak several times, stopping himself. Finally he said, "Eathalin told me something. That she saw Reyker—his spirit, I suppose. He was there, fighting with the Dragonmen to overthrow Selkie's Quay."

A draft blew across the raw wounds inside me. "She was wrong. Alive or dead, Reyker would never fight with them again."

"I guess not." He paused. "Do you want to talk about him?"

"No."

"Because if you did, if it would make you feel better—"

"I can't." Not with Quinlan. Not with anyone.

In front of us, a sliver of sea stretched across the horizon. Along its edge, the cottages and shops and docks of Stalwart Bay were spread out across green dunes that sloped down to the water. A channel had been dug around the entire village and the drawbridge was the only way to enter without a boat. From here, I could see Dragonmen—some guarding the bridge, others patrolling both sides of the channel.

The crystal dagger had been a constant presence at my side since I'd found it, but I couldn't risk it being taken from me, falling into Draki's hands. I held the dagger on my palm, wondering if I should give it to Quinlan for safekeeping or bury it beneath a tree and come back for it later. Neither felt right.

As if it read my thoughts, the dagger melted to a pool of liquid crystal in my hand. The liquid circled my wrist, hardening into a bracelet. When I tried to pull it off, it didn't budge.

Quinlan's brows rose. "No dull moments with you, eh? Vengeful gods, mind-controlling warlords, shape-shifting daggers around every corner." There was no mockery in his tone, nothing but wonder. He was the only person left who never looked at me like I'd become a stranger, who made me feel like I was still that same girl who'd punched him for tugging on my braids. "You're sure about this, Lira?"

"I am."

He slid off his horse and climbed onto Wraith behind me. "Whether it works or not, Garreth's going to kill me."

Passing Wraith's reins to Quinlan, I leaned into him, closing my eyes, letting my limbs go limp as his arms settled around me. Shouts rang out as we reached the bridge, demanding us to halt. I heard the threat of steel as the Dragonmen clanged their swords and axes together in warning.

"I serve King Madoc," Quinlan called. "I've brought a gift for your warlord on the king's behalf. A highborn lady, young and fair. Come and see."

The Dragonmen came forward. I felt their eyes on me.

"What's wrong with her?" one of them asked in heavily accented Glasnithian.

Quinlan told the story just as I'd instructed. "She tried to run, so I had to hit her in the head. She'll need a gifted healer if you want her to live."

Suspicious, the Dragonmen conferred in Iseneldish. One suggested summoning the warlord.

I'd expected this. Draki's men weren't complete fools.

"There are more girls where this one came from," Quinlan said, "even prettier than her. I can bring them to you, if it pleases the Dragon."

That was all it took.

"Give her over," the Dragonman said. "We'll take her to the healers.

Be more careful with the next ones you catch. The warlord doesn't like his possessions damaged."

As the Dragonman started to pull me away, Quinlan held on.

My chest constricted. He was going to ruin our ruse and get himself killed.

Go, Quinlan. You have to go.

His arms loosened, releasing me. I didn't breathe until I heard him riding away. The Dragonman who held me carried me across the bridge, and just like that, I was inside the sieged village.

I cracked one eye open, making note of the path the Dragonman took to get to the infirmary. He entered the wooden building and laid me on a table, calling the healers over, telling them of my condition before he left us. The door closed.

I looked up into the faces of two women not much older than me, one with chestnut hair hanging down her shoulders, the other with strawberry hair tied into a braid, their eyes foggy and faraway. We were in an herb-scented room lined with shelves full of vials, so much like Ishleen's cottage I had to bite down against the memory of it. I counted nine other girls in the room, sitting or standing or pacing aimlessly, all of them trapped within the web of Draki's spell.

My blood responded to their presence, effervescent, like calling to like.

The healers touched my head, examining me, but when I pulled away, they didn't try to stop me. They only stared in silence.

There was a scalpel on one of the tables. I took the brunette healer's hands in mine, wrapping her fingers around the instrument. Without touching the scalpel myself, I guided her hand with my own, cutting a *skoldar* into the wrist of the red-headed healer: a small knot meant to resemble hands holding a heart, the symbol of healers. Then I took the redhead's hands and did the same to the brunette, before pressing their bloody wrists together.

Though they hadn't so much as flinched during the entire procedure, now they both blinked as if waking from a long sleep, awareness seeping slowly into their expressions. The brunette gasped, and the redhead backed away from the bloody scalpel I held. "Who are you?" she asked.

"I'm Lira of Stone," I told them. "In the name of the Fallen Ones and blessed Aillira, I've come to free you."

———————

When every Daughter of Aillira bore a shield-scar, and their minds were their own again, they introduced themselves. Along with Mabyn, the brunette blood-healer who could treat wounds that couldn't be seen, and Keeva, the redheaded bone-healer who mended fractures, there was also a well-washer who could take toxic water and make it drinkable, a tract-seeker who could lead people to any destination she sought, a harvest-reaper who could make crops grow faster and fuller. There were tide-tellers, a sea-farer, a star-mapper. Some of them I knew from memories the temple ruins showed me.

They listened as I explained what I wanted to do. "You're linked now. That's an advantage, but it won't be enough to fight the Dragon. I can offer you more. Traces of the Fallen Ones' power, to make you stronger." The mystic had transferred the fallen gods' power to me through her blood. I could do the same, but I would grant these Daughters of Aillira the choice I was denied.

Mabyn cocked her head. "You want to give us your blood because there are gods inside it?"

I touched her hand and she jerked away like I'd burned her, staring at her fingers.

"Sweet Silarch! I felt them through your skin," she said. "The Fallen Ones. They really are inside you."

The women gazed at me, fascinated and fearful. Mabyn held her wrist out to me. "The Dragon sacked our temple, killed our teachers. This is war. We need every advantage we can get."

I sliced my palm, wrapping it around the healer's *skoldar*. Something tugged free inside me, like a single leaf plucked from a tree by the wind—a trickle of the Fallen Ones' power, leaving me, flowing into Mabyn. She felt it, too, staring down at her wrist, curling her hand into a fist.

Every Daughter of Aillira accepted my blood.

Power thrummed from them, a shadow of what lived within my veins, but strong enough that the whole room seemed to vibrate. "Your gifts might overwhelm you at first," I warned them. "You need to practice using them to get used to it."

Keeva folded her arms. "I can't practice mine, unless someone wants to volunteer to break an arm."

Alane, the tract-seeker, closed her eyes. "I can see outside! The village, the bay. The Dragonmen." She rubbed at her temples. "Gods, this is making me dizzy."

"Can you check on the other girls?" Mabyn asked.

"There are other Daughters of Aillira here?" I said. "Where?"

"Ten more, brought from Aillira's Temple," Bronagh, the sea-farer answered. "The ones the warlord deemed the most dangerous."

"They're all right." Alane's brow furrowed. "They're locked in the manor, with two guards outside the door, two more stationed outside the building. There's no way to get to them."

I ran my fingers across the crystal bracelet. At my touch, it turned liquid, molding back into a dagger and solidifying once more. "There is, if you help me."

The guard came a few hours later with a basket of food. Alane signaled us just before the Dragonman entered, and I ducked behind the door as it opened.

Keeva lay silent on the floor, eyes closed. The others stood around her, staring at nothing. A good impression of how they'd looked when I first found them.

"What's this?" The guard set the basket down and edged closer, bending over to peer at the girl feigning illness. I pushed the door shut and snuck quietly toward the Dragonman, stabbing the dagger into the back of his neck.

As he staggered and fell, there was a sound like a belching drain, and a moment later, crimson clouds danced inside the dagger's clear blade from tip to hilt, trapped within the crystal, redder than blood, redder than fire.

The Dragonman's soul.

I felt the brush of his soul through the shell of crystal, crying out as it was sucked from his body and transported to that hollow prison-realm where the Fallen Ones had been sent. I had been to the prison-realm, when I dove into the loch in the Grove of the Fallen Ones, and it was like being torn to pieces and suffocating and disintegrating, all at once. Not even a Dragonman's soul deserved an eternity in that dark oblivion.

I tapped the dagger against my forearm and it transformed back into a bracelet, tightening around my wrist. I vowed not to use it on another mortal unless I had no choice.

I helped the other Daughters of Aillira drag the Dragonman's body beneath a table. Mabyn hid the key he'd dropped while the rest of us concealed our crime, sopping up blood, placing sheets and plants around the table so nothing would seem amiss.

Mabyn hugged the other girls, whispering *goodbyes* and *good lucks*, then she followed me out of the infirmary into the night. Stalwart Bay was quiet, its paths empty, its cottages and shops dark. We walked slowly toward the manor on the opposite side of the village, but still I heard Mabyn's pulse racing, beating in time with my own.

"It will be all right," I said. "Follow the plan, and we'll all be free soon."

Footsteps marched toward us. I squeezed Mabyn's shoulder and ducked behind the nearest building, watching. The patrolling Dragonman stopped her. Mabyn said nothing, keeping her expression blank, her eyes unfocused.

"The warlord will flay me if he finds out one of his magiskas wandered off," the Dragonman said. There was a risk he would take her back to the infirmary, but it was far enough away that I thought it unlikely. Sure enough, the guard gripped Mabyn's arm and pulled her into the manor.

The healer had her scalpel and a vial of my blood hidden beneath her clothes. She would help the rest of the Daughters of Aillira mark one another, as I'd done, guiding their cuts into *skoldars*. Returning their minds to them, so they could tear themselves free from Draki's compulsion and meet us on the battlefield when the time came.

I crept through Stalwart Bay, noting the guards and what areas they patrolled. If Garreth and his army had left shortly after Quinlan, and they pushed the horses and marched all night, they could be in Stalwart Bay as early as dawn tomorrow. I had to ensure the drawbridge was open and take out as many Dragonmen as I could, to better their odds.

But when I found the cellblock, I stopped, remembering Draki's words from my dream. *I have a gift for you—someone you thought lost. Someone you might like returned.*

For a mad moment, my heart screamed for Reyker.

I eased closer on quiet feet, closing my eyes, letting my senses reach out like extensions of myself—probing the sounds and smells and essence of who was in the cell, brushing against something dark and dangerous, but familiar, and I grappled to put the pieces together. I knew whoever was down there. I'd touched his soul before.

This was what I was focused on, absorbed in, when another familiar soul blotted out the first, saturating my senses, soaking me in dread. I floundered, trying to clear my mind and defend myself, but a hand was already around my throat, slamming me into the wall behind me.

"You shouldn't have come, Lira," Madoc said. "Now you've forced me to kill you again."

CHAPTER 12

REYKER

Reyker dozed atop the horse's back as the mare crossed the Green Desert. He'd not bothered to change clothes, still wearing his bloodstained jerkin and half-burned tunic. Soon he would return to Stony Harbor, to ensure Draki upheld his part of their bargain and released the captives, but first, he had to ride to Stalwart Bay—Dragon Bay. Draki had summoned him upon word of his victory in Selkie's Quay, and Reyker wanted to take stock of the port's survivors, to save as many as he could.

He'd cut through the center of the moorlands, riding over rocky hills and scraggly brush, before the desert spit him out into the verdant fields beyond. The horse had displayed otherworldly endurance, never faltering, rarely needing to rest.

Reyker really should stop calling his mount *it* or *she* or *horse*. He should give the animal a name.

He was thinking on it when he spotted something odd in the air over the field in front of him, a shimmer that made it seem like the landscape shifted. The kind of thing most people would never notice unless they'd seen it before, as he had in Ghost Village, and again in Selkie's Quay. It was the sign of a spell, a veil meant to hide something.

Eathalin. She was here.

He dismounted and snuck closer, crawling across a hilltop, ducking behind trees until he was at the edge of the veil, pushing his way through.

What the spell concealed was a mass of people, some on horseback, others in horse-drawn carts, all carrying weapons and dressed for battle. At the front, he spotted Zabelle. Beside her was a brown-haired warrior who wore Torin's face, but it was twenty years younger.

Garreth, the Ghost Prince. Leading his nomad army.

Gods aflame. There was only one place they could be heading. If they attacked Dragon Bay, the warlord would crush them.

Reyker considered going to Garreth, trying to talk him out of this, but he'd gotten an inkling of the kind of man this warrior was from Lira's stories. Garreth's homeland had been invaded, his entire clan wiped out. Reyker knew the sort of vengeful madness that came from losing everything. Garreth would not be dissuaded.

That left only one option—help the nomads win. The best chance he could give them was by thwarting the Dragon from within, a thing he'd done many times, to his own detriment. A thing he'd risk again, if it meant keeping Lira's brother alive.

He crept back to the other side of the hill, keeping out of sight. "Vengeance," he called to the horse, and she whickered. It was a good name, an apt one.

Reyker climbed onto Vengeance and rode hard for Dragon Bay.

Vengeance gained on the scout's mount, legs flying, mouth foaming. Reyker hurled his axe across the gap between him and the Dragonman. It spun, end over end, and found its mark. The man went down. It was the third scout he'd killed. Though Eathalin's spell was strong, it wasn't impenetrable. Reyker would not risk the message reaching Draki that a nomad army was marching in his direction.

He arrived at Dragon Bay far ahead of the army, and Dragonmen met him at the bridge. The guards let him pass, directing him to the beach.

Three piers jutted from the shore into the bay, and Draki stood in the bow of a caravel tied to one of them. It was the same ship Madoc had sent to run Reyker down when he sailed to Iseneld, the spur that sank his cog still attached to the caravel's prow. Dragonmen milled about on the other ships, inspecting them.

When Draki saw Reyker, the warlord grinned. "What do you think of my armada, brother?"

Reyker dismounted and walked onto the pier, eyeing the twenty-odd ships—some falling apart, others so new the wood gleamed, some tiny fishing vessels, a few big enough to sail the world.

"Inferior to those of Iseneld," he said. True for some of the ships, untrue for others, but it was meant to force Draki into a corner in front of his men, to admit his stolen fleet was middling or insult his own country's shipbuilders.

The Dragon only laughed. "Then it is good you will soon sail them to Iseneld, where our shipwrights can adjust them to our superior standards."

"*I* will sail them?"

Draki vaulted out of the caravel's bow, landing on the pier beside Reyker. "The Fjull Uprorsmund are here in Glasnith, attacking villages that belong to me. You will take this fleet and a contingent of Dragonmen to hunt them. Once the Renegades are dead, you will join me in Iseneld to celebrate our victories."

Home, home, home.

"I can't," Reyker said, to himself as much as to the warlord. He'd made a vow to protect Lira's people, and he wasn't about to break it now, with her brother on his way here. "Find someone else."

Draki frowned at Reyker's burned tunic, his blistered arm. "We'll discuss this later. I won't have my Sword looking like he's been roasted on a spit. Go to the infirmary. Tell my pretty healers to treat you well."

Reyker didn't bother arguing. He mounted Vengeance and headed back toward the village infirmary. He felt Lira's presence here, stronger than it had been before, as if her ghost was calling out, trying to tell him something—to save her sister magiskas at all costs.

The bone-healer wasn't under Draki's control. None of the Daughters of Aillira kept inside the infirmary were. Though they gazed off into space, their features neutral, Reyker was all too familiar with what compulsion looked like. These women were pretending.

If Draki found out . . . he could not let Draki find out.

The healer had already erased his burns. He'd felt the blisters dissolve, more unsettling than painful. Now she worked on his knuckles, melding the cracks in his bones from when he'd punched Draki's unbreakable skull. "Are you all right?" he asked her. She didn't respond, but her blank expression slipped for an instant. "You don't have to be afraid. I'm not like the other Dragonmen. I promise I won't hurt you."

The healer's eyes darted to the table behind him.

"What has you so frightened?" There was a bloodstained bandage on her wrist. "Who did this to you?"

She snatched her hand away. "Please. Just leave us alone."

Besides the healer, there were seven other magiskas here. He needed to go—it wouldn't be long before Garreth's army arrived—but when several of the women glanced at the same spot the healer had been looking at, Reyker couldn't stand it. He went to inspect the table, pushing the plants aside.

"Don't," a raven-haired magiska said. Several of the other girls whimpered, clinging to one another.

Reyker lifted the sheet covering the table and saw the dead Dragonman's body. He turned, stepping toward the magiskas, a question on his lips.

"Stop!" The bone-healer lurched forward, palms lifted as if she was blocking a blow.

An invisible force slammed into him. From under layers of skin and muscle came the sick crack of bones, his entire rib cage splintering into kindling, pinching his lungs in a vise. He gasped, and it was like breathing razor blades.

Pain hit him in a red wave, and he sank to his knees, the healer's screams filling his ears.

CHAPTER 13

LIRA

The cells of Stalwart Bay were nicer than those in Stony Harbor—cleaner, airier, with floors of stone instead of dirt. These were my observations as Madoc dragged me past the guards and threw me into one of the cells, slamming the bars shut in my face.

The crown he'd worn in Taloorah was perched on his head, a gaudy gold circle studded with sparkling gems. *I am no chieftain*, he'd confessed during Gwylor's trial. Because he thought he deserved more. A kingdom. All of Glasnith.

"Where are your subjects, Uncle? Where is your throne? You're squatting in a village conquered and held by a foreign warlord. It seems you're king of nothing."

Madoc stared at me, fingers drumming on his sword hilt.

"You can't touch me," I said with a smile, "and you know it. I can call Draki with my mind. I can tell him where you are, what you've done, what you're threatening to do. He wants me alive. Kill me, and he'll hunt you down. But if you take off that crown and run, I won't tell him anything."

His eyes narrowed. "And why is that?"

"Because I don't want him to kill you. Your death belongs to me."

Someone coughed in the cell next to mine. "Lira?"

My back was a constellation of scars, every one of them twinging at the sound of his voice. The smile fell from my face.

As Madoc observed my reaction, his grin widened into a gulch. "I need to think," he said. "While I decide your fate, I'll give you two time to get reacquainted."

He left me. Left *us*.

"Lira," the man said again. He sounded too much like my father. I didn't trust it.

"I thought you were dead," I whispered to the man, the thing, in the cell beside mine. "How did you survive?"

"I ran." There was a shame-filled pause. "I didn't know I was leading the Sons of Stone into an ambush. When Dragonmen surrounded us, I abandoned my men. Madoc found me the next day and gave me to the warlord, and Draki brought me here for you. He said you would come."

Had this all been a trap? Were my choices ever my own, or were Draki and the gods manipulating my actions at every turn?

"Is a part of Gwylor still inside you?" I asked.

"Yes." He sighed. "But he comes out less, now that he doesn't need me. Just to taunt. To gloat."

Part of me felt this was what Torin deserved for his foolishness and pride, for inviting the god of death into his soul. Another part—the pieces of me that could never let go of the father I knew had loved me and my brothers more than anything—pitied him and wondered if there was any way to ease his suffering, to release him from that darkness.

"In the desert," Torin said, "I didn't run out of cowardice. I ran because Gwylor gave me my mind back for a moment, and all I could think of was you and Garreth. I didn't know if you were safe. And after what I'd done to you both, the thought of never seeing you again, of never making it right . . ."

I sank down, forehead on my knees, resenting the sadness flowing through me, the little girl inside who wanted to hug her father. The soul-reader who wanted to fix him. "Did you know Mother followed the Forbidden Scriptures? That she worshipped the Fallen Ones?"

A long silence. "I did."

"You could have exiled her."

"By the time I discovered it, we'd been married for years. You had just been born, Garreth was only a child. I was so in love with Iona, I couldn't bear to lose her, so I helped her hide it instead. She said she'd denounced the Fallen Ones, and I believed her."

But she hadn't denounced them. She'd named me after Aillira, as if daring the world to discover her secret. "Was she a Daughter of Aillira?"

"If she was, she never told me."

My fingers went to the hollow between my breasts, seeking a medallion that wasn't there. My parents had loved each other, the sort of love I'd only just begun to discover before it was torn from me. Mother would want me to save the man she'd loved.

My gift was strong. The discordant forces inside me had made me a weapon when I walked through Andrithur's soul, but I had a better handle on it after my practice in the temple. Perhaps there was a way to use that weapon for good.

"Torin, if I could free you from Gwylor's grip, would you want me to?"

"Yes." The hope in his voice shook me.

"I need to put my palm on your chest. It will hurt. My touch will burn you. If it becomes too much, you must pull away. Do you still want to try?"

I heard him shuffle closer, the rustle of him adjusting his tunic. "I trust you, daughter. I will do whatever it takes to be rid of this curse."

I angled my arm around the wall of stone between us, my hand just inside the bars of his cell. He moved so my palm settled on his chest. "Ready?" I asked.

"Begin."

"Show me where Gwylor hides," I said, blowing out a breath as I opened myself up. I expected to be assaulted by sensations, but Torin didn't fight me as Andrithur had, and he was weak, so little of him left inside his diseased soul. I pushed through memories and impressions, meeting no resistance as I sought the rot eating him from within. I could feel the splinters there, pieces of the god of death piercing Torin's essence.

Slowly, carefully, I reached for one of the splinters. At my touch, the splinter warmed, charring along the edges, but it remained intact. I pulled, but the splinter didn't give, not even a fraction.

It would take every ounce of strength I had to remove the hooks Gwylor put in him. "This man is a prisoner, just as you are," I whispered to the Fallen Ones. "Help me fight Gwylor's influence over him. Help me release him as I will release you."

My power churned and my blood burned hotter. The splinter lodged in Torin's soul bubbled and blistered, melting enough that my fingers slipped. I tightened my grip and pulled hard, harder, until finally the splinter came free, disintegrating, leaving my hands sticky with oil and ash.

When I reached for another, the remaining splinters shuddered. They lengthened, curling like talons as they dug in deeper. My father, whatever was left of him, screamed. Images of my mother and brothers, of me, flickered across the inside of his soul, and then were torn asunder.

"Father?" I called, even though he couldn't answer.

Something wound around my ankle, tripping me, dragging me—a tendril of the rot in Torin's soul, drawing me closer, into itself, its malevolent sentience.

I severed it with my fist, but others wrapped around my arm, my calf, my waist, until I was covered in inky vines, just like what I'd seen dancing in Torin's eyes for months. Fragments of Gwylor that had been consuming Torin's soul.

Kicking, howling, I was wrenched into the god of death's darkness, my mind smoldering as he branded it with memories.

A man who is not a man stands over three bodies: Aillira's father and brothers. Lord Llewlin has a sword through his chest, another in his back. Andras and Cynfor still have their hands wrapped around each other's throats even in death.

The god of death grins from inside the human shell he wears.

The scene shifts, and a battering ram smashes open the gates of a village. Gwylor storms through them on his warhorse and dismounts, ordering the men behind him to burn everything, to kill everyone they see. And they do.

"*Gwylor!*" *A man stands in the center of the field, his gleaming sword held high. Handsome, noble Veronis. "You can't have her, cousin," he says.*

"We cannot allow her to live." The death god steps closer, tapping his temple. "She's a mind-reaper. She's seen inside our heads and holds all our secrets. Aillira must be destroyed, along with her descendants."

"You don't mean . . ." Veronis glances at the castle behind him, his eyes wild. In a window high above, five faces peer out: Aillira, arms wrapped around two girls, two boys. "Stay away from my children."

"Gods are not meant to breed with mortals. Their offspring are unstable."

"I'm no longer a god," Veronis says.

"That body is mortal, but your essence, your memories, your mind—that immortality cannot be shed. Some of it leaked into your progeny. It will stain every generation that comes after."

"I know how to end you, Gwylor. Aillira told me." Veronis lowers his sword, running his palm across the blade. "Let her and my children live. Swear it, and you can do what you want with me and our brethren who stood against you. The secret to your destruction, and your sister's, will remain hidden." He holds out his bleeding hand to seal their pact.

Gwylor grips Veronis's hand. "Are you so certain I'll honor this agreement?"

"Gods cannot lie to one another. You know that."

"Yes. But as you mentioned, cousin, you are no longer a god." Gwylor draws something from beneath his cloak—a crystal dagger—and stabs it into Veronis's chest.

Veronis's mouth freezes on a silent cry. The sound is brought to life from the window above, where Aillira and her children watch and scream.

"I will let them live." Gwylor twists the dagger and Veronis groans. "Ildja and I will send such plagues and sorrows upon them, they will wish they died this day. Should any of your descendants call me to this realm again, as Lord Llewlin and his idiot sons did, I will

consider our deal broken. The war will begin anew. And this time, I will sever your line. I'll ensure every last child of your blood dies in torment."

The life drains from Veronis into the dagger, and Gwylor lets his body fall, ripping out the blade.

One by one, he goes after the other gods, plunging the blade into each of them, drawing out their immortal spirits. Gwylor flicks a finger against the blade, sloshing the swirls of color floating inside it—the souls of seven gods and goddesses.

He rides to a spot on the north of the island, in the middle of a forest, and tosses the dagger into a loch. The waters of the loch begin to boil, the trees around it start to rot.

The dagger washes ashore, the crystal blade empty.

The memory faded, but I was still inside Gwylor's vision, standing on the shores of the loch that lay above a prison-realm in the otherworlds, surrounded by the decaying Grove of the Fallen Ones. Gwylor was there with me, not wearing a mortal's skin, but in his god form—a blinding prismatic light that hurt to look at, forcing me to turn away.

He spoke into my mind: THE FALLEN ONES THINK TO USE YOU TO FREE THEM.

"I didn't ask for this power, this quest. I don't want it!"

IT MATTERS NOT.

I was done worshiping the god of death. I was done fearing him. "You and Ildja's monster of a son destroyed everything. My father, my clan, my home. Isn't that enough?"

IF YOU SIDE WITH THE GREAT BETRAYER, YOU SIDE AGAINST ME, AGAINST ILDJA, WHO CONTROL THE REALMS OF THE OTHERWORLDS. CHOOSE CARE-FULLY. WE CAN DAMN EVERY ONE OF YOUR BELOVED DEAD TO THE HALLS OF SUFFERING AND THE MIST FOR ETERNITY.

Mother. Rhys. Reyker.

My knees gave out, and the putrid waters of the loch lapped around me. Not long ago, Gwylor told me my life meant nothing to him, but now . . .

NOW, LITTLE SACRIFICE. NOW YOUR LIFE OFFENDS ME.

CHAPTER 14

REYKER

Reyker's eyes were closed, but voices swirled around him.

"What did you do, Keeva?"

"I don't know." He recognized Keeva's voice—the bone-healer. "I think it was the blood she gave me. I think it was the Fallen Ones."

"Just put him with the other dead Dragonman."

Reyker's head swam as he focused on trying to breathe around the splinters in his chest. Something touched his side, over the broken ribs.

"I'm going to heal him," Keeva said. "He wears a medallion of Aillira."

"He probably stole it."

"Why hide it under his clothes, Alane? Dragonmen flaunt their stolen prizes. Perhaps he's a spy working against the Dragon. Veronis already sent one harbinger to us. Who's to say there won't be more?"

Warmth flowed into Reyker's body, sliding around his fractured bones, shifting and smelting his ribs back together. He bit down, trying to keep still.

The infirmary door flew open. The healer's hands fell away from him.

Reyker forced his eyes open, his gaze landing on a Dragonman who stood in the doorway. "What's all this? Where's the guard who's supposed to be stationed here?"

Reyker's mind and body snapped to attention. "I dismissed him." He sat up slowly, blinking at the table—the corpse—behind him that, thankfully, had been covered with a sheet and hidden behind plants once more.

"On whose authority?"

"Mine." Reyker stood, willing his legs not to shake. "I wanted privacy for my healing. Among other things." He jerked his head at the Daughters of Aillira.

The Dragonman ran his eyes over the young women. "Thought you were above that, little lordling."

"You've heard the rumors." He made himself spit out the foul words. "The Sword of the Dragon has a taste for Glasnith girls."

The Dragonman grunted. "Lock them in when you're done."

Once the man was gone, Reyker leaned into the wall, gulping air. The magiskas shuffled backward, Keeva in front, holding up her palms to him. "Come near us and I'll crack your skull open."

"I don't doubt it, but there's no need. I'm going. Stay here and barricade the door. There's an army on its way to free you, and the battle will be dangerous."

"We know about the battle," said the raven-haired girl, the one Keeva had called Alane. "We're going to fight."

"You'll die." The bone-healer, with her deadly gift, might survive, but the rest of them? Unless they all had similar gifts, they wouldn't last long in the storm that was coming. Not with the way the Dragonmen fought, cutting down everything in their path.

"Then we'll take as many Westlanders with us as we can."

Reyker dragged a hand across his jaw, hating how familiar this all seemed. Hating that now he had to choose between protecting Garreth and the nomads or the Daughters of Aillira.

"Remember me," he said, gesturing at his face, his clothes. "I'm not one of them, so don't crack my bones if you can help it. I'll watch out for you all as best I can."

"Why?" Alane asked.

He put his hand over the medallion. "Because I made a promise I couldn't keep to one of your own. I owe her a debt I can never repay, but protecting her god-gifted sisters is a start."

The magiskas glanced at one another. "All right," Keeva said, speaking for all of them. "We'll spare you from harm, invader. If you stay out of our way."

He almost grinned, imagining Lira and these women working together, wondering if they would have been close friends or fierce rivals. Then he slipped outside and whistled for Vengeance, his blade out, heart racing. Ready for battle.

CHAPTER 15

LIRA

My hand glowed bright crimson as I held it in front of me, and I knew I'd left a matching print on Torin's chest. Gwylor's influence had overtaken him, and he screamed at me, telling me that I wasn't really his daughter, that I'd killed Mother and Rhys, that everything he'd done to Garreth was my fault. There was nothing more I could do for him.

Ignoring Torin as best I could, I puzzled over the god of death's threats.

I had to choose a side. Should I trust that the Fallen Ones would save my island and those I loved who still dwelled on it, but at the expense of those I'd already lost? Or forsake Glasnith and obey Gwylor, in order to save my dead loved ones from eternal torment?

No matter what I did, I would damn people I loved.

I felt the Dragon before I saw him, a beat of power, striding closer—lazily, as if he had all the time in the world. The door to the cells opened.

"Little warrior." Draki sauntered in, dressed in boots and trousers, a woolen vest left unbuttoned to reveal broad muscles and tattooed skin. "I see you found my gift. I kept your father safe for you."

I stood up straight, shoulders squared. "That *thing* is not my father. Not since your uncle's poison infested his mind."

"You would prefer I put him out of his misery?"

I wanted to punch the easy smile that split Draki's face. "Where is Madoc? He's the one you should be offering to kill."

"Your uncle is as poisonous as you claim mine to be. He's run off, in fear of my censure, but I shall hunt him down soon. We could hunt him together."

"I want to hunt him now." To get out of this cell, to draw Draki away before Garreth's army arrived.

"Patience, little warrior. We have other matters to discuss." His serpentine eyes locked with mine, their greenish gold hues brilliant and shimmering. Hard to look at, like sunlight on a mirror. "I return to Iseneld soon. You will accompany me."

"No." I didn't care what the Fallen Ones wanted; I would not go to the Frozen Sun with Draki.

"I have taken the Green Isle. I sail home a conqueror of two countries, the beginnings of an empire. I need a powerful consort at my side, one who secures the ties between our nations."

"You need a valuable hostage, you mean." I crossed my arms against the sparks prickling them, Draki's presence energizing the air around him like the threat of lightning. "The clans of this island care nothing for a beast-loving soul-reader."

"They will if I make you a symbol. A god-blessed child of Glasnith, daughter of its greatest clan's chieftain. You represent this nation and its people. If I shame you, I shame them. But if I revere you . . ." His gaze roamed over me. "Your choice. To be shamed or revered. For yourself and your country."

"All you want is the blood in my veins. The power it gives me."

"All conquerors want power." He tilted his head, silver hair spilling over his shoulders. "Yours comes in a package that pleases me. Mine pleases you as well. It is a victory for us both, on the throne and in the bedchamber."

My cheeks flamed. "I'll never let you touch me."

"Never? I will take that bet." He slid a key from his pocket and unlocked the door, stalking toward me slowly. "Despite what you may think, I do not ravish the women I lie with. There is no sport in stealing affection. I prefer to seduce."

"Stay away from me." My back was pressed to the wall. The dagger was a circle of crystal around my wrist, ready to be wielded. If it could imprison a god, surely it could imprison a demigod. I tried to reach for it, but a gentle pressure kept me in place, my arms frozen at my sides. "Stop touching me."

"I'm not," he said softly. "When I touch you, it will be unmistakable." He'd paused a few inches in front of me, but the heat coming off his skin, the fire in his gaze, was as potent as a caress. I was eye level with his chest, and when I blinked, the sinuous black ink that covered half his body in knots and tails and dragon heads slithered as if it were alive.

"You killed my brother," I said. "You burned my village."

"Desire and morality do not exist on the same plane." When he finally touched me, it was the barest brush of his fingers along my cheek, gliding down to lift my chin until his breath was a warm breeze over my lips, daring me to give in.

Teeth gritted, I jerked my head away. "Try that again and I'll find another cliff to jump from."

He opened his mouth, full lips parting as he leaned in. To argue? To kiss me? I braced myself.

From outside came a series of shouts, followed by the sounds of horses, the clatter of steel.

Draki sighed. He threw the key to the cells, and it bounced off the wall, landing in front of Torin, just out of reach. The chieftain stretched his arm through the bars, straining. "If you manage to get free, wreak whatever havoc you wish," Draki said to him. Then the warlord gripped my elbow and hauled me from the cellblock.

We stepped beneath a sun-drenched sky into a scene fraught with chaos. The corpses of Dragonmen guards littered the ground, their throats slit. From here, I could see the drawbridge to the village was down. Nomad warriors clamored over it, weapons drawn, clashing with the Dragonmen and mercenaries surging forward.

I pulled free from Draki, and he smiled—that beautiful, savage smile he wore so often. "I know what you truly came here for, little warrior. What your god-touched blood can do for the gifted girls of your clans. Let us match the Fallen Ones against Ildja and see whose blood wins."

He turned and headed away from the battle, moving so fast my eyes couldn't keep track of him.

I spotted Garreth on the drawbridge, wielding a spiked vambrace and gauntlet on his impaired right hand, using his short sword to slice through a Dragonman with his left. Quinlan was behind him, the two of them fighting back to back. Zabelle was perched on top of the drawbridge, firing arrows, taking down one Dragonman after another.

I was about to run to them when someone touched my arm.

I spun, staring at the gray-eyed young woman before me, remembering where I knew her from: Selkie's Quay, a case full of blades, bloodstained gloves. How she'd acted so cavalier about torturing the man I loved. Her name came to me, and I spit it out. "Sursha. Pain-wielder."

She returned my cold greeting. "Soul-reader."

I punched her in the face.

She stumbled, blood oozing from one nostril. "That was for Reyker," I said, raising my fist again. "And this is for Mago."

"The Bog Man's death wasn't my fault." Sursha wiped her bloody nose with her sleeve. "The Dragon compelled me. I took no pleasure in brutalizing him."

Mabyn moved between us. "Settle this later. We're here to fight the Dragon's forces, not one another."

I glanced at the five Daughters of Aillira behind her and Sursha. All of them bore marks on their wrists—*skoldars*. Their eyes were clear, signaling that they were no longer under the warlord's control. These were the Daughters of Aillira that Draki had deemed dangerous. "I thought there were ten girls. Where are the other four?"

"The warlord took them before I arrived," Mabyn said. "But I gave the rest of them some of your blood. It strengthened their gifts, as it did mine. We've been practicing."

"Good." I picked weapons off a dead Dragonman. "Arm yourselves."

They did, searching the corpses, pocketing knives and daggers. I strapped on a sword and Sursha grabbed an axe. The sun burnished the village roofs, the bridge, the flying steel, as we moved closer to the battle underway. I closed my eyes and channeled Veronis's gift, sending a message into the depths of the wilderness, the forests and hills, the caves and brush. *Come now. Come to me.*

"This," I said, "is for Aillira's Temple and all her daughters. For the priestesses and pledges who died. For our island. Our people. Our home. Show no mercy."

Two Dragonmen were climbing the towers on either side of the drawbridge, going after Zabelle. The wind-wafter reached her arm toward the bay, harnessing the gusts and hurling them at the Dragonmen, knocking them from the towers.

Sursha threw knives at the mercenaries, every blade hitting its target in a spray of blood. The two earth-shifters pulled dirt from beneath Dragonmen's feet, and the nomads took advantage, setting upon the men who fell. The pair of fire-sweepers drew flames from a torch, using them to burn our enemies where they stood.

Dangerous indeed.

I called the horses from their stables and commanded them to trample every Dragonman they came across, as the other beasts I'd called crept nearer. *Hurry*, I urged them.

A mercenary, one of the Ravenous, came rushing at us with his scythe raised. There was something wrong with his eyes—like the Bog Man who'd tried to kill Garreth, dark hairs swirled around his pupils.

Or were they vines?

Bloody fates. Torin wasn't the only one Gwylor had infected. How many mercenaries were now the god of death's puppets? How many chieftains and warriors across Glasnith did he control?

Mabyn held out her palms toward the mercenary, and he jerked, his skin shriveling. The healer curled her fists and red rivers flowed straight through his pores as she wrung every drop of blood from him. He crumpled, nothing left of him but a dried-up husk.

I caught up to Mabyn as her knees buckled. She trembled, staring at the dead man. Her first kill. I squeezed her hands, looked into her eyes, as someone had once done for me. "You did what you had to," I told her.

She nodded, brushing away tears.

Something plunged through the air and landed a few paces away from us—a flaming stone. I searched for where it had come from. My acute vision shuddered into focus, revealing Draki and four girls standing on the roof of a watchtower that bordered the sea. Draki waved hello.

Dread coiled inside me. "Get down!" I shouted, pulling Mabyn to the ground with me just as the burning stone exploded in a spray of sparks and shards.

Sursha and the earth-shifters screamed as bits of rock sliced into their flesh. Mabyn was already up, hurrying to heal them. I glared up at the watchtower where one of the girls opened her palms, ripping stones from the tower's walls with her gift, and another girl touched a finger to them, setting them aflame. A third girl flicked her wrist and sent the rocks sailing above the battle, dropping at the feet of nomad warriors.

At my brother's feet.

"Garreth, get down!"

Somehow he heard me. He looked from me to the burning stone, then spun toward Quinlan, calling out a warning. The two of them dove flat to the dirt just as the rocks shattered, spitting fire and debris.

Warriors and Dragonmen screamed. Another volley of rocks fell, but with them came glass jars. When the jars broke open on impact, gusts of gray smoke coated the surrounding area, blinding the fighters.

On top of the tower, Draki held a jar out to one of the girls. She put a palm over it, and a tiny gray cloud filled it. The wind-wafter launched the jar toward us. It slammed into the ground, and smoke filled my eyes, my lungs. I crawled through it, coughing, choking.

Sursha grabbed me, her tunic pulled up over her nose and mouth. "How are they so powerful?" she asked, pointing at the Daughters of Aillira standing with Draki.

"The warlord must have given them his blood." The blood of Gwylor, the death god. The blood of Ildja, the serpent-goddess, the eater of souls.

Dragonmen and nomads fled the battle to escape the smoke and exploding stones. Cracks opened in the earth, swallowing warriors before closing again, burying them alive—a powerful trick from Draki's earth-shifter.

Something glimmered above our heads, spreading across the battlefield. On the other side of the field, I saw Eathalin, her hands in the air, casting a veil to hide us all from the Daughters of Aillira on the watchtower.

It was no use. They didn't need to see to do damage, and Draki had no qualms about sacrificing his own men. A wave of fire crashed over nomads and Dragonmen alike, followed by a hail of stones. My brother's army thinned as one nomad after another succumbed.

"We have to stop them," I said. "We can knock them from the watchtower and use the wind to catch them when they fall."

Mabyn looked at the wind-wafter. "Can you do that?"

"I think so."

"It's too risky," Sursha said. "You could kill them."

"They're going to kill everyone. Do you have a better idea?"

No one spoke. The women glanced around, seeking confirmation from one another. The wind-wafter nodded first, then the rest of them bobbed their heads in consent. "Careful," Mabyn said. "Our sisters are innocent. We mustn't harm them."

We stood shoulder to shoulder, surrounded by a shield of wind and earth and flame, throwing everything we had at the tower. I called for every bird who could hear me to dive at the Daughters of Aillira, but they had their own shields. Wind met wind, flame met flame, the gulls and cranes and crows that swooped over the tower caught fire and fell in a scorch of feathers or were thrown back by gusts.

The wind-wafter on the tower sent a gale shrieking toward us, scraping across the field, stirring up cyclones of dirt and hurling men through the air. Wind slammed into our line, ripping us away from one another, dragging us along the ground in different directions.

Draki's mind touched mine. *It doesn't have to be this way. We can be allies, Lira.*

His voice forming my name made me shiver. Had he ever used it before? "Our gods won't let us be allies," I said as I climbed back to my feet.

Then we will become gods ourselves.

I didn't want to be a god. All I wanted was to be a soul-reader, to be given the choice to use my gifts of my own free will, to help those who needed it. At least, that's what I told myself.

But when the packs of catamounts and coywolves I'd called from the wilderness finally arrived, paws running across the drawbridge, my pulse spiked. I felt the burn of the animals' muscles in my own as they leaped at the Dragonmen, claws and fangs ripping through the invaders, the scent of death in my nostrils, the tang of blood on my tongue—it sent a thrill up my spine.

We were created for greatness, little warrior.

I licked my lips, tasting salt and iron. "I was created to avenge my ancestor, Aillira. To cut down anyone who gets in my way."

Just like that, I made my choice. Damn the god of death and his serpent-bitch sister. Damn the twisted monsters Veronis and his brethren had become. Whatever choices I made from here on would be to right the wrongs that had been done to the first gifted girl of Glasnith, a girl who'd been betrayed by her family and her gods just as I had, whose life and love were stolen from her as mine were. The woman my mother named me after.

The Daughters of Aillira on the watchtower raised their hands, preparing for their next attack.

I screamed Aillira's name like a battle cry as I lifted my palms toward them, guiding another flock of birds to the tower's rooftop. This time, I urged the birds closer together, sending them to attack the shield not as a scattered mass but as a single entity, a crushing boulder of talons and beaks and wings that burst through the barrier. In their wake, the warlord remained as steadfast as a statue, but the Daughters of Aillira swayed and stumbled.

Where was our wind-wafter? I looked around, frantic.

There—she lay on the ground not far from me, blood dribbling down her forehead. Unconscious.

The Daughters of Aillira toppled over the watchtower's edge, into open air, and crashed into the sea.

CHAPTER 16

REYKER

He couldn't see what was happening at the drawbridge. He'd done all he could, quietly executing guards, lowering the bridge, disabling the warning bell. The rest was up to Garreth and his army. Reyker had his hands full with the battle for the bay.

He'd seen the fleet of longships from one of the watchtowers—Iseneldish ships, the same symbol painted on the sides of every hull: a circle with crossing axes in its center. The Mountain Renegades, coming to attack Draki's largest stronghold on Glasnith, to undermine his great victory. To turn more of Iseneld against the Dragon.

A thing Reyker would gladly help with, if not for the nomad army crashing through the front gates. The Mountain Renegades would cut through the Dragonmen and keep going, straight through every last nomad, until the village was theirs, and the nomads would see no difference between Dragonman and Renegade as they aimed their blades.

The Daughters of Aillira were just opening the infirmary door when he leaped off Vengeance and skidded to a stop in front of it. "I need your help," he said.

He convinced them to follow him to the shore, to watch the longships edging toward the bay. They didn't trust him, but they recognized the threat. Any ship from the Frozen Sun was considered an enemy.

"What's your plan?" Keeva asked.

"Are there tide-tellers among you?" Two women stepped forward. "Can you propel a ship if you aren't on it?"

The tide-tellers shared a glance. "We couldn't before," one of them said, "but we're stronger now. We can't control the ships like a sea-farer could, but I think we can push them forward, if that's what you're asking."

"Good. Are any of you fire-sweepers?" As the magiskas shook their heads, Reyker said, "Then we'll do this the old-fashioned way. Come with me."

They started on the largest of the three piers, climbing aboard the ships—Reyker on his own, the Daughters of Aillira working in pairs. They searched the ship holds for flint, using sailcloth as kindling, turning each vessel into a bonfire before unmooring it. The tide-tellers took turns, one shifting the Renegades' longships so they drifted away, the other ferrying the burning ships forward, creating a fiery blockade that stretched across the mouth of the bay.

Only the caravel remained. Reyker had nothing but an armful of arrows and a few spears. It would have to be enough.

Vengeance danced nervously on the pier. "Stay," Reyker ordered the horse as he boarded the caravel.

Three of the Daughters of Aillira were right behind him, climbing aboard without being asked. Then the damned horse took a running leap from the pier onto the deck, rocking the whole ship. The tide-tellers stayed behind, pushing the caravel into the current before Reyker could protest.

"Go back," he told the magiskas.

"You can't fend them off alone," Alane said. "Bronagh is a sea-farer." She pointed to the curly-haired young woman. "You already know what Keeva can do." The bone-healer. "And I'm a tract-seeker. I can glimpse what's happening on those ships. You need us."

Vengeance nudged Alane with his muzzle. Traitor.

One of the Renegade longships had slipped free of the tide-tellers and was creeping between two of the burning vessels.

Reyker met each woman's gaze in turn, noting how their eyes shone as much with fury as with fright. "If any invader makes it aboard, you all get below and lock the hatch." He looked to Alane. "How many warriors are on that ship? What sort of weapons do they carry?"

Alane's eyes closed, her forehead wrinkling in concentration. "Two dozen. Swords and axes. Arrows." Her eyes flew open. "Their archers are gathering along the railing."

The Renegade ship broke through the line of fire and headed for the caravel. "Stay low, all of you," Reyker said. Keeva lifted her hands as Reyker raised his bow and nocked an arrow. "Maim them, if you can," he told her. "Kill them if you must." The Renegades were Draki's enemies, and that made them valuable. It made them worth keeping alive.

The sea-farer trimmed the sails with more finesse than the most adept sailors he'd ever known, and the caravel circled the longship. Smoke from the burning ships coated the bay like a fog, obscuring his vision, but Alane used her gift to guide Reyker's arrows, showing him where to aim to take out the Renegades' archers. He had to kill some of them—it couldn't be helped—but others, Keeva took out, shattering the bones in their hands to keep them from firing their weapons.

The tide-tellers regained their grip on the Renegades' longship and shoved it back toward the blockade, but the fleet was pressing through. It wouldn't hold. The caravel would have to retreat to the shore. He gave the order to the sea-farer and she turned the helm.

"Can you see the fighting at the drawbridge, Alane?" Reyker asked. "How the nomads are faring?"

Alane's eyes were already closed. "It's hard to see clearly. There's smoke everywhere, and a veil of some sort. I think there's a spell-caster here."

Reyker looked at the smoke rising above the village rooftops mingling with the smoke from the burning fleet, and movement caught his eye: flocks of birds diving at one of the watchtowers before bursting into flame. And on the watchtower roof, five silhouettes.

"Daughters of Aillira." Alane's eyes flew open. "On the watchtower. The warlord must have compelled them to use their gifts against the fighters on the battlefield below."

Vengeance brayed in alarm, and Reyker's attention shifted to the nearing shore just in time to watch a man he hated nearly as much as Draki cross the sand. Torin stopped before the Daughters of Aillira clustered at the water's edge. They were focused on the bay, the ships, unaware of the sword rising behind them.

Reyker's shout came too late.

The sword sliced through air, then flesh. Several magiskas tried to fight back, but Torin's blade was quicker. One by one, the Daughters of Aillira on the shore crumpled to the sand.

Atop the watchtower, another flock of birds dove. Four silhouettes teetered on the roof's edge, hovering between life and death.

Life lost.

Alane, Keeva, and Bronagh wept as ten of their sisters died in the span of heartbeats.

There was no time for grief. Ahead of them, the barrier of burning ships was already drifting apart. They'd have to take their chances against Torin. "Get us ashore," Reyker shouted to the sea-farer, but the magiskas were hugging each other, not listening. "To shore, now, or we all die!"

That got them moving, Bronagh hurrying to adjust the mainsail and the mizzen, but without the tide-tellers' help, the caravel was slower than the sleek longships that had rowers as well as sails. The longships surrounded the caravel.

At the back of the fleet was a knarr, larger than the other ships, carrying cargo—a wooden crate big enough to hold a horse. If the rumors Reyker had heard about the Mountain Renegades were true, everyone in the village was doomed.

The Renegades let go of their oars and leaped for the caravel's gunwale, pulling themselves aboard. There were male and female warriors, equally fierce, equally deadly.

"Go." Reyker shoved the Daughters of Aillira toward the hatch, ensuring they locked it before facing the Renegades, drawing his axe and sword. Vengeance snorted, guarding his back.

One of the Renegades stepped forward, a young woman as tall as Reyker and dressed in worn leather armor, her white-blond hair cropped at her ears. "A lone man and three little girls. That's who attacked my warriors? That's who the warlord leaves to defend his coast?"

"Not just any man, Jarl Solvei," another Renegade said, gesturing to the tattoo of black flames over Reyker's eye. "That's Reyker Lagorsson. Sword of the Dragon."

"Draki's notorious little lordling brother, risen from the dead? Now there's a prize worth crossing an ocean for." Solvei signaled her warriors. "Take him. Alive."

The black river seethed. *Let me out.*

If he gave in, his battle-madness would claim him. He could kill at least half of them before they brought him down, but he needed them. The Renegades were the only organized opposition in Iseneld with enough warriors to stop Draki.

"Wait." Reyker spoke to the river as much as to the Renegades. His hands trembled, aching to use his weapons. He forced his fingers to open, to drop the blades instead. "I surrender. I'm not your enemy."

It was no use. The Renegades surged. Even though he didn't fight, the Renegades pinned him to the deck, wrapping lengths of chain around his arms and legs. He called to Vengeance, telling her to submit as ropes were thrown over the horse's neck.

"Chain the lordling to the mast," Solvei said, and Reyker was dragged to the mainmast, more lengths of chain fixing him to it, a cocoon of metal he'd never break through.

"Inside the crate on the knarr . . . is it truly one of *them*?" he asked.

"It is," Solvei answered.

Sjaf save us.

"Listen to me," Reyker said. "There's a battle in the village, Draki's forces against the natives. Speak with the native leader, Garreth of Stone. You don't have to harm them. You can ally with his army to overthrow the Dragon."

Solvei's eyes narrowed, inspecting Reyker's neck—the Sons of Stone brand marking him as a slave. She poked it with the tip of her dagger. "I don't want to overthrow the Dragon. I want to hunt down everything he covets, everything that gives him a sense of pride or pleasure, and beat it into dust. Including you." She pointed to several warriors. "Take this vessel. Sail ahead of us back to Iseneld with our prisoner so the warlord will be forced to follow. The rest of you, don your battle armor and prepare for war."

Several Renegades scrambled to the caravel's helm and sails, while the rest climbed back into their longships.

"At least let the girls in the hatch go!" Reyker called. "Please. They are blameless."

"No one is blameless." The jarl's boots clomped across the deck. Over her shoulder, she said, "Time for you to go home, Reyker Lagorsson."

In spite of his failure, his broken vow, his captivity, peace settled over Reyker. He closed his eyes, letting that kernel of hope take root.

Home.

CHAPTER 17

LIRA

The dirt had turned to mud from so many lives spilled out upon the field in floods of red. My hands drooped at my sides. I clenched them into fists. *I had to stop them. I had to.*

Didn't I?

I wanted to stay curled inside myself, with my grief and loathing, but the dregs of battle raged around me. Many of the warriors on both sides were either dead or too injured to fight, though bands of Dragonmen and nomads still staggered across the smoky field, Garreth and Quinlan among them.

Draki was conspicuously absent, no longer on the watchtower roof.

The Daughters of Aillira pulled injured nomads off the field. Mabyn healed them as quickly as she could, but she was struggling, fatigued. We all were. I hurried to help Sursha drag one of the larger nomads to Mabyn, catching the women's wary expressions.

I'd struck the blow that killed four of our sisters. Though my choice had saved many lives, I doubted they would forgive me anytime soon.

I had to.

"Who in Gwylor's name is that?" Sursha hissed.

A man lumbered toward us, his strides awkward, like he'd only just learned to walk. Torin looked so unlike himself, I hardly recognized him. He held a sword in one hand, but his other arm dangled limply, the shoulder bulging—he must have torn his arm out of the socket to reach the key to his cell.

"Father?" I whispered.

"He's in here too." The chieftain's eyes danced with the darkness of the death god. He lifted his sword above Mabyn where she was crouched over an unconscious nomad. Sursha threw a knife at Torin's throat, but he ducked. I drew my sword and rushed forward to meet his blade with my own.

Our swords locked together. "I won't let you hurt them," I said.

Torin grinned. "Too late for that. I left you a gift on the beach—six Daughters of Aillira, dead. I will kill every bitch with Aillira's blood in her veins. I'll save you for last."

"Torin!"

We both turned at the shout that had come from the battlefield. Garreth stood in a calm patch amid the turmoil, looking more like a leader, a prince, than he ever had. "Last time we fought, you had your lackey hold me down," Garreth said, pointing his short sword at the chieftain. "Care for a rematch?"

Shadows shuddered around Torin's irises and he shoved me backward. He dropped his sword and picked up a scythe from one of the dead mercenaries, stalking to where his firstborn waited.

I started to run to my brother, but Quinlan blocked my path. He was panting, sodden with sweat and blood. "Garreth needs this," Quinlan said. "Give him his chance."

Father and son faced each other for the first time since Torin cut off Garreth's warrior-mark and banished him from Stony Harbor. The swirling dust and smoke seemed to stand still as the two men squared off. Torin gestured at the gauntlet and vambrace on Garreth's right hand. "It seems dishonorable to thrash a cripple, but if you insist."

Torin's scythe sang, arcing toward Garreth's neck.

Garreth leaped sideways, thrusting his sword, but Torin dodged the strike easily. "If you weren't so weak," Torin said, "you'd have let Gwylor in and you would've been chieftain, boy."

The scythe came at Garreth again and he parried with his vambrace, steel scraping along iron. "At the expense of my soul? A man is nothing without his morality. My father taught me that."

"For all the good it's done you." Torin swung his body so his limp arm whipped out, clamped fingers opening, releasing a handful of dirt into Garreth's eyes.

In the wake of pain and blindness, Garreth dropped his guard for an instant. The scythe curved toward his torso.

Zabelle's arrow struck first, sinking through Torin's mangled shoulder until it came out the other side. From her perch on the drawbridge, she nocked another, bow trained on Torin.

She could have killed him, but it wasn't her life to take.

Torin ripped the arrow out, bellowing his fury, and Garreth followed the sound, blinking dirt from his streaming eyes, punching with the gauntlet. The strike cracked Torin's jaw, splitting the skin from chin to cheek, until the knuckles of the gauntlet and the side of Torin's face were glazed red. Garreth's knee slammed into Torin's gut, knocking him flat.

"You're a shame to our family," Torin said. "I'm glad your mother and brother died, so they didn't have to witness your betrayal. I wish your sister was dead too."

Garreth bent down, his sword ready. "Don't make me do this, Father."

I felt my brother's anguish. I wouldn't let him bear this burden alone. "I read his soul, Garreth," I called out. "Father is gone. Gwylor buried him beyond our reach."

"As I will bury you both." Torin rolled away from Garreth, snatching up the scythe, charging.

Garreth's sword came up, aiming for Torin's chest.

There, on the edge of a blade, the parasite abandoned its host. The shadows in Torin's eyes left him, streaking down pupils and irises, oozing into his lashes, until the darkness inside him was nothing more than trickling black tears.

Torin stilled. "Garreth?" he whispered, and then his son's sword plunged through his chest, just below his heart.

"Father?"

Garreth caught him as he fell. Torin's hand came up, holding Garreth's face, gazing at him with nothing but love and pride. "Forgive me, Son."

Garreth took a shuddering breath. "I already have."

Blood surged around the blade in Torin's chest. I looked to Mabyn, but she shook her head. Her gift had been drained, and she lacked the strength to heal such a severe wound. As Garreth laid Torin on his back, I went to them—my father, my brother.

"Lira?" Father's smile was brighter than it had been since Mother died. "You're here."

"Of course I am, Father." I squeezed his fingers in mine.

He was fading, the flow of blood slowing, his eyes growing dim, just as Rhys's had. It was this thought that caught in my throat, a sob I couldn't swallow.

Father understood. "I'll tell them . . ."

Rhys. Mother. If the world was just, if Gwylor was just, Torin would see them soon. But my trust in such things had waned. Father's gaze flickered between me and Garreth, trying to remember us, to take a piece of us with him, wherever he was headed.

"We'll take you home," I promised him. To entomb him in what was left of Stony Harbor, with his father and the other chieftains. He deserved that much, for who he'd been before the Culling.

Even though I was watching, I missed the precise moment he was gone, the lines blurring into obscurity. He was there, and then he wasn't. He was my father, and then he was a shell. I let go of his hand and took Garreth's instead, the two of us holding tightly to each other.

It was then we noticed the silence around us.

The battle was over. Every warrior still standing, nomad and Dragonman, was frozen, staring at the army marching up from the direction of the bay—a hundred of them at least. At first, I thought they were all disfigured, but as they drew closer I realized it was just the helms they wore, monstrosities with the curling horns of rams jutting up from either side. At the back of their procession was a massive, wheeled crate that took ten men hauling thick ropes to drag forward, one inch at a time.

The voice that rang out from beneath the helm of the foremost warrior was feminine and it spoke in Iseneldish. "Where is the usurper who calls himself the Dragon?"

No one answered. The remaining Dragonmen snarled at the horned warriors but made no move to attack.

"Draki!" The woman spun in a circle, head angling toward the windows of cottages, then up at the watchtowers. They looked empty. I couldn't feel him, but Draki had to be here somewhere, watching, listening. "Are you too afraid to show yourself?"

Words writhed across my mind. *What do you think, little warrior? Do you want me to come save you? You need only agree to my terms.*

I will make no deals with you, I replied, shoving at that invading essence, trying to slam shut whatever door he used to slip into my head.

When the woman spoke again, it was in crisp Glasnithian. "Natives of the Green Isle, I am Solvei Snorrisdottir of Iseneld, jarl of the Fjord-lands and leader of the Mountain Renegades. This village and its bay now belong to me. Surrender, and I will consider letting you live. Refuse, and you will die with the bastard warlord's soldiers."

Garreth slid his legs from under our father's head and stood. "This village belongs to the clans of Glasnith, not a tribe of the Frozen Sun. If you want it, you must take it."

Solvei smiled, a wicked flash of teeth. "I was hoping you'd say that."

One of her warriors started to open the crate. I tried to sense what was inside it, but the tendrils of awareness I sent toward it were immediately repelled, bouncing off an impenetrable wall. Whatever it was, I couldn't let it be set free.

Instinct pushed me to my feet, arms outstretched, doing the only thing I could—sending out a call to those loyal to Veronis and his blood. *Come to me.*

The response didn't come from moorland wildlife, or horses, or even birds. This call had been unfocused, born from a place of exhaustion and grief. I felt cornered in the dark, and it was creatures who lived in dark corners that answered, scurrying from the walls and floors and thatched roofs of every building, scuttling out of the ground itself. Rats and mice, spiders and roaches and maggots.

I gave the command: *Attack.*

And they did, climbing the legs of these Mountain Renegades, biting and clawing, slipping beneath clothing and armor, tangling into hair. Warriors yelped, swatting at the vermin, trying to shake them off.

Garreth didn't waste the chance I'd given him. He ran forward, with Quinlan and what was left of the nomad forces right behind him. The Daughters of Aillira were drained from the battle, but they pushed the last reserves of their power at the jarl's army.

Eathalin wrapped a veil around Garreth so his opponents couldn't see him coming.

The crate the Renegades brought had been loosened, and the thing inside wanted out. Hammering sounded from within, and the wood shook and splintered until the lid gave way. A monster stepped from the crate into the light, and I saw red eyes, curled horns—the same as the ones the warriors wore, but five times larger—and fangs like a wolf. A demon of mountains and ice. Slaver dripped from its mouth, soaking its muzzle. It slunk forward, surveying the scene, waiting for something.

Solvei snapped her fingers. "Now, Skrim!"

Jaws stretching, neck arching, the beast threw its head back and roared. The sound of it nearly split my skull. The earth shook beneath me and the buildings of Stalwart Bay groaned, cracks spiderwebbing through the stone. They began to crumble, one after another, into piles of rock and rubble that crashed down on nomads and the Renegades who'd not retreated fast enough at Solvei's signal, dust and debris eddying through the air.

There was a scream, and I saw Zabelle falling from the drawbridge as it dissolved beneath her. I watched in horror, but I had to turn away as Solvei ran at Eathalin—the spell-caster's hands stretched toward the invisible force cutting down Renegades left and right in the center of the field. The Ghost Prince.

I moved between Eathalin and the jarl, both our swords poised to strike. "Stay back," I said in Iseneldish, my ears still ringing, muffling every sound. Ash swirled around us, the remnants of what had been Stalwart Bay only moments ago.

"You're another of the warlord's precious magiskas," the jarl said. "A powerful one at that. How the Dragon must covet you." A roach crawled across Solvei's cheek, a spider nested in her hair, but she didn't flinch. "Call off your swarms or I will tell my pet to eat your people."

This was not a woman to be trifled with. I released the tether I'd put on the vermin, severing the bond, and they reverted from soldiers to animals, fleeing in fright, scattering into the toppled cottages and towers.

"Drop your sword, magiska. We both know you're too weak to fight me."

Solvei was as tall and muscled as any man, brandishing her weapon with obvious skill, and I was exhausted from using my gifts. I made a show of struggling to lift the sword higher, only to let it fall. When I dropped it, she grabbed me by the hair, lowering her guard, assuming I was disarmed and powerless.

My hand went to my bracelet. I didn't want to use the dagger on her, but I would—if it came down to her life or mine, her life or any of the nomads or Daughters of Aillira, she would die on the end of its crystal blade.

Her fingers dug behind my ear, finding Draki's mark. "You are coming with me to Iseneld," Solvei said.

I let go of the bracelet and nearly laughed.

Iseneld?

The jarl was going to take me right where I needed to go.

I had experience being a captive. It was easy to play the frightened damsel, to stumble and tremble and let Solvei drag me past the battling warriors, to let her think she'd won. To let her underestimate what I was capable of.

As we passed the ice demon, its red eyes followed me, daring me to try and call to its mind. I couldn't—even if I'd not been drained, this monster was not of my island, had never worshiped Veronis. It would not listen.

The jarl stopped at the shore, and I saw the bodies of Daughters of Aillira I'd met in the infirmary, the ones Torin had bragged about cutting down. Solvei shoved me when I slowed to stare at the dead girls, pushing me into one of the waiting longships before I could commit the faces of my fallen sisters to memory.

These ships looked just like the ones that had come to Stony Harbor, wooden sea beasts with a single tall mast and square sail, oars sticking from each side into the water. The only difference was the carved figurehead;

instead of dragons, a rendering of a half-wolf, half-ram creature adorned the front of each ship.

Solvei locked my wrist in a manacle attached to the inside of the bow, one of several lining the gunwale. I felt the hands of something far bigger than myself at work here—gods, fate—pushing us like pieces on a game board, sending these Renegades to escort me over the sea to the Frozen Sun, where I'd been commanded to go, but in the worst, most shameful of ways. Shackled to a boat, at the mercy of enemies.

Last chance, Lira, Draki drawled, breaking through the weakened barriers I'd erected around my thoughts. *Come to Iseneld as my consort, or as their prisoner.*

Was that why he'd hidden, letting the Renegades destroy the village he'd seized, to force me to bend to his will?

I'm a prisoner either way, I told him. *Better an unwilling captive than a culpable one.*

After a pause, he murmured, *As you wish.*

I felt his presence recede and squashed a desperate impulse to summon him back as more Renegades trickled out of the ruined village, returning to the ships, their blades wet with the blood of both Dragonman and nomad.

Garreth. Quinlan. Zabelle. The Daughters of Aillira.

How many of them lay dead among those ruins?

The ice demon padded toward the boat as Solvei beckoned, coaxing it in a language I didn't understand, something older and stranger than Iseneldish. The huge beast let itself be led back into its crate once the Renegades rolled it down to shore, and they loaded the monster onto the largest of the Renegade ships. Other Renegades returned carrying looted goods: weapons, saddles, sacks of things I couldn't see. Anything of value they'd managed to pluck from the rubble.

A group of Renegades climbed into Solvei's ship and suddenly we were drifting over the shallows, the waves nudging us away from land. Solvei barked orders for the rest of the warriors to hurry.

"None of you are staying?" I asked. "You came all this way, killed my people and sacked the village they just reclaimed, and now you're leaving?"

"We stopped at the largest coastal villages along the way to this one, reduced them to rubble and killed every Dragonman who didn't flee. Our job is done." She regarded me like I was lowlier than the roaches that had crawled over her. "Iseneld is our home. The Green Isle is a dung heap infested with inferior gods and craven tribes. I would never curse my warriors to stay in such a place."

There were likely Glasnithians in all those villages, kept as prisoners and slaves. How many of them had died during the jarl's attacks? Was Stony Harbor among the villages she'd routed?

My temper heated, my tongue about to get me into more trouble, but then I saw a Renegade pushing another captive down the beach toward the boats that hadn't yet cast off. Quinlan—limping, bloody, but alive.

"Everyone else either fled or died, but this one surrendered," the Renegade shouted. "Practically begged me to take him prisoner."

Quinlan met my eyes briefly, and my heart stammered. With too many Renegades to fight, no way to help me escape, Quinlan had surrendered so he'd be taken as a captive to Iseneld alongside me. Stupid, brave fool.

Solvei took one look at me and read all she needed to know in my expression. "Bring him," she said.

The Renegades onshore pushed Quinlan into one of the longships. Some of the warriors on Solvei's ship took their places at the oars, others hoisting the square sail so it caught the wind with a jolt, tugging us out to sea.

The village shrank to a smear of green and gray.

"You are not the Dragon's prize anymore," Solvei said, standing over me. "You belong to me now, magiska."

"I belong to no one," I replied, but it was a lie. Until I freed them, I was beholden to the Fallen Ones, a vessel at the mercy of their whims. I had to end it—Ildja, the war, the gods' power over me.

I *would* end it.

By the time the sun sank, Glasnith, the only land I'd ever known, had melted into shadows. It was just a speck on the horizon, and then it was gone.

PART TWO
HEART OF
THE FROZEN SUN

CHAPTER 18

LIRA

"I love you."

The thorntree swayed above us, the ruins of Aillira and Veronis's kingdom spread out around us. It was cloudless, but the storm in Reyker's eyes reflected the one raging inside me. "You're not really here," he said, trailing his thumb along my cheek.

"Neither are you." I reached for him anyway, pulling his head to my chest.

Because you left me, you are gone, you are dead.

Something had changed. How many times had I dreamed of him, of us, like this, not understanding until the end that it wasn't real? But this time, I knew, and so did he, though neither of us wanted to say why, to give voice to that irrevocable truth.

Dead, you are dead, you are—

"I don't want to go." His arms slid beneath me, circling my waist. "If it was my choice, I would never leave."

"But you should." Whatever this was, this place between worlds where we'd managed to find each other, it wasn't a blessing as I'd first assumed. It was a torment. "Knowing this isn't real, that it won't last, that we'll lose each other again and again will drive us mad. It will keep us from moving on as we must."

I needed my wits to face what awaited me when I woke, and Reyker— Reyker needed to let go of me, so his spirit could find peace in Skjorlog Felth, the afterworlds of his people, where his family surely waited for him.

"What are you saying, Lira? That you don't want to see me again?"

"Nothing." I shook my head. "Don't listen to me. If this is all we get, let's not waste it."

He tried to be gentle, but I had no patience, no restraint. My mouth was hard against his, my hands digging into his skin, using my body to beat back the words I'd almost spoken, the words I must say eventually because I knew he never would.

We cannot return to this place. This is the last time.

The last time.

The last.

CHAPTER 19

LIRA

The sea had been kind when I'd fallen asleep, a placid silver mirror, but I woke to an angered ocean, its frothing hills rolling across an infinite expanse of gray. The expressions of the Renegades were grim, but not fearful. Solvei stood on deck, arms spread wide, grinning at the pelting rain like a gleeful child.

We'd been sailing for three days. Every bit of my power had been expended during the battle at Stalwart Bay, so I waited for it to slowly seep back. Solvei had anticipated this. She'd moved Quinlan onto our ship, chaining him in the stern, threatening to kill him if I tried to use my gifts.

The longships had crossed into the realm of the Ice Gods, and beneath the water, shadows glided—whales and sharks and tentacled monstrosities big enough to rival the Brine Beasts. I could feel them, but not the way I'd felt the animals on Glasnith, and I doubted these creatures would listen to me if I called. This was Sjaf's kingdom, and every animal here belonged to him and his kin. Power sloshed through me, useless and restless, like sap in a tree that could not be tapped. My heightened senses had dulled, still sharper than a mortal's, but only a sliver of what they'd been. I wondered if I could even read a soul this far from my gods and home. I could feel the Fallen Ones in my veins, but the farther we got from Glasnith, the quieter my blood became.

Alarmed as I was at the loss of my strongest weapons, it was a relief to feel the fetters binding me to Veronis slacken.

Quinlan was watching me, as he often had on the journey. His head tilted, asking if I was all right, and I nodded. He needed the assurance, even if it was a lie.

For the thousandth time, I tested my manacle, pulling at it with all my strength. There was no way I could break it. If only there weren't so many eyes on me, I could try to pry it open with the crystal dagger.

"Where do you plan to run to, magiska?" Solvei asked over the roaring of wind and waves. "You are no child of Sjaf. If you jump, the sea god will drown you."

"If this ship capsizes, the manacle will drown me," I told her, rattling it for emphasis.

"This is *my* ship. It is unsinkable."

A wave crashed over the deck, soaking us. I shoved wet hair out of my face. "Do you enjoy tempting fate?"

Solvei was already gone, giving orders to the Renegade at the helm and encouragement to the men and women rowing to keep the longship from turning sideways as we plunged down the swells.

The storm lasted half a day before blowing itself out. We had a few hours' reprieve of sun, enough that my clothes almost dried, before the next storm hit. I might have frozen, had it not been for the mercy of one of the Renegades, a young man who threw me a wool blanket when no one else was looking. I saw him give one to Quinlan too.

An uneventful sea crossing, Solvei declared. How could they stand it, being tossed about on waves ten times larger than our ship, soaked to the bone, cold and wet for days on end?

When land appeared on the horizon the next morning, I felt something like relief, until I realized it wasn't land, but islands of ice floating in the middle of the sea. The longships drifted between them, and I craned my neck to take them in, their icy faces smooth and glistening, each one like a pile of crushed jewels—turquoise and topaz, diamonds and moonstones—sitting in the ocean's palm. Though I'd witnessed such sights in Reyker's memories, it stunned me that ice could be so beautiful.

Behind us, a silhouette continued to stalk the Renegade ships. It was a dark cloud riding the waves, far enough back that I couldn't get a clear view of the other ship, close enough to be certain it was following, as it had been since we'd left Glasnith.

Draki. I didn't dare call out to him.

Solvei raised a spyglass to her eye, trained on the creeping shadow. "What a prize you are, magiska. He'd attack us if he wasn't certain we'd kill you for it. You may prove to be of more value than his cursed brother."

"Brother?" I sat up straighter. Reyker hadn't mentioned Draki having any family beyond the warlord's serpent-goddess mother. "The Dragon has a brother?"

"I found him in the bay, just before I found you. Another token I stole from the Dragon."

Draki's brother had been in Stalwart Bay?

"The Dragon is my enemy as well," I said. "He killed my brother and burned down my village. Let me go and we can fight him together."

She lowered the spyglass, knuckles whitening as she squeezed it in her fist. "Draki killed my father and sister. He killed my wife. Now I will repay him. I'll destroy him by destroying everything he cares for, just as he did to me."

If that was the case, then I wasn't a prize, I was a hostage. Innocent or not, deserving or not, Solvei would hurt me to get to Draki. "If you do, you're no better than him."

The insult cut her. Solvei leaned in, teeth bared. "For your sake, magiska, pray that you are wrong."

—✦—

We spent another two days sailing through ice fields before Iseneld was spotted. A cheer went up, all the Renegades celebrating and giving thanks to their gods.

Part of me felt like celebrating with them. I couldn't wait to get off this boat—my skin was crusted in salt and my manacled arm throbbed so much I was ready to chew it off. But then I looked at Quinlan, pale and gaunt after a week on the sea, what little food the Renegades had offered him having crawled back up his throat during the worst of the storms.

As a captive, Reyker had suffered at the hands of my people, his enemy. Would I watch the same things happen to Quinlan here?

The Renegades lowered their sails when we were a league or so from the coast, slowing as we came upon some sort of frozen jetty sticking up from the water. We glided closer, and the jetty seemed to twitch. It inched higher above the surface.

I gripped the gunwale, defying my boneless legs to stand, and stared in awe.

Eyvor, the island-serpent, guardian of Iseneld. This was how the Frozen Sun had remained shrouded in mystery, why so few foreigners had ever made it to the country's shores. She was a living barrier, circling the entire island.

White as snow, with cracks and crevices like stone, but it was skin. Scales. Her body was wider than three longships and longer than I could guess, pocked with barnacles and garnished in seaweed. Her head broke through the waves, her jaws stretched wide, full of her own tail. Reyker had told me the story: Eyvor had been a goddess, sister to Ildja, and some slight of hers had angered the serpent-goddess, the eater of souls. So Ildja turned her sister into a giant snake, but to keep Eyvor from attacking her, Ildja threw the snake into the sea and cursed her to devour herself. She'd damned her own sister.

Eyvor's eye was a bright blue marble with a slitted pupil cutting through the center. The eye swiveled, taking us in.

Renegades bowed, pulling trinkets from their fur-lined vests and dropping them into the sea—rock carvings, gems, broken bits of silver and gold. Offerings.

I had no baubles to give her. The blue eye narrowed on me as I reached my hand out, stretching as far as the manacle allowed, pressing my palm to her sleek scales.

"This is what I offer," I told the cursed goddess. Veronis's gift flared to life, just enough to put my thoughts into the serpent's mind as the crystal bracelet brushed across her skin. I couldn't make Eyvor obey, but I could ask a favor of her. For help avenging other gods Ildja cursed, for a chance to end the reign of Ildja and her monstrous son. Though Eyvor couldn't respond, I sensed her pain—years of longing and loneliness, of chewing on sorrow and rage as much as her own body. Beneath the misery was a deep longing to make the sister who'd done this to her pay.

She pulled away, sinking below the surface to let our ships pass.

I looked at Quinlan, trying to communicate what was about to happen, that he needed to be prepared, but he was gaping at me. So were the Renegades.

"No one touches the island-serpent," Solvei said. "It is forbidden."

"I didn't know."

"Throw her to Sjaf," someone whispered. "She will curse us."

Yes, I would. The longships were already drifting forward on the current. It wouldn't be long now.

"We need the magiska to lure the warlord into our territory." Solvei's hands were on her hips, studying me. "The boy, however, is nothing but an extra mouth to feed. We can offer him to Sjaf to appease any insult on the girl's behalf."

The ships were still far enough from shore that being dumped overboard was a death sentence. The tides were too unforgiving, the water so cold it would sap a man's energy before he made it to land. "Don't," I growled as Solvei nodded and four Renegades moved toward Quinlan, unlocking his manacle and hauling him to his feet.

She pointed at me. "You did this. You violated a sacred law."

"Damn your laws. Damn you all."

Behind the ships, Eyvor breached the surface once more. The Renegades turned at the sound, and the crystal bracelet slithered from beneath my manacle, into my cupped palm, taking on its dagger form. Eyvor bobbed on the water, once, twice, her heavy head stirring up the sea, spinning off swells that rolled toward the fleet.

The manacle was made of dense iron. Whatever powers the dagger possessed, cutting through solid metal wasn't one of them, so I worked at the rusted lock, pushing the tip of the dagger into it.

Eyvor's body undulated, her head rising as high as it could, slamming down hard enough to make a wave that dwarfed the others, even the ones that had hurled us about in the storms. Coiled with power, pushing as fast as a fist through the water.

Despite the icy air, sweat sprinkled my forehead. I dug at the lock, hearing the tumblers give, but slowly, so slowly.

Across the fleet, Renegades screamed. Eyvor's wave was almost on top of us.

Solvei's head whipped toward me. "Tricky little witch. What did you do?"

The manacle opened a fraction. I turned the dagger, prying at the lock. Wider, but not wide enough.

The screams melted into a roar as the giant wave's shadow fell over us. The longships behind ours were dragged up the wave's face, vanishing on the other side. Then it was our turn, the stern sucked backward, our vessel teetering on the crest.

With a groan, the lock broke and the manacle yawned wide enough for me to slip free. The dagger molded to my wrist. I took a deep breath and held on.

The ship somersaulted, tumbling into the wave's trough. I clung to the gunwale to keep from being torn away, dangling from my fingertips as the boat spun above me, cracking my shoulder against the hull as the ship landed and sank from the force of its own weight.

Cold water embraced me. The sun was gone. Everything went dark and quiet.

Then the sea spit us out, buoying the vessel up to the surface. The ship righted itself, rolling violently in the wave's wake. As soon as I let go of the gunwale, I fell to my knees, pushing hair from my face, blinking salt from my eyes.

I was alone in the boat.

I scanned the water. Some of the longships were upright, but others had capsized. Renegades clambered into longships, clutched at overturned boats, swam or treaded water or floated facedown. The ice demon's crate had busted open, and the horned beast paddled in circles, yelping in confusion.

"Quinlan!" I didn't see him anywhere.

"Kill her!" Solvei stood in the bow of another longship, dripping, bedraggled, her furious gaze trained on me. But her warriors were too busy saving themselves or their comrades to obey.

Behind the damaged fleet, another ship drew closer to the island. It was a massive galleon, the wood decorated with carved knots and reptile scales, and a Dragon figurehead boasting a sharp-fanged snarl. A lone figure stood on the deck, lounging against the rail.

"Quinlan!" I called, louder this time, as if that mattered. I slung a leg over the side, about to jump in after him, just as something rocked the ship.

I turned in time to see Quinlan climb over the stern and flop onto the deck, and I rushed to his side. He was scratched and bruised, coughing up water, but otherwise unharmed.

"A little warning would've been nice," he said without opening his eyes.

"I tried. Pay more attention next time."

One eye cracked open. "You're planning a next time?"

"Hold on." I went to the mast, checking that the sail was undamaged.

Now, I called to Eyvor, and the serpent rose again. She angled her huge scaly head toward me as best she could, exhaling in a long huff that billowed our sail and sent us skating along the water, leaving Solvei and her broken army floating there, with the Dragon on their heels.

Before me was an island I knew well, but only through another's memories. Seeing it with my own eyes made my blood pump faster, despite the ache in my heart.

I made it, Reyker.

If only you were here with me.

CHAPTER 20

REYKER

He woke with her name on his lips, as he so often did. Always expecting to find her beside him, in those gilded first moments between waking and dreaming, as if some part of him had never left the ruins and still lay with her beneath the thorntree.

It wasn't branches he saw above him when he opened his eyes, but a hatch.

The caravel was fast, and they'd reached Iseneld days sooner than any longship could. Once they'd gotten within a day's sail from Iseneld, the Renegades had unchained Reyker from the mast and shoved him into the hold to keep their destination's location hidden from him. Even after they'd docked, no one had come. His body was cramped in the tight space, and all he could see was a square outline of light. If he pressed his eye to it, sometimes he could make out a pale sliver of sky. They'd left him a skin of water, and a tiny bucket to relieve himself that sloshed with the heaving waves, dampening the floor of the hold with his own stale piss. He'd started to wonder if the Renegades had left him locked in here to die slowly when the hatch finally opened, filling with sun, leaving Reyker squinting at the figure hovering over him.

"Paint me pink and call me a horse's ass. It *is* you." The man gripped Reyker's arm, helping him out of the hole he'd been curled in for the last however-many hours—or, more accurately, lifting him out like a cat would lift its kit. This hulking man was not one of the Renegades who'd captured him.

"Do I know you?" Reyker rubbed the heels of his hands against his bleary eyes. The sky around him was pale blue, the caravel's deck empty.

"Been a while, hasn't it?" The man dragged his fingers through a thick beard, black streaked with rust-red, that matched the hair on his head. "Seven years."

Reyker counted backward, remembering where he was seven years ago: a boy, in Vaknavangur. Heir to a village and a title, his parents still living, his life not yet destroyed. He stared at the warrior in front of him, familiar features standing out—light-brown skin that marked him as having a foreign-born parent, jovial expression that put everyone around him at ease—and recognized the boy inside the man. "Brokk?"

The man laughed, slapping Reyker's back hard enough to hurt. "Knew you'd remember eventually, clever bastard."

Reyker had to tip his head back to look up at him. "You've grown." His childhood friend had been lanky, but now he was as broad as a bull.

"And you've changed." Brokk's demeanor darkened, his gaze latching onto the flames over Reyker's right eye. "You obey the Dragon now."

The last time Reyker saw Brokk was the day Draki and his Dragonmen stormed into Vaknavangur and killed his father. Brokk's older brothers died that day as well—one on the battlefield, the other by an executioner's axe while Brokk and his mother watched. Brokk had been twelve, the same age as Reyker. A year older, and he'd have met the axe too.

"It's not what you think," Reyker said.

Brokk's arms were so bulky it was a wonder he could cross them. "Explain."

"I will. But first, will you tell me what's been done to the other prisoners on this ship? Three Glasnithian magiskas—"

"They're fine. So is that creepy mare of yours that stares like she can see straight into your soul. The Fjull Uprorsmund don't harm horses or unarmed girls."

After having his rib cage shattered by the bone-healer, Reyker knew it was naive to call any Daughter of Aillira unarmed, but he nodded, glancing at their surroundings. The caravel was docked at a pier in a narrow fjord, one he couldn't name. There were no signs of inhabitance except a worn path that led up a hill, into the mountains beyond. He took a deep breath and tasted hints of salt and snow, soil and rain. *Home.* "You're one of the Mountain Renegades?"

"I joined Solvei's army last year, after my mother died."

"I'm sorry," Reyker said. Before Brokk was born, Brokk's mother had been a war widow and a sword-maid, sailing across the seas, marching into battle. Brokk was the result of her dalliance with a Savannan warrior, though she'd treated him the same as his older brothers and threatened anyone who insulted him for his mixed heritage. A strong woman, who'd raised a strong son. Reyker had admired her.

Draki had made a show of sparing her from execution when he sacked their village. It wasn't a mercy—women from tribes Draki considered enemies were forced into servitude, and if they refused to submit, they were given as playthings to the Dragonmen. Reyker couldn't bring himself to ask what had become of Brokk's mother in the years between when Vaknavangur fell and her death.

Brokk shifted awkwardly. "I'm supposed to tie you up. The others don't trust you. *I* don't trust you, even though I want to."

Reyker put his arms out, no stranger to chains and ropes. He'd spent the last seven years in one form of captivity or another: hostage, pawn, slave. Brokk leaned in, looking at Reyker's neck, eyes widening at the sight of the brand. "Gods a-fucking-flame. What happened to you, Lagorsson?"

"It's a very long story. I'll tell you all about it over a bowl of stew and a pint of ale."

That earned him a snort. "I should offer you a bath as well, I suppose. You reek of piss."

"At least it's mine."

The snort turned into a hearty laugh. Brokk put a hand on his shoulder and pushed him toward the pier, a gesture both welcoming and threatening. "Don't try anything, old friend. I'd hate to have to kill you."

The path was long and winding, ending behind one of the mountains, where the Renegades had set up a spot that was half village, half camp—dozens of wooden buildings and grass-roofed cottages beside twice as many sheepskin tents. Fjullthorp, Brokk called it. It reminded Reyker of Ghost Village, only there were no families, no children. This was a war camp. Everyone here was a soldier, all of them glaring at Reyker as he walked at Brokk's side.

Everyone, except the three frightened girls huddled together around a fire. The Daughters of Aillira were unharmed, as far as he could see, and left untied as well. Their eyes found him, following him desperately—the only familiar face in a sea of Iseneldish warriors who didn't speak their language. Reyker nodded at them, trying to offer reassurance, waving Alane off when she started to rise.

They were here because of him. He had to find a way to free them and get them back to Glasnith where they belonged.

Brokk led him into what must have been the meeting hall, a rustic structure of wood and rock, the walls decorated with the same curling ram horns the Renegades wore on their helms. A fire blazed in the center of the room, and they sat down at a table near it. Brokk called for stew and ale, and a young woman brought out a tray from the kitchens attached to the back of the hall. Reyker held a bowl in one hand, a tankard in the other, too stunned to eat or drink.

"Easy, Lagorsson. You look like you're about to cry into your ale." In less than a minute, Brokk's tankard was already half empty, as was his bowl.

Reyker took a swig of the bitter liquid, letting it heat his stomach. "It doesn't feel real. I never expected to make it home. I thought I was going to die on Glasnith."

"You did die." Brokk pointed a spoon at him. "According to our informants."

"For a time." Those months between when he washed ashore in Stony Harbor to the day Draki burned it down, between when Lira found him and when he watched her jump from the bluffs. He'd never been more alive than he had during that period he was presumed dead.

"The other Renegades want to lock you up. When Jarl Solvei returns, she'll want to cut off pieces of you and send them to taunt the warlord. I'm the only friend you have here. The last time I saw you, you were a child taking on a villain, fighting Draki for Vaknavangur, for *us*, its people. I want to know how that brazen boy became the Sword of the gods-damned Dragon."

Reyker tossed his head back, draining his tankard, clunking it against the table. "We're going to need a few more of these."

CHAPTER 21

LIRA

Once we were far enough out of reach, we had to abandon the longship. The ship stalled when the winds died, and we were too exposed, sitting out on open water in a boat that took more than two people to steer. Quinlan and I trudged through knee-deep surf with sacks full of supplies we'd pilfered from the ship slung over our shoulders. We held on to each other for balance, struggling to keep our footing as the current fought to suck us back out, and made it onto the black-sand beach.

The moment my foot touched shore, the bracelet on my wrist grew tighter, as if the key knew where it was and was urging me on.

There were pillars rising from the sea here, like those around Stony Harbor, but these were sharp blue-black rock instead of worn brown stone, some hollowed in the center where the ocean had carved out arches and caverns. The cliffs looming directly in front of us seemed to be made of thousands of miniature versions of those pillars, the jagged black slabs combining to form a tower of spikes.

"Up?" Quinlan asked, nodding at the cliff wall.

"Up."

At least the jutting rock made the cliffs easy to scale, though we had to move slowly to avoid slicing ourselves open on the serrated edges. The dead wind sprang back to life as we climbed, whipping up from the sea to tug at me like restless fingers, sending waves crashing at the foot of the cliffs and spindrift misting my skin. By the time we reached the top, we were both breathing hard, our palms scratched and bloody, our clothing torn in places.

All those aches disappeared as we took in the view from atop the cliffs.

Spread out below us was a valley carpeted in green moss and yellow wildflowers, crisscrossed with dozens of meandering streams formed by snowmelt trickling down the mountainsides. The mountains themselves were scattered, lonely rock giants punching up defiantly through the earth wherever they pleased, their summits capped with snow.

"I thought it would be nothing but ice," Quinlan whispered. "A frozen wasteland, like the legends said."

"So did I, once." Before Reyker showed me how wrong I'd been, how beautiful his island was, vibrant and lush outside of the winter months, except for the deepest parts of the glacial Highlands—those were frozen year-round. And, unfortunately, they were exactly where we needed to go.

"Do you know where we are?" Quinlan asked.

I shook my head. Reyker's memories were still fresh in my mind, but they were flashes across time and place with no way to organize them into a map of the island. "We're on the coast now. That means we have to head inland."

To the heart of the Frozen Sun, Veronis had said. The center of Iseneld.

Quinlan swept his arm out and bowed. "Lead the way, Lady Lira, enchanter of sea creatures, explorer of uncharted terrain."

I unstrapped the ice axes from the supply sack and handed one to Quinlan. They'd be essential on the glacier, and for now we could use them as walking sticks. I skidded down the rocky slope in my stolen boots to the floor of the valley, with Quinlan right behind me. From there, we picked our way over a rock field buried under moss and tussock grass. The air was cool, but the valley was protected from the gusting wind. I was dressed in clothes I'd found on the ship—a heavy wool coat that came to my knees, and trousers so loose I'd had to tie them with rope just to keep them from falling off. For the first time since we'd left Glasnith, I felt warm.

Quinlan was dressed similarly, looking almost at ease. It was his nature, adapting to whatever the circumstances required without losing his wit or composure. I envied it.

"What do you think Garreth and Zabelle are doing right now?" he asked.

"Arguing."

They were both alive—that was the first thing Quinlan had said after we'd sailed out of sight of Solvei's fleet, filling in what I'd missed while Solvei dragged me down to the longship in Stalwart Bay. When the drawbridge collapsed, the wind-wafter had used the last of her strength to slow Zabelle's fall. She'd suffered a broken ankle, nothing more. Garreth helped her onto a horse and gave the command to retreat. Zabelle led the Daughters of Aillira and the nomads out of the village, bow in hand, taking down anyone who tried to stop them. Few did. The Renegades and Dragonmen were too busy killing one another.

Garreth had debated coming after me. It was Quinlan who convinced him to stay so he could lead the nomads and reunite the clans of Glasnith, because our country needed its prince. Quinlan had to come in his friend's place, to follow me wherever I was taken and keep me as safe as he could.

"Maybe Solvei and her warriors killed all the Dragonmen," Quinlan said. "Maybe Garreth is already prince of Glasnith."

"She only stopped in coastal villages that were on her route, only killed the Dragonmen who didn't run. The Dragonmen are spread too far. I'm sure she thinned their numbers, but the way Draki bragged about being an emperor . . . I doubt he'd have left Glasnith if he thought he'd lose control over the island. And there's still Madoc and the mercenaries, Draki's supposed allies, to contend with. Not to mention the god of death."

"Ever the optimist." Quinlan nudged me with his shoulder. "If Garreth can convince the clans to unite, they might stand a chance."

"That's a very big *if.*"

We reached a shallow stream, splashing through rock-strewn rapids, the water clear and cold. This one was easy, but there were many more to cross that would be deep with strong currents. It felt like madness to do this with no guide, no map—nothing but a key I didn't understand how to use, and the vague instructions of a god.

I let my mind quiet with the stillness around me. *Veronis? Are you here?*

There was no answer but the cry of gulls overhead.

"It nearly killed Garreth, letting you go," Quinlan said. "But I made him promise not to come after us, no matter what happened."

I imagined Garreth and Quinlan clasping hands, the insinuation of that promise burning between them. If Solvei used us as hostages, or if Garreth never heard another whisper about our fates, he would put our island and its people first. I couldn't fault him for it. Garreth had his duty, and I had mine. "Thank you for talking sense into him."

Our boots crunched over the rocky slope as we emerged on the other side of the stream. "I didn't just do it for him," Quinlan said.

I kept my eyes forward, focused on the hills and mountains, the journey ahead. Anything to keep from acknowledging what I heard in Quinlan's voice, what I knew lived in his heart, things that I once thought I felt for him too. Things that seemed impossible to ever feel again, for anyone, when my own heart belonged to a dead man.

⸻

The plan was to stop and make camp at the first glimmer of sunset. We kept pushing onward as the valley became a mossy canyon, steep rock walls rising on either side of a foaming river. Our stomachs grumbled, our legs shook. Still no hint of dusk.

"Wait." I halted suddenly on the canyon's lip, sending a spray of pebbles over the ledge. "It's summer. So it's nighttime already, in a sense. The sun won't set until around midnight."

Quinlan looked at me like I'd lost my mind. "If the sun is up, how can it be night?"

"It just is. Trust me." I'd scoffed, too, when Reyker told me that in his country, the sun burned during summer nights, and sank long before daytime ended in winter. "We should stop as soon as we're clear of the canyon."

He rubbed his hands over his face. "I'll agree that day is night if it gets me fed and off my feet."

It was another hour before the canyon walls gave way to a flat sandy plain, leaving us on safer ground. I dropped my satchel at the foot of a boulder and slid down it, my back against the stone. Quinlan joined me, pulling dried fish from his pack, offering me some. We shoveled bits of fish into our mouths, not bothering to light a fire.

"Either hunger has made me delusional or this is the best meal I've ever had," he mumbled.

"Likely a bit of both." I washed the fish down with a skin of fresh water, filled from a stream. Even the water here tasted different—cleaner, crisper, like it was bubbling up from the source where all water was born. "I'll take the first watch."

Quinlan didn't argue. Between bouts of seasickness and the beating he took from the island-serpent's wave, we both knew he was in worse shape than I was. He wrapped himself in a wool bedroll. "How can I sleep with the bloody sun still out?"

"I'm sure you'll manage."

Minutes later, he was snoring.

Climbing atop the boulder, I watched the sun dip slowly to the horizon, drenching the clouds in beams of pink and orange. The sky it left behind was a velvety blue, darkness mingling with light rather than smothering it. A pair of bleating sheep wandered by, a few cooing loons nested in the brush—I could sense them, their energy, their souls, but only faintly. The burden of carrying so much power had eased since leaving Glasnith, and this respite was welcome. And yet . . . I'd begun to miss the hum in my blood. I missed feeling strong enough to defend myself against monsters and men, and those who were both.

Was this what Torin had felt? Was it why he'd not fought harder to resist the god of death?

I tried not to worry about Garreth, tried not to be speared by grief over my father and Reyker, and failed. The sun rose again a few hours later, and I woke Quinlan so I could sleep awhile.

It was hard to know what time it was when we set off once more, after a small meal of dried fruit and hard bread. The landscape turned rough, as did the weather. A labyrinth of jagged black rock stretched out as far as I could see, liquid fire that had spewed from a mountain and hardened into uneven stacks that we had to step, and climb, and sometimes crawl across.

Above us, the gray-bellied clouds broke, joining forces with the wind to pelt us with raindrops that fell sideways and stung like falling needles. We shivered in our soaked clothes, but we didn't stop.

Half a day crept by as we crossed the lava field, and the closer we got to its end, the louder the sound of water on the other side became. When we cleared the rocks, another canyon stretched out before us, but this one had a wide river above it that rushed over the edge in a roaring wave, as beautiful as it was violent. Mist veiled the air like smoke, and it would have drenched us if we weren't already wet. There were thousands of waterfalls all over Iseneld, named and unnamed; it felt like I should know what this one was called, like not knowing was disrespectful. I wished Reyker was here to tell me.

Quinlan and I stood as close to it as we dared. Beside the falls, we were small, insignificant. Mortals in a land of gods and beasts.

By the time we made camp, we were both too tired to keep watch. We'd gone far enough that I wasn't worried about the Mountain Renegades tracking us, and if Draki found us there would be no outrunning him regardless. Our clothes were still damp, as were our bedrolls, so we lit a small fire and huddled next to each other for warmth.

———◆———

I let myself dream of Reyker, even though I shouldn't have, even though beneath the bliss of those stolen moments I felt the ache in my chest worsening, the pit of grief widening. When Reyker tried to speak of anything beyond the ruins, I shushed him, and when he tried to get me to speak, I ignored him.

"I'm losing you, aren't I?" he said.

"My wolf. My love." I pressed my fingers to his lips. I did not say, *We are already lost to each other*, but he heard it still.

———◆———

Sometime later, I woke, confused by the pale sun, until I remembered where I was. Confused even more by the arm slung across my waist, the breath rustling my hair. Before I could think better of it, I shoved the arm off me and pulled away.

Quinlan sat upright, blinking, half asleep. "What's wrong?"

"You can't touch me like that."

It could have been dawn or dusk, based on the gray light. It illuminated Quinlan's face, the hurt written there that I tried to ignore. "You were shivering. I was just trying—"

"Don't," I said. Then, calmer, "Whatever you were trying, just don't."

Color rose on his cheeks. "Fine. Next time, I'll let you freeze." He rolled over, putting his back to me, pretending to sleep.

We barely spoke the next day as we trekked around a series of grass-lined lakes and what appeared to be a mountain that had collapsed in on itself, leaving a wide, empty maw.

A blanket of fog squatted in the distance and, as we got nearer, the tussocks turned from green to brown, tapering off, until there was nothing but dirt and stone beneath our feet. The ground was stained with streaks of yellow and red, like it was covered in rust.

The fog turned out to be steam pluming up from holes in the ground, curling across the barren terrain. There was another lake here, its water a glowing turquoise, steam drifting along the surface. Even stranger were the fountains of water bubbling up from the earth, some of them erupting toward the sky in white waves.

"Geysers," I said before Quinlan could ask. When he started to move closer, I pulled him back, pointing to the boiling mud pools. "The water is hot enough to burn the flesh off your bones."

"He turned you into a walking library for this island, didn't he?"

The words were doused in bitterness. I let go of Quinlan's arm and kept walking, skirting the scalding puddles. He hurried after me.

"Sorry. I didn't mean it to come out like that."

"How did you mean it to come out?"

Quinlan pressed his lips together, and something seemed to snap inside him. "Fine. I hate him. For stealing your affection, for giving you things I never could. For dying and leaving you alone. He ruined you, Lira."

All this time, I'd thought Quinlan was the only one who didn't see me differently. How wrong I'd been. "Ruined. That's what you think I am?"

"The girl I loved was full of joy. She put other people's needs first. She put her clan and her country first." He shook his head. "Tell me this mad quest we're on has nothing to do with him, that you don't have some scheme to compel the Fallen Ones to bring Reyker back from the dead if you free them."

Quinlan knew me too well. It was easy to forget sometimes.

"This mad quest might save Glasnith," I said. "I'm here, fighting for my people, despite what they did. My clan betrayed me. My country abandoned me long before I left it."

"I didn't." When I met his gaze, he let me see it: What he felt for me. That he was still waiting . . . for something I could never give him.

Because I was ruined.

Despite the cold, we slept far apart that night.

CHAPTER 22

REYKER

Solvei stood over them, hair matted and damp, her eyes filled with fury. With no better target, she aimed it at Reyker.

"Why is he in my hall and not in a cage?" Her glare flickered to Brokk. "With all his fingers still attached?"

"Because I heard him out and decided he makes a better ally than he does a prisoner."

The caravel had beaten the longships to the Renegade camp by two full days. Reyker and Brokk spent most of that time talking and planning for this very moment, when Solvei would decide his fate.

Her hands went to her hips. Somehow she made the giant warrior seem small. "Thinking has never been your strongest asset, Brokk. Lock him up, sharpen your knife, and bring me his fingers, his tongue, his balls, I don't care—something I can send to goad the warlord."

"No." Brokk lifted his chin. "I took an oath to his father, and to him, long before I pledged myself to you and the Uprorsmund. He is as much my lord as you are my jarl, and he's our best chance at dethroning the Dragon. Let him tell you his plan, and if you still want his balls after that, you can take them yourself." He slapped his dagger onto the table.

Reyker resisted the urge to cross his legs.

Slowly, the jarl lowered herself into a chair and picked up the dagger. "I've had quite the day, little lordling. If your tale disappoints, your flesh will pay its debt."

Leaning forward, Reyker pressed his palms to the table and let it pour out of him. Not the same things he'd told Brokk—he left out the most painful, intimate details, a sketch of what Draki had done to him, his parents, and his village, how the warlord had twisted his mind up and forced him to fight, catching him every time he tried to run, every time he tried to end his own life to escape, taking out Reyker's refusals and misdeeds on the innocent and anyone he dared to care about, until he gave up, gave in.

And then, Lira. How she'd saved him from himself. How she'd died. He kept this part brief, vague, concealing the gaping wound that lay beneath it.

Lastly, his plan. He would go back to Draki, feeding the warlord false information about the Mountain Renegades, gathering his own reports on the villages Draki chose to attack, when and where the Dragonmen would be dispatched, their numbers, anything that could be of use. And, if he could get close enough, if he could find a way to kill what could not die, he would end it. The Dragon would be slain by Reyker's hand, or not at all.

By her expression he could tell Solvei's interest was piqued, but she still didn't trust him. "You will swear loyalty to the Fjull Uprorsmund?"

"I will support anyone who has the strength to defeat an army of Dragonmen," Reyker said. "No one can be worse than Draki and those under his command. Once they are gone, you can have your chance at being high jarl of Iseneld. If you prove unfit to rule, I will come for you next."

Brokk glanced nervously at Solvei, like Reyker might find himself castrated for that declaration, but the jarl nodded. "An honest answer, and a noble one. I will let you keep all your body parts and consider you an ally *if* you prove yourself."

He raised a brow.

"If I cannot keep you as a hostage, I need the other one I acquired in Glasnith. A powerful, valuable magiska, marked with the Dragon's star. She and her companion escaped," the jarl said with a scowl. "I hear you are a formidable tracker. Find my hostage, and you will have your alliance. Brokk will accompany you and kill you if anything seems amiss."

"I will?" Brokk said.

Reyker cursed inwardly. To gain the resources he needed to overthrow Draki, he had to help the Renegades capture a Daughter of Aillira so they could use her to bait the warlord. He let none of his reluctance show as he said, "Tell me everything you know about the girl, her companion, where you last saw them, and how they got away."

As Solvei described the girl, Reyker's breath caught in his throat.

Short, slender. Green eyes. Red hair.

A coincidence. Like the fire-sweeper Draki had taunted him with, there were many girls in Glasnith with such features.

"What is the girl's power?" he asked carefully.

"Animals. She can call them, make them obey her. Rats and bugs, even the island-serpent." She explained how the girl used Eyvor to break free, how the Renegades had to leave half their ships and a few floating corpses behind to stay out of Draki's path.

Not her. Reyker hated the sinking in his chest, the churning in his stomach, as his brittle hope shattered. This girl wasn't a soul-reader.

Of course it isn't her, you fool. She is dead. You saw her die.

"I'll find the girl, and the boy with her," he said. They couldn't have gotten far, two children of Glasnith lost in the wilds of Iseneld. If they were even alive, not drowned or frozen or broken at the bottom of a canyon. He would find them, to save them, and then . . . then he would have a decision to make. "When I bring them back, you let the other three magiskas go."

Two lives in exchange for three. A trade he could live with, if he had to—the sort of bargains he'd made during his time with Draki, justifying one wrong with another, weighing consequences, making choices no one should have to make.

Solvei tapped a finger against her chin. "We shall see."

━━━━◆━━━━

They found the stolen longship floating a few leagues out to sea. From there, the hardest part was determining where along this side of the island the Glasnithians had gone ashore.

The black cliffs his people called Sjaf's Staircase, he decided, since the entire shoreline was covered in steep cliffs and these were the easiest to climb. The Renegades rowed the knarr as close as they could, and Reyker and Brokk jumped into the surf, Solvei's monstrous pet right behind them.

A skrikflak—elusive beasts of legend that lived in the mountains around the fjords. He'd never seen one until Dragon Bay, but according to myth, they'd once been a tribe of men blessed with beatific voices they used to seduce the wives and daughters of their rivals. Like so many stories, it ended it with them being cursed for their crimes: the men became monsters, their sweet voices twisted to ruinous shrieks. They couldn't harm anything living, but they could topple buildings, shatter rock and ice. With enough of them, they could bring down a mountain.

"Why did you drag that beast along?" Reyker asked. The skrikflak carried most of their supplies on its back so they could move faster, but Reyker doubted that was the reason.

"That beast has a name. We call him Skrim, and Skrim has a better nose on him than you do. He's also had a whiff of the ones we're chasing. He'll keep us on the right path."

"Then why am I here?"

Brokk gave him a look as they gained the shore.

Ah. This wasn't just about finding the Glasnithians, it was also a test of trust to see if he would obey Solvei's orders.

Reyker chose his path up the cliff carefully, trying to think like the escaped captives might, selecting what looked to be the least hazardous route.

There—drops of blood on some of the sharpest rocks, still red, not yet faded by weather. "They were here a few days ago," he told Brokk. He went up, to the top of the cliff, eyeing the valley below, the clear skies overhead. "Our trek today will be easy."

"Thank the gods' favor," Brokk muttered.

"So we must cover it quickly to make up for lost time." Reyker broke into a run.

Brokk cursed, jogging after him. The skrikflak plodded along lazily, bringing up the rear.

The world narrowed to a fine, familiar pinpoint: tracking his quarry, like the elk or reindeer or foxes he'd hunted with his father. And sometimes with Aldrik.

Quarry. That's all they are, he told himself.

CHAPTER 23

LIRA

As the days passed, the land sloped upward. There was no more grass, only rolling dunes made of black rock and sand that scoured our bare skin and snuck into our boots. The air grew colder, until I could see the fog of my breath every time I exhaled. Our supplies dwindled. We could gather fresh water from streams and lakes, but food was another matter.

"I need to hunt," Quinlan said, looking skeptically at the sparse, snow-dusted dunes. Yesterday, the sky had showered us with flakes, and now our footsteps followed us everywhere, flat hollows crushed into the white earth.

We were nearing the Highlands. My crystal bracelet was growing tighter, as if the key was impressing its impatience upon me.

It wasn't as if Quinlan hadn't been trying to hunt all along. He'd kept the ice axe we'd stolen from the Renegades close at hand, but the animals here were few, and Quinlan had never been taught how to hunt them. We had no traps to set, and no time to wait for them.

"Reyker was a good hunter," I said.

"Lovely for him." Quinlan dropped his pack and scrambled to the top of a low ridge at the edge of a fast-flowing stream, lying on his belly, watching something in the water.

"What I mean is that he might have shown me something helpful," I called, but Quinlan waved at me to be quiet. His arm jerked, hurling the axe like a spear. There was a splash, and then Quinlan cursing as a skein of ducks took to the air.

"We need both axes," I told him. "If you lose yours—"

"I won't." He turned to me. "If you really want to be helpful, call out to something we can eat and make it stand still for me."

"They serve the Ice Gods, not Veronis. They won't listen."

"The sea-serpent did."

He was right. I hadn't forced Eyvor, but I'd coaxed, and she'd done as I'd asked. Maybe the other creatures of Iseneld would do the same.

The axe jutted from the middle of the stream. Quinlan slid down the rocks, wading in the knee-deep water to grab it, ignoring my warnings. As he pulled the axe out, one of his feet sank into the streambed and he teetered. The current did the rest, ripping his legs out from under him, sweeping him downstream.

"Quinlan!" I ran after him, moving as fast as I dared on the slippery banks.

He got his arm around a rock and pulled himself onto it, then across the rocks next to it, still clutching the axe. When he was close enough, he reached for my outstretched hand. I helped pull him onto the shore and we both sat down, breathing hard. Quinlan was soaked, trembling. He started to laugh, amusement edged with despair.

I put my arms around him, my chin resting on his shoulder. "Don't do that again. Don't leave me alone out here."

"You're already in love with this island. It strengthens you. You'd be fine without me."

There was no bite to his words, only truth. I'd loved Iseneld before I ever saw it, because Reyker had loved it and showed me all the reasons why. Being here only made me love it more, even as it tested me, exhausted me, tore me open with grief—grief that might make me reckless if I had no one to care for but myself. "I'd be lost without you, Quinlan."

"We've been lost since we got here."

"You know what I mean." I scanned the fields around us for the best spot to make camp. "We need to start a fire and get you dry."

We could afford to slow down, and an extra day of rest before reaching the Highlands would do us both good. Silently, I made a fire, set out our bedrolls, and unpacked the last of our food. I turned my head as Quinlan stripped, wringing out his wet clothes and lying them flat to dry before settling into the warm wool blankets. He fell asleep soon after.

I looked at him, the dark circles under his eyes, the sharp angles of his cheekbones. A warrior used to hearty meals and heavy training, he was losing weight faster than I was, growing weaker by the day. We both had wounds around our wrists where we'd been shackled to the Renegades' longship, but while mine had scabbed over, Quinlan's remained raw and red. Over the course of our travels, he'd twisted his ankle in a rockslide, burned his hands when he mistakenly tried to drink from a hot spring, and now he'd almost been swept away by a swollen stream.

A sudden realization made me shudder, the mystic's prediction dragging its nails up my spine. *Many forces seek to destroy him.* She'd been talking about Reyker; Glasnith had tried to kill him—a trespasser who did not serve my island's gods—in many different ways. Was Iseneld returning the favor, trying to kill Quinlan?

"I won't let you," I said.

I pulled a knife from its sheath. There were many ways to die in Iseneld, some easier to avoid than others. At least I could keep us from starving.

Unwilling to leave Quinlan, I didn't go far, just to the edge of the stream, taking a net with me. I closed my eyes, seeking that spark of Veronis's power in my blood, using it to call to the fish floating below the surface. They heard me, crowding together into a school, inching closer, but they darted away from the net I tried to toss over them.

I threw the net aside and called to the ducks clustered in the rocks and drifting along the calmer waters upstream. It was the same as the fish—they came out of curiosity, but they did not obey. The ducks were gone in a flap of feathers as soon as I started to raise my knife.

With a hiss of frustration, I screamed in my mind.

Come to me! Come, now!

I sent the call to every creature who could hear me, waiting. Waiting. But nothing listened. I wasn't sure why I'd expected them to—if fish and birds eluded me, what hope was there that anything bigger would come?

Finally I stood up, brushing off snow, heading back to the fire.

A forlorn creature crouched at the bottom of a dune. A small wolf with white fur, its outline barely visible against the snow. Watching me.

Answering my call.

The wolf, lean and blue eyed with youth, cocked its head, creeping toward me. It barely came up to my knees, but its claws and fangs were sharp. I extended the hand that held the knife, and the wolf sniffed it, licking my fingers. Bowing its head willingly beside the blade in understanding.

"Why?" I whispered.

Sorrow swam in the creature's eyes. Wolves traveled in packs, but this one was alone. Lost, or forced out, or the only one of its family still living.

I looked from the wolf, to Quinlan, and back. One life in exchange for another. There was no other choice.

I put the blade to the wolf's throat. "Thank you."

It was swift. I held the wolf as it twitched, its lovely white coat stained red. When it was over, I sliced the fur from its body, cut open its belly and pulled out its organs. I'd only done this once before, to a grouse I'd brought down with an arrow, because Garreth insisted it was a skill I might need one day. I was clumsy then, and I was clumsy now, my stomach roiling at the scent of blood. This creature had given its life for me, a willing sacrifice.

When I closed my eyes, I saw my mother's face, smiling at me from beneath the waves.

"Lira?" Quinlan said softly as he kneeled beside me.

Only then did I realize I was shaking, a keening noise rattling my chest. Quinlan's arms came around me, and I let them, keeping my blood-stained hands in my lap. "How many people have you killed?" I asked.

The question seemed to startle him. "I don't know. Ten? Twenty? Some I wounded, and I have no idea if they lived."

"How do you bear it?"

He pulled back to look into my eyes. "Because the only thing worse than bearing it is letting it eat you alive."

I wiped my nose on my sleeve. "Who knew you were so wise?"

"I'm not. Garreth told me that once, and I stole it."

Together, we finished preparing the wolf. With the meat sizzling over the fire, hunger erased any reluctance I might have otherwise felt. We ate our fill, silent, staring into the flames. Our bellies full, we lay down once more. I moved beside Quinlan, nestling close. For warmth, and for necessity—his presence was a barrier between me and the gnashing teeth inside my head.

I was half asleep, thinking out loud. "I don't want to be ruined, Quinlan."

He sighed. "Then you must let yourself laugh without guilt. And care about people. And fight for your own causes. If you hold too tightly to the dead, you'll live halfway in the pyre."

"Did you steal that from Garreth too?"

"Those bits of wisdom are all mine." There was a long pause, and then he said, "You'll love again, Lira. Not soon. Perhaps never as much. But you will."

Maybe, I thought, and it was enough to soothe me into a deep, dreamless sleep.

I woke before Quinlan did, bleary-eyed. There was a woman sitting beside me.

I bolted upright, drawing my knife. "Who are you?"

Her hair was black, her eyes shiny gold like a pair of coins. She wore garments of thick fur the color of grass, the sort of coat no native animal of the Frozen Sun possessed.

The woman waved at my weapon. "There's no need for that. I'm only here to warn you."

"Quinlan," I called. He should have woken at the sound of our voices. Something was wrong.

"Let him sleep," the woman said. "The words I bear are for your ears, not his."

"Did you do something to him?"

She smiled. She wasn't pretty, but she was striking. I was drawn to her, frightened of her. She felt almost familiar, though I was certain I'd never seen her before. "He will wake when our discussion ends. When he does, you must leave this place. Turn around. Go back the way you came, and all will be well. You will find what you seek."

"What I seek lies before me."

Her right eye slanted to the west, while her left eye looked to the east, and the sight of it made me cringe. "Death lies before you," she said. "Sacrifice. Misery."

"You're a seeress." That was why she seemed familiar—she reminded me of the blind mystic, speaking like she knew things, saw things, that others could not. A vassal and harbinger of her gods.

"The last seeress in Iseneld," she said, her crooked eyes straightening again. "I am the vision and the voice of the Ice Gods."

"You live out here?" Around us was nothing but plains and hills of black sand. "In the middle of nowhere?"

"Magiskas do as we must to survive." She tipped her chin up pridefully. "But not you. A foreign girl bearing gifts bestowed by rival gods, calling to the creatures of this land, using your abilities without asking permission. Taking a life that was not yours to take without giving thanks to the gods who created it, who shaped this island and breathed life into the souls inhabiting it. This is a grave offense to the Ice Gods. There is a price to pay for your insult. You must turn back and find a temple, make an offering, beg forgiveness of Sjaf and his kin. It will be granted, if you are sincere."

Her clothes. They were *moving*. What I'd thought was fur was actually moss, full of insects and small animals, crawling all over her. "Stop speaking in riddles and tell me exactly what the cost will be if I keep going."

"I can't. I do not know."

I stood, glaring down at her. "Tell your gods I'll be off their island soon enough, but first I have a task to complete."

"What simmers in your blood was never meant for you. There is another, a stronger vessel, who it must be passed to. In the meantime, it spreads and stains and corrupts you." The seeress touched my arm and every vein in my body seemed to tighten.

My knife found her throat. "Keep your hands off me."

"It may be too late for you already." She brushed her palms together, indicating she was done with our conversation.

I kept the knife up but stepped back. "If I'm a lost cause, then why did you come?"

"That is the curse of the seeress. To know too much, and yet not enough. To be listened to, but rarely heeded, compelled to offer warnings that will only be ignored. And forgotten. That is the worst curse laid upon me by the gods, for abandoning my duties to save my own life. No one will remember me. You will forget this meeting as soon as I am gone, and the omens I shared will mean nothing more to you than a feeling, a dream. But we will see each other once more, on the other side of this choice, and you will wish you had listened. So will I."

With that, the seeress turned in a flourish of her swirling, living cloak, stark against the dead black sand.

Quinlan rolled over and looked at me, yawning. "Are you ready to be off, then?"

I glanced to where the seeress had been, but the sand was empty. I hadn't trusted the mystic in Glasnith, and I didn't trust Iseneld's seeress either, but briefly, I let in the possibility: What if she was right? Quinlan was sick, growing weaker. My gifts were nearly useless in this strange land. We could go back, seek out a village. I could make an offering at one of the Ice Gods' temples. We could rest, wait for Quinlan to grow stronger while I practiced using my gifts. Then we could try again, later.

But we had come so far. We were so close. And I was tired of living in fear of gods, tired of begging them for favors. I wanted to end this. I needed it to be over.

I was already forgetting why I had doubted in the first place, who it was that had made me think this was the wrong choice. "Do you want to stop, Quinlan? Do you want to turn back?"

I would if he wanted. I owed him that, and more, for everything he'd done for me.

He grinned, running fingers through his sleep-mussed hair. "We were bloody daft to attempt this in the first place. We'd be completely mad not to finish what we started, don't you think?"

Simple, sage advice from my oldest, dearest friend.

"Completely," I agreed.

CHAPTER 24

LIRA

Spilling out between the mountains was what looked like a soft blanket of endless snow. It was a glacier covering the middle of Iseneld, an island unto itself, and the main source of the streams and rivers we'd crossed to get here. At its very center was the Mountain of Fire, the blazing heart of the Frozen Sun. It was a sacred place, and Reyker had made the trek here with his father and other villagers once to pay tribute to the Ice Gods.

Circling the glacier's base were half-frozen rivers crowded with broken chunks of ice, floating slowly downstream, the beginning of a long journey to where the river met the sea. The crackle of melting ice, of glacial fragments scraping against each other, was the only sound.

"You're certain you want to do this?" Quinlan asked.

We'd braved Iseneld's hostile weather thus far, but it was nothing compared to the Highlands, where the wind brushed along the glacier, sucking up its chill, so it could tear at us with freezing claws. There were no animals to hunt here. Half the wolf meat was wrapped up in our packs, and it would keep in the cold, but once it was gone, we'd go hungry.

"It's not about want. I'll never be free until I do this." I touched the crystal bracelet. It had become like the manacle on the longship, molding so tight to my wrist that it hurt. Even with Veronis's voice muted, I could sense his impatience—a twitch under my skin, a shudder in the back of my mind. I needed to right the wrongs of Ildja and Gwylor and be rid of this burden. "But you can wait here. You don't have to come with me."

"Aye, I came all this way just to quit on you right before the finish," he said.

There was no obvious path for climbing onto the glacier, only places that were less hazardous. Crossing the river risked falling through the ice sheet. The caves were unstable, and parts of them could collapse at any moment. Other spots had pools of gray leaking off the glacier where the water had weakened the sand, turning it to loose, deep mud pits that could easily swallow someone foolish enough to step in them.

I led Quinlan to a boundary where the rock and a lolling tongue of glacier met, taking a length of rope from the bag. "The snow hides cracks in the ice. We need to tie ourselves together in case one of us falls in." That was what Reyker and his father had done.

"You won't be able to hold me up. If I fall, I'll pull you down with me."

"Why do you think we lugged the ice axes all this way?" I held mine up. The staff was longer and lighter than an ordinary axe, the head small and curved. "Before we step, we anchor ourselves."

"Lira—"

"It might be me who falls, me who drags *you* down. Are you so certain you can hold me?"

Quinlan stared at me for a long moment, like he was working through a puzzle and his answer might change everything. I met his gaze. Maybe there was something stirring inside me, water flowing under ice. I wasn't certain, but I thought it might be possible. Someday.

He took the rope and cinched it around my waist, tugging me closer as he tested the knot. "If it happens, I'll catch you. Believe me."

I did.

Axes in hand, we started up the glacier, snow and ice crunching under our boots. Fear twisted my chest, making it hard to breathe. It was easier not to dwell on the last part of my task when we were so far from our destination, but now there was no ignoring it. I had come to battle a goddess, the eater of souls, empress of the damned.

She would not go quietly.

The snowdrifts got deeper. It would take at least a full day's trek to reach the center. We went slowly, our steps light, not advancing until our axes were secure, our grips on them steady. It was tedious work, but we edged past holes and crevasses in the glacier that warned us not to go faster. In the distance, the Mountain of Fire rose up, a stone tumor bursting from the frozen earth.

We didn't stop until our muscles trembled so much it was dangerous to keep going. Resting side by side, cold seeping up through our trousers, we passed a waterskin back and forth and finished off the wolf meat.

"If I can't defeat Ildja, you have to run." I wouldn't stop Quinlan from entering the Mountain of Fire, but I had to be the one to fight the goddess, to stab her in the heart and capture her soul in the crystal dagger.

Quinlan gestured at the glacier. "Running isn't exactly an option."

"Get out, then. Away from the spiteful goddess trying to eat your soul."

"Back to the Mountain Renegades, to be a prisoner? Or to the Dragonmen, so they can put an axe through me?" He shook his head. "We leave together, or we don't leave at all."

"Don't say that."

"This isn't just about you. I made promises. To Garreth. To Reyker, before he died. And to myself. That I'd protect you with my life. Don't ask me to break those promises."

"What did Reyker say to you, before Torin forced him on the ship?" We'd not gotten a proper goodbye. I'd been so drowsy with potions, I'd thought Reyker's visit was a dream.

"Are you sure you want to hear it?"

"No. But tell me anyway."

Quinlan paused. "That he owed you his life. That at the first opportunity, he was going to run his sword through everyone who'd hurt you. That I was the only one he trusted to keep you safe in his absence. I—" He bit his lip, glancing at me. "I hate him, for reasons I've already shared. But mostly because I thought no one else could love you as much as I did. He proved me wrong."

I swallowed around the tightness in my throat. "Thank you," I whispered.

"I won't break my promise," he said again. "I'm with you to the end."

"To the end." Whatever end it might be—victory or death. Despite my fear, I was relieved. This journey was almost over, and because of Quinlan I wouldn't have to finish it alone. "Come on, then. Let's go destroy an evil goddess."

Once more, we crept and crawled across the frozen plain, taking our time. More and more often, one of us put a foot down only to jerk it back at the sound of creaking ice. The mountain grew closer, closer, until it was just over the next ridge.

When the ice creaked again, I listened harder, not certain the crackles were coming from us. I looked over my shoulder at how far we'd come. There it was—the crunch of footsteps. Something heavy. Big. "We aren't alone," I said.

Quinlan squinted into the distance. "I don't see anything. What do you think it is?"

"I don't want to find out. We need to get up the mountain."

Above us I could see the entrance, an opening carved in the middle of the frosted rock emitting a golden-red glow from within. We picked up our pace as much as we dared, but the sounds of something following us sped up too.

We'd made it to the bottom of the mountain when the whole glacier seemed to groan. Quinlan and I were a rope-length apart, with me in front, my axe dug deep into the ice as I climbed the first slope of rock.

"What was that?" he asked, one foot hovering in the air, not daring to move.

I scanned the white landscape. A head peeked up out of a dip in the glacier. Horns. A muzzle. Claws dug into the ice, and the beast dragged itself over the ridge.

"Oh, gods," I hissed. "It's an ice demon, like the one the Mountain Renegades brought to Stalwart Bay."

Maybe it was the same one. Maybe I'd called it here, when I'd sent out the summons that brought the white wolf to me—I heard someone telling me there was a price to pay for such acts, though I couldn't remember whose voice it was.

I held tight to the axe, reaching for Quinlan, but it was too late. The demon saw us. It threw its head back, opened its mouth, and released a howl fit to bring down the sky.

Except it wasn't the sky that cracked, but the ground. My ears rang, the demon's scream vibrating my skull, and the glacier shook. Were the mountain not Ildja's sacred domain, it might have cracked too. All around us, fissures widened and hidden crevasses revealed themselves as sections of the ice sheet turned brittle and collapsed. The ice under Quinlan's boots crumbled.

He fell.

The jolt on the rope knocked my legs out from under me, and nearly ripped my fingers from the axe. My feet dangled over the crevasse, not far above Quinlan's head. Only my grip on the axe kept us from tumbling into the chasm.

"Your axe!" I shouted down at him. If he could swing to the wall of ice, he could use it to climb up.

"It's gone." There was something wrong about his voice. It was too even, too calm.

I tried to pull myself up, but my arms trembled and refused to budge. My muscles already ached from the strain of holding us up. "You'll have to climb the rope between us, then climb over me to get out." He didn't answer.

I dared a glance down and saw the knife in his hand. "Quinlan. What are you doing?"

"The axe won't hold."

He was lying to spare me. It was my grip that wouldn't hold. He pressed the knife to the rope that linked us. "No! Quinlan, please. Please don't."

"You're almost there. You can make it to the fire. But not if I drag you down with me." The blade cut into the rope.

"No, no." My mind was racing. Everything was happening so fast, yet somehow it felt as if we'd been hanging here forever. It was only hours ago we'd been looking at each other, speaking in code about a possible future, a fragile hope. "We leave together, or we don't leave at all, remember?"

"This was always your journey." The fibers of rope frayed, coming apart. I was coming apart, too, each slice of the knife undoing something inside me.

I'd lost the only man I'd ever loved. How could I lose the only man who might be worthy of taking his place? How could I bear it if both of them were stolen from me?

The knife. Oh gods, the knife was still sawing. This couldn't be happening. "Quinlan! Please, no. Not you. I can't . . ." My fingers were cramped. Slipping.

"You can, Lira. You will." He smiled at me. Not a boy's smile full of mischief, but a man's smile full of promise. All the love he'd kept hidden, not wanting to guilt or pressure me—he let me see it, and it burned like a sun, setting him aglow. Turning me to ash.

The rope snapped.

His smile grew smaller as the distance between us widened. The light couldn't penetrate the shadows of the crevasse. The glacier swallowed him in its dark depths and he was gone.

That burning sun, that boy I'd loved, that man I'd taken for granted. Gone.

I screamed his name into the void that took him, telling him I was sorry, telling him I loved him. Begging him to come back, even though it was pointless—he'd gone to a place I couldn't reach. Not unless I let go too.

It would have been easy to do nothing, to wait until my arms gave out. Join Quinlan. And Rhys, Mother, Father. Reyker. But Quinlan gave his life for me, so I could finish this journey. Everyone I'd lost, in ways small and large, had died to get me here, to this place. This moment. I couldn't waste it.

Better to die fighting a goddess and take her to the otherworlds with me.

I kicked and clawed, hauling myself onto the ice, lying beside the axe and staring at the unfeeling sky above. "I'm going to end this," I told it, because there was no one else left to hear.

I made myself stand and take the axe. Made my arms wield it, my legs bracing as I pulled my way onto the foot of the mountain. The slope was steep, barely climbable, and I kept scrambling up only to slide back down again, displacing ice and snow.

"I'm going to end this!" I said again, slamming my fist against a bare spot of rock. The crystal bracelet circling my wrist brushed the slope.

Pebbles tumbled and rolled, and a thin ray of light appeared, spilling from an odd-shaped hole in the rock. The hole had perfectly cut lines and curves, and it was the size of my thumb.

The size of a key.

The bracelet was so tight my whole arm throbbed. I ran my hand over it and the bracelet released its grip, liquefying in my hands, molding into a large crystal key. It slid into the hole in the rock, an exact fit. I turned the key, and a gap opened in front of me. A tunnel.

With tears frozen on my cheeks and the weight of so many deaths pressing me forward, I entered the Mountain of Fire.

CHAPTER 25

REYKER

He knew something was wrong as soon as the tracks he was following left the green canyons and headed into the desolate dunes. No one trying to survive would abandon fertile land for stark wilderness.

"They're going somewhere." His gaze raked the black sand that stretched as far as he could see. There was nothing that way except . . . "The Mountain of Fire."

Brokk gripped his knees. "Why would they go there?"

"Some Glasnithians know our legends. Maybe they think the goddess in the mountain can help them."

"Then they're as good as dead," Brokk said. "Ildja will bite off their heads and feast on their souls."

"Not if we find them first."

Reyker pushed on.

Ildja had taken his brother from him. Aldrik was flawed, but there had been goodness in him—he could have been saved, had he not gone to his mother and let her poison his mind. For years, Reyker had revisited that moment when Aldrik left, wondering what would have happened if he'd shrugged off the hateful words Aldrik said to keep him away and ridden after his brother. Could he have prevented it all—his parents' deaths, the battles and bloodshed, the conquering of Iseneld and Glasnith?

Ildja had taken enough. He would not let her have these Glasnithians.

They had made good time. Unlike the quarry they stalked, the two warriors were at home here, accustomed to trekking through harsh terrain in volatile weather. He knew the cold that nipped at him, no worse than a gnat, would slow the blood in a foreigner's veins. He could see it in the tracks the Glasnithians left—their strides had begun to flag, the traces of their camps growing closer together.

Reyker set a brutal pace, pausing only for short rests, until he was certain they were less than a half day behind.

"Sjaf's balls," Brokk wheezed as they knelt at a stream in the middle of the black sand desert. "How are you not tired, Lagorsson?"

"I am." The lure to lie down in the sand and sleep under the open sky was strong, though it was nothing compared to the exhaustion he'd felt in Glasnith. Being in his homeland, close to his gods, was already healing the damage that had been done to him while he'd been away, fading scars, soothing aches. Even the weight of his grief had lightened, something that both relieved and shamed him. "But we have to hurry if we want to find them alive."

And he did, desperately, for reasons he couldn't quite understand, reasons that went beyond nobility or need. Something deep in his gut pulled him along, urging him to go faster.

The skrikflak was beside Brokk, slurping from the stream. Its head jerked up suddenly, swiveling toward the distant dunes. Its nostrils flared, and then it trotted off, surprisingly swift on its mismatched legs—paws in front, hooves in back.

"Skrim! Get back here, you rotten furball!" Brokk shouted, but the beast ignored him.

"Solvei said the girl can control animals." Reyker noted how the ducks struggled to swim upstream briefly, in the direction the skrikflak had run. Overhead, a pair of gyrfalcons dropped out of the air as if stunned, catching themselves before hitting the ground. "She spoke to them, just now. If she can turn that monster pet of Solvei's against us—"

"She can't. If she could, she'd have done it during the battle for Dragon

Bay or on the sea crossing here. And stop calling the skrikflak a monster. If I have to refer to that phantom-eyed horse of yours as Vengeance, you can call him Skrim."

Reyker was already on his feet, pulling on one of the packs he'd taken off Skrim while they rested, and then he was running, keeping pace with the skrikflak.

They ran for an hour, with Brokk complaining about his blistered feet, the stitch in his side, his heavy bladder, but to his credit, the oversized warrior didn't fall behind. Not until he grabbed Reyker's arm and said, "I'm not going to walk around in piss-soaked trousers. Slow down a bit, and I'll catch up."

Reyker slowed to a jog, not letting Skrim get out of sight. Space fell between him and Brokk.

He didn't notice the woman until she was right in front of him. He skidded in the sand, stopping just shy of her.

He knew what she was instantly. Dark hair, fiery-gold irises that burned like twin stars, draped in garments made of the earth itself.

"Seeress," he breathed. "I thought your kind was dead."

There had been a seeress in Vaknavangur when Reyker was a boy. Draki had taken her captive when he seized the village, marked her, forced her to remain in the netherworlds between life and death for days, awaiting visions of the Dragon and his fate. It had driven the woman mad. Reyker didn't know if she'd killed herself, or if the visions had drained her life. He just remembered her body burning on a pyre, one of many magiskas whose end came too soon under Draki's rule.

"I am the last, like you." The seeress reached up, running cold fingers across his cheeks. "A male magiska, allowed to live only because you share blood with the Dragon. Turn around, magiska. Go back."

"I can't. What I seek lies before me."

She smirked, a deeply unsettling expression on her uncanny face. "Death lies before you. Sacrifice. Misery. Abandon your chase and the two you followed here will die, but the Dragon will be weakened, perhaps enough to be killed."

Reyker did not question how the seeress knew—as with his battle-madness, the nature of her visions was beyond her control—nor did he question the truth of what she saw.

Let the Glasnithians die. This was the cost of crippling the warlord. "Is there no other way to weaken him?"

"There is always another way." Her gold-rimmed eyes lost focus, one looking toward the ground and the other toward the sky. "He is part god, born of the womb of Ildja, eater of souls, to defy a death by mortal hands. Because you are the same flesh as the Dragon, he keeps you close. That makes you his weakness. You carry the answer to his death inside you." She tapped his forehead. "You've already witnessed how it can be done."

Something he had witnessed? A memory of Draki, or of Aldrik?

Something insignificant enough that he'd missed it, or terrible enough that he'd entombed it beneath the black river of his soul so he wouldn't have to relive it.

"Turn back," the seeress said, "and you won't need the answer. Others will make sacrifices. Others will fight this war."

"I fight my own wars." He pulled away from her icy hands. "And I don't let innocent people die if I have the power to stop it."

"No," she whispered. "But you will."

Reyker heard Brokk calling him. The moment his gaze left the seeress, she was gone, as if she'd melted into the earth itself. Her words faded from his mind, until he could hardly remember what she'd said, and then he could hardly remember her at all. He pushed away the sense of foreboding and took off running, continuing with his hunt.

Brokk came up behind him. "Talking to ghosts, Lagorsson? Has the wilderness scrambled your wits?"

Reyker shook his head, speeding up so they could catch Skrim. "I wasn't talking to anyone."

When he found the wolf carcass, Reyker knew the Glasnithians were as good as caught—the organs and blood hadn't frozen yet, nor had the remnants of their fire been buried by snow. "A few hours more," he said.

"Soon as we find them, I'm going to make those Glasnithians rub my feet. The girl can call us up some dinner. I could eat an elk whole."

"Is that how you got so big?"

"If I can't get an elk, I could always gnaw the flesh off your scrawny bones. Don't think I'm above it."

"These scrawny bones bested you a good many times on the training field, as I recall."

They traded barbs and reminisced about their boyhoods in Vaknavangur, to make the time pass. Reyker let himself enjoy it, laughing in earnest about their escapades. Things had been simple back then: hunting, swordplay, wooing village girls. That's all they had cared about before the Dragonmen came. Before they were forced to become men in the span of a day.

In his loneliest moments, Reyker had tried to befriend several of the Dragonmen, but the ones who didn't sicken him rarely lasted—Draki sensed the honor in them, that these men wouldn't do his bidding long, so the warlord sent them on the most dangerous missions or executed them for disloyalty as a warning to others.

Brokk was his only friend. All the rest were dead.

"What about the other children of Vaknavangur?" Reyker could still see them, boys and girls his age and younger, screaming as they watched their brothers and fathers die. They would have been rounded up, enslaved by the Dragonmen. "What happened to them?"

"That bastard didn't tell you?" Brokk grunted. "After the warlord took you away, he left his soldiers to march us through a valley to one of the other villages he'd captured. There was an avalanche in the mountains that killed most of the Dragonmen, so those of us who survived were able to escape. We separated into groups, changed our names, and went into hiding for years, afraid the Dragon would return for us. Some of them I've lost track of, but I can get a message to the others. They'll want to see you."

Alive. His people, the ones his father had been responsible for, the ones *he* was supposed to be responsible for.

"When all of this is over, I'm going to rebuild Vaknavangur," Reyker said. "I'll give them back their homes, their land. I'll be the leader my father wanted me to be."

"That's a mighty big job for scrawny bones like yours. Suppose you'll need some help."

"There might be an elk in it for you." The grin dropped from Reyker's face as the glacier came into view.

Two sets of tracks led straight to it. He saw their footprints in the snow, the wounds in the ice where axes had dug in. The Glasnithians were on the glacier, heading for the mountain.

"Stay here, Skrim," Brokk said.

The skrikflak lurched up the glacier, leaving them behind despite Brokk's threats and curses. "That stupid ball of fur is a danger to all of us," Reyker said. He knotted one end of the rope they'd brought around his waist before handing the other end to Brokk. The big warrior looked nervously at the ice sheet, but he tied himself to Reyker.

Both of them were used to trekking across ice, and they traversed the glacier with swift efficiency, the mountain drawing closer with each step. They passed one crevasse after another, and Reyker peered over the edge of each, thinking to see the boy and girl lying at the bottom. How had two Glasnithians made it here, with no knowledge of the island? He wanted to meet these brave souls who'd traveled across his land faster than he'd expected and gotten farther than he'd thought possible in their state. Before he turned them over to Solvei and her Renegades to use as bait for the Dragon.

"Skrim, you bastard! Wait for us."

Reyker's head snapped up in time to see hooves disappear over a snowy ledge far ahead of them, just below the mountain. He scrambled after the skrikflak, as fast as he could with Brokk still tied to him, fearing what the beast might do if he reached the Glasnithians first. It was too much ground to cover. They'd never get to Skrim before—

The skrikflak howled in the distance.

The glacier crackled like glass.

Reyker dug his axe in and jerked the rope, pulling Brokk back from the hole that yawned over the ice shelf, widening until it was as big as a house.

Brokk stared at the spot where he'd just been standing, which was now an empty space above a blue chasm. "Don't expect me to be grateful, Lagorsson. You just saved your own ass from being dragged in after me."

Another sound was carried to them on the wind—a scream, unmistakable even though it was far enough away to be no louder than a whisper.

"We have to move," Reyker said.

Quick as they dared, they crossed the fragile ice in silence, concentrating. They made it up to where the skrikflak had been and found it struggling to escape a massive trench of its own making, claws and hooves scrabbling up the ice, finding no purchase. There were holes and cracks all over the ice shelf here.

"Damn you, Skrim. I told you to wait."

"There." Reyker pointed at an indentation marring the edge of a crevasse. The mark of an ice axe, deeper than the ones they'd been following. The cry they'd heard had come a full minute after the skrikflak's roar. "The ice gave. The axe held." It had been pulled out from above, not ripped free from below. "One of them fell here."

"How do you know?"

It wasn't a question he could answer. The bottom of the crevasse was cloaked in darkness, so there was no telling how deep it went. He couldn't see a body. But his hunter-instincts were screaming at him, and he needed to listen. "I just do. I'm going down."

"What? Have you lost your gods-damned mind?"

Reyker pulled an extra coil of rope from his pack, untying himself from Brokk and knotting the two lengths of rope together. "Whoever is down there is either hurt or dead. We need to know which."

The girl—it was the girl that screamed, wasn't it? He didn't want to see her, a Daughter of Aillira, lying broken at the bottom of this hole. But if he didn't see, he would always wonder.

"The rope isn't long enough," Brokk said.

"It will get me close. I'll use the axes the rest of the way." He took Brokk's axe and his own, strapping both to his back before taking hold of the rope. "If I don't make it out, help the three magiskas get home to Glasnith. And look after my phantom-eyed horse."

With Brokk's weight anchoring him, Reyker eased over the cracked edge of ice, into the crevasse. Hand over hand, he descended.

The white walls of the crevasse were glassy and rippled, as if they were made of streams that had frozen as they purled, and the ice seemed to glow with bluish light. It felt like being underwater. He went deeper, passing into shadow. The walls disappeared from view first. Then the rope. Then he could see nothing at all. He heard his own labored breaths, and all around him, the crackle of ice, shrinking, expanding, and the trickle of water feeding it. The chill in the air sank its teeth deep into his muscles, making them tremble as much from cold as exertion.

The rope ended. He pulled one of the axes off his back and slammed it into a wall he couldn't see, then did the same with the other. Above him the light was a distant dream and Brokk was nothing more than a smear of color against a patch of gray sky.

One axe, then the next, dangling one-handed above a bottom he wasn't certain was there. He went lower, doubting himself. What if the crevasse was endless? What if he didn't have the strength left to climb back up? What if he'd cheated death over and over just to die in the belly of the soul-eater's glacier?

The sound of running water echoed up the walls. His boots touched ice, solid beneath the shallow stream flowing over it. He reached into his tunic for the cloth and flint he'd tucked there, wrapping the cloth around an axe head, lighting it to make a torch. The flash of fire was a trespasser here, just as Reyker was. He almost dropped it when he saw what the dark concealed.

The crumpled warrior lying at the bottom of the crevasse.

It was impossible.

"Quinlan?" Reyker stabbed the axe's shaft into the ice and knelt beside the warrior, checking his injuries, the numerous fractured bones. Blood danced in the stream as it flowed away from him. His chest still rose and fell, but the sound was wet and rough. He was too broken to be moved.

The warrior's lashes fluttered. Quinlan opened his eyes and stared at Reyker. Blinking in confusion. Then alarm. His lips parted, trying to speak, but only blood spilled from his mouth.

"It's all right," Reyker said, clasping the warrior's hand. But Quinlan knew better. Reyker could see it in his eyes.

Death could come for him in the next minute, or it might creep up slowly, pouncing only after untold pain-filled hours.

"I can end it now." The offer tasted like rotten meat on Reyker's tongue.

Quinlan squeezed his hand with what little strength he had left.

Reyker bent over the warrior, one hand on the top of his head, the other beneath his chin. Quinlan kept his eyes open, focused on him. Reyker spoke the words Lira had taught him. "The god of death has claimed you. May Gwylor accept you into his palace."

His hands thrust up and to the side, until he heard the snap.

The light drained from Quinlan's eyes.

Reyker bowed his head, whispering prayers to the Ice Gods and the Green Gods. He put his face in his hands, breathing hard, trying to make sense of this—how he'd found himself on his knees inside Ildja's glacier, killing Lira's dearest friend.

In the flickering torchlight, he noticed an opening in the wall of ice behind him.

He should go. Brokk was waiting for him. But his instincts, his blood, pressed him toward the ice tunnel, telling him to see where it led, and his mind was too muddled to think better of it.

He ducked through the fissure. It was short, ending in a nook that had tunnels branching off in every direction. Here, the walls were flawlessly smooth, the ceilings carved into archways. These were part of Ildja's palace. He'd stumbled into the Mountain of Fire—he could see it, a red shimmer at the end of one of the tunnels. There were voices on the other side, faint even though the distance wasn't far.

He followed the voices, the firelight, the tug on the line between himself and whatever he was moving toward that kept reeling him closer.

CHAPTER 26

LIRA

One tunnel led to another, and another, winding and twisting, finally spitting me out into a lofty, hollowed-out space, as big as ten great halls put together and as hot as a kiln. I walked along a rocky ledge coated in ice that should have melted in the heat—there must have been magic here, sustaining it. High above me was the volcano's crater. Far below was a boiling cauldron of liquid fire.

This was the Frozen Sun, a volcano in the heart of a glacier. The doorway between Iseneld and the death realms Ildja reigned over. And I was standing in the middle of it.

Smoke swirled along the outskirts of the fire, veiling what lay beyond. The Mist—where the Destroyers dragged the souls deemed unworthy of joining their kin in the endless meadows of Skjorlog Felth. Where souls would be tortured, devoured slowly by the serpent-goddess.

From the depths of the Mist, a voice spoke, blazing like it was born of the spewing fire. "Have you come to capture me, soul-reader?"

"I brought you a gift, Ildja. Show yourself so I can present you with it." I ran my hand over the crystal key and it pooled like wax in my palm, shapeless, before transforming back into a blade.

"Did you think it would be so easy, mortal child? Cross an island, climb a glacier, cage a goddess. With my own ice dagger, no less, forged in this very mountain."

I held the dagger up, examining its bluish-white sheen, its glassy texture. Not crystal, as I'd assumed—unmelting ice, like the sheet beneath my feet.

Laughter curled around me, reeking of sulfur. "Did you learn nothing from the story of the Fallen Ones?" Ildja asked. "Gods cannot be trusted. Veronis did not tell you everything."

What was I meant to do with the dagger? How did I bury it in Ildja's heart, as Veronis had instructed, if she wouldn't manifest into a body I could stab?

I squinted at the fire, the heart of Iseneld.

The core of Ildja's realms, the gate between the world of the living and the nightmares of the dead. The heart . . . of Ildja herself.

BURY IT IN THE HEART OF ILDJA.

I squeezed the dagger, staring into the crater. It couldn't be as simple as tossing the key in the fire. With gods, nothing was ever what it seemed. Veronis had said to bury it, but how could something be buried if it burned? To bury a blade required either dirt or flesh.

There was no dirt here. No flesh but mine.

"Your mother only delayed the inevitable," the voice in the Mist said. "You were always meant to be a sacrifice. Destroying the key in my fire will break the lock on Veronis's cell, but the prison-realm does not let its prisoners out without an exchange. To free Veronis, one who shares his blood must take his place. You."

Ice and snow and fire blurred around me.

Bloody fates.

Veronis had misled me all along. He was never going to bring Reyker back or reunite us in the otherworlds. To free him, I didn't just have to die—I had to damn my soul, to become an eternal prisoner. I could never see any of the people I loved again, even in death. Separated forever, as Aillira and Veronis had been.

It wasn't fair. I could accept dying, but this? This was a fate worse than death.

But if I didn't go through with it, there would be no gods to rise against Gwylor and Ildja, and they would continue to bolster Draki. Glasnith would fall. Garreth would die. And other countries would follow, conquered by the Dragon as he built his empire.

"Such a dilemma," Ildja said.

"No." I stepped up to the edge of the crater. "It really isn't."

What was one life, one soul, compared to thousands?

The blade was meant to be buried in a heart, so I turned the dagger on myself, its tip pressed beneath my breastbone. I wondered how fast a body could fall. Would I be dead before I hit the fire, or would I burn alive? Would my sacrifice be enough to turn the tide of this war, or might Draki win anyway? Was I about to die for nothing?

Had Quinlan died for nothing?

With a deep breath, I let the uncertainty fade. The rest was out of my control, but this choice was mine. I had made it once before, leaping off a cliff to save myself from becoming Draki's slave. I could make it again, to give Glasnith and Iseneld a chance.

Hanging my toes over the crater, I positioned my arms, elbows out, angling the blade so it would pierce my heart. I leaned forward, preparing to thrust the dagger and let myself fall.

I hesitated.

The ice beneath me trembled, shifting suddenly, like a rug being yanked out from under my feet.

Laughter crackled around me, Ildja's mirth searing my ears.

I stumbled backward, and something heavy slammed into me, knocking me sideways. I fell hard against the ice and skidded, the dagger slipping from my grasp. It spun across the frozen floor, close to the lip of the crater.

The key. My one chance.

With a cry, I dove for the dagger. I would grab it and leap into the crater, stab myself on the way down, before Ildja could stop me. My knees bent, preparing to jump. My fingers grazed the dagger's hilt.

A hand wrapped around my ankle, jerking me backward. The dagger slid over the edge and was gone.

No.

Just like Quinlan was gone.

No.

I screamed, clawing at the ice as if I could still catch the dagger, as if all hope wasn't lost, but the hand that held me wouldn't let go. I turned to confront whoever Ildja had sent to ruin this for me, my fists balled, ready for a fight.

The breath froze in my lungs.

Reyker was crouched on the ice, one hand around my ankle. Staring at me like I was the strangest thing he'd ever seen.

For a moment, I believed it was him. The *skoldar* on my wrist came to life, tingling with warmth. I almost reached for him, almost threw my arms around him.

But I knew better. I'd failed, and Veronis was punishing me. The throb of my *skoldar* was just a clever new part of this trick.

"Get away from me." I scooted back, putting space between me and Not-Reyker.

"Lira?"

"Don't say my name."

"How did you get here?" He looked from me to the crater with something like horror. "Did you come from the Mist? Did Ildja claim your soul when you crossed over?"

I put my hands over my ears. "Stop talking to me. You're nothing but a lie."

He crawled to me on hands and knees, stopping right in front of me, pulling open his wool coat and the top of the tunic beneath. "Touch my soul and tell me I'm a lie."

The shell of Reyker that Veronis sent before had felt wrong to me instantly. It had been too perfect. But the man before me now had stubble on his jaw and tangles in his hair. His skin was dusted with black sand. His eyes were older than the rest of him, carrying burdens far beyond his years. My hand inched toward him before I remembered my gift wouldn't work in Iseneld the way it had in Glasnith. What I noticed beneath his tunic stopped me cold.

My medallion.

I lifted it, and the thorntree shone in the firelight, the carving stained red with Reyker's blood from a mercenary's blade in his chest. The kind that must have caused the fresh scar running beside the heart of the man kneeling in front of me.

"Reyker?" I whispered, running a fingertip over the scar. "Is it really you? How—"

His lips stifled the words on my tongue, his arms pulling me closer. He felt exactly the same, so much that I couldn't let go. I opened my mouth to his, my fingers sinking into his hair.

A growl echoed from inside the crater. Smoke filled the space around us, stinging my eyes, scalding my throat. A fountain of liquid fire spewed up from the hole, steaming as rivulets hit the ice, melting the ledge beneath us.

"It's Ildja," Reyker said. "She's coming. We have to run."

His hand laced with mine, pulling me up, away from the crater, into the ice tunnels. A wave of smoke and fire followed us, and the whole glacier rocked, worse than it had when the ice demon roared. Walls and ceilings cracked, pieces crashing down on us, tripping me.

My hand slipped from Reyker's as I stumbled.

One moment there was solid ice beneath me, and the next it was slush. My legs sank through the melting ice sheet, into one of the many rivers flowing through the glacier's veins. My fingers grappled for purchase, finding nothing. I slipped the rest of the way into the water, so cold it knocked the breath from my lungs. I kicked and paddled, trying to swim, but my head still went under and the river's current dragged me beneath the ice sheet, deeper into the glacier, until frozen white walls surrounded me like a prison. Like a grave.

CHAPTER 27

LIRA

My flesh felt like it was filled with needles. I couldn't open my eyes. I raked my fingers over them, trapped in darkness, whimpering.

Someone grabbed my wrists. "Your lashes are frozen shut."

The voice wavered, distorted by the water clogging my ears. I tried to say his name, but my breath hitched wetly in my chest. A coughing fit seized me, wracking my body so hard I thought my ribs would break.

A hand touched my back. "You swallowed a lot of water before I pulled you out."

The memory was vague, colored by pain and fear: being sucked under the ice sheet, certain I was going to die. Then an arm braced around my waist, hauling me against the current, up to the surface. Easing me onto my side as I spit up water. After that, consciousness had trickled away.

My head was fuzzy, my thoughts sloshing about as if my mind was still underwater. "Cold," I managed to say through chattering teeth.

"Do you want me to warm you?"

"Yes."

Heat fell like a blanket over my shivering muscles. Arms wrapped around me, a body fitting itself along mine. That was when I realized my clothes were gone. I wore nothing but a thin sleeping gown, just a layer of cobwebs between my back and his bare chest.

I turned in his arms, nestling closer.

"Do you want me to touch you?"

"Yes."

His hands began to move, like flames brushing over my skin, reviving me. I didn't know what he was—a gift, a ghost, a dream. I didn't care. Gods, how I'd missed him.

My lashes thawed enough to open. Spots danced across my vision, but I could tell we were lying on a pallet inside an ice cave. A single oil lamp burned in the corner. Reyker was a silhouette bathed in shadow, the blue of his eyes the only thing I could clearly see.

"Do you want me to kiss you?"

I answered by pressing my lips to his. My mouth stilled. Unease rippled through me. He tasted different, smelled different. Even the pressure of his lips felt different—rough, unyielding. Like he was trying to conquer me.

"Lira." His voice changed. He scraped his teeth along my neck before kissing behind my ear, over my scar. "I want to hear you speak my name."

"Reyker?" It came out a strangled sob—a hope, a prayer, a lie.

"Guess again, little warrior."

The blue of his eyes shifted to greenish gold. Fire burst from a row of sconces frozen into the wall. The shadows coating him drew back like a second skin peeling away, revealing black tattoos crawling up one side of his body.

A trick.

All of it.

Reyker had never been here. Reyker was dead.

Draki had abused Reyker in life and was still using him in death, fooling me into thinking he was alive, touching me with his hands, kissing me with his mouth. Fear and rage tangled inside me. Rolling out from the blankets, I grabbed Draki's sword from where it lay beside the bed, unsheathing it. I lunged at him, screaming out my fury.

Draki didn't move. He didn't flinch. The blade crashed into his chest.

It shattered into silver dust that spilled across the blankets and onto the white floor.

"What . . . ?" I backed up until my spine hit a wall of ice, never taking my eyes off him. There wasn't even a scratch where I'd stabbed him. "What are you?"

His laugh was colder than the river that tried to drown me. He stood, crossing the space between us with slow, lethal grace. "I am your savior. Your master."

When he was close enough, he cupped my chin and lifted it so I was forced to look at him, towering over me in all his beautiful, savage glory.

"Your god."

CHAPTER 28

REYKER

Fire streaked toward the twilight sky. Inside it, a man burned to ash, pieces of him breaking off into the wind to join the snow and black sand.

Reyker stared numbly into the pyre. If Brokk wasn't watching him so closely, Reyker would have gone back up the glacier. Trekked over the brittle ice sheet with no one to anchor him. Climbed down every crevasse, searching, screaming a dead girl's name.

Dead. Alive.

Spirit. Illusion.

What had she been?

It was her in the mountain, standing over the crater. Those were her lips he'd kissed, her fingers he'd held in his own. She'd been right behind him in the ice tunnels, and then her hand slipped. He'd turned around, and—

And the ceiling caved in on him. Chunks of ice that buried him and knocked him unconscious. Or so he thought. When he woke, there had been no broken ceiling, no tunnels. Nothing but jagged ice, as if the corridor he'd run through had vanished.

Or never been there at all.

He'd spent hours searching, calling for her. He'd combed the glacier, but there was no trace. He'd tried and failed to climb the mountain itself, sliding back down, losing every bit of ground just as fast as he'd gained it. The liquid fire had churned inside, and he could feel Ildja's laughter in each bursting bubble, the goddess's secrets drifting beyond his reach, deep in the swirling Mist.

Brokk eventually forced him off the glacier, but Quinlan was the reason he'd agreed. The warrior deserved a pyre. Reyker had hauled his body out of the crevasse, and Skrim had carried the dead warrior on his back, across the ice sheet, to the edge of the dunes. This final flame was meant to be lit by kin or a priest. It shouldn't have been Reyker, the man who stole the girl Quinlan had loved for half his life, the brother of the warlord who'd razed Quinlan's village and ravaged his country. But Reyker had lit the fire because there was no one else.

As it burned lower, he looked behind him. The glacier glittered in the fading light.

"Try it, and I'll beat you senseless," Brokk said, coming up beside him. "I'll drag you back to Fjullthorp if I have to."

"We didn't find the girl. What if . . ."

What if Lira was the girl, the one Solvei had captured.

Brokk grabbed him by the shoulders. "You saw her jump off a cliff. Do you really think she could've survived that fall?"

Reyker closed his eyes, forcing himself to go back to that moment. He'd stood on the edge of the bluffs and stared into the sea. The fall. The rocks. The water was rough and unforgiving, the shore an impossible distance to swim. "No." The words were spikes tearing at his throat. "It was too much. No one could . . ."

Reyker pulled out of Brokk's grip and faced the glacier. His head pounded. He could hardly see straight, between the blow to his skull and the days he'd gone without sleep. If he went back up the glacier, he might not come down again.

Will she be waiting for me on the other side?

He must not have been ready to die yet because he turned and followed Brokk and Skrim over the dunes.

The land passed below his feet, but he hardly felt it, no more than he felt the passing of days. His body moved across rocks and streams and sand, but his mind wasn't there. It was back inside the glacier with a ghost.

When the peaks around Fjullthorp came into view, he stopped.

"I'm not going back." Reyker cut Brokk off before he could argue. "Solvei wants me to bargain and beg, but she's wasting time. I need to be gathering information from the warlord and his men. Tell your jarl I'll send word as soon as I have news to share."

Brokk's eyes darted between Reyker and the path to the Renegade village, his allegiance torn. Finally, he nodded. "I'll keep the three magiskas safe until you can get them home. What about your creepy horse?"

"Open the stable. Vengeance will find me."

They turned to part ways.

"Lagorsson."

Reyker waited.

"You've tried this before," Brokk said. "Undermining the Dragon from within. What makes you think you'll succeed this time?"

A good point. If Draki could be overthrown, why hadn't Reyker done it years ago?

"Because back then, I was afraid of him."

It was a half truth. He'd feared what Draki told him about himself. Draki said he was weak, a spoiled little lordling who'd not earned what fate had given him, and Reyker had believed. He'd watched it all burn, and when Draki said he deserved his punishment, part of him agreed. Every attempt he'd made to stop his brother had been tainted by fear that Draki was right, that somehow all of it was his own fault.

But a soul-reader had shown him he was wrong.

"I don't fear the Dragon anymore."

There was nothing Draki could do that would break him, nothing left for Draki to take from him that he couldn't bear to lose.

CHAPTER 29

LIRA

Dragon's Lair wasn't a village, it was a fortress.

I'd been dozing in the saddle, chin against my chest, but I snapped to attention as soon as it came into view. For the tenth time, I called to Draki's horse, a large stallion with a coat the color of shadows, begging it to buck the warlord. The horse merely flicked its ears in annoyance.

Behind me, Draki chuckled. "You must be careful with those shiny new powers of yours. When you cry out, you never know what sort of monsters will hear and come running."

I bit my lip, hard enough to hurt.

The call I'd made, desperate to find food for Quinlan—it had brought the wolf, but it also brought the ice demon that caused Quinlan's death. And it led the Dragon straight to me.

"I can help you understand your gifts," Draki said. "I will teach you to use them properly here, so far from your Green Gods. You will need them, now that you have lost your pretty dagger." He leaned in. "If you wanted to meet my mother, you could have just asked."

I threw my head back, trying to slam it into his face.

He dodged the blow without seeming to move at all. "Welcome to my home, little warrior. Our home."

After Draki had herded me through a long series of tunnels cut through the center of the glacier, we'd come out at the bottom, through a hidden entrance within the ice caves where Draki's horse was waiting. From there, we'd ridden a full day, over black dunes and yellow hills, to the vast, twisting paths of a lava field. The lava formations rose like a forest of obsidian trees, and on the other side was a strip of land where the island ended—sea cliffs as tall as the northern bluffs on Glasnith, only instead of a sheer drop, the cliffs' edges jutted upward, taller than a man, jagged fingers of rock hemming in the land between them. Stretched along the cliffs were long, narrow buildings, designed to fit into the oddly shaped terrain, with bridges and balconies connecting each one to the others. Dragonmen patrolled the area, pounding their fists against their chests in salute as Draki and I rode past.

The buildings were coated in ice. Beneath the frost, I could see the walls were constructed from gray stone, black lava, white branches.

No. Not branches. Bones. Skeletons, broken into pieces. Femurs and skulls stuffed between stones.

"My enemies," Draki said, following my gaze.

There were more inside—chandeliers made of spines, tables and chairs erected from arm and leg bones, a staircase banister forged from stacked skulls. They were mixed among wolf-skin rugs, stuffed foxes, reindeer heads mounted over a hearth. The whole place reeked of death.

"Are you hungry?" he asked.

I spat at his feet.

"I'll have something sent to your room."

He led me up the staircase, his fingers trailing fondly over the skulls. I wasn't tied up, he didn't push or drag me, but I knew what this was—I was a prisoner. I'd tried to run from him in the glacier tunnels, but he'd caught me. I'd stabbed him with a sword and it had done nothing.

Draki stopped at a door at the end of a long hallway. "You will learn to accept my kindness, Lira. Despite the dramatics of that ridiculous sword-maid who calls herself a jarl, my forces still hold the Green Isle. Even without my Dragonmen, your island's death god favors me above your people, and your father was only one of Gwylor's many sycophants. I could make your uncle king and help him hunt down the last of your kin. Or I could make your brother king and allow him to rule as he sees fit."

It took effort not to fall to my knees and beg for Garreth's life. "You always do exactly as you please. I'm not stupid enough to think my choices will change that."

"Is that truly a gamble you're willing to take?" He smiled and left me standing in the doorway.

I crossed the threshold, relieved to find this room free of bones. It was spacious, with a table and chairs in one corner and a sink and tub in the other. Between them was a large wooden bed frame piled with pillows and wool blankets. A fire crackled in the hearth. There were bookshelves, and I thumbed through several of the books, all of them written in Iseneldish. I could speak the language, but I couldn't read it. I would have to teach myself; there was no way I'd ask Draki to teach me.

Our home, Draki had said. Nowhere had ever felt less like home to me.

I didn't weep for myself, or for Quinlan. I pushed away the impulse to fall apart. When a servant brought me a tray of lamb stew, I ate. When several servants filled my tub with hot water, I bathed. After, I crawled into bed and slept. Tomorrow, I would agree to let Draki show me how to control the powers the Fallen Ones had given me now that I was in Iseneld.

I needed every advantage if I was going to fight my way out of here.

———

Draki's first lesson was about letting go.

We walked the length of the fortress, saluted by Dragonmen, bowed to by servants. The wind snuck in through gaps in the jutting cliffs, tugging at my hair and the thick cloak I was wrapped in. I was Draki's prisoner in much the same way I'd been Torin's: free to move about the fortress, but always with a guard on my heels; kept away from weapons; never spoken to beyond pleasantries, not even by my guards or the servants, no matter how much I prodded—whether out of loyalty or fear, I didn't know. I wasn't locked into my room, but there was a rotation of Dragonmen stationed outside my door at all times, and many more patrolling the fortress and grounds.

My only chance at getting away was with my gifts.

"Forget about Glasnith and its gods," Draki was saying. "They gave you power, but it lives in you. It is yours to wield. Now that Iseneld is your home, you must ask the Ice Gods for permission to use it."

He took me to the fortress temple. On the outside, it was no different from the armory or the feasting hall or the kitchens, but stepping through the door, I saw the temple was decorated with bones, just as Draki's parlor was. The bones were arranged on the walls and ceilings in artistic patterns to form garlands and murals, and many of them were black and brittle.

"More enemies?" I muttered.

"We don't allow the remains of enemies in this sanctuary." It wasn't Draki who answered, but what I assumed was the priest, a robed figure bending over an open book sitting on an altar of bones. The figure straightened, and I was surprised to see a woman in her midtwenties, her white-gold hair pulled up in a knot atop her head. A long scar marred each of her cheeks. "These are the bones of our ancestors and fallen soldiers, taken from the ashes of their funeral pyres."

I reached absently to touch the mural, and the priestess moved to block me. "Don't disturb the bones," she warned, "or the dead will haunt you." On the other side of the temple, Draki batted a garland of dangling femurs so they clanked like chimes. I glanced at him pointedly, and the priestess pursed her lips. "The dead know better than to bother the son of the soul-eater."

"The magiska is here to be cleansed, Hilde," Draki called.

"Well." Her hands went to her hips. "Let's get you undressed."

Draki must have trusted this priestess, because he left me alone with her in the temple. I stripped off the plain dress his servants had brought me that morning and stepped into a dry tub. Hilde lit a censor of incense, and the smell of the earth during a rainstorm filled the room. She held up a bucket, and I saw that the three middle fingers on both her hands were too short, amputated at the knuckle. "Do you renounce your ties to your homeland and its gods?"

"What?" I stared at her, my arms wrapped around my chest. My blood seemed to fizzle in my veins.

"You must be cleansed of everything that ties you to places outside of Iseneld. You must commit yourself to this island and the Ice Gods."

"If I don't?"

She smiled sadly. "It is the only way for your gifts to be your own. Otherwise, you are nothing but a conduit for the warlord."

My hand traveled to my *skoldar.* "Draki can't control me."

"Draki controls everyone on Iseneld, in one way or another." Her tone was even, though I sensed bitterness. "This is your one chance to keep some of that power for yourself."

All it cost me was forsaking my home. My brother.

But I was also severing ties with the Fallen Ones.

I thought of the dagger I'd nearly stabbed through my heart, of Quinlan vanishing into the jaws of a crevasse, of an illusion that looked like Reyker pinning me down. If I renounced the Fallen Ones, they couldn't make demands of me.

The Green Gods couldn't help me here, and neither could Garreth. It was up to me to survive, and I needed power to do it.

"Yes." My voice shook as the hissing in my blood swelled, as loud as it had been since I'd left Glasnith's shores. "I renounce all ties to my homeland. And its gods."

Hilde tilted the bucket over my head, dousing me with saltwater. "Do you accept Iseneld as your new homeland, embracing the Ice Gods as your own?"

Disavow Veronis and Gwylor, in exchange for Sjaf and Seffra. With the key to the Fallen Ones' prison gone, what choice did I have?

My blood burbled like a death rattle.

"Yes." All except Ildja.

The next bucket was full of what must have been melted ice. My teeth chattered.

"Will you fight for Iseneld against all foes, using your gifts to defend this land and its people?"

"*Yes.*" Especially Draki. Hilde dipped her thumb in ash and drew a symbol over my heart: a jagged star like the one Draki carved behind my ear, surrounded by flames like the *skoldar* Reyker had cut into my wrist. "The symbol of our country," she explained. "You're one of us now."

Silence trickled through my veins.

Was it that simple? Water and ash, and now I was Iseneldish instead of Glasnithian?

"You've done this to others like me?" I asked, accepting the cloth Hilde brought me to dry myself. "God-gifted girls from Glasnith?"

"From your island, no. But from other isles, near and far. They're all gone now, though. You are the first magiska I have met in some time."

"Gone where? And what of your own people with gifts? Where are Iseneld's magiskas?" For some reason, I thought of my journey to the Mountain of Fire, sleeping in the cold dunes, a dream of black hair and gold eyes.

"Some fled. Most died."

The cloth fell from my fingers. "Draki killed them?"

"The males, yes. Men and boys alike, from Iseneld or foreign lands, he kills them so none can rise against him. The girls and women, he collects. The female magiskas of Iseneld went into hiding. When Draki finds them, he uses most of them up quickly as weapons in his war, and their bodies fade with their gifts. The servants whisper about a door in his bedchamber that leads to a magiska prison. Pray you stay in his favor and never see the inside of those cells."

I wanted nothing to do with anything inside Draki's bedchamber—that's what I would pray for. "You said he uses up most of the magiskas. What does Draki do with the rest?"

"He feeds them to his mother."

A shudder ran through me, and I dressed quickly, trying to stave off the chill. Draki had first sought me out as a sacrifice for Ildja—he would have given me to her, had the Fallen Ones not chosen me as their vessel and strengthened me with their blood. "Is that why Draki came to Glasnith, an island with only female magiskas? To add more of us to his collection?"

"It was Ildja's will. She told him to end the Daughters of Aillira."

Not take. Not enslave.

End.

The door to the temple opened and a Dragonman beckoned. I had so many questions, but there was no time for them. Draki was waiting.

The priestess touched my arm. "Come visit me again, when you find yourself in need of holy guidance."

Beneath the invitation was a message: *You seek answers that I can provide.* I nodded, thanking her before the Dragonman ushered me away.

My first day in Dragon's Lair, and it seemed I'd already found an ally.

With my cleansing complete, Draki took me to the barn to select a sacrifice. Like the Green Gods, the Ice Gods wouldn't answer requests without a bit of blood. I tied the sheep's legs together, thinking of the stew I'd eaten the night before, and Draki slung the animal over his shoulder.

He led me to a bolted metal door in the fortress cellar. The Dragonman guarding it removed the bolt and stepped aside, handing Draki a torch, and I followed the warlord into a cramped tunnel. The rocks here weren't stacked, but hewn, carved straight through the cliffs. We passed several openings where other tunnels branched off, stretching into darkness, but Draki didn't turn. Our tunnel wound on and on, sloping downward like we were traveling into the belly of the earth, steep enough that I had to hold on to the wall to keep from losing my balance. At the tunnel's end was another barred door, and we emerged from it onto the beach at the bottom of the cliffs.

There was an enormous sea cave, a fleet of longships bobbing in its maw. The gray cliffs above us and the foaming slap of the sea against the sand reminded me of the home I'd just renounced, except rime glazed every surface.

At the edge of the water, Draki offered me a knife. Because I knew I couldn't hurt him with it, I didn't bother trying.

Wading into the icy surf, I cut into my palm and bled into the sea. Then I sliced open an artery in the sheep's neck, holding it still—this wasn't like killing the wolf, but it wasn't easy watching the creature's life slip away.

When the water swirled with red, Draki drew a symbol in the sand and motioned to the sea. "We begin with Seffra, wife of Sjaf. She is the womb of Iseneld, the life-giver, goddess of beasts and goddess of water.

Her bounty keeps us fed, sustains us when crops die and winter reigns. First, you must give her your tears."

"My tears?"

"Your sacred water in exchange for hers."

I didn't want to cry in front of Draki, but I'd spent so much time holding back, swallowing grief, that it was a relief to let go. I allowed myself to relive the moments I kept tucked beneath my sternum, close to my heart yet far from my thoughts: holding my father's hand as he told me goodbye; Quinlan's arm around me, promising I would love again; Reyker's lips on mine, calling me his deer.

Tears slipped down my cheeks, dripping into the sea.

"Now, pray to her," Draki said.

I imagined Seffra, a generous goddess floating beneath the waves, caring for the children of this island, guiding the fishermen's nets to ensure Iseneld's people never went hungry. Closing my eyes, I beseeched her, telling her how I came to be in Iseneld, asking her to accept me as one of her own. Calling on her kingdom's creatures to give me a sign of her answer.

A minute passed. Nothing happened.

Had I renounced Glasnith only to be rejected by the gods of Iseneld?

"Look." Draki pointed in the distance, where shapes slid through the waves. A pod of whales, spraying pillars of water into the air. One of them breached, its massive body leaping high out of the sea before splashing back down.

Awe dredged my soul up from the depths of mourning, the beauty of this moment singing along my nerves. It faded as Draki smiled at me with pride—the same sort of smile he'd given twelve-year-old Reyker when the boy had challenged him to a sword fight, stabbing at the warlord even after his arm was broken.

"Summoning animals was Veronis's power," Draki said, "but your veins carry blood from each of the Fallen Ones, and they all have an equivalent, a counterpart, here on Iseneld. You can awaken those gifts. I can make you the strongest mortal alive."

Glasnith had erased the names of those defeated gods, and the victors had taken control of their gifts in the mortal realm. I only knew of Veronis through blasphemous stories and scraps from a forbidden book, and I knew nothing of the rest of them. But Draki did, from his serpent-goddess mother who'd helped Gwylor imprison them.

"Why would you help me? What do you want from me?" I wouldn't pretend to care for Draki, wouldn't touch him willingly, not even as a ruse to get me out of this place. Maybe not even to save Garreth.

"When you finally give in to me, little warrior, your power will become my power."

I met the intensity of his gaze and did not flinch. He had his reasons, and I had mine. "Teach me more," I said.

—◆—

Reyker was there that night, as soon as I slept and dreamed, awaiting me in the ruins. He opened his arms and I backed away. "How do I know it's you and not him?"

"Who?"

"How many times have I been fooled, in these dreams and now when I'm awake, into thinking you are alive? I've hoped and wanted and let myself believe, only to have you torn away from me. You are dead! And I cannot stand it!"

Reyker shook his head. "I am alive. You are dead, Lira. Aren't you?"

He sounded too much like he had inside the Mountain of Fire, that false version that Draki had worn to trick me. "Stop! Do not seek me here again. It hurts too much. I cannot trust you, and I cannot trust myself."

"Where are you?" he asked. "What's happened to you?"

The answer was too difficult, too absurd. "I am in the Halls of Suffering. I am in the Mist. Or I might as well be."

He reached for me, and this moment mingled with others—he was Reyker, he was Draki, he was both and neither, a nightmare, a dream. I screamed in frustration, in agony, digging my fingers into my hair.

"Lira?"

"Whatever you are, you only make it worse. Please. Go."

The despair that twisted his features made me want to take it back.

Draki had never made such an expression, had never felt so deeply. "I don't know what I've done to hurt you, but I will stay away, if that is your wish. I'm sorry I couldn't . . ." He stopped and closed his eyes, pressing his fists against them. "I love you."

The sunlight dappling the ruins dimmed.

"Reyker?"

Where he'd stood a moment before, there were only crushed clovers, a swirl of moonflower petals trapped by the wind, the hulking shadow of the thorntree.

CHAPTER 30

LIRA

The village of Sjoglen was in the countryside not far past Dragon's Lair, between the misty foothills of a mountain range, but it felt like a different world from the fortress. There were rows of houses, and villagers wandered between them, chatting with their neighbors as they went about their chores, laughing at the packs of children chasing goats around the valley. The only similarity was the stacks of black stone that cupped the village on three sides. Hardened lava that had spewed from the sun burning inside the island, giving western Iseneld its name—the Lavalands.

All the cottages had sloping walls and roofs of bright green. On closer inspection, I noticed the fuzzy outline of moss and grass. "They build houses out of plants?" I asked.

"There's wood and stone underneath," Hilde said beside me, "but the plants keep in the heat. I wish we could do the same in Dragon's Lair. It gets quite drafty during the Ice Season."

"You can't grow a garden out of bones." I glared at Draki's back where he walked, a few paces ahead, along the shore of a glassy loch where villagers fished and bathed, rinsed their clothing, and gathered water for cooking. "Were you born in the Lavalands?"

"No, I'm from a small village in the Streamlands, a good ways south of here."

Vaknavangur was in the Streamlands, just beyond the Lavalands' border. I wondered how far her home village was from it, but I didn't dare ask with Draki so close by.

Bending down, I skimmed my fingers through the loch's cold waters. I called to a school of fish and sent them swimming straight into the fishermen's nets. The men laughed, struggling beneath the weight, calling for help to drag in their catch.

These people seemed kind enough, but they bowed and waved to the Dragon, stopped to speak with him, offered him fruit and wine, which he accepted with a smile that lacked his usual severity. "I don't understand," I whispered to Hilde as we made our way deeper into the valley, following after Draki. "Don't the villagers know what he is?"

A savage. A villain. Not the hero they greeted him as.

"The last overlord of the Lavalands took more than his fair share of the people's bounty. He didn't help Sjoglen or his other settlements when outlaws attacked, when storms caused the lochs to overflow and flood the villages, when plagues broke out. Then Draki rode into Sjoglen, put meat hooks through the jarl's heels, strung him upside down from this tree"— she gestured to the large birch tree in front of us; children scaled its trunk, swung from its branches—"and invited the villagers to pelt the jarl with stones, offering a reward to whoever struck the killing blow. The people of Sjoglen view Draki as their liberator, as many in Iseneld do. Those who benefit from his wrath rather than being its target."

A small girl—six years old or so, with blond braids whipping about her head—was perched on the edge of a branch, looking at the warlord. Turned away, he didn't seem to notice the girl. She flung herself forward, leaping from the tree and landing on Draki's back.

I took a step forward, ready to intervene on the girl's behalf.

The Dragon lifted her with one hand and set her on the ground. They eyed each other, and the girl laughed. "I won, Jarl Dragon," she said, holding out her palm. "I told you I'd catch you off guard one day."

"So you did, Magda." He took a knife from his belt and offered it to her. Magda accepted the weapon with wonder, holding it up in the light. "Don't stab anyone unless they deserve it."

She nodded at this sage advice and ran off, announcing her prize to everyone within earshot, prompting a trail of children to chase after her, begging to see.

Draki's gaze slanted toward me. "Commence your studies with the priestess, Lira." Then, almost as an afterthought, he said, "I let her win."

I shook myself, not sure what I'd just witnessed. Draki, feigning kindness by giving a *blade* to a child?

No. Draki, putting on a farce to manipulate me. That was why he'd brought me today—not to show me more of the Lavalands, as he'd claimed, but to display how beloved he was by his people. I wasn't falling for it.

Hilde sat beneath the tree, a book in her lap, and I joined her. A Dragonman stood behind us, monitoring our conversation. Spying for his master.

"Did you always want to be a priestess, Hilde?"

She touched the stub of one of her knuckles to the scar running down her left cheek, her gaze distant. "Not always."

The Dragonman cleared his throat in warning.

I rolled my eyes, but Hilde opened her book and began.

"This book is the Gud Sager, a chronicle of the Ice Gods. Once, magiskas could use their gifts freely throughout the world, but that was before the Gud Rift, when all the gods were forced to choose sides. Now, for each gift the Green Gods gave you, you must make a sacrifice to the corresponding Ice God. Only with the god's blessing will your power flow unencumbered, with no further price to be paid."

I pointed to a symbol on the page: three connecting triangles, overlapping. Draki had drawn it in the sand when I prayed to Seffra. "What's this mean?"

"Sacrifice. A blood offering, in exchange for a god's favor."

This was the same symbol my uncle had drawn in front of his home when he promised his wife and daughter to Gwylor. It was the symbol he'd etched in the dirt of my cell in Stony Harbor before he tried to burn me alive. If it worked for both the Ice Gods and the Green Gods, he must have found it buried in the pages of the Forbidden Scriptures.

"That's it?" I said. "Make an offering, draw a symbol, pray to the right god."

"In the simplest of terms, though each god's demands are dependent upon the gift you're requesting. But, Lira, these rituals are dangerous. You cannot pretend. Whatever you ask for, whatever you promise, you have to mean it with the whole of your heart. Otherwise, the gods might strike you down."

These rituals were about asking for power, to be stronger, better able to defend myself and what I held dear. "I will mean it."

"You have the blood of seven gods inside you. Draki was very specific about which of their gifts he'll allow you to claim until you've proven your loyalties. In accordance with his wishes, there are certain gods' rituals I am not permitted to teach you."

I threw a glance at the Dragonman shadowing us. "Of course."

Hilde showed me pictures and read me stories about the gods and goddesses Draki had chosen for me. Jardun, goddess of crops and soil. Velder, god of wind and sky. Leggi, goddess of health and fertility. "Shall we start with Leggi?"

My mind churned with possibilities. Earth and wind made worthy weapons—I'd seen it myself in Stalwart Bay, the strength of the earth-shifters and wind-wafters I'd fought beside—but how was I supposed to attack someone with fertility? "Is it truly my choice, or has the Dragon dictated the order in which I am to receive my gifts?"

Hilde offered me a wry smile.

"Leggi it is."

The priestess's smile faded. "To gain power over health, you must sacrifice your own. A common illness in Iseneld is *sor mund*. It's rarely fatal, but it's quite unpleasant. A man in Sjoglen came down with it a few days ago." She stood, beckoning me to follow.

"Wait. That's why we're here? So I can catch this man's illness?"

"Yes." Hilde paused. "Unless you do not wish to gain this gift."

It might not make an effective weapon, but curing illness was a valuable gift. I nodded, and Hilde led me to one of the cottages, where a man lay shivering in a bed pushed close to the hearth. Heat radiated off him, and he was only half conscious, babbling to himself. All of the gods' rituals required blood, so I pricked my finger, using the droplets to draw three overlapping triangles across the sick man's forehead. Then I prayed to Leggi to heal this man, to transfer his illness to me and use it to make me stronger.

By the time we left the cottage, my skin was flushed and my bones had begun to ache. I leaned heavily against a cart filled with straw. "The Ice Gods don't dally, do they?"

"We should get you back to the fortress."

"Don't," I said as she came closer. "You'll catch it too."

Hilde huffed, wrapping her arm around my waist, supporting some of my weight. "I'm a priestess. Leggi will protect me."

On the ride back to Dragon's Lair, I began to shiver and sweat. Draki had let me ride to Sjoglen on my own horse instead of on his, a thing I'd been relieved about on the way there but was starting to regret now as I teetered in my saddle. I stopped my horse several times so I could lean over and retch.

Sor mund, this sickness was called. Sour mouth.

I laughed, then retched again. My limbs felt fuzzy, like they weren't really there. My head felt fuzzy too. I closed my eyes, just for a second.

I woke in my bedroom in Dragon's Lair. Hilde was there, murmuring encouragement, mopping the sweat from my skin. She held a bucket beneath me as I vomited up everything I'd ever eaten, wiped my mouth, and settled the blankets over me when my stomach finally calmed. "I think your gods are punishing me," I told her.

"If that's true, you must have done something to deserve it."

She was teasing, but an image rose in my mind: four young women falling from a watchtower. "You hardly know me, Hilde. Why are you so kind to me?" The priestess's hands came in and out of focus, the scarred knuckles, the empty space where her middle three digits should have been. "How can you be kind, after everything the Dragon has done to you?"

"The Dragon didn't do this. He's never touched me. There is no kindness in him, but rarely is he cruel without cause." She sat back, folding her arms around herself. "There is kindness in me because of the compassion others have shown me. I offer it to you because you're in need of it, and I believe you will share it as I have."

Inside me were cavities of rage, hollows of grief. There was little room left for kindness. "I will try."

The room tilted, and the world faded once more.

The next time I woke, it wasn't Hilde at my bedside. I was too weak to sit up. A hand slid behind my neck, lifting me so I could purge my stomach. A glass touched my lips, and I drank. It chafed to lie there, frail and wasted, letting my enemy care for me. I should have told him to go, but I didn't want to be alone. The sickness had sapped my pride.

"Where's Hilde?" My voice was little more than a croak, leaking from my raw throat.

Draki dipped a cloth in a bowl of water, draped it over my forehead. "Resting. She's been watching over you for the last two days."

Two days? No, no, I'd been sick for years. Every inch of me was swollen, my flesh stretched too tight over my bones, my eyes wobbling like marbles in my skull. "Are you enjoying this, Draki? Watching me suffer?"

"I enjoy cutting down warriors on the battlefield. I relish crushing my rivals, torturing my foes. But you . . . your suffering does nothing for me."

"And what of the Dragonman you called your Sword? Did you relish his suffering?"

Draki's face swam in my vision, his features beautiful and cold and cruel. "Do not speak of things you cannot understand."

Before I could form a proper retort, my eyelids fluttered, my tongue too heavy in my mouth. I was half asleep when I heard it.

"I will break you, little warrior. So no one else can."

Maybe he said it aloud, or in my head, or maybe I dreamed it and he'd not spoken at all.

———

The sickness left me a few days later, and I was finally able to get out of bed. My legs were still weak, but I managed to dress and make my way to the bone temple, a Dragonman guard trailing after.

Hilde was standing over a table lined with weapons, polishing a giant axe covered in runes. She smiled as I stumbled in. "Nice to see you without vomit coming out of your mouth."

"You said *sor mund* was unpleasant." I shook my head. "A thorn in your foot is unpleasant. A bee sting is unpleasant. Retching up my guts for four days was a bit more troublesome than you'd led me to believe."

"But now it is over, and if all went well, Leggi has blessed you."

I hefted one of the swords, picking at the rust on its blade. "What are these?"

"Treasures. Ancient, sacred weapons used by our ancestors, the warlords who built the first settlements on Iseneld. The first children of the Ice Gods."

Gingerly, I put the sword back on the table. "I'm ready to test Leggi's gift, Hilde."

She pursed her lips. "Not yet. Give yourself another day or so to rest."

"No." I needed to gain the Ice Gods' gifts as quickly as possible. I didn't want to remain in Dragon's Lair any longer than I had to. "I'm fine. I can do this."

The priestess set the axe down and braced her knuckles against her hips, assessing me. She must have known what I was up to. "Who am I to stand between you and the will of the gods?" she said.

I wanted to return to Sjoglen and heal the man who'd given me his illness, but Hilde had already been to visit him and assured me he'd recovered. Still, in a place as large as Dragon's Lair, with servants and soldiers mingling with one another and the villagers in the surrounding areas, we were bound to find a sick patient in the infirmary.

Sure enough, there was a stable boy of about fifteen lying in one of the beds, afflicted with some sort of ague not unlike *sor mund*. I approached the boy, explaining who I was and what I wanted to do, but in his feverish condition he couldn't respond, could hardly keep his eyes open. I put my hand on his head.

Hilde's books had detailed how to ask permission to use my gifts, but not how to wield them. I'd never healed anyone. It was different than soul-reading, different than summoning beasts.

Or perhaps it only seemed that way.

I opened my mind and sought the sickness inside him just as I would have searched for guilt in a soul. When I found the source, a pulsing sludge that coated his organs, I called to it as I would a horse or a hawk, and it came—viscous fluids leaking from his pores like sweat and tears, bile spilling from his mouth.

The boy cried out. Hilde grabbed a rag and cleaned his face. "What is your name?" she asked gently.

"Olaf."

"And how do you feel, Olaf?"

"Sleepy. But better." He grinned at her, at me. "Thank you."

"Sleep, Olaf," Hilde said, brushing the boy's damp hair from his temples. "Leggi has granted you mercy. Tomorrow you can go home."

The healer came to check on Olaf, confirming the boy's fever had broken.

I walked with Hilde back to the temple. "I want to complete Jardun's ritual. Today. Now."

"Slow down, Lira. You'll run yourself ragged. There's no rush."

"Yes, there is. I can't wait. I can't . . ." *I can't stay here, with* him. "Please."

She lifted her palms in surrender. "All right, I'll get my book. But you should know—" She peered at my Dragonman guard strolling behind us and lowered her voice. "This plan of yours plays right into Draki's hands. The Dragon is fickle, but he appreciates ambition. Your tenacity will only make him covet you all the more."

"Draki's desires are not my concern."

Hilde linked her elbow with mine. "Careful. The god of lies will hear you, and it's clear you have not been blessed by his grace."

CHAPTER 31

REYKER

The Dragonmen stopped him at the edge of the lava field, and though he hardly recognized their faces, their expressions were familiar—suspicious, hostile, as most Dragonmen were to him. They barred him from entering the path cut through the lava. In the distance he could see Dragon's Lair, a place that still haunted his thoughts. This was where he'd spent most of his days in the years after Draki razed Vaknavangur, where he and his mother had lived as prisoners. It was where she'd died.

He waited as a Dragonman rode to inform Draki of his arrival, waited as the warlord mounted his beast of a horse and came out to meet him.

If Draki was surprised to see him, the warlord didn't show it. "Have you taken care of the Fjull Uprorsmund?" he asked.

"Taken care of them?" Surely Draki knew Reyker had been the Mountain Renegades' prisoner for a time, the way he knew—through his goddess-mother or some unearthly means—so much of what happened, far and wide, on Iseneld.

"We had a deal," Draki said. "You fight for me. You remain my Sword. Or do you wish to break the bargain, now that we are both home? Shall I send word to the remaining Dragonmen on the Green Isle to round up the Daughters of Aillira and bring them to me?"

"No." Reyker gritted his teeth. "Look, I already convinced the Renegades to let me go, that I would ally with them. If you want more—"

"I want them all dead." Draki eyed Vengeance, his brows lifting, and the mare eyed him in return, her glassy pupils throwing the warlord's reflection back at him.

"I need time," Reyker said, thinking, plotting, as quickly as his mind could spin. "If I kill Solvei, someone else will take her place. They're more than an army—they're an idea, a belief that the Dragon should not rule Iseneld. If you want me to quell this uprising, I must pluck it up by the roots, or another will rise behind it."

He waited for Draki to see through his deception, to tell him he'd just sealed the fate of the Daughters of Aillira.

Draki's smile was a flash of white against the backdrop of black rock. "My clever brother, always one step ahead. That is why I keep you around. However, it has not escaped me that you've spent a great deal of time among my enemies recently, on Glasnith and Iseneld. If you want to serve me again, you must prove you have not turned traitor. Meet me here at sunset in three days. You will accompany me to an assembly where your guidance may be of use."

"What sort of assembly?"

"You will see." Draki waved a hand in dismissal.

Reyker held his breath for a beat, letting it out slowly. He turned Vengeance, but Draki called after him.

"Until you have proven yourself," the warlord said, "you are not welcome in Dragon's Lair."

Reyker glared at the stark gray outline of the fortress. He wished he could burn it down or dump the whole monstrosity into the sea. "Good."

Vengeance carried him away in a flurry of hooves, Dragon's Lair shrinking fast, but never fast enough.

———◆———

Three days. Not enough time to get to Fjullthorp and back, but enough time to visit a place he hadn't been in years, a place that haunted him as much as Dragon's Lair.

Reyker rode for the better part of a day, crossing from the Lavalands into the Streamlands, until the sparse woods of his childhood home came into view. Riding over the hills to Vaknavangur didn't feel real. He'd done it hundreds of times as a boy, but only a handful as a man.

He expected it to be a ghost of what it once was, tumbled stones and rotted wood sticking up from below a sea of frost, just as it was the last time. But someone else had been here recently, digging up the remains of cottages and the feasting hall.

They were still here.

A boy of ten or so was walking up a path through the woods, carrying a bucket. When he noticed Reyker, the boy gave a shrill whistle and darted through the trees toward the far corner of the village. Reyker followed and came across a group of children. They were about to run, but one girl stepped closer, eyes wide. "You're him."

"Who?" Reyker caught himself looking around, as if someone might be behind him.

"The Wolf Lord."

"The . . . *who?*"

"Get away from them!" someone shouted. From different directions, twenty young men and women rushed out, all Reyker's age or a bit younger. Their swords and axes were raised, ready to defend the children.

The girl pointed, bouncing with excitement. "The Wolf Lord is here! He's come home!"

They stared at him—men and women, boys and girls. The oldest among them, a sandy-haired man who held his axe like someone who'd used it before, spoke first. "Who are you?"

They knew. Everyone knew. Draki had made certain of it, tattooing Reyker's identity onto his face for the world to see. Reyker's hand went to the hilt of his sword, an unspoken warning. "Who is asking?"

The axe inched higher. "I am Hamund Akesson of Vaknavangur. And you?"

Hamund, son of Ake. Reyker remembered Ake, a quiet man with a hearty laugh, good with a spear, better with a fiddle; he'd had one daughter, one son. Hamund—Reyker knew this boy from long ago. His eyes grazed their faces, recognizing some of the others. These were his people. Like

Brokk, they'd been children when Draki destroyed their village, forced to watch the men in their families fall beneath the Dragonmen's swords.

"I am Reyker Lagorsson of Vaknavangur." It came out strained by the knot in his throat.

"Are you here on behalf of the Dragon?"

"I do not serve the Dragon." He looked at the ruins around him. Somewhere beneath the frost was his father's body. Draki didn't cut Lord Lagor's corpse up and put his bones into the fortress as he had with the other fallen men of Vaknavangur. A kindness, for Reyker's sake, so he would not have to pass the bones of his father every day—this was what his brother had claimed, not acknowledging the insult of leaving their father to be buried by winter, ravaged by animals that came to gnaw at his frozen flesh. "I am here for my father, Lord Lagor, to reclaim and rebuild these lands. Our lands."

"We've heard stories of what happened to you in Dragon's Lair, how you fought to resist the warlord. Are they true?"

Memories of those days rumbled in Reyker's soul, pressing at his mind. He shoved them back down again, somehow kept his voice even as he said, "They are."

Hamund kneeled, holding his axe up on his palms. "Then I pledge my aid and my axe to you, Reyker Lagorsson, in the name of your father and mine."

The others followed Hamund's lead, kneeling on the cold ground, swearing their lives to him. Something twisted in his chest—shock and pride and gratitude. He dismounted and went to kneel with them. "I pledge myself to you, heirs of your fathers, and to Vaknavangur. May it rise to greatness once more."

One by one, they introduced themselves. Not all of them remembered Vaknavangur's destruction, but all had been there for it. Children who had been just babes in their weeping mothers' arms circled him, cheering and chanting. "Wolf Lord! Wolf Lord!"

"Wolf Lord?" He looked at Hamund, who grinned.

"Dragons and serpents are Ildja's creatures, but wolves belong to no gods. They rule themselves, and each leader is sworn to protect his pack. That's what you were to us when you raised your father's sword against the warlord. A wolf fighting a dragon. A boy fighting a god."

That twinge came again, beneath his ribs. He hadn't earned their esteem yet. He didn't deserve the title they had bestowed upon him, but he could try. With the Mountain Renegades' help, he could finally end the battle he'd started that moment he picked up his father's sword. But it would have to be done carefully—this was a walk along a rope strung above Ildja's crater. One misstep and everything would burn.

Hamund showed Reyker what they'd accomplished, leading him past buildings in various stages of reconstruction, to the only one that was livable, a half-finished cottage in the center of what had once been Vaknavangur. Reyker's father's home.

His home.

"With a few more days of work, it will be done." Hamund passed Reyker a large stone from the pile beside the doorway. "It will go faster now that you're here."

They entered the house and Reyker's breath caught. Their possessions were long gone, the floor was filthy, but the space was the same. How many times had he sat here before the hearth with his parents? With Aldrik? "If the warlord finds out . . ."

If Draki found out about the survivors of Vaknavangur, he would see them as weakness. He would turn Reyker's plans, and everyone they touched, to ash.

"We were all there," Hamund said. "We all lost someone. The dead would want us to reclaim what is ours. It is worth the risk, Lord Reyker. Or do you prefer Wolf Lord?"

They stacked their stones onto others that were patching a hole in the back of the room. "Just Reyker." No one had ever called him lord, except as an insult—*little lordling*, a taunt Draki and all his men had hurled at him like arrows meant to wound his pride, to remind him that he was lord of nothing.

Hamund chuckled, turning to fetch more stones. "That is not a name befitting a legend. Your story belongs to your people now. Let them have their dreams. Let them believe in the boy who took on a god."

Wolf Lord.

He could still hear Lira whispering from the ruins, calling him *my wolf*. The stories Reyker told her of his gods and the great heroes of Iseneld had fascinated her. How amused she would have been to know Reyker was a legend now himself.

CHAPTER 32

LIRA

Draki's second lesson was about many things. Patience. Desire.

Death.

Though he'd overseen my rituals to Jardun and Velder, he'd been busy in the days since, and I'd spent most of that time under Hilde's tutelage, practicing my newly acquired gifts, and the rest of it wandering the fortress aimlessly, bored enough that I couldn't suppress the flare of excitement when the warlord finally summoned me to meet him that afternoon. If nothing else, he presented a target for my restless energy.

I showed up to the feasting hall early. Finding it empty, I ambled through the adjacent halls, passing silent servants who bobbed their heads at me as they swept up dirt tracked in by careless warriors. Most of the doors along this hallway were closed, many of them leading to the private quarters of Dragonmen. The bone-cluttered walls made me long to be back in Sjoglen, where the homes were clad in greenery.

It gave me an idea.

I picked up a clump of moss dragged in by a Dragonman's boots, placing it at the bottom of the wall. Head bowed, I channeled the gift I'd gained from the goddess of crops and soil. Jardun's ritual had required me to spend hours buried in a clay coffin, to convene with the earth. In the quiet dark, struggling to keep my breaths steady and my panic at bay, I'd heard the earth speak, heard the deep rumble of trees and the chattering of flowers. An ancient, mystic tongue my ears couldn't decipher, but my soul could.

It was my soul that whispered to the moss I'd placed against the wall of bones, coaxing it to grow, to spread. The moss expanded into a blob, green tendrils extending out like legs crawling over the bones, until a thin carpet of green trailed from floor to ceiling. It was only an arm-span wide, but it was progress from my previous attempts, a confirmation that my gifts improved each time I used them.

Inspired by this small victory, I called up Velder's gift next, pulling wind from outside through the cracks in the walls. With a wave of my hand, I sent a swirling breeze across the floor to eddy the rest of the dirt into piles.

Wind was the easiest gift for me to wield—strange, since gaining the god of wind and sky's favor had been the most taxing ritual I'd endured thus far. I had prayed for a storm, and when it came, I'd sat on a swing made of a plank with lengths of rope attached on either side that Draki lowered over the edge of the cliffs of Dragon's Lair. Dangling in midair, with only a slab of wood between me and the frothing sea far below, tossed about by wind and pelted by rain, I'd given myself over to Velder's mercy. The storm lasted hours, and when it finally died, I was soaked and shivering, my nerves in tatters. Draki hauled the swing up and set me on solid ground, prying my stiff fingers from the ropes. Rewarding me with a nod of approval.

"Stuff it up your arse," I'd replied, hating how his scant praise made my cheeks flush.

I made my way farther up the hall. The wind I sent through it rattled the bones and knocked open several of the doors. I peered into each room before shutting the doors—some were messy and reeked of sweat, others were pristine and orderly. All were empty.

The room at the end of the corridor was the only exception. I sensed someone inside, and I toed the door open a bit wider.

There was Draki, his back to me, sitting by the hearth in a dust-coated room similar to mine. The bed was unmade, the desk was cluttered with books. It was unremarkable, yet something about it spoke to me. It felt warmer than the rest of the fortress. The scent that lingered was cinders and salt and thyme.

It was Reyker's scent, clinging to every surface, soaked into the sheets.

"You are trespassing, little warrior," Draki called without looking up.

"Who lives here?"

The Dragon sighed as he stood. "No one."

I was too stunned to press him, too gutted to make sense of it. When he grasped my elbow and led me from the room, I didn't protest.

———✦———

The warlord took me to an unmarked building, this one with a high roof, and inside was a large open area, bigger than the barn. The room's floor was made of cool black sand. Weapons lined the walls, but it was not an armory. "We call this the Blood Ring," Draki said.

"Is this where you train your warriors?"

"Warriors train outside, even if the snow is deep or the rain is heavy. The Blood Ring is for sport and entertainment. But you and I will train here, in a contained space."

"Train? To fight?"

He walked in a wide circle, digging his boot heel into the sand as he went. "Everyone of age in Dragon's Lair is required to train. They must know how to defend themselves and their home from an attack. Do you think I would expect less from my consort?"

"I am not your consort." It would have sounded bolder if my voice hadn't cracked like an egg on that last word.

"Yet." Draki completed the circle. He'd not even paid attention as he made it, but the ring was as seamless as if it had been drawn by an artist or carved by nature's hands: the haloed heart of a flower, a corona encompassing the sun. "If you want me to help you strengthen your gifts, you must earn it by strengthening the rest of you. Come here."

I did as he asked, dragging my feet through the curves of the circle as

I crossed it, marring its perfection. As soon as I reached the center, Draki disappeared.

A hand brushed my shoulder, and I spun, but he was already gone. He moved around me, touching my neck, my hip, my calf. My kicks and punches only hit air.

With a growl, I went for the weapons. Many of the swords hanging on the wall were as tall as I was—heavy blades meant for giants—but there were a few smaller ones. I pulled one down and took it to the circle, slicing at the breeze, the only sign of Draki's position.

"How am I supposed to learn anything if you won't stand still?"

The sword flew out of my grip and then Draki was there, taking my hands, spinning me into his arms. "The god of war teaches us that battle is a sort of courtship. Sometimes you pursue. Other times, you let the object you desire come to you. Understanding which option is best requires patience, something you are sorely lacking."

"So let me pray for the gift of war, if I have it."

I did. Hilde wasn't supposed to tell me, but she'd found subtle ways of revealing which gifts I carried, and the Dragonmen who spied on us had yet to catch on.

"Few mortals have embraced the war gift without descending into madness. You are not ready. Not until you've mastered restraint." I pressed against his arms, but he held me tighter. "Focus all of your senses on me. I am the object you desire, the only thing that exists for you in this moment. Seek me with your eyes. Listen and hear my body as it moves. Every muscle. Every breath. Every heartbeat." His fingers trailed along my collarbones, resting at the curve of my breast, over my heart.

It beat faster beneath his hand.

"Feel every single part of me and you will find me," he whispered in my ear, and then he vanished.

I took several seconds to collect myself, shaking off his touch, and then I focused on my desire. Draki. I wanted to beat him. I wanted to hurt him. I wanted . . .

There. I felt a shift in the air to my left. I waited, concentrating, and saw a glimmer of silver. I heard a drum, faint to my ears, even though I could tell it was a loud and powerful thing. I felt him, the way he moved through the world as if it belonged to him, as if the very elements it was composed of would bend at his command.

I reached out, keeping my desire sharp in my mind. I wanted to stop him. To show him I could. To touch the man who thought himself untouchable.

My fingers met solid flesh. Draki came back into view, standing before me, my hand on his arm. He stared down at me, at my fingers curled around his biceps, like I was some new species he'd just discovered. His desire was plain in his eyes. Draki was here to teach me, but he was also here to learn, to explore. He wanted to know me, inside and out—my kindness and cruelty, the beauty and the ugliness.

Did I pull away first, or did he?

When there was space between us, Draki glanced at me again, and the look I'd seen before was absent. He was cocky and cold once more. "What weapon do you prefer?"

Every weapon imaginable was right there at my disposal, but it didn't matter. I would fight as my father and brothers had, as the Sons of Stone had. I gestured at the blade I'd chosen, lying in the sand. "A sword."

"You have not earned a sword."

"Then why did you ask?"

Draki went to the wall and removed two throwing knives. "Start with these. Master them, and I will reward you with another god's gift."

I held the blades in my hands, wondering if I could plunge one into the scar behind my ear—to be rid of Draki once and for all, even if it killed me. "I don't know how to use them."

"A conundrum."

I stomped my foot like a child. That's what it felt like, being in Draki's presence. I was a petulant child and he was my long-suffering mentor. A mentor who might kill me if I stepped too far outside the invisible circle he'd drawn around me. "Fine. Show me."

"How could I resist such lovely manners?" He held the knife hilts lightly, the back of each blade resting between his thumb and forefinger. With a flick of his wrists, they shot forward, hard enough to bury the blades in the stone wall.

He waved for me to retrieve them, knowing I couldn't, chuckling as I jerked at the hilts with angry grunts. "Pitiful little girl."

"Deceitful savage."

He spun me so my back was against the wall, the knife hilts digging into my spine. One hand stroked my throat, a flirtatious threat. "Do you want to live, Lira?"

The question caught me off guard. "I . . . I think so."

"You think? No, that is not good enough." His fingers tightened. I could breathe, but just barely. "Do you want to live?"

"Yes." The word was little more than a hiss of air from my lips.

"Liar." He picked me up as if I weighed no more than a speck of dust, hurling me across the room, into the center of the Blood Ring. "You jumped off a cliff. You would have leaped into Ildja's fire. Just now, you were staring at those knives like you longed to embrace them and bleed yourself dry. You think dying is noble, but it is weakness. When death comes for you, will you cower and let it suck the flesh from your bones?"

I tried to stand, but he knocked my feet from beneath me. I tried to crawl, but he grabbed my leg and pulled me backward through the sand. He rolled me over, straddling me, his hands closing around my throat, cutting off my breath.

"Shall I put you out of your misery?"

I clawed at his fingers, at his face, but it did nothing. My lungs itched and burned, starved for air. My vision was fading. Draki was a blur of silver hair and green-gold eyes dancing in front of me.

"Would you prefer to join all the loved ones you've lost?"

I'd been asking myself that since Reyker died. Seeing his room in Dragon's Lair had unlocked all the pain I kept trying to cage, and I still couldn't answer Draki's question. I didn't know.

Yes, I did.

Darkness closed around me like a falling curtain, but Draki's voice drifted through it, a tether keeping me grounded even as my soul began to rip free.

Do you want to live, Lira?

Living hurt. I'd lost almost everything, and so much of it was my fault, and sometimes I just wanted the guilt and the pain to be over.

Sometimes.

But not all the time. Not really. Because, in spite of everything, there was still joy in me. There was still love. There were things worth fighting for.

Worth living for.

A scream built in my lungs, and deeper—in my gut, in my nerves, in every fiber of my being. It burst out of me from every pore, a storm howling from my mouth, a wave crashing in defiance. The world shrank to the head of a pin, expanded to infinity. I was floating in a sea of stars, flying over Glasnith, over Iseneld, over a thousand unknown lands I'd never heard of but wanted to explore. I saw a girl, standing in the Blood Ring in Dragon's Lair, her back to a wall.

And then I was that girl, blinking awake in my body, the knife hilts still poking at my spine, Draki's fingers resting lightly around my throat.

"You tried to kill me," I said.

Draki raised a brow. "Did I?"

No. My throat should have been on fire, but it didn't hurt. The sand in the circle on the Blood Ring's floor was undisturbed, because he'd never thrown me into it. Draki had only made me think he was hurting me. Killing me.

"I just taught you the most important lesson of all." His hands slid down my back as he pulled the knives from the stone, muscles barely shifting. "Before you learn to fight, you must be certain of the value of what you're defending."

I started to shove him, but he stepped away. "Stay out of my head, Draki."

"I would, if only you stopped leaving the door wide open." He twirled the throwing knives, skipping them across his knuckles, spinning and catching them without ever looking. "I will take you back to your room to rest. We can begin tomorrow."

I snatched the knives from him. "We begin now."

When the Dragon smiled, he seemed to glow from within, too strange, too beautiful to be wholly human. "As you wish, little warrior."

CHAPTER 33

REYKER

As instructed, he met Draki outside Dragon's Lair at midnight. He'd been loath to leave Vaknavangur—for a full day, he'd lugged stones and gathered logs and scrambled about, patching the roof, until repairs on his childhood home were nearly complete. It had been a soothing reprieve. One that could not last.

Draki waited by the lava field's gate, wearing his traditional war garb—wool trousers, boots, and nothing else. He left his torso unclothed, exposing the black ink that marked what he was, not that anyone could miss the distinctive yellow sheen of the warlord's eyes. Together, they rode south in silence. Reyker had learned long ago how pointless it was to ask the warlord questions, so he didn't bother.

After a few hours, they arrived at Hidden Falls. Draki slowed his mount and Reyker followed suit, the horses winding their way along the sloped path, curving around hills and ledges, until the falls finally came into view. The wide river that fed the falls rushed over the edge where land ended, spilling into a canyon. From here, Reyker couldn't see into the canyon, so it seemed the falls crashed into nothingness, a hole ripped straight into the earth.

Jutting above the falls was a rocky cliff, flat and gray, contrasting against the white water, the green hills, the brown canyon. On it stood a group of men, thirteen in all.

Night was already seeping away, the deep blue of the sky paling to light indigo. Enough to see the faces of those gathered at the falls, and the way they startled as the Dragon came closer. Reyker recognized some of the men, and he noted the expensive clothing they wore, the ceremonial weapons they carried. These were lords and jarls from across the island, a meeting of Iseneld's leaders. One Draki had not been invited to attend.

Reyker stiffened, knowing what was to come. He scanned the leaders again, but Solvei was not among them. A small mercy.

"My friends," Draki called, dismounting when he reached the cliff. "You should have told me this was a party. I would have brought wine."

There were wary gazes, some shuffling.

"We meant no offense," one of the lords finally said, shouting to be heard over the thundering water. The lord was younger than his companions, a nervous-looking man who dropped into a bow. "We did not wish to burden you with our petty debates."

"How thoughtful." Draki strode toward him, and the young lord cowered. Somehow the warlord's voice was louder than the falls even though he didn't raise it. "But no discussion is too trifling when it concerns the future of *my* country."

"This is not your country." A scowling man unsheathed his sword— Jarl Sigmundsson. His village had been the last to accept Draki's reign, and only to avoid bloodshed. Reyker had gone to Sigmundsson on Draki's orders to kill him and had instead convinced the man to surrender for the sake of his people. The overlord was gray haired, but his years didn't temper his bravery. "You have brought suffering upon the people of Iseneld. You made an enemy of men who have been rulers here since before your serpent mother spat you from her womb."

Draki smiled. "Is that what you all think?" No one else said a word as the warlord circled them, though many rested their hands on their weapons. "It appears I have made a terrible mistake. I shall rectify it immediately and step down as high jarl." He stopped in front of the gray-haired jarl. "Is that what you came here to debate? How to overthrow me?

And who would take my place? You, I suppose." He flicked Sigmundsson's chest, and the jarl fumed. "You are kin to my predecessor Jarl Gudmund, are you not?"

"I am brother to the rightful jarl of the Streamlands, the one you stabbed in the back."

"Figuratively and literally," Draki said, steepling his fingers. The lords murmured. Their panic was growing, and the warlord was a leech, feeding off it.

"I, too, understand the importance of brotherhood." Draki's eyes slanted to Reyker. "Such bonds make us blind to our brothers' faults and misdeeds. Sometimes they are undeserving of the faith we put in them. It is the same with all of you. I offered my trust, believing we wanted the same things for Iseneld: to see it triumph, ruling over the rest of the world. For our strength to unite us so that we might conquer those lesser nations across the sea and enjoy their bounties for ourselves, as the Ice Gods created us to do. But it seems I misjudged my countrymen. And as I punish my brother when he fails me, so must I punish the lords who hold Iseneld back. You weaken our people, and that is a thing no jarl should abide."

The lord who had bowed to Draki shuffled backward, as if he could escape. Draki struck, quick as a viper, his hand lashing out, curling around the lord's throat. "Weak men deserve a coward's death."

Draki launched the lord into the air, off the ledge. The man shrieked as he plummeted, and then the noise was cut off as the falls drank him down. It was replaced by the sound of swords and axes being drawn.

Draki walked between the men, amusement curling one side of his mouth. "Brother, clean up this mess."

The roar of the falls filled Reyker's ears.

He could refuse. But that was a path he'd stumbled down many times, one that ended with Draki killing these men anyway, only their deaths would be far worse. This was a punishment, a test, a game. If Reyker did as Draki asked, the warlord would take him back into his confidence. He could gain the information he needed to aid Solvei and the Mountain Renegades.

A choice that was not a choice.

Reyker's sword and axe came free. He stepped onto the cliff, his breath heavy in his lungs. The black river whispered, and he gave it control.

For Iseneld, he told himself.

His limbs flowed like liquid, sliding beneath the weapons that swung at him. His blades were silver ripples that danced across the air, meeting flesh, opening veins, until he was surrounded by crimson waterfalls instead of lords. Sigmundsson was the last man standing, and the river drained to a trickle as Reyker met the overlord's sword with his own. The man was a good fighter, but it was only a matter of moments before Reyker disarmed him.

"You're worse than the Dragon," Sigmundsson said. "His mother made him a demon, but you chose to be a demon's lapdog. There is a dark pit in the Mist with your name on it, boy."

Reyker's sword silenced the man.

He stood in the center of a ring of corpses, trying to catch his breath. As soon as the fog of battle lifted from his mind, his stomach recoiled, spilling bile onto his tongue. He could feel the lords' blood drying on his skin, stiffening his clothes.

Draki watched him, looking bored. "You may return to Dragon's Lair after you bring me the head of Solvei Snorrisdottir."

All this carnage, and Draki still would not give him what he needed. "I'll leave for Fjullthorp as soon as the bodies have burned."

"These are traitors, brother. Enemies." Draki kicked Sigmundsson, whose lifeless complexion was as white as the moon. "You know what must be done."

The warlord held out a knife.

Reyker shut his eyes. Images of the fortress in Dragon's Lair floated across the backs of his lids, a nightmare made of rocks and bones. He took the knife and knelt beside the first body, fighting the shake of his hands as he began to slice away the skin.

CHAPTER 34

LIRA

The days began to blur together, one lesson after another. Sometimes it was weapons and combat training in the Blood Ring with Draki. Other times, I was in the temple with Hilde, who taught me more about Iseneld—its people, its legends, its gods. With respect and humility, I prayed to those who'd granted me permission to use my gifts, and little by little, my abilities strengthened.

"If you forget who this island belongs to, you will lose the Ice Gods' favor," Draki cautioned. "Your gifts will run dry."

"And you still garner their favor?"

We stood in the stern of one of the warlord's many longships, cutting through the waves as I reached out with my senses to find Seffra's current and harnessed Velder's wind to billow the sail.

"I am Ildja's son. That is all the favor I need."

Over the past weeks, Draki had taken me to another nearby farming village, so I could push my hands into the soil and speed the growth of their crops. He'd tasked me with transforming jars of salt water into fresh water. In the fortress infirmary, I'd helped heal small ailments—a Dragon-man's sprained ankle, a cook suffering from gout.

Modest powers, useless to me as a captive. Though Hilde and I had lessons every day, he would not let her teach me the rituals for the last of my untapped powers—gifts of metal and war—knowing what I might do with them.

"Tonight," Draki said, "I'm meeting with emissaries from my holdings outside of Iseneld, including the Green Isle. You may accompany me, if you like."

He held the favor out to me, but I couldn't snatch it up without knowing the cost. "Why?"

"Call it a reward for your hard work."

Draki was planning something, that much I could tell. He wouldn't let me in on his schemes, and I wasn't willing to turn down his offer out of spite. "I'll go."

Taking hold of wind and current, I angled the ship parallel to shore. After so many hours of practice, it was almost effortless—I envisioned what I wanted the vessel to do and wrapped a cirrus of power around whatever force was needed to make it happen, pulling them to me like reeling in a fish. I wondered if I could pitch the ship hard enough to throw Draki overboard and command the tides to ferry me away from here.

Draki was watching me as he often did, like he knew what I was thinking. I'd watched him, too, these last weeks, as we'd trained during the day, and on the evenings when the inhabitants of Dragon's Lair gathered in the feasting hall to listen to one of the storytellers or musicians display their talents. He was constantly surrounded by servants who worshipped him, warriors willing to die for him, but they were merely decorations in the background of his existence. They served their purpose, nothing more. When he didn't force me to dine with him, he took his meals alone. When he didn't make me accompany him on his rides through the countryside, he traveled alone. He had no companions. Draki wasn't a mortal or a god—he was both, the only one of his kind, fitting in with neither.

Beneath his callous visage, Draki seemed almost . . . lonely. The word was too sympathetic, too human, but there was no other description for it. He was as isolated as the island he called home.

There had to be a way I could use this against him.

"I want to speak with the priestess this afternoon," I said. "Privately."

Every time I met with Hilde, the Dragonman accompanying me stood inside the door, listening to our conversation. She was teaching me to read Iseneldish, and we'd talked lightly of our lives and pasts, but we guarded every word knowing anything we said could be reported to Draki. Why was I free to roam the library, the parlor, and the stables without a Dragonman hovering nearby, but not the sanctuary?

"For what purpose?"

I used Hilde's words. "Holy guidance."

Draki laughed. "I'm not a fool, Lira. Neither are you. Visit the temple alone if you wish but remember that your choices have consequences. Hilde is replaceable."

"You would execute a priestess?" I shouldn't have been surprised.

"I will dole out a fitting punishment to anyone who betrays my trust, be they kin, comrade, or priest." The longship went suddenly, completely still. Though the wind blew and the waves lapped, the boat did not move, and I knew it was the Dragon's doing.

Draki looked at me. Without arrogance. Without his usual pomp and flair.

This was his true power—he was inhumanely strong, impervious to weapons, he could move so fast he was rendered invisible, he could speak into people's minds and enter their dreams. But all of it came from this gift, this inability to be affected by forces or boundaries, unyielding to entities of nature or men. Draki was immovable. Unconquerable.

"Future consorts are not immune to my wrath either."

The threat came softly. In all this time, Draki hadn't touched me except when we sparred in the Blood Ring, and though his gaze and his hands often held desire when he trained me, he'd made it clear there was a line he would not cross. He didn't want to force me—like a wild horse, he wanted to break me, and so he waited, testing me, teasing me, holding back, certain I would submit eventually.

His restraint might dissolve, if I pushed him too far. *A fitting punishment.*

Draki released his hold on the longship. He nodded at the pier, a silent command to head back.

I didn't hesitate, turning us directly toward the shore.

———◆———

Draki sent an elegant dress to my room that evening, and servants to help me into it. The women brushed my hair and fastened the buttons and ties along the back of the gown. Once I was ready, guards escorted me to the feasting hall, where Draki and two men sat at the largest of the tables. These men weren't native to the Rocky Isles or Glasnith—they were just better-dressed Dragonmen, the ones Draki had left in charge of the countries he'd conquered while he played emperor in his homeland.

The warlord didn't stand when I entered, though the emissaries did. Draki inclined his head toward me. "Jarl Lira, formerly a lady of Glasnith, and my honored guest," he said.

The title startled me. He'd named me a jarl, but I had no lands, no coin, no power. The emissaries bowed awkwardly before taking their seats once more.

Servants brought out tray after tray, piled with a variety of meats and cheese, breads and pastries. They refilled the men's tankards, and brought me a fresh chalice of wine even though I hadn't touched the one already sitting in front of me.

Draki interacted with his emissaries as he did with everyone, keeping his distance, revealing nothing of himself beyond the almighty sovereign. They ate and drank, studying the cloth maps unrolled across the table, brushing away crumbs that fell on the painted lands and seas, staining the borders with ale sloshing from their mugs. It was far less dignified than any council Torin ever held.

The warlord noticed my curled lip and laughed. "The Green Isle raises its children to be quite uptight. But when the world belongs to you, formalities can be tossed aside."

"What of the laws?" I looked to Glasnith's emissary. "Are those thrown out as well in the countries you govern?"

The Dragonman shifted nervously. This was a test for him as much as it was for me, a delicate balance of showing respect for Draki's guest without seeming cowed by a foreign girl's questioning. "The Dragon's Law rules all of Iseneld's holdings, my lady," he said through a tight smile. "The strongest command the weak. Those chosen by the gods decide the fate of each country's citizens."

These Dragonmen were different from the others I'd met. There was shrewdness beneath their brawn. To finish the wars Draki started and make his conquests profitable, their minds had to be as sharp as their axes.

"Who is the strongest in Glasnith?" I asked.

"In the absence of the Dragon, it would be myself or one of his other trusted commanders. But if you mean among the natives, there have been ongoing battles between the armies of two men from the same family. One calls himself a king, the other a prince."

Madoc. Garreth.

"Will Iseneld support one of these men to rule alongside the Dragon's commanders?" My gaze lit upon Draki.

"That is what we are here to discuss," he replied.

The emissary pointed at villages on the map of Glasnith, detailing the bloody conflicts between the clans who'd thrown their support behind King Madoc and those who fought with the Prince of Ghosts. Madoc's men had better training and weaponry, but Garreth had the numbers, enough green soldiers to swamp the seasoned warriors on the battlefield.

"What are your thoughts on the matter, Jarl Lira?" Draki asked.

It was a taunt, but he was also curious. I squared my shoulders and tried to sound more confident than I felt. "You made an alliance with Madoc, but he's meddled in your dealings with the mercenary clans. He abandoned your army on the eve of the battle for Dragon Bay. He's done nothing but look out for his own self-interest and it's unwise to maintain agreements with one so untrustworthy. Besides, the nomad prince has proven himself to be the stronger adversary, so according to the Dragon's Law, he's the one you should ally with."

The emissaries glanced from me to Draki, who nodded. "I will take this into consideration. Let us convene again tomorrow night."

At this dismissal, the two Dragonmen took their leave. Alone with Draki, the air thickened. He leaned forward, his arms folded into an X across the map of my homeland. "Your assessments are biased, but they are not unsound."

"The people of Iseneld see the people of Glasnith as dogs to be kicked and conquered. Your alliance with Madoc was clearly a short-term charade. Would you really ally with my brother and let him rule?"

"The people of Iseneld believe whatever I tell them. If I say Garreth of Stone is a bastard with the blood of an Iseneldish father in his veins, I can make him a true king."

"And slander my mother."

"Your mother is dead. Your brother is not. Do you think she would do everything in her power to protect her son, whether it be spread her legs or spread a lie that she had?"

My jaw dropped, indignant on both fronts. "Of course she would."

"Would you?"

My mouth snapped shut on bared teeth.

"For your brother?" His serpent eyes scraped past my expression, digging through flesh and bone to reach my shameful thoughts. "No. Not for him. But there was another, once."

"Enough." The chair clattered as I stood and spun away from the table, hiding my face.

I didn't hear him move, but Draki was suddenly right behind me, his breath grazing my ear. "I can save Glasnith or set it aflame and sink it into the sea. I can make your brother a king and you a jarl, consort to an emperor. Or I can add Garreth's bones to my collection and dump you back in the Mountain of Fire for my mother to feast on."

The room twirled around me, the two paths playing out in my head— lose everything but my pride or give up my soul and gain the world.

I couldn't say yes. I couldn't say no.

The warlord took my arm and led me back to my room, opening the door. There were gifts from Glasnith scattered across my bed, and he watched me sort through stacks of books in my own language, tins of shortbread biscuits, sticky balls of incense that smelled of clover. And a note from my brother.

It shook in my hands as I read.

Dear Lira,

Iseneld's emissary informs me you made it safely to the Frozen Sun and are under the protection of the Dragon. I do hope they are treating you well, as they claim. I've been promised that if circumstances become more favorable, I will be allowed to visit and confirm your safety myself. Until then, know that part of my heart is there with you.

Always,

Garreth

It was short, terse. I could imagine his anger as the emissary pretended I was a guest and not a hostage, his shame that he could not help me, that as long as I was under the Dragon's roof I was out of my brother's reach.

Garreth would put Glasnith first. He would not surrender, even if Draki threatened to kill me. But if Draki offered an alliance along with my life, if it was the only option other than a full-scale war that would ravage our country and result in countless deaths . . . that might force him into a truce.

I didn't want a truce. I would accept nothing less than Draki's defeat and Glasnith's unconditional freedom.

"These tokens were brought for you at my request," Draki said from the doorway. "Is there anything you would like my emissaries to bring from your island on their next visit?"

"My uncle's head."

His mouth twitched in amusement. "That is another boon you must earn. My patience and hospitality are not boundless. By the turn of the moon, you will make your choice."

"Why me?" I called after him as he started to go. "Is it only for my gifts?"

Draki paused, inhaling deeply. "Something in you appeals to the remaining shred of my gentler nature."

"You don't have a gentler nature."

He stared at me. There it was again—that loneliness, a hole inside him I could almost see. And something else, something between longing and desire. A presumption that I could fill what was missing. "If I didn't, you would have been dead long ago. Happy birthday, little warrior."

Then he was gone, the door shutting me in.

Birthday? I counted the days in my head.

Yes, I'd turned eighteen today. I'd forgotten, losing track of how long I'd been in Iseneld, yet somehow Draki had known. This was meant to be the day I chose whether to marry on behalf of my clan or pledge myself to Aillira's Temple, but that was a lifetime ago, before the temple fell and my clan was massacred. Even if those options had still been available to me, there was no one left to hear my choice.

There was no one here to care.

My need for holy guidance was no longer a ruse.

The next day I went to the bone temple, and the Dragonman guarding me stopped at the entrance, letting me go in alone. There was no sign of Hilde, so I circled the sanctuary, careful not to brush against the skeletons. At the back of the room was a harp I'd never seen before, as tall as I was, its frame constructed of wood and bone. Were the strings made from sheep gut, or were they human too? I risked dragging my fingers across them, throwing a string of buoyant notes through the still air.

"Greetings, magiska." Hilde emerged from a curtained alcove behind the altar, glancing around. "You have misplaced your guard it seems."

"For the time being," I said, letting her know it was safe to speak freely. "Where did the harp come from?"

"A gift from the warlord, for helping you." There was something tight in her voice, a meaning I didn't grasp yet.

"Do you play, priestess?"

She held up her mangled hands, and I blanched at my thoughtlessness. Before I could apologize, she said, "I did play, ages ago, it seems. I was studying to be a priestess, but the elder women declared that I was blessed by Frigmer, the goddess of music and poetry, and they advised me to devote myself to this gift. That's why I moved from the Streamlands to Dragon's Lair, for the honor of entertaining the warlord and his guests. I was young and poor, and it made my parents proud that I served the most powerful man in Iseneld."

"What happened?"

"It was Season's Eve, the night we celebrate the transition between the Sun Season and the Ice Season. After the gala, a Dragonman who'd had more than his share of mead decided he wanted a private performance."

My stomach knotted.

"The refusal I gave was . . . harsh. Mocking. He attacked me, seeking to wound my pride as I'd wounded his." Absently, she touched her thumbs to the long scars trailing down her cheeks. "The Dragonman might have killed me, had it not been for the warlord's brother. He heard me scream. When he found us, he pulled the Dragonman off me. The man was dead before he hit the ground."

Brother. Jarl Solvei had mentioned him as well, when I was a prisoner on her ship. "I assumed Draki's brother would be just like the warlord."

"His half brother wasn't kin to Ildja. They shared a mortal father. And though the brother was no innocent, he was very different from the warlord. Draki meant to throw me out after I could no longer play my harp. I was worthless to him, my gift insignificant enough that I wasn't even worth feeding to his mother. But I had nowhere else to go. The fortress had become my home. It was Draki's brother who found a place for me, suggesting I resume my studies of the gods, apprenticing with the elderly temple priestess. At his request, she took me in and trained me."

"You never say his name."

Her eyes misted. "I received word that he fell during the conquest of Glasnith. It is unwise to speak the names of the dead in a sacred place. I do not wish to disturb him in the afterworlds."

I couldn't mourn a man, honorable or no, who'd helped his vile brother steal my country, but I could sympathize with Hilde and what he'd meant to her. Should I tell her that Solvei claimed Draki's brother was alive and the Mountain Renegades had captured him? Or was it crueler to offer what might be false hope?

I glared at the harp. "So Draki's gift is actually a taunt."

"Or a threat."

Everything Draki did was one or the other. "The warlord made me an offer," I whispered.

Hilde listened as I explained what Draki wanted, all the things I stood to gain and lose. When I finished, she asked carefully, "What are you going to do?"

"I can't let Draki use me. As long as I'm a hostage, so is Garreth. So is all of Glasnith, no matter what Draki promises." I'd gone in circles about this, always coming back to my original plan. "I'm going to run. I'll go to the harbor, steal a boat, and sail home to my brother."

"The Dragon will catch you. You cannot outrun him."

"Not without a stronger gift." I went to the holy book sitting on the altar, flipping through pages of words I could only partially understand, luminous illustrations of gods and goddesses whose names I'd yet to learn. "You told me I have the gift of metallurgy in my blood. Which of the Ice Gods controls it?"

"All-God Sjaf is the god of steel, silver, and iron. You would need to offer him a weapon of great power in exchange for his favor."

"I thought Sjaf was god of the sea."

"He is. He's also the god of war. Your Green Gods are quite lazy, only ruling over a single aspect of life. The most powerful Ice Gods are masters of many things."

Sjaf. Strongest of all the gods, alongside Ildja. Could I carry out a ritual that would make him pay attention without Draki finding out?

The book fell open to two nearly identical pages. Painted on the first was a goddess with hair like dripping fire and eyes as black as obsidian. A serpent was coiled around her neck and smoke swirled behind her. In her hand, she clutched a thrashing shadow, edging it toward her open mouth. Ildja. Eater of souls.

On the opposite page was another goddess, sitting in a green meadow dotted with wildflowers. Her hair and skin were a shifting rainbow of colors, her eyes as soft as Ildja's were hard. In her cupped hands, she held more shadows—souls—but these appeared content. I read the name written beneath her: Eyvor. Ildja's sister.

"What was Eyvor's power before Ildja turned her into the island-serpent?" I asked.

"Before she was cursed, Eyvor was the soul-keeper. As Ildja rules the

Mist and lords over the Destroyers, Eyvor ruled Skjorlog Felth and the veil-dwellers. Eyvor laid bare the deeds of each soul, guiding those who were worthy to the great meadow."

It was so like my own gift. Eyvor was Gwylor's sister, too, so she had a connection to Glasnith—the ability of some Daughters of Aillira to read souls might have come from her, and perhaps that was why she helped me. "Who watches after Fortune's Field if she's gone? Who guides those souls?"

Hilde shrugged. "The few veil-dwellers that are left."

The goddess of souls was gone, but that didn't mean I couldn't ask her for permission to use my gifts. She'd granted me a favor once before. I could convince her to do it again.

My fingers traced the gold outlines haloing the soul-eater and the soul-keeper. "What did Eyvor do that made her sister so angry? Why did Ildja curse her?"

"For being herself. Ildja was stronger, both feared and respected, but Eyvor was beloved. One sister damned souls and the other offered them salvation. Ildja could not stand that her weaker sibling was so adored." Hilde glanced at the nubs of her fingers. "That's how it was between Draki and his brother. Everyone fears the warlord's strength, but some of us who follow him believed his brother would make a better ruler for Iseneld. His strength was tempered with reason and mercy. Draki saw his brother's mercy as weakness and punished him for it. I waited for him to rise up against it. One day, he would have. But with him gone, there is no one powerful enough to stand against the Dragon."

"What if he isn't gone?" The question slipped out before I could stop myself.

Hope kindled in Hilde's face, and she lit up like the paintings of the goddesses. "There are those who did not believe the news of his death. There was no body, no witness to his end. If the Sword of the Dragon returned, perhaps he could change things."

It took a moment for me to understand what I'd heard, and another for my mind to unravel its meaning. The floor tilted beneath me, and I stumbled into the bone altar, knocking books and candles over.

Hilde rushed to help me. "Are you all right?"

I gripped her arms, needing to hold on to something. "What did you call the warlord's brother?"

As she spoke, each word slammed into me like a blow, driving me toward the ground. Like thunder, warning of a coming storm. Like fate, swallowing the stars and spitting them back out again, rattling a world that had tried to be its own master.

"That's what Draki called his brother. His Sword. The Sword of the Dragon."

CHAPTER 35

LIRA

Eyvor, I prayed, *goddess of Fortune's Field, keeper of souls. Hear me, please.*

There was a rumbling from beneath the waves.

The water lapping around my boat was red. My hands and clothes were coated in blood—some mine, some from the animals I'd called: a blue ice skink that slipped from a hole in the frosted cliffside, a shark with a beaked nose and teeth like fishhooks that leaped into the bow. There were three longships behind me full of Dragonmen who'd abandoned their posts to chase me as I'd stormed through the tunnels leading to the sea and seized the smallest boat I could find. I'd only had to hurt two Dragonmen, using a gust of wind to slam the one guarding me outside the temple into a wall, stabbing the axe Hilde had given me into the foot of the one stationed at the tunnel entrance.

With wind and water and earth dancing at my fingertips, I'd kept the Dragonmen at bay, letting them follow at a distance. Now I rocked the three longships, whipped the Dragonmen's hair so it lashed their cheeks, drenched their boots under sea and foam I sent splashing into the hulls.

Draki's men wouldn't touch me. They were only here to keep track of me until the Dragon arrived. But this wasn't about escape. Hilde had been right—if I ran on my own, Draki would hunt me down. I needed help. So I'd come to make offerings to the gods, to gain a few new gifts.

And to cause a distraction.

Before me, the island-serpent rose from the water. Her blue eye locked on me. I'd cut the symbol for sacrifice into my palm, and I pressed my hand against her scales.

I pledge myself to you. Allow me to use the gift I was born with, to see what mortals seek to hide, to be a mistress of souls in this realm as you once were in the otherworlds.

Eyvor hissed, spraying water from her nostrils.

Deep within me came an answering susurrus, the click of a lock breaking. Vibrations traveled up my arm, into my body, followed by a rush of power unlike anything I'd experienced with other Ice Gods—a portion of what had lingered, trapped inside Eyvor all this time, as much as she could spare without leaving herself vulnerable. As much as I could handle without sinking into madness.

With my gift restored, I saw into Eyvor's soul. The bright fields of her home realm, the souls she'd tended.

"Thank you, Eyvor," I whispered. "If I can, I will find a way to free you."

She hissed again, sliding back below the water.

"Little warrior." I turned to see Draki standing in the bow of a longship. He was the only one in the ship, and the Dragonmen were all heading back to shore. "If you had asked, I would have taken you sailing. What are you doing out here without me?"

I lifted my bloodstained hands. "What does it look like?"

Draki's lips twitched. He jumped from his longship into my boat, rocking it hard enough to make me stumble, though he remained steady, his balance undisturbed. "So you have regained your soul-reading gift."

In response, I stepped toward him and slammed my bloody palm to his chest.

The last time I tried to read Draki's soul was moments after he'd killed Rhys. The space inside him had felt hollow, and I'd have sworn the warlord had been born soulless. But now, with my wits about me and my power stronger than ever, I realized I'd been wrong. The pit inside him was slick with residue, traces of the soul that had once been here, the one he'd traded to Ildja for immortality. There were only scraps, the images void of context, but I found what I was looking for. A woman, a man, a village.

A gold-haired boy with ocean eyes.

The emotions wrapped around the images of Reyker were a tangled mess of rage, envy, disappointment. Pride. An inexplicable fondness that shocked me into letting go.

"You are his brother." And his jailor. His torturer. I'd believed Hilde, but it was different seeing it for myself. "Is he alive?"

Draki's eyes churned with things I lacked the language to read.

"Is he alive?" I screamed it, shoving at him, but the warlord was unmoved. I punched Draki, and it was like hitting a boulder, but I beat my fists against his body and howled the question over and over. "Is he alive? *Is he alive?*"

My gifts slipped their reins and the air became a vortex pivoting around us, the boat jouncing so that I had to hold on to Draki to keep from tumbling out. Draki stood as still as one of the stone pillars jutting from the sea, saying nothing, his unblinking gaze fixed on me.

"Where is my medallion?" I tore at his tunic, but there was no necklace. "Where did you find me at the Mountain of Fire? In the crater? Or when I was drowning in the glacier?"

The Dragon said nothing.

I'd known something was wrong in the ice cave the moment I'd kissed Draki. But the kiss in the crater—it was real. It was Reyker.

We'd found each other. And lost each other again.

"Where is he?" My voice had frayed to a strangled whisper. "I want to see him."

The storm circling us died, and I wasn't certain if I'd let it go or if Draki had smothered it. Finally, Draki spoke, gripping my flailing wrists. "Give me what I want, and you will get what you want."

Be Draki's consort, knowing Reyker was alive?

I spit in his face.

He smiled, my saliva dripping down his perfect nose and cheekbone. "Your outburst caused quite a scene. Consequences must be dealt out. The guards you slipped past will be executed for their mistakes, and dear Hilde will have to be punished as well, since she must have helped you. Shall I whip her with a branch from a thorntree? I had the Green Isle emissary bring me one of those too."

It was my turn to smile. "Good luck finding her."

Draki pulled me onto his longship and tied my boat to it, steering us back to shore. Dragonmen met us on the beach. "The priestess is missing, Emperor," one of them said. "We're searching, but no one has seen her since the magiska ran from the temple."

Draki turned to me, eyes narrowed.

I waited for my punishment, for him to strike me, or order me to be whipped as my father had, but he only shook his head before vanishing into the tunnel. Still I heard him speak, as if he was standing right next to me. "You will be the death of him, Lira. You will damn yourself and drag him down with you."

CHAPTER 36

REYKER

"You look like shit, Lagorsson."

Reyker rubbed at the ache between his eyes. "Good to see you, too, Brokk."

The big man clapped him on the back hard enough to jar his bones. "I mean it. I've seen you look like all sorts of horses' asses, but this is by far the ugliest. What's wrong with you?"

"Nothing."

When he'd first left for Dragon's Lair, Reyker had slept restlessly. His dreams were empty without Lira, but he would not go to her—whatever her reasons, she had asked him to stay away. He worried that something had happened to her spirit at the glacier after he'd left her. He feared that he would never see her again.

Since the slaughter at Hidden Falls, he had barely slept at all. Every time he tried, the fleshless corpse of Jarl Sigmundsson was there, jawbone wagging, reminding Reyker that his soul was damned to the Mist. The nightmare tossed him back into wakefulness quicker than being doused with a bucket of fjord water. To ward off facing what he'd done, he had hidden in Vaknavangur for the past weeks, helping Hamund and the others with the rebuilding, wearing himself ragged until he finally felt steady enough to make the journey to Fjullthorp. To tell Solvei that the only way the Mountain Renegades would get the information they needed to stop Draki was for her to give up her head.

"I need to speak with the jarl," he told Brokk.

"She went to meet someone at the mead house, though I bet she'd want you there. Another Dragonman contacted her, willing to turn traitor."

"Who?" A trap—that was his first thought. No one considered betraying Draki and lived long enough to tell anyone about it. No one but him.

"Let's go find out."

Brokk headed to fetch a horse from the stables, and Reyker was about to mount Vengeance when a voice stopped him.

"Reyker!" It was Alane, the tract-seeker. She ran to him, as if she might throw her arms around him, but stopped herself at the last moment. "I was afraid you wouldn't come back."

"Are they treating you well, Alane?" She looked no worse than the last time he saw her. He glanced around for the sea-farer and the bone-healer. "And your sister magiskas?"

She spoke haltingly, a mix of graceless Iseneldish and Glasnithian. "Jarl Solvei treats us well enough. She made us pray to her gods and bleed a goat and—well, it was strange, but it allowed us to use our gifts here. She sends Bronagh out with her sailors and Keeva with her patrols. She makes me spy on the Dragon. And on you." The girl stared at her feet, chewing her lip. "I saw what you did to those men at the waterfall, but I told her the warlord did it."

"Alane . . ." He felt like he might be sick. "Gods aflame, I'm sorry you had to witness that."

"I know it wasn't your fault. He made you do it. Right?"

There it was—a flash of doubt, of fear. It was justified, yet it still wounded him. "I was forced," Reyker agreed, not sure if the lie was more to comfort her or himself.

Most of her distrust ebbed. There was a rosy warmth to her demeanor he'd not seen before. Though he barely knew her, she seemed a much different girl than the one he'd fought beside in Dragon Bay. But then, the man he was off the battlefield was nothing like the monster he was on it.

"Are you staying in Fjullthorp?" Alane asked. "Have you come back for good?"

"I can't." He cringed as her face fell. "I'm only here to speak with Solvei, and then I must leave again. I promise as soon as I'm able, I will take the three of you back to Glasnith."

"Take Keeva and Bronagh. There is nothing left for me in Glasnith." She brushed her fingertips along the cuff of his coat, tugging a loose thread from his sleeve. "I would rather stay here."

"Here? You want to join the Renegades? But—"

Brokk cleared his throat loudly behind them, where he waited atop his horse.

"I'm sorry, Alane. I have to go. We'll talk again soon." He gave her an awkward pat on her shoulder and mounted Vengeance.

Alane watched them go.

Once they were out of sight of the camp, Brokk raised his barrel-deep voice, singing as they rode. "*Oh, I had a pretty girl, but she spent up all my gold. I had a pretty girl, but she only brought me strife. I had a pretty girl, but she left me for a blacksmith. So I gave up on pretty girls, and now I have a wife.*" On the last word, he gave Reyker a pointed look.

"Something you want to say to me, Brokk?"

"You are a lodestone for god-gifted Green Isle girls."

"Alane is lonely and heartsick over what was done to her country. If she sees anything in me, it's because I'm the only man here who speaks her language and understands her homeland."

"If you wait to escort that magiska home yourself," Brokk said, "she'll become another casualty in the war between you and your brother. If you care about her and the other two, send them away now. You can always go back to Glasnith and fetch her later."

"Why would I do that?"

"Because she's young and fair and she looks at you like she cannot wait to tumble into your bed."

Reyker flushed. "There is more to love than that."

"Who said anything about love?" Brokk shrugged, whistling another bar of the cheery, obnoxious tune.

They reached the mead house, a communal feasting hall and inn of the Fjordlands, where a certain class of people from the surrounding mountain and fjord villages gathered whenever they could to drink and gamble, eat and fight, find a mate for a night or two—be they patrons or prostitutes. Reyker was no stranger to such establishments, having visited them with fellow Dragonmen; an attempt to escape his misery by diving into the brief pleasures they offered, though no amount of wine or women ever healed the fractures within him.

Music and laughter poured out as soon as they opened the door, and it reeked of sweat and smoke and liquor. They had to navigate through crowds of carousers, but people dancing and talking parted like a wave for Brokk, tossing him nods of recognition or smiles of appreciation. Reyker garnered a few smiles from the women, but just as many glares. Even on the other side of Iseneld, far from Dragon's Lair, people he had never met saw his infamous warrior-mark and knew exactly who he was.

Solvei sat at a table in the far corner of the mead house, across from a man with lanky yellow hair. Reyker couldn't see his face yet, but as they got closer, something else caught his attention. On the table between Solvei and the man was a knife.

There was nothing special about it—a beveled blade of steel and iron, a wooden handle wrapped in leather. Except he knew this knife. He had held it several times, once to his own throat. She had held it to his throat once too. And she had used it to slice her wrist, to bleed for her gods so they would purge his body of venom.

This knife had saved him. And now, for some reason, it was here in Iseneld, lying on a sticky table in a mead house, covered in smudges from a Dragonman's fingers.

Reyker didn't feel the black river sweep up. He was himself, and then he was that other man, drowning in rage. Reveling in it.

He blinked, and his hands were on the Dragonman, pinning him against the wall. It was a face Reyker had seen before, but it swam before him now, and he could not place it. "Little lordling," the Dragonman singsonged. "You survived after all."

Reyker hardly recognized his own voice. "Where did you get that knife?"

"From a sweet young witch on the Green Isle. I believe you might know her."

The Dragonman's grin turned bloody under Reyker's fist. Far away, people shouted at him, just noise buried by the pound of his pulse in his ears. A meaty hand tried to pull him back, but he threw out an elbow and followed it with a kick, and the hand was gone. He roared at the Dragonman, words rushing out of him without pause, without thought. *"You're-lying-where-was-she-did-you-touch-her-I-will-kill-you!"*

The knife was in his hand, though he didn't remember reaching for it. He pressed it to the Dragonman's neck.

More hands grabbed at him. He was about to turn and stab them, but a chair crashed down on his head. Before he could recover, something hit his legs, sweeping them out from under him, and he was on the floor, the breath crushed from his lungs as an anvil dropped on his chest. The knife vanished.

He didn't know how long he lay there, struggling and growling like an animal, before the fog cleared from his mind. Solvei held one of his wrists to the floor, a stranger restraining the other. Brokk was sitting on top of him, blood dripping from the giant warrior's nose. The music had stopped, replaced by mutters from the crowd pushing in around them.

"It's over," Reyker said. "I'm all right now."

"I don't give a damn how you are." Solvei's hand squeezed tighter on his wrist. "You almost killed us."

"I'm sorry. I lost myself."

"You'll lose your head to my sword next time." Brokk's body was tense, like he was waiting for Reyker to turn rabid again. "So make sure there isn't a next time."

They let him up slowly, everyone watching him. All he wanted was to be alone, to calm down and pull himself together without fifty sets of eyes on him. Brokk gripped his shoulder, steering him to the door. Outside, Brokk's fingers dug in deeper.

There was the Dragonman he had beaten.

"Don't make me hurt you, Lagorsson," Brokk said.

"I'm fine." He took a step toward the Dragonman. "But stay close, just in case."

The Dragonman held a cloth against his swollen face. "Keep that mad dog away from me."

Reyker left a few paces between them. He curled his fingers, the ache of his knuckles keeping him grounded. "I just want to ask you some questions, Andrithur." That was the Dragonman's name. He'd been a guard in Dragon's Lair, fought beside Reyker in the Rocky Isles.

"I have a question for you." Andrithur spit out a tooth. "If you love your witch so much, why did you leave her? Why did you let her think you were dead?"

"I didn't—" He swallowed the anger with deep breaths. "When did you see her? Where?"

Andrithur told his story, and Reyker remained silent and still despite the squall building inside him.

Alive.

Somehow Lira had survived jumping from the bluffs, falling into the sea. She had made it to her brother in the Green Desert. But where had she gone from there?

If she was not dead, then she could not be a spirit. Which meant when he saw her on the glacier . . .

Reyker was already running to Vengeance, his legs moving before his mind finished sorting through the memory. Lira had been there with him, in the Mountain of Fire, and he had left her in Ildja's jaws.

"Wait," Brokk called, chasing after him. "Think this through. You can't go up there alone, without supplies. I'll come with you, just give me an hour—"

"I've already lost too many gods-damned hours!" His foot was in the stirrup, reins threaded through his fingers. Ignoring Brokk's protests, he was about to tell Vengeance to go.

"Lagorsson!" Solvei came up behind them. "Someone has been hanging about since yesterday, asking after anyone who knows you. He told the innkeeper it's about a woman."

The fight went out of Reyker all at once.

A boy he'd never seen was waiting beside Andrithur, bouncing on his heels. "You are the Sword of the Dragon?" the boy whispered as Reyker took him aside.

"I am."

"Then you must go quickly to the Temple of the Mountain. She doesn't have much time."

The boy would say no more. He ran off, and Reyker agonized over his options, but he'd already left Lira twice—on Glasnith and at the glacier—out of ignorance. He would not risk doing it again, even if it cost him time. Reyker bid Brokk and the others to wait, and rode to the temple.

Another hour, gone.

The Temple of the Mountain was the largest of many sanctuaries dotting the foothills of the Fjordlands. Light leaked out between the slits in its wooden walls, and he knocked on the door, not knowing what to expect.

An aged priestess answered, wrinkled and hunched, scowling at him. "Took you long enough. She has held on longer than she should." The priestess waved him into the candlelit room. There was a bed inside, and several priestesses hovered around the prone figure in it.

Not Lira.

Disappointment was a thundercloud roiling under his ribs, but once he got past the hair that was blond instead of violet, the eyes that were blue instead of green, he registered who he was looking at. "Hilde?"

The other priestesses moved aside, and Reyker went to her, kneeling beside the bed, folding her damaged hands inside his own. Hilde smiled at him, tears spilling into the scars cutting down her cheeks. "You *are* alive," she said.

She was too pale, her skin too hot against his. Feverish. There was a pile of bloody bandages by the bed. "What happened, Hilde?" The fresh bandage wrapped around her middle was seeping red.

"A Dragonman's arrow."

"You need help. Healers." He looked to the other priestesses. "Why have you not sent for one?"

"I am a healer, boy," the old woman who'd let him in said. "The infection has spread. There is nothing more to be done. The veil-dwellers await her."

"No—"

"All I needed was to see you one last time," Hilde said, "to know the man who will save Iseneld still lives. When I told you what I read in the runes, you did not believe. But you do now. Your faith glows beneath your skin where darkness used to dwell. Your magiska's doing, is it not?"

Reyker shook his head, thinking he'd misheard her.

Hilde glanced at the old priestess and the woman took a slip of parchment from beneath her robes, pressing it into Reyker's palm. When he looked back at Hilde, her eyes had closed. "I will be watching from the afterworlds with your family," she murmured. "Make us proud, Reyker Lagorsson."

"Hilde." He touched her scarred cheek. The heat was already leaving it. "Hilde?"

"Let her go," the old priestess said, pushing Reyker from the bedside.

He watched helplessly as the priestesses held hands and sang hymns to send Hilde on her way, and to welcome the veil-dwellers who would lead her to Skjorlog Felth. All the people he had lost over the years, and it never got easier.

Reyker clenched his fists. The parchment crinkled in his hand.

He unfolded it. Read it. Stared.

It was Hilde's handwriting, but it was written in code, and there was only one person it could have come from.

A brave deer is trapped, dreaming of thorntrees. When the midnight moon is full, she will spring from her cage, hoping a kind-hearted wolf awaits her on the other side.

CHAPTER 37

LIRA

The garden must have been lovely once, a private world where a woman dug her hands into the soil to be one with the earth, but the flowers and herbs had withered long ago, and weeds grew with reckless abandon, held at bay only by the stone walls encompassing them.

No one had tended it since Reyker's mother died.

This was where Draki brought me after the execution. In front of the fortress, with everyone in Dragon's Lair bearing witness, he had taken the heads of the two guards I'd fought my way past to slip into the tunnels. The Dragonmen had not begged for their lives, they had simply kneeled and accepted their fate, and the Dragon's sword had been swift, almost merciful.

Because their deaths were not truly about punishing their mistakes, but mine.

"Katrin came here often for solace," Draki said now. He stood behind me, looking over the tangles of vines and moss. "It is yours, if you want it. Jardun's gifts will serve you well here. Perhaps it will bring you solace too."

Since Hilde's escape, Draki had not trusted me to be alone with his guards. The door to my room was kept locked, and the only time I could leave was if the warlord escorted me. He told me Hilde was dead, felled by an arrow, but I knew better. If the priestess had been caught, Draki would have brought her body here and dropped it in front of me. He might have made me watch as he took her bones and fixed them to the fortress walls.

"You're giving me a garden." A laugh bubbled in my chest. "The same garden you gave your mother before you killed her."

"She was not my mother."

"She was, once." I turned to face him. "She loved you like a son. And you loved her, as much as your tainted heart could. As you loved your father. And your brother."

Draki's jaw twitched, the only sign of his annoyance.

"That's what I found in your soul. Or what's left of it, since you threw it away for power, to win the favor of a goddess who abandoned you at birth."

Before I could move, Draki had pressed me to the stone wall with his body, his mouth too close to mine. "Hate me if you must, Lira. Curse my name. But do not speak ill of my mother." His thumb trailed up my neck, and I shivered. "I did not kill Katrin. Reyker killed her."

"You're lying."

He pressed the scar behind my ear. "Reyker cut my mark from her skin. But such a mark is forever. It was part of her. Without it, she withered like one of her flowers. So will you, if you try to leave me."

Instinctively, my eyes went to the horizon. Though night had not yet fallen, the full moon had begun its slow ascent—a phantom in a gauzy dress, a cold white eye that watched everything but never intervened. Nesper was the god of the moon on Glasnith, but here, it was the goddess Manott shining down upon us.

"I know your secrets, Draki. You torment Reyker because he's all that's left of your humanity. You hate that you care for him, so you punish him out of shame for your own weakness."

"I punish him to make him strong, to keep him fighting when he wants to give up and die. Just as I've done for you." He gathered my hair in his hand, draping it over my shoulder. "I made Reyker what he is. If you love him, as you claim, you should thank me."

I slapped his hand away. "You tried to poison the goodness inside him, but I brought it back to life."

"Then you will be responsible for his death." It was the smallest of gestures, just a brief furrow between his brows, but I saw it. Some part of Draki hated the thought of Reyker dying. That piece of Draki's missing soul that he was using me to fill—that he yearned for, though he'd never admit it—was because of Reyker. I wasn't the cure he wanted, I was a temporary fix.

Draki leaned in close, taking hold of my hair once more, twirling it around his fist. He brushed the strands beneath his nose, inhaling my scent. "I can take away your memories of him, if that makes it easier for you."

"Let go of me." He did as I asked, smiling like this was all some sort of harmless courtship ritual. "I could never forget Reyker. Never."

"There you go again, making bets you cannot pay. Your time is almost up, little warrior. Tomorrow you will give me your answer." He went to the door, beckoning me to follow.

As I stepped through the garden, I imagined Reyker's mother kneeling here, mourning her dead husband, her razed village, her lost freedom, watering the blooms with her tears just as Aillira had done with her thorntree.

In a far corner of the garden, I spied a patch of color. A single tiny flower with plum-colored petals, nearly hidden among the vines, had punched up through the weed-choked soil. It was a sign that the Dragon could not conquer everything.

I lay awake in bed, counting down the minutes.

Draki had brought me to Dragon's Lair just before the last turn of the moon. One of those first nights, I'd watched from the small window in my room as he mounted his stallion and rode off, an elderly male servant tied up and slung over the horse's haunches. When I'd asked Hilde about it, she told me Draki rode to the Mountain of Fire and made a sacrifice to his mother at midnight on the first night of every full moon.

Tonight, he tossed a trussed-up goat on the back of his horse—perhaps Ildja preferred variety, or perhaps Draki was short on disposable servants. The stallion broke into a gallop, and the warlord vanished into the winding aisles of the lava field. He would be gone for hours.

I would not be here when he returned.

Would I be leaving alone, or would Reyker be out there, waiting for me?

I hadn't dared let myself dream of Reyker—the Dragon had haunted Reyker's dreams since he was a boy, and haunted mine since he'd marked me. The risk that he might find us there in the ruins and unearth our intentions was too great.

Once enough time had passed for Draki to be well away, I shoved aside the tub in the corner of the room and pried up the floorboard beneath it, where I'd hidden a spoon brought by a servant with one of my meals. I wrapped my fingers around it, pressing it to the lock in my bedroom door, pouring every ounce of focus into reshaping it. And I prayed to Sjaf—the god of metal—as I had on the boat I'd stolen to reach the island-serpent.

Before leaving the temple and running to the tunnels, Hilde had given me the axe that had belonged to her ancestors, the earliest settlers of Iseneld. The first children of Sjaf. I'd used the axe to kill the shark I'd called, sliced the symbol of sacrifice into my palm with its blade, dripped my blood and the creature's into the sea and tossed the treasured weapon in, offering them all to the god.

Draki thought Eyvor's was the only gift I'd sought that day. He was wrong.

The spoon softened in my hand, its form shifting. It had taken a great deal of practice over the last week, trying and failing over and over, before I could finally bend the metal to my will. Reshaping it to fit the lock like a key, as I did now.

I turned the key slowly, cringing at the click that seemed as loud as a scream, as loud as the pound of my heart, certain to alert the guards, but when I eased open the door, the two men at the end of the hall still had their backs to me, chatting and laughing quietly. On silent feet, I inched toward them.

The key squeezed in my fist became a long, slender blade.

I pushed the knife through the back of one Dragonman's neck. He gurgled, blood dripping down his chest, and the second Dragonman's arm whipped out, striking the side of my face. He drew his sword as I hit the ground and looked up at him. I could already feel bruises budding along my jaw.

The Dragonman had acted on instinct, but now his eyes widened, realizing what he had done. My guards had permission to restrain me, nothing more. No one touched a woman Draki had put his mark on, not in anger or affection or lust. Anyone who did paid a painful price. And I wasn't just another one of Draki's toys, I was his chosen consort.

The Dragonman lowered his sword, backing away. I gathered a thread of the breeze whistling through a half-open window and flicked it in the man's direction, knocking him down.

For this last ritual to work, I couldn't use my gifts. Sjaf demanded the blood be shed by my own hands.

Tearing a femur from the wall of bones, I swung it into the Dragonman's temple and he slumped to the floor. I swung again, and this time there was a *crack* that turned my stomach.

I took a breath, staring at the bodies. Hesitating. Hilde, and even Draki, had warned me against this. Was I ready?

No. But Draki would come after me. I had to be stronger. I needed it.

On my knees, I mixed the blood trickling from my swollen lip with the blood from the two Dragonmen, drawing overlapping triangles on both men's chests. Pausing long enough to pray to Sjaf for one final gift.

I was halfway to freedom. Moving swiftly along the balcony, I made it to the next hallway and from there I crept through the shadows to a narrow stairwell. Then I was through the kitchens, to another set of stairs, these leading to the cellar. I hit the bottom stair, running into the cellar with the small knife I'd pulled from the dead Dragonman's neck, to surprise the guard at the tunnel entrance and disable him quickly.

Standing in front of the tunnel's barred door were four Dragonmen, none of them shocked to see me. "Put the knife down and surrender," one of the men said, stepping forward.

Why had I not expected Draki to bolster security after I'd made it into the tunnels the last time?

If I used my gifts, everyone above us would hear. A guard would be dispatched to alert Draki. But if I didn't silence these Dragonmen, the result would be the same.

"Draki will kill you if you harm me," I reminded them.

"The Dragon killed the last guards who let you escape," the Dragonman closest to me said. "I'll take my chances."

I raised my knife, but just before the man reached me, one of the others sank his sword through the man's back.

Everyone froze as the body fell, looking at the Dragonman with the sword. In the cellar's dim light, I'd not recognized him.

"Andrithur?"

He spun to meet the other two men's swords and axes. "Go now, witch!"

I raced past them, unbolting the door. It didn't seem right to leave Andrithur, still fighting for his life, but again he yelled for me to go.

The torch I grabbed from the cellar was nearly burnt out, and the tunnel was long. If I didn't reach the intersecting tunnels before the fire died, I would have to grope my way blindly. It would slow me, increasing the risk of choosing the wrong tunnel.

I ran faster.

When I got to the other tunnel branches, the torch flickered, not much more than an ember. I ducked under the archway into the middle tunnel, as Hilde had told me to, slowing just enough to keep from running into the walls. Footsteps echoed in the archway behind me.

If it was Andrithur, he would have called out. I tried to quiet my breathing, my footfalls. Maybe the Dragonman would pass by, thinking I'd headed for the shore.

I heard him stomping up the tunnel I was in, fast. Too fast.

I dropped the extinguished torch and ran.

This tunnel stretched beneath the lava field. I had no idea how long it was, so I pushed myself to run as if any step could be the end, heedless of the scrape of stone against my skin when I drifted too close to the walls. My side ached, my breaths were no more than gasps, but I kept on.

The footsteps were louder, nearer.

There—a flash of silver in the dark. The bolts barring the door leading outside. My feet carried me forward, until I was only a few paces away. Someone pounded on the other side of the thick wooden door, trying to break it down.

The Dragonman caught me from behind, knocking me to the dirt, landing on top of me. I bent my arm and stabbed with my knife, hitting flesh, and he grunted, his iron grip wrapping around my wrist, slamming my hand into the ground. My hold weakened and the knife slipped from my fingers.

There was no wind or water here to use as weapons, and the metal bolts were out of my reach. I could use Jardun's gift of earth to bring part of the tunnel down on his head, but it would crush me as well. The Dragonman had one hand dug into my hair, the other around the back of my neck. He lifted me, shoving me in front of him through the dark, back the way I'd come. Away from the door, away from freedom.

Inside me, something quickened. A beast cracked open its eyes, took its first breath. It was me, and yet *not*. It was a girl made of rage, dark and sinister and lovely, stirring beneath my skin—my war gift, awakening. Reminding me of the strongest weapon in my possession.

Spinning in the Dragonman's grasp, my palm slid inside his tunic, slapping his chest. I dropped into his soul, light as a petal, steady as a root. His essence was a mosaic: loves and losses, victories and sins, memories, thoughts—everything that made him who he was. I drew it toward me, calling his soul as if it was a creature, and it bowed to me, its mistress. His soul was mine to control.

I commanded it to shatter.

Fissures formed along each piece of him, splintering. For a moment, all was static, a final interlude. Then his soul broke apart, the fragments scattering, until he was unrecognizable to himself, lost in his own mind, a sad, mangled mess of pieces that couldn't be put back together.

When I let go, I could see. The Dragonman was on his knees, hands pressed to his head, rocking back and forth. Screaming. Whimpering. Drool trickled from the side of his mouth and his eyes bulged in his head like those of a fish.

"What did you do, witch?" Andrithur stood there, the candle in his hand drizzling light across the three of us.

"I unmade him." My voice came out flat. I was staring at a horror I'd created, and I was too numb to care.

"He was my friend, once," Andrithur said, setting the candle down so he could hold his sword with both hands. "I won't leave him like this. You go on."

Darkness fell around me once more as I moved away from the candlelight. There was a whoosh of air, the squelch of severed flesh. I stumbled at the sound, and at the void it left when the broken Dragonman fell silent. It was filled a moment later with Andrithur's prayer for his dead friend, chanted across the stillness.

I reached the door at the tunnel's end and tossed the heavy bolts aside. I'd barely pulled on it when the door was thrown inward, and I had to jump back.

Moonlight spilled into the tunnel, framing the figure in the doorway. Golden hair and blue-gray eyes, tall and broad and starkly handsome. My *skoldar* thrummed, as loud and fast as my pulse. I wanted to go to him, but something kept me rooted where I was.

We stared at each other, motionless, silent.

Andrithur shoved me through the doorway, straight into Reyker, startling us both. He caught me, and I looked up at him.

"Are you all right?" His hand rose toward my face.

I flinched. I didn't mean to, but I'd been fooled by Draki, by Veronis, and my body reacted involuntarily.

Reyker's hand fell to his side.

"Time to go," Andrithur said, hurrying up the slope that led away from the tunnel. "Unless you want to stay for a family reunion?" He looked at Reyker pointedly. Reyker glanced at me. For the first time, I noticed the angles of his brows and cheekbones, the cut of his jaw. Features he must have inherited from his father. Just as Draki had.

Anger simmered within me suddenly. Reyker had lied—not just with words, but in his soul. He'd taken care to never let me glimpse a memory that revealed Draki was his brother. After everything we'd shared, he still hadn't trusted me enough to tell me the truth. If he'd lied about this, what else had he hidden?

I hurried after Andrithur, past the slumped figures of three Dragonmen—guards who'd been stationed outside the tunnel, I gathered, dispatched by Reyker before they could raise an alarm. From the top of the slope, I could see the lava fields spread out behind us. Before us was a hummock covered in moss and wispy brown grass. Two horses waited, and Andrithur mounted the dappled gray. The other was a chestnut mare with dark eyes.

"Victory?" I ran to her, and pressed my face into her muzzle, inhaling the scent of Rhys's horse. "Bloody fates! How did you get here?"

"A long story," Reyker said softly. "I will tell you later, if you wish to hear it."

I pulled myself into the saddle, and Reyker settled in front of me, offering me a heavy fur cloak. Andrithur was already galloping ahead. "Hold on," Reyker said. His voice was stiff, and so were my arms as they wrapped around him.

Why was this so hard? All I'd wanted for so long was to have Reyker back, and now that I did, it didn't feel as I'd thought it would. Had Draki ruined this, too, as he'd destroyed everything else I cared about?

Victory took off, flying across the hummock, catching up with Andrithur's horse and then surging ahead, faster than she'd ever been on Glasnith. Night lightened to dawn, the sun rising as the moon set. The hummock gave way to meadows dotted with wildflowers, and then to a sparse forest. Victory slowed as we rode up the path to a village, or what would soon become one—the place seemed empty, most of the buildings incomplete, with stacks of wood and stone piled beside them.

Reyker dismounted. I let him help me down, but he didn't look at me as he held my waist and lowered me to the ground. I walked through the village, taking it in, wondering why it felt familiar.

Andrithur rode up and handed his horse over to Reyker, who was bringing out a fresh mount from the half-built stables.

"Thank you, Andrithur," I said. "I know you put yourself at great risk to help me."

"I owed you a debt, witch. Consider it repaid." He climbed onto the horse and addressed Reyker. "I'll make sure the ship is ready, lordling."

Reyker bristled at the title, but he nodded, and Andrithur kicked his mount, disappearing into the forest. Leaving the two of us alone.

"What ship?" I asked.

All of my focus had been on getting out of Dragon's Lair. I wasn't sure what to do now. Stay on Iseneld with Reyker, fighting to overthrow the Dragon? Or go back to Garreth and help him push the Dragonmen out of Glasnith? Both seemed impossible feats, especially since I'd renounced my homeland and pledged myself to Iseneld's gods. Would they let me leave? Would the Green Gods allow me to return to their shores?

"A ship sailing to the Auk Isles." Reyker walked toward the largest of the grass-roofed cottages in the village, the only one that was finished. "A place without Dragonmen."

I ran to catch up to him. "Who is going to the Auk Isles?"

"You are." He entered the cottage, holding the door for me.

As soon as I was inside, he moved, and I kicked the door shut. "I just spent the last month with a man who tried to control me. You don't get to make decisions on my behalf."

"This is not just about you." He whirled on me. "If you stay in Iseneld or go to Glasnith, Draki will find you. As long as you are his captive, he will use it against me. He will use me against his enemies. He will hold your life at stake and force me to kill the only warriors who might be able to overthrow him. The fate of my island is tied to your fate, Lira."

He was right, and I felt like a fool for not having realized. But it was also unfair, and I couldn't simply give in. "I still deserve a say in this choice."

"I wish I could offer you that."

"What will you do if I say no? Throw me over your shoulder and drag me to the ship? Tie me down so I can't jump overboard?" I'd stepped closer to him, and there was only an inch of space between us. I wanted to beat my fists against his chest. I wanted to grab his head and pull his mouth down to mine.

"I will do what I must to keep you and Iseneld safe." He went to the hearth, kneeling beside it to start a fire.

I leaned against the wall. "Everything is different now, isn't it? Everything has changed."

He blew on the kindling until the sparks caught, crackling to life. "Not everything." His gaze slid over me briefly before returning to the fire.

"Why didn't you tell me?" I whispered. I didn't have to say Draki's name. It lay between us like a chasm.

"You know why. You would have hated and feared me. You would have looked at those darker parts of my soul and seen him there, always worrying that one day I would turn into him."

"Those sound like your fears, not mine."

There was a *pop* as he snapped a branch in half and fed it to the flames.

"Reyker." I crossed the room, determined to break this strange barrier that had risen between us. Above the hearth was a wooden mantel with scratches along the surface. Symbols. Words. From Hilde's teachings, I understood some of it. These were protection runes, spelling out blessings and prayers.

I'd seen this mantel in Reyker's soul.

"This is your family's home." I ran my fingers along the grooves in the mantel. "We're in Vaknavangur. But how? I thought it was destroyed."

"We're rebuilding."

I peered out through the cottage shutters. "There are others here?"

"Not now. I sent them to a nearby village for their safety, in case Dragonmen followed us. But yes, I've been working with those who survived Draki's attack on Vaknavangur. In time, we will return it to what it once was." He came up behind me, pointing out different buildings. "The stables. The barn. The feasting hall. The workshops will go there, the gardens there. The well is already running."

His entire demeanor was lightened by this sense of purpose, by the sort of joy I'd only ever seen in him once before—the night we'd spent in each other's arms beneath a thorntree. We had lain beneath that tree, speaking of being in Iseneld together, and here we were. It wasn't how we'd imagined, but we had made it.

I took the first leap, because I knew he wouldn't. I leaned into him, my spine against his chest, pulling his arms around my waist.

With a sigh, he rested his chin on my head. "I missed you, my deer."

The dam I'd built inside myself over the last months, the only thing that had kept me sane, began to crumble. I turned, my fists balling into the fabric of his tunic, trying to hold back a torrent. "I thought you were dead.

I dreamed it. I saw it when I touched the medallion." My fingers slipped beneath his collar, pulling out the circle of silver. "How did you get this?"

Reyker took my hand and pressed my palm to his chest.

The memories were jagged rocks jutting up from the swift currents of his soul. All I did was brush them with my fingertips, and they poured into my mind, every moment that had passed since we parted.

The attack on his ship, when he'd been stabbed, and the monks who pulled him from the sea and saved his life. His return to Glasnith, how he'd searched for me, how he'd watched me jump from the bluffs. His battle with Draki. The horrible things he'd done to try and save the survivors in Stony Harbor and the Daughters of Aillira. His capture. His journey to the glacier.

Quinlan's death.

I could bear no more. I ripped free of his soul, weeping. Reyker pulled me to him, leading me to the hearth, and the two of us sat before the fire. There was a blanket of soft fur beneath us, and Reyker wrapped another around us. He held me as I let go of every tear I'd refused to drop, every sob I'd caged, every scream I'd swallowed over the past months. He cried with me, his chest heaving against mine.

I wasn't certain when the shift happened, when our breaths melted from sobs to gasps, when touches that had sought to soothe gave in to need.

"I love you," we said with our mouths.

I am here, I am alive, and you are still mine, we said with our bodies. We kissed each other's scars, dried each other's tears. Long after the fire burned down and the cottage grew cold, we kept each other warm.

CHAPTER 38

LIRA

My hands were hot against Reyker's skin, and he groaned.

"Be still," I said, focusing the small healing stream inside me, pouring it into the bruised flesh and strained muscles in his shoulder. "Did you really think you could knock down a door as thick as your arm and reinforced with iron?"

"If you'd been the one standing there waiting for an hour, knowing I was on the other side, you'd have tried it too. I was about to claw through it with my fingernails when you finally came out."

"As often as you get injured, I'll have ample opportunities to practice my healing gift. How's that?" The bruises weren't gone, but they had faded. I was better at removing sickness than I was at mending flesh and bone.

Reyker rolled his shoulder, groaning again. "Much better."

I ran my fingers over the scar beside Reyker's heart as he pulled on his tunic. "With enough practice, I might get strong enough to erase this. Maybe even remove your brand and your warrior-mark."

"I don't want them erased." He glanced at the puckered flesh on his chest, scratched at the slave-brand on the side of his neck. "Every scar is a story. When I die, I take my stories with me, written across my skin."

"Not every story is worth keeping."

"Yes. Every story." He bent to kiss one of the scars left across my back by the thorntree knout. He'd kissed them all many times as we'd lay tangled together in the fur blankets, telling me they were part of me, they were beautiful. "These scars tell the story of our love. What we fought through and sacrificed to be together. If you erase them, you erase us."

"I would always have this," I said, lifting my wrist. The scar of flame that told the story of how we'd met, that connected us evermore. Reyker kissed my *skoldar*, and it heated beneath his lips, sending sparks up my arm, warmth flowing in all directions until I was reaching to rip off the shirt he'd just put back on.

It was the third time he'd tried to get dressed.

"Lira." My name was a groan of desire, amusement, frustration. "Later, I will give you every minute left of my life. But for now, we must go." In contrast to his assertion, his hands traveled down my ribs, across my stomach, along my thighs.

"Did I betray you?" I didn't know where the words had come from, why they were spilling out at this of all moments, but now that they were out, I pushed on. "By getting close to Quinlan, thinking of him as more than a friend? Am I betraying him, tumbling into bed with you so soon after he gave up his life for me?"

Reyker's hands froze, but he didn't pull away. "Quinlan would want you to live. He loved you enough to value your happiness above his own. I don't blame you for loving him in return. Nothing is gained by the dead envying the living, nor the living envying the dead."

Could it be that simple? Choose to live, choose happiness, and still be granted forgiveness? Love Reyker, love Quinlan, without guilt? Maybe as long as I let myself keep loving Quinlan, it would feel like he wasn't wholly gone.

Even so, the loss of him was still raw. The possibility of losing Reyker, too, so soon after I'd gotten him back, was like ripping open stitches on a half-healed wound.

"I'm not getting on that ship without you," I said.

He closed his eyes, his breath leaking out in a sigh. "You would force me to choose between you and my people?"

"I'm asking you to stay at my side, no matter what comes. We can return to Glasnith, where I can seek answers from Veronis that might help us stand against Gwylor and Ildja. Or we can stay here and fight Draki, together."

"That is not an option." He let go of me, stepping into his trousers with his back turned.

I let the blanket fall and reached for my own clothes, discarded on the floor. The cold air prickled my skin. "I spent a month as his prisoner, and I'm still standing."

"Are you so eager to go back? To be his captive again?" Reyker held up my cloak for me to step into, fastening it around my shoulders. Tension seeped into his expression, his every movement, and it struck like flint against my own ire.

"Snarl all you want. Stomp your feet and punch the walls. I can bear it. I'd rather live with your anger than live without you again, my wolf."

It was the wrong choice of words. Wolf Lord was the name his people had given him, those who had survived Draki's attack on Vaknavangur and helped rebuild it from the ashes. They were depending on Reyker, and I was pressing their lord to leave them once more.

"You don't know what you're asking, Lira." Reyker stormed out the front door. I stepped into my boots and hurried after him.

Before I could speak, he was yelling at me. "You don't know him like I do! The lengths he will go to, the harm he will cause you, just to hurt me. Every time I cross him, he finds some way to make me regret it. Every time I care about someone, he uses it against me. That is why he took you. What I have done, going to his home, taking a woman he viewed as his possession, he will view it as an act of war!"

Reyker paced, breathing hard, his shouts so loud the birds in the trees had taken flight. "You matter more to me than anything, and he will tear you to pieces because of it. He will take you apart and make me watch, as he did with my mother, and the gods-damned truth is that I cannot protect you any more than I could her!"

The blacks of his pupils were spreading, as they did when he fought. I grabbed his hands and squeezed, pulling him to me before he slipped over the edge. "Then we run. To Savanna or Sanddune if we must, or farther, to the unknown edges of the earth." Like cowards, abandoning our countries, our kin, our comrades. "We don't stop until we're beyond his reach."

Reyker laughed as if the idea of such a place was a joke, but his eyes cleared, his breaths slowed. His stiff muscles loosened as I rested my head on his chest. "It is your turn to ask me to run with you," he said. "Though our last attempt didn't quite work out as planned."

"Something brought us back together, Reyker. Against all odds, we are here, on Iseneld, in your home village. We didn't find each other after all this just to lose each other again."

"Are you so certain?"

"Yes." I wasn't, and he knew it. But we wanted to believe the lie, so we did.

The ride to the sea took several hours, yet they passed like minutes, just as our time in the cottage had. There was still tension between us, but it mattered little. My arms were around his waist, and Reyker held the reins in one hand, his free hand linked with mine. Every so often, he looked at me over his shoulder, assuring himself I was still there.

Darkness had fallen once more by the time we arrived. We skirted the fishing village, heading straight for the pier we would set sail from at dawn. Andrithur was supposed to have returned to Vaknavangur to warn us if something had gone wrong with the ship or its crew. But as we got closer to the pier, my chest tightened. My stomach sank with dread, chilling me down to my bones.

There was no one on the pier. No one on any of the longships or knarrs docked there. No lights or sounds coming from the village. A thick fog had settled over the water.

"It's too quiet," Reyker said. "There should be fishermen up and about. Andrithur should have been waiting for us."

Victory sensed it, too, sniffing at the briny air, snorting and shaking her head.

Reyker dismounted, drawing his sword. "Go back to the cottage and wait for me."

"No."

Someone whistled, the sound low and grating, echoing across the water as a knarr appeared out of the fog. There was no mistaking who was on it.

A tremor rippled through Reyker. "Don't fight me on this, Lira, please. You must go."

The only thing that frightened me more than facing Draki was leaving Reyker to face him alone. "He'll find me. There's nowhere for me to run. We do this together."

Reyker cursed under his breath. He took hold of Victory's reins and led her to the end of the pier, where the knarr waited, a stone's throw from the pier's edge.

Draki stood in the bow, watching us. He held the ship still upon the sea, letting waves and wind pass by without moving the vessel out of place. There were a handful of Dragonmen with him, and two dozen others on the boat whose faces were unfamiliar to me. But not to Reyker. He inhaled sharply, his eyes widening, and I understood.

These were the survivors of Vaknavangur, men and women, some older than me, some younger, some no more than children. They had gags in their mouths and their wrists bound behind their backs. Rope was tied around their ankles, and on the end of each length of rope was a large stone. They looked at the lord who had fought the Dragon for them before, pride and hope shining through their fear: their Wolf Lord would save them.

"Leave them alone, Draki," Reyker said. "Your quarrel is with me, not them."

"Do you hear yourself, brother? You sound like a silly little boy who still believes honor matters more than strength and goodness triumphs over evil. No matter how many times I try to smother that boy, he lives in you still. Maybe we will change that tonight."

I slid from the horse and moved to Reyker's side. "What do you want, Draki?"

"Little warrior." His gaze shifted to me. "Did you enjoy your last day of freedom? Did you think I did not know of your plans?" He kicked a wooden chest in the bow onto its side, and Andrithur rolled out. "You bewitched another one of my Dragonmen. Such betrayals cannot go unpunished, as you are well aware."

Andrithur glanced at Reyker and me. He nodded once—a salute, a farewell.

There was a rope slung around the top of the mast. Draki looped one end around Andrithur's neck and pulled on the other end so Andrithur was jerked into the air, his legs kicking futilely at the sail.

My hands balled into fists. I pushed wind at the knarr, testing it, but the ship didn't shift an inch. Draki's head swiveled toward me and he wagged his finger.

The life ebbed out of Andrithur, his complexion a spectrum drifting from red to blue to violet. When he stopped moving, Draki dropped the rope and Andrithur's body crashed to the deck.

"You took something that belongs to me, Reyker. You will return her." Draki stepped over Andrithur and grabbed one of his captives, a broadly built young man with dark yellow hair. Draki forced the man onto the railing, setting the rock beside him. "For every minute you make me wait, I will take something that belongs to you."

Draki let go of the rock. It wobbled. Fell. Splashed into the water.

A single second passed—enough time for me to gasp, enough time for the children to scream through their gags, enough time for the man to look at Reyker and for Reyker to look back, to shout, "Hamund!" before the rope went taut and the man was dragged off the railing into the sea. Hamund's frightened face was a blur below the surface, and then it was gone as he sank into the dark.

Reyker tore off his coat and sword-belt, checking that his knife was secure in the sheath at his ankle, about to dive in.

"Take another step, and I'll shove them all in at once," Draki called. "That goes for you as well, little warrior. I feel you reaching out with your gifts, thinking to buoy that drowning boy up on the waves. I have been very tolerant of your rebellions thus far, but if you test my patience these children will pay."

He grabbed a girl who couldn't have been more than fourteen. Tears streaked her cheeks as Draki pulled her to the edge and propped the rock she was tied to up on the railing.

"Wait!" Reyker and I screamed at the same time.

Draki paused, keeping his hand on the rock.

"Please, Draki," I begged, searching for the shred of a soul that lingered within him. "Don't do this."

Reyker didn't bother begging. He'd spent far longer than I had trying to find mercy in the Dragon and was more certain than I was that none existed. "You're a gods-damned monster!" he shouted. "These are your own countrymen, scions of Iseneld, children of Sjaf! How can you do this and call yourself our king?"

"Do not waste your righteous indignation on me," Draki said. "I am high jarl because I make choices no one else has the stomach for. A ruler must be willing to do whatever is necessary to keep what is his. Lira is *mine*. We all know how this ends. The only difference is how many of these sad little remnants of Vaknavangur will lie at the bottom of the ocean when you two finally give up. You have ten seconds to decide."

I took Reyker's hand. "I have to go."

"No. No, we can find a way out of this, there must be a way." Reyker looked at the girl Draki held, her life dangling by a thread, then back at me. He couldn't let her die. He couldn't turn me over to the Dragon. Caught between those damnable options, he was paralyzed.

I had to choose for him.

"They need you, Reyker." I brushed my lips against his. "Our fates are twined. We will find each other again."

"Your time is up," Draki said.

As he released the rock, I leaped off the pier.

The cold was like a punch to the gut. I kicked for the surface and came up sputtering just as the girl went under. I found Reyker staring at me as if he was the one drowning, and I was the stone dragging him down. Then he went after the girl, diving below the waves.

I swam to a spot halfway between the pier and the knarr, treading water. "Let them go first, and I'll come with you."

Draki swept his hand toward an empty longship gliding out of the fog, its sail bearing the warlord's Dragon Star. When it was near enough, the Dragonmen jumped onto it. Draki leaped last, soaring through the air with unnatural grace. As I swam toward the longship, I heard Reyker surface with the girl. She was coughing and crying, but alive.

Once I was close enough, Draki leaned out, extending his hand to me. I wanted to defy the Dragon, to curse and slap him away, but this wasn't just about me. It was about Reyker's people too. I wouldn't let Draki steal anything else from them.

I took the Dragon's hand.

Draki pulled me from the water and wrapped someone's cloak around me—not his, since he never wore one. Even now, he was dressed in a fur vest left open in front, like the cold couldn't touch him. Draki spun me so I faced the other longship. His arms snaked around my waist, pulling me against him. "Now, Lira," the Dragon purred in my ear, "you are truly mine."

I didn't fight. There was no point anymore.

This was my choice.

Reyker had hauled the dead man from the water and was laying him gently on the knarr's deck. He hurried to cut the others free from the ropes at their wrists and ankles, found a blanket to wrap around the shivering girl. The Wolf Lord, protecting his people, ensuring they were unharmed. The survivors gathered around Hamund's corpse, weeping, and Reyker let them grieve. He came to the bow, standing there like a figurehead, his body motionless, his expression blank.

I knew I looked the same.

We stared at each other as our ships drifted farther apart, until the fog swallowed the space between us. My hand moved, reaching toward the white veil where Reyker had just been, but he was gone.

PART THREE
ASHES OF DREAMS

Dear Brother,

I invite you to attend the upcoming grand ceremony in Dragon's Lair, in the month of Loksomar at dusk on Season's Eve, when I will officially introduce my chosen consort, Jarl Lira of Drakin to my most loyal and esteemed comrades. Together, let us feast and drink and mend old wounds.

Dress formally.
Gifts are appreciated, but not required.

Sincerely,
High Jarl Dragon of Iseneld,
Emperor of the West and Eastern Isles

CHAPTER 39

REYKER

The invitation arrived by messenger. Draki sent a servant to the mead house, knowing Reyker was likely to kill any Dragonman he came across.

When Reyker entered the mead hall, Brokk at his side, he spotted the servant immediately. She held up the envelope with the Dragon's seal. Reyker ripped it from her hand, fast enough that she brought her fingers to her lips as if to check that she hadn't lost any. He tore open the envelope, unfolded the thick parchment, and read the words that were written in the Dragon's own intricate looping script, caged inside a decorative blue border.

Reyker crumpled the invitation in his fist.

The black river did not ask his permission—as it had done before, it sensed what he needed. It tried to possess him completely. He heard the growl rising in his throat, knew his pupils were widening to swallow the blue of his irises.

No.

His muscles shook from the strain as he fought to keep the darkness inside him leashed, to make it answer to him.

Just as he regained the river's reins, Brokk's punch crashed into his jaw. It held the force of a swinging hammer and sent him stumbling into a wall. "Not again, you bastard," Brokk said.

"I'm all ri—"

A glass bottle shattered over his head.

"Wait, Brokk, I—"

Meaty hands grabbed him by the collar and shoved him out the door, gripping him by the hair and plunging his head into stale, icy water. A trough. Brokk was drowning him in horse spit.

Finally Brokk pulled him out and slung him to the ground. "Gods-damn it!" Reyker sputtered. "I told you, I had it under control."

Brokk glared down at him. "At the first sign of your madness, you lose the right to be listened to. Besides, I was reading over your shoulder. I saw what it said."

"Fuck." Reyker flopped onto his back, staring at the sky, slamming his fists against the dirt. "*Fuck!*"

"Behold, the great Reyker Lagorsson, throwing a tantrum like a child. Back when we were boys, you had fits over broken swords and bruised pride. Sometimes a girl. Or your brother. Or your brother and a girl. Gods, he's been at this a long time, hasn't he?"

"Do not make light of this."

"I will make light of this. It's what I do. It's what you need to keep you from sinking into a puddle of pity." Brokk held his hand out. "You're a lord. Act like it."

Shame burned through him. What would his parents think, if they could see him now? He shoved wet hair out of his eyes, sat up, and took his friend's hand.

"It was nice to have an excuse to punch that pretty face of yours," Brokk said, untying the horses.

"Feels like I got kicked by a skrikflak." Reyker sniffed at his hair. "What was in that bottle you hit me with?"

"Only some of the finest whiskey on the island. A gods-damned waste. You owe me another bottle, by the way."

The horses ran for home, or at least the closest thing he had to one. Fjullthorp—another temporary dwelling, while he pined for a place he would never call home again.

After Draki had left with Lira, Reyker and the others took Hamund's body back to Vaknavangur to set his funeral pyre. Reyker feared they would find the village destroyed, but no, it was still standing. In fact, it was occupied. Dragonmen were finishing the rebuilding work, placing belongings inside the cottages. A flag flew from the roof of his parents' cottage: the Star of the Dragon. Another thing Reyker loved, laid claim to by Draki.

With nowhere else to go, Reyker had brought the survivors to the Fjordlands, to make a new home. To give them another chance to live, or to fight, if they chose—to join the Renegades' army, as he had. With his people settled and safe, he was ready to head to Dragon's Lair. To do . . . something.

He'd not quite thought it through.

"I'm going," he told Brokk. "I have to get her out of that place."

"And get yourself killed in the process. You know it's a trap."

"Yes." A trap to draw him out, so Draki could shove his victory in Reyker's face. So he could reveal whatever sinister plots he had in store that he would force Reyker to be part of, using Lira's life as collateral. To remind Reyker that nothing in this world was his, that when the Dragon came and took Lira away he had just stood there and let it happen.

Brokk read the thoughts Reyker could not bear to speak aloud. "You couldn't have stopped him, Lagorsson."

But he'd not even tried. He'd not rushed to the knarr's helm or jumped in to swim after the longship, because even a wolf could not defeat a dragon. Draki would only have laughed and beaten him bloody, left his body as wounded as his heart.

Lira had sacrificed her freedom to save his people.

He should have done *something*.

Reyker had sought her in his dreams, in the ruins. He could feel her there, like she was standing right in front of him, but a veil was clouding his eyes, keeping him from seeing her. He'd wandered to the edges of their shared dreamworld and screamed her name, carved messages into the thorntree for her to wait for him there, but she hadn't come.

"I won't leave her in Dragon's Lair. How can I be of any use to the Renegades, my people, my country, when all I can think about is what he's doing to her right now, what he'll do to her tomorrow? I have been his prisoner, and I would not wish it on my worst enemy. How can I sit back and do nothing as it happens to the woman I love?"

Brokk watched him carefully, weighing his words. "Well. I suppose it's time we start planning an assault on the most secure fortress in Iseneld in order to take down the most dangerous bastard in the whole gods-damned world."

A foolish hope sparked in Reyker's chest. He reached out to grip Brokk's shoulder. "Have I ever told you that I love you like a brother?"

"No. And judging by your ill luck with brothers, you probably shouldn't start now."

A few hours later Reyker stood on Fjullthorp's pier with his back to the fjord, certain Solvei was about to shove him into it. "You want to do *what*?" she asked.

She'd granted him a private audience, agreed to hear him out. Now all he had to do was convince her they could achieve the impossible.

He repeated himself calmly. "I want to attack Dragon's Lair."

"Ah." She squeezed her fist around the hilt of her sword. "I suppose you have a plan for this idiotic endeavor?"

"Yes. It must be a joint effort, attacking from two fronts. I will be inside the fortress. You will be outside the lava field with a legion of Mountain Renegades." Reyker told her the details, what he and Brokk had come up with on their ride from the mead house.

When he was done, the jarl laughed in his face, and the sound echoed over the water and across the mountains. "You're joking."

"I'm not."

"You want to risk losing the war, losing our entire army, to win a single battle? All to save your woman?"

"This is not just about Lira, and it is not just a battle." Reyker slapped his palm against the hull of the longship floating beside him. "This *is* the war. It is where we make our stand. Where we end his reign."

"Or where we all die."

"Then at least we die fighting instead of waiting for Draki to slit our throats while we sleep."

She snorted. "Brave declarations from the man who has failed to foil the Dragon over, and over, and over again."

Though it was late, the sun still hung above them, a dimming circle of gold dripping honey-tinted light across the waves. It gilded the pier and the mountains, a deception that made the world feel kind and full of promise.

"You aren't wrong," Reyker said. "But my failures have taught me a great deal about how the Dragon plots. If we wait much longer, he will come here. You will lose *this*." Reyker gestured to the fjord and the village beyond. "All of it will burn. With every other threat to him dead, his focus will turn toward the Renegades. Toward all of the Fjordlands. I know him better than anyone. What drives him, what distracts him, what stays his hand and what forces it."

"Knowledge is good, but it is not enough," she said. "Can you kill the Dragon?"

He considered lying, but Reyker had spent a great deal of time with the jarl, and had grown to respect her. He would not let her risk herself, her people, on false assurances.

"I don't know," he said. "With his dying breath, my father told me I was the only one who could. Mystics and priestesses and fallen gods have prophesized that I would. If there is a way, I will find it. If I must, I will give my life to end his."

Solvei chewed the inside of her cheek, glaring at him. Finally, she said, "I curse the day I found you on that ship in Glasnith, Lagorsson. I hope you know that."

Reyker reached his hand out. "Are you with me, my jarl?"

She gripped his hand, her mouth stretching into a half-mad grin. "Let's wage a war, Wolf Lord. Let's bring the walls of Dragon's Lair down on Draki's head."

CHAPTER 40

LIRA

The knife I threw was aimed at Draki's eye.

Draki plucked the blade out of the air and hurled it back at me, so fast I had to drop to the ground to avoid it. There was sand in my clothes, my hair, under my nails. This was all I lived for these days—the moments when I could release the anguish pent up inside me. On him.

The Blood Ring spread out around us, but we could have been anywhere—on the beach, in the snow, floating in a void. All I saw was him. All that mattered was unleashing the beast curled around my heart. The hate that kept me alive, the rage that wouldn't let me give up.

All of it. All for him.

Draki had fortified Dragon's Lair, surrounding me with guards and locks. He had moved me to a larger bedroom in the fortress, right beside his own, with a door leading from his quarters to mine. He hadn't used it yet, but it was only a matter of time.

In less than a fortnight, he would parade me before his commanders and emissaries, officially declaring me his consort. I'd held my tongue when he showed me the invitation, when he'd had servants take my measurements for a gown, because this—as he never ceased to remind me—was the choice I'd made.

There was a phrase Reyker used to describe Draki's manipulations, the torment of unbearable decisions: *A choice that is not a choice.*

I pulled a sword from the wall and rushed at Draki. In these last weeks, I'd grown stronger, swifter—from practice, from the gods I'd pledged myself to, from sheer fury, I didn't know. Stalking the Dragon, I slashed and stabbed, enough to keep a strong warrior on his toes, running for his life.

But Draki wasn't a strong warrior. He was the strongest. He never tripped, was never winded, never even sweat. And he never, ever bled.

Though he didn't seem to move, my blade missed again and again.

With a cry of frustration, I lunged. Draki disappeared.

I called the sand up in a wave, suspending it in the air, searching for a telltale shift that would reveal Draki's position. It didn't come, so I kicked open the door to the Blood Ring, drawing in the wind, spinning it into the floating sand. A swirling sandstorm stretched from floor to roof. There—the hint of a shape. I ran for it, swinging the sword wildly. Something hit my ankles, knocking my feet out from under me. I landed flat on my back in the dirt, and Draki materialized on top of me.

I shoved at him, and when he rolled, I went with him, throwing my legs around his hips. I screamed at him, punching and clawing at his face, his neck, his chest. It was like slamming my body against a marble statue, but I didn't stop. Not until Draki rolled again, pinning my arms above my head.

"When you try to hurt me, you only hurt yourself."

"I don't care." I flailed under his grip. When I sought water, a stream of it came burbling up from the closest well, spilling through the open door, and I lashed him with it. When I reached for the earth, vines sprouted from the ground around us, lengthening, coiling, and I wielded them like whips.

The water evaporated, the vines withered. Nothing could touch him. His skin was armor.

"I know what you did," Draki said. "Offering those two Dragonmen you killed to Sjaf, gaining his war gift. This is what it does to mortals. You can't control it on your own, no more than my brother could when his gift first surfaced. It will only get worse. You need my help."

Reyker—oh gods, his battle-madness, his curse . . . it was Sjaf's war gift?

He didn't know. Draki had clearly never told him, and Hilde must not have realized. The Ice Gods had forced the gift on Reyker, but I had begged for it, *killed* for it. I'd made it a part of me—just as Draki had planned all along. As he'd done to Reyker, Draki had molded me to fit his purpose so he could wield me for his own gain.

"I want nothing from you!" The vortex of wind and sand kept churning, scraping at my skin, sticking in my lungs.

"Enough, little warrior."

I called to Seffra's creatures. I heard birds slamming into the roof above us, horses screaming and bucking in the stables. Far away, in the mountains and valleys, wolves howled. I thrashed and bucked and howled too.

"Lira. Stop."

I called to the weapons hanging from the wall, a thing I'd never done before, something I wasn't even aware I could do, but they answered—not as the horses did, but as the wind and water did, a force bending to my will. Sjaf's power over metal rippling inside me. I beckoned the weapons to me, all at once, and they came.

Knives and swords, axes and spears, maces and halberds. They flew off the wall and shot forward in a shining storm, slipping out of my control. I closed my eyes, waiting for the blades to collide with us. To glance off Draki. To impale and flay me.

It wasn't the slice of sword or axe that I felt next. It was Draki's lips, sudden and firm, sliding over my own.

The abyss of power that dwelled inside him beckoned to the gifts that lived in me, and my blood roared in response. Like the rest of him, Draki's mouth wasn't warm or soft. His touch was silken darkness, and he tasted like sin. Tempting. Forbidden. His kiss was a walk through perilous lands, knowing I could turn back to safety or forge deeper into the unknown.

For a moment, I let go of who I was, who he was.

My lips took what he gave and made their own offering. He released my wrists, and I twisted my fingers into his hair, pulling it roughly, biting down on his tongue. Draki moaned into my mouth, and every inch of me shivered, my back arching as his hands slid down my ribs. His mouth crushed me, feeding my hate, devouring it, reveling in it. I pushed back, struggling to brace myself, but there was nothing to hold on to but him, so I gripped him tighter. I wondered how much time had passed, if I'd forgotten to breathe, if I'd died and this was the serpent-goddess's form of torture.

If I didn't get out now, I never would.

I pulled away with a gasp, my head spinning, my pulse racing at the sensation of Draki's weight pressing me into the floor, his lips suspended just above mine.

The weapons I'd called spun overhead, dancing amid swirls of sand and water. I blinked and the blades fell like silver rain around us, sticking hilt-up in the sand, forming a perfect circle along the edge of the Blood Ring.

It was a full minute before I caught my breath, before I could arrange my thoughts enough to speak. "Why did you kiss me?"

"To calm you. And because, for the first time, you wanted me to."

"I didn't."

He brushed a lock of hair behind my ear. "We are past lies, Lira."

"I hate you."

"Yes. But just as desire and morality do not exist on the same plane, neither does hate live alone in its castle." His finger circled my temple. "Your mind is crowded. Disgust and abhorrence are tangled up with confusion. Curiosity. Lust."

"I don't—"

"And denial, deep as an ocean." His eyes glimmered with something like mirth. "I am not the only one you hate. You hate yourself, your desires that woke when I marked you, that strengthened when your gods fed you their blood. You hate the part of yourself that draws you to me. You know if you only give in, I can fulfill those needs."

For a heartbeat, I thought he would kiss me again, and though it shamed me, I didn't know what I would do if he did.

The guilt that ate away at me for the awful things I'd done, the grief for all I'd lost, the loathing, loneliness, desolation—it had planted a bit of grit in my soul. Using my gifts seemed to feed it. Draki had cocooned it with his darkness, coaxing it into a tiny, hard pearl. It was growing, and I wasn't certain I was strong enough to stop it.

The blood howling through my veins made me fear I no longer *wanted* to stop it.

My fingers went to my chest, to the place where my medallion used to rest, the place where it lived against Reyker's skin instead of mine. I'd made him keep it. That night in the cottage in Vaknavangur, lying in each other's arms, he'd sworn to me—as he had once before—that he would never take it off. A small comfort, thinking of him carrying that piece of me with him.

Draki's lips paused a hairsbreadth from mine. He studied my expression, all traces of amusement vanquished. Rolling off me, he stood and extended his hand. "Right now, what you feel most is exhaustion. Your gifts deplete your energy. You need food and rest. Come."

I didn't take his hand—I never did, not since the night I'd left Reyker, no matter how many times he offered—but neither did I slap it away. I followed him without protest as he led me to the kitchens and called for food. He watched me eat, then escorted me to my room.

Before he shut the door, he said, "Some part of you hates my brother as well, for letting you go, for not being strong enough to keep you. Forget him, and nothing will stand between us." He stroked his knuckles along my cheek. "Sleep well, Lira."

I did not sleep at all. I lay awake all night, waiting to hear the creak of the door between our rooms, sickened by the prospect. Thrilled by it.

No. *No.*

Bloody fates, what was happening to me?

Why this day? What had cracked the shield I'd raised against Draki? Beyond my hate, what had I been thinking about as I'd fought him, as I'd raged and screamed and lost control?

A single, simple thought, whispering through my mind: *Eighteen days.*

That's how long it had been since I swam to Draki's ship and pledged myself as his prisoner, since I'd watched Reyker drift out of my reach, out of my life. Eighteen days, and there had been nothing. No attacks on the fortress. No secret letters. He had not even come to me in my dreams. When I wandered the ruins, calling for him, I found that I was alone.

I'd known what I was doing when I jumped off the pier, when I stepped onto Draki's ship, and yet . . . some part of me had thought Reyker would come after me. That he would show up at the fortress and beat down the door. That he would find a way, if not to see me, at least to send a message, telling me he was all right, and he understood why I'd done what I did. Telling me that he would never stop trying to get me out.

I had clung to that hope, that belief, for eighteen days. Then, for an instant, I had doubted. I gave in to the fear that he would never come. I gave up on him, if only for a moment.

Draki had slithered in to take Reyker's place.

I'd kissed him. The scourge on my country. My brother's murderer.

"Never again," I said.

I pressed my face into my hands, clinging to the hateful beast guarding my heart, begging it to keep Reyker's memory locked there, where it could not be touched, and to let no one else past its snapping jaws.

As Season's Eve drew nearer, Draki brought me gifts, one for each of the seven days leading up to declaring me his consort. A silver comb lined with pearls. An ornate glass bottle filled with floral perfume. An exquisitely crafted sword, the blade studded with diamond spikes. And the one gift I truly did cherish, another terse letter from my brother, telling me he missed me but all was well with him.

Each of Draki's gifts was beautiful, eerily thoughtful. Each was a symbolic step closer to my doom.

When Draki said he had another gift for me, three days before the ceremony, I assumed it would be similar to the others, but he led me to the stables and put me on his horse. We rode beyond the lava field, to a copse of trees at the foothills of the mountains, where a circle of Dragonmen guarded someone. A man on his knees, tied up with rope. Bright red ribbon was wrapped around the man's face, knotted into a bow.

Even without the gaudy crown pinned to his head, I would have recognized him.

I hurried over, ripping off the bow, revealing features so like those of my father and brothers. "Uncle," I greeted him. "I warned you about making deals with gods and dragons."

Madoc put on a show of indifference, his eyes darting between Draki and me. "Rumor has it you've made your own unsavory deals, niece. My only regret is that I was caught. I suppose your husband will take my head as punishment."

"My consort prefers to kill you herself," Draki said, passing me my diamond-encrusted sword. "Execute him however you see fit."

Anticipation flowed into those pain-filled parts of me that couldn't let go of the past, that longed for my enemies' blood. I looked Madoc over. "I won't kill a man bound and on his knees," I said. "Release him."

Draki nodded, and the Dragonmen cut Madoc free.

"Run," I told my uncle.

He laughed like I was joking. The sound was quickly stifled as he took in my stance, my focus. A hunter, preparing to take down her prey. The arrogant tilt of his mouth flattened.

Madoc turned and fled into the woods.

I stalked after him through the trees, ducking beneath branches, picking my way around boulders. Taking my time, my keen hearing catching every subtle hitch of his lungs, every snap of a twig under his skidding boots as Madoc bumbled his way across the tricky, unfamiliar landscape. How it must have chafed, running from an insignificant, wayward girl—that was all he'd ever seen me as.

I would show him how wrong he was.

My wind shook the trees, branches clawing at Madoc and blocking his way. I whispered to the gray clouds above us, and when they split open at my command, I seized the rain as it fell, dumping a waterfall over Madoc's head. The raptors swooped from the sky when I called—falcons, razorbills, great skuas, diving at my uncle, slicing at him with beaks and talons. He stumbled, screamed, ran.

Where the forest ended, the mountains began. Madoc tried to climb, slipping on gravel, sliding back down. I was close on his heels.

He spun and threw a handful of rocks at me. With my earth gift, I grabbed ahold of the rocks, hurling them back at him.

"Lira." He kneeled before me. "You don't want to do this. It's murder, and you aren't a killer. You have a pure heart. It's what makes you better than the rest of us."

I took a step closer.

"It's beneath you to harm an injured, unarmed man. Give me a weapon and I will kill myself. Your hands, your soul, can remain clean."

With the toe of my boot, I drew a symbol in the dirt—three triangles overlapping. A sacrifice to a god, in exchange for a favor. The same symbol he'd drawn on the floor of my cell in Stony Harbor.

Madoc saw it and paled. "I'm your family, your father's brother! I have known you since you were born. Do this, and you will bear the stain of kin-slayer. It will taint you."

"You helped destroy my father, my village, my entire clan. You betrayed our homeland, tried to assassinate my brother, and nearly burned me alive to keep your secrets. You are no kin of mine."

Madoc reared up, lunging for my sword. I stabbed it straight through the center of his torso, diamond spikes ripping the wound wider. The sword's tip burst through his back. I jerked the blade out, leaving a red gulch in the space between his chest and belly.

"Oh." The exclamation came out a gurgle. He stared at the hole I'd left in him. "Oh."

I tore the crown from his head. The false king of Glasnith fell over and died.

Draki emerged from the woods behind me. He noted the symbol on the ground. "Which god did you offer him to?"

"None. His life was mine to take, and his death belongs to me."

The Dragon placed a hand on my shoulder, and in that touch I felt what he would not say. He was pleased. Proud.

The darkest, sickest parts of me basked in his praise, glowing with delight. The desolate pearl in my soul hardened and grew.

CHAPTER 41

REYKER

Plans were in motion. Reyker poured all his focus into carrying them out, grateful for the distraction from his thoughts. From his dreams.

They all had a part to play. Solvei was meeting with her commanders, strategizing, working through every possible scenario. Brokk was in the mountains with Skrim and the Renegades' best hunters, tracking down more of the Fjordlands' most elusive quarry. Reyker had stayed in Fjull-thorp to run drills with the rest of the Renegades, dividing Solvei's forces based on skill level, determining the best position to place each warrior in during the attack.

Alane found him as he sat alone in the feasting hall, his stew growing cold beside him while he wrote down lists of names, scratching some out, moving them around. Warriors were not game pieces, yet he must treat them as such if they were to win—he knew which ones would be sacrificed, placed in roles that could only end in their deaths. Playing a god did not sit well with Reyker.

The slap of a full tankard at his elbow startled him out of his deliberation. "I figured you could use this," Alane said.

He thought it was ale at first, which he wouldn't touch while making battle plans, but then he sniffed the contents. It was an herbal tea the healers made, a concoction of bark and petals and spice meant to soothe aching muscles. "Thank you," he said, bringing the tankard to his lips.

"I saw you out there, training the other soldiers for hours. You've done it every day since Jarl Solvei left. Don't you ever get tired? Sore?"

"Of course."

"Doesn't seem like it." Alane sat in the chair across from him as if she belonged there, craning her neck to peer at the list. "What are you working on?"

Reyker admired her boldness. She fit in well with Solvei's army. "Nothing. Just deciding men's fates."

"And women's."

"Yes. Women's too." The Mountain Renegades had plenty of sword-maids, women who guarded the backs of their warriors in battle with blade and shield, even some like Solvei who were strong enough to fight on their own. It was hard sending a man to his death, but every female soldier made him think of his mother. Of Lira.

"Where is my name?" Alane's finger slid across the parchment. "Why is it not here?"

"Because you are not going. Neither are Keeva and Bronagh."

Her nostrils flared. "We have been training alongside the other Renegades since we arrived. Our skills will be useful. Solvei says a wise leader uses every asset she has and does not let emotion cloud her judgment. She promised us—"

"Solvei is not responsible for you. I am." The list crumpled under his hand. "It is my fault the three of you are here, and I will not let you die for my country. Besides, if you were to be captured, the warlord would have a dangerous weapon to use against us."

"He already has a dangerous weapon. I thought that was the point of this mission. Saving your precious soul-reader, or whatever she's become."

Something in the girl's voice sent a chill up Reyker's spine.

Alane's gift allowed her to spy on places from a distance. This was how she'd seen the atrocities he'd committed at Hidden Falls, when Solvei had her spy on the secret meeting between Iseneld's overlords. Although Alane never saw the Dragon clearly—the strength of Draki's magic cloaked him from her visions—she caught glimpses of his affairs in and around Dragon's Lair.

"Alane. What have you seen of Lira?"

"She's changing. Her powers are growing stronger." Alane started to say something else, then stopped.

"What?" He kept his tone calm, even though he was about to crawl out of his skin.

"Let me come with you. This is why you need me. I can see into the fortress before you enter and ensure nothing is amiss."

She was right, loath as he was to admit it. "If I agree, you must do as I tell you. You take my orders, not Solvei's, and you follow them precisely. You don't get closer to the fortress than necessary. You spy and report, nothing more."

Alane gave a mocking salute and pointed at the parchment. "Write it down."

He smoothed out the list and added her name to it. "Tell me what you saw."

"Your soul-reader hunted a man down and murdered him in cold blood as he begged for his life. And she . . . she gave her body to the Dragon."

Reyker jerked, sending the tankard crashing to the floor. He squeezed his fists, fighting the black river's rage—if a man had said such things, Reyker might have broken his bones, turned his face to pulp. The river wanted blood. It *always* wanted blood.

Alane flinched but did not run. The magiska held her ground.

When he had himself under control, Reyker said, "You are mistaken."

"Believe whatever you wish. I'm only telling you what I saw: the soul-reader, lying on a bed of sand, with a dark shadow atop her. Shadow lips and hands on her body. But she wasn't fighting him. She kissed him back. She lay beneath him willingly."

Alane rose from her chair. Numbly, he watched her leave. At the door, she turned and said, "I'm sorry. I know you love her. But you must accept the possibility that when you attack the Dragon, she will fight at his side, not yours."

Reyker would never believe that. He would bet his life on Lira's loyalty, her love.

He would bet all their lives on it.

When Alane was gone, Reyker stared at his reflection in the spreading pool of tea at his feet. He did not look like a man capable of leading an army and seizing a fortress. He looked like a boy, lost and haunted.

There is some explanation, he assured himself. *She would not betray me this way. She would not betray herself.*

He tore up the list in his hand, the one he had carefully compiled while seeing each warrior's face in his mind, considering their ages, whether or not they had a family. Stupid, sentimental. This was no way to win a battle, much less a war.

Banishing his guilt, he took out a blank sheet of parchment and began anew.

He did not mean to sleep, yet some time in the hours between midnight and dawn, the list before him blurred, and the weight of his eyelids became too much.

Then came the sensation of falling, of shifting between worlds. If he must sleep, he would at least make use of it.

The ruins spread around him, broken stone, charred land. He ran through the wreckage, calling Lira's name, as he had done many times before. He ended at the thorntree. The messages he'd left her—one line for each time he'd searched—were still there, carved into the bark with a sharp stone.

> WAIT FOR ME HERE.
>
> I MUST SEE YOU.
>
> WHERE ARE YOU?
>
> WHERE ARE YOU?
>
> WHERE ARE YOU?

He knelt and found the rock at the base of the tree. He carved another message.

> I'M COMING FOR YOU.

"She won't see it," a voice said.

He whirled, the rock raised in his fist. A gold-eyed woman stood behind him. "Seeress," he greeted her. "How are you in my head?"

"This is the only escape left to me." She ran her hand along the messages in the thorntree's trunk. "Your words are wasted. The Dragon has shielded her dreams against you. She could be here, right now, but the two of you will never find each other, never see the signs of love you leave."

He'd suspected this, of course, but knowing it, knowing she was in Dragon's Lair, alone, with no way for Reyker to reach her, to offer the smallest shred of hope . . . He had lived that life himself for many years, with one crucial difference. The torments he'd suffered in the name of Draki's twisted obsessions were from one brother to another. Reyker had given in and become Draki's demon, his Sword.

It would be worse for Lira, as Draki's consort. Far worse.

She lay beneath him willingly.

"Have I lost her already?" he asked.

"Does it matter?" The seeress crouched beside him. "Either way, the Dragon must die. You did not heed me before. You stopped the girl from sacrificing herself and freeing the fallen god who could have weakened Ildja and her spawn. Now you must confront the Dragon at full strength. I cannot tell you the secret. The gods did not show me. I only know it is buried inside you, waiting to be unearthed."

"How am I supposed to do that? Why would the Ice Gods create me to be a weapon but leave no instructions for how I'm to be used?"

She shoved him and the ground gave way beneath his feet. The ruins were gone. He was floating in a black expanse—the sky-well, where his people once lived as gods before falling through a hole in the sky to live on the earth as mortals. The spiraling arms of galaxies stretched out as far as he could see in ethereal shades of cobalt and violet. He couldn't see the seeress, but he heard her, her voice echoing between the stars.

"Why do you think I was sent to find you that day in the wilderness? Why do you think I am here now, planting these seeds in your slumbering mind where you are best able to comprehend them? Sleep. Dream.

Untangle what I've told you. When you wake, you will remember nothing, but you will have a light to guide you through these uncertainties."

The stars shuddered. The brightest one, right in front of him and yet infinitely far, exploded in a bursting wave of color and dust—rocks the size of countries, crashing down to create new worlds.

This was where he'd come from.

Draki was a god, but long ago, in this realm, Reyker had been a god too. Had they been brothers even then?

Perhaps Lira had been here as well, a goddess drifting beside him through eternity. Had he loved her before this life, sought her across time and space in their mortal bodies to be the light of his earthly soul?

Reyker woke with a jolt in the feasting hall. His head lay on the table, strands of his hair floating in the forgotten bowl of stew. The quill was still in his ink-stained fingers. He looked down at the list and saw another name had been added, though he didn't remember writing it.

Lira

She was grouped with the other magiskas, her gifts listed alongside her name.

Beasts
Water
Wind
Earth
Healing
Metal
War

This last skill, he had written larger than the others, underlined and circled it. For what purpose? He knew what she was, how she could dip into the deepest parts of his being and draw out his very essence. Thoughts. Emotions.

Memories.

Words swirled around his head, as if from a long-forgotten dream. *You carry the answer to his death inside you. You've already witnessed how it can be done.*

A vision. An omen. A thread of something he knew from the past: rose-colored droplets, trickling down skin inked with scales and knots.

Red.

Blood.

Not Aldrik, who'd borne no tattoos, who could be wounded, who'd bled and healed. Draki, who'd returned from the Mountain of Fire as an immortal, rendered invincible by Ildja. Or so it had seemed.

"Gods aflame," Reyker whispered. Draki had bled.

The Dragon can bleed.

He only had to remember how. There was nothing else to the vision, just that infinitesimal flash. But Reyker had spent more time with Draki, with Aldrik, than anyone, knew both versions of his brother better than anyone. The secret was there, somewhere—the detailed memory, trussed within the chaos of his mind and soul. Lost, but not irretrievable.

Not from the plundering of a powerful magiska.

This was why they'd found each other across oceans, why they'd lived in spite of all the things that had tried to kill them. There was a way to destroy the Dragon. And together they would find it—the Ice Gods' Sword and the Green Gods' soul-reader.

CHAPTER 42

LIRA

I stared into the oval mirror. It was taller than me, framed with a trim of silver and gold, etched with knots and dragons—another gift from my soon-to-be consort, this one ensuring I could never look at myself without seeing traces of him surrounding me, confining me to living inside whatever boundaries he chose.

Even so, I couldn't stop staring. That woman inside the mirror was not me.

First, there was the gown—my final gift—made of a rich blue silk that clung to every curve. The left side was void of decor, but the right side had markings like the mirror. Like the Dragon. The right sleeve, neckline, bodice, and waist, down to the hem of the skirt, bore the same design as Draki's skin, embroidered black silk instead of ink, but otherwise an exact match of his tattoos. Servants had twisted my hair into tight spirals and pinned them around my head, letting a few ringlets dangle at my neck.

Then there was the warrior-mark. If I was to be Draki's consort, I had to show the world, to prove my devotion with a tattoo similar to the ones his Dragonmen wore. Draki had tattooed me himself, his face too close to mine, the pain insubstantial in comparison to the meaning that tiny needle branded into the skin above my right eye: the twisting branches of a thorntree.

The design I had chosen.

That tree had been the only thing left of Aillira and Veronis after the gods destroyed their lives. Draki had ripped it up from its roots, but I would carry it with me. A symbol of the love Reyker and I had shared, even if symbols were all we had left. Even if everyone else saw only a mark of ownership, a sign that I was the Dragon's most prized possession.

No, the woman staring back at me from the mirror was not Lira—not any version of her I'd ever known. She was aloof. Resigned.

This was Jarl Lira of Drakin. The Dragon's consort. Empress of a broken world.

When a servant brought me a goblet of sweet wine, I drank deeply and asked for more. Maybe I would get drunk and make a scene, trip and rip my pretty gown, knock over a table. Anything to embarrass Draki, to disrupt this fancy Season's Eve party I wanted no part of, despite being its focal point.

There was a knock on the door. Draki entered without waiting for my permission. Once he made his public announcement at the ceremony, and I accepted, the last barriers between us would be gone. There would be no more courtesy knocks. There would be no more courtesy.

I stayed where I was. Draki came and stood behind me at the mirror, dressed in deerskin trousers and a tunic made from the same blue silk as my gown, and they fit him just as snugly, revealing every lethal bit of strength in the body they concealed. The tunic's top buttons were open, and the inked knots and dragons climbed from beneath it, across his chest and throat, the side of his face, vanishing beneath his hair. He was a glowing, otherworldly presence encompassing me. A gilded god.

"Our guests have begun to arrive," Draki said. "Your presence will be expected soon."

"A few minutes more. Please." Imploring him was like chewing planks, smiling around the splinters in my tongue.

Draki's hand slid along the curve of my neck, taking hold of my chin, lifting it gently so our eyes met in the mirror. That such a powerful, savage man could be gentle always set me off-kilter, defying the lines I'd drawn around him.

"When you accept me as your consort, Lira, we will be near equals. You will never bow or beg, not to anyone for anything, not even me. Unless you choose to, of course." His mouth quirked, and I flushed hot and cold at once, enticed and repulsed. Draki had caused a rift inside me—I was two women, trapped in the same skin, each struggling for control.

"Take as much time as you need, little warrior." Draki traced his thumb over my bottom lip. "But do not leave me waiting forever."

He drifted from the room, and the air grew lighter, the room larger. I took a deep breath and turned away from my reflection.

My door was unlocked. There were no servants or guards hovering in the hallways, all of them diverted to other areas because of the gala. Either Draki trusted me not to run or trusted I wouldn't get far enough for it to matter if I did.

This was Draki's wing of the fortress, and I'd been allowed to explore it on occasion. There was a small library, a sitting room I doubted he'd ever used, three bedrooms and three bathing rooms—one for him, one for his consort. Another for his lovers.

I'd heard the servants' whispers. Draki was the most powerful man in his country, and he was intensely alluring; he could have anyone he wanted, and he had, from jarls to peasants, Iseneldish and foreign, women and men alike. And he'd made it clear he would continue to share his bed with whomever he chose, even after our vows were spoken. A consort was not a wife. Any promises we made would have nothing to do with fidelity, only consolidating power. For him, at least.

If I was ever caught with another lover, they would die. Brutally.

On impulse, I went to the door I feared most, the one connecting my room to Draki's. It swung open at my touch.

I was looking for something, anything—a clue about who Draki was beneath his facade, what he wanted from me. I slipped into the Dragon's private chamber, disappointed at how plain it was. The room was large but sparse, with a stone hearth that took up half of one wall, a wooden table and two chairs, a massive bed with a frame made of elk antlers, the mattress topped with white fur blankets.

I tore my gaze quickly from the bed.

There was a wardrobe in the corner, and I rummaged through it. Inside were trousers, jerkins, tunics, things I'd never seen him wear, some the simple garb of peasants, others richly crafted and fit for a lord. At the bottom of the wardrobe, behind a row of boots, was a sword. I pulled it into the light, drew it from its sheath. It had a tapered cross guard, a crown-shaped pommel.

This was Reyker's father's sword—the one he'd fought Draki with as a boy—which would have passed to him the day he became lord of Vaknavangur. I recognized it from Reyker's memories, but it had been altered. An inlaid pattern of flames was etched into the blade. A design that matched the tattoo over Reyker's eye.

Reyker thought Draki had the sword destroyed, but here it was, in pristine condition, recently oiled and sharpened. By Draki? To what end?

I put the sword back, searching the rest of the room, finding nothing of interest. Then I looked at the doors. There were four: One led to my chambers, another into the hallway, one was attached to the bathing room. The last door, at the back of the room, was shut tight. I crossed the floor and opened it.

Behind the door was a passageway that ended at a narrow staircase, twisting downward.

Hilde had warned me about this door, and where it led—a prison where Draki kept the magiskas he captured. *Pray you stay in his favor and never see the inside of those cells*, she'd said. But I needed to see. This was where Draki would put me, consort or no, if I did not please him. If I did not obey.

I followed the hidden staircase down to a well-kept dungeon. Two rows of wooden doors had windows cut into them, revealing cells with beds and chairs and sinks. Comfortable, as much as a prison could be. Five of the cells were empty, and I shuddered at what that meant, at how many magiskas the Dragon had pushed to their breaking points, draining their gifts until their bodies gave out.

In the sixth cell, a woman lay on the bed, a blindfold covering her eyes. I'd have thought her asleep, she was so still, but her lips moved.

The cell keys hung on the wall. Carefully, I opened the door and went to her bedside. "Hello?" I touched her shoulder, but she didn't stir. "Are you all right?"

Her dark hair fanned across the pillow beneath her head. I eased the blindfold away. Beneath it, her eyes were open, turned in opposite directions. They were an odd shade of shiny gold.

Her murmurs were barely audible, words running together in an endless stream, and I leaned in, listening. "The blood will spill the gods will cry the world will shake the meek will kneel the strong will break the ice will crack the fires will burn the blood will spill . . ."

Who was this woman? What was Draki doing to her?

I stretched my hand out, until my palm was flat against her chest.

Hers was different than any soul I'd ever touched. It resembled a public garden, a fertile plot filled not with her own essence, but with the essence of other people's lives. Leaves and roots stretched up, flowers bending toward me. I ran my hands over them.

I was assaulted by visions.

A patchwork of faces and names I didn't recognize. There were births and weddings and battles and deaths, across time and distance, each life its own unique flower or bush or tree, growing, flourishing, wilting. And then, three thorny, tangled vines, three blackening blossoms, unfurling inside her soul, revealing their secrets.

Draki, sitting on a throne of ice, giant wings sprouting from his spine.

Me, floating on my back above an altar, surrounded by a circle of stones.

Reyker, his face bloody, his heart faltering as some unseen force wrenches his soul from his body.

The visions shifted to other people, other things. Briefly, I saw into the past through this woman's eyes, saw myself meet her in the Highlands. I heard the warning she gave, heard her tell me how I wouldn't remember it. She was a mystic. A seeress. And she'd predicted Quinlan's death—the price I paid for killing the white wolf in the Highlands, for using my gifts without the Ice Gods' permission.

I pulled myself together, enough to speak. "Show me what's going to happen to Reyker. Show me how to stop it."

"Kill me, soul-reader," the seeress said. "You must kill me before the Dragon returns."

"What? No. I can't."

The seeress persisted. "Last time you did not listen to me and look what happened. Listen to me now: As long as I live, he will have a window into what only gods and seers should know. He will see who betrays him before it happens. He will recognize attempts to take his throne and stop them before they begin. He will be invulnerable."

Kill the seeress, as I'd killed the white wolf. A willing sacrifice.

"Hurry!" she said. "He's coming. Do as I say, or we will both regret it."

I had no weapon on me, and there was no time to fashion one from the key in my hand. The only quick death I could offer was what I'd done to the Dragonman in the tunnels, but this time I would have to follow through. Not simply break her soul, but sunder it from its vessel.

I gathered her soul to me—the stalks of flowers, roots and vines, sprawling bits of other lives she carried inside her. Beneath those images, I felt the seeress's peculiar essence brushing against mine, pulsing with life. "I reap this soul in the name of the Ice Gods," I murmured, "in the name of Eyvor, the soul-keeper. May her veil-dwellers welcome you into Fortune's Field."

"Do it, magiska!"

With a silent cry, I pulled, ripping her garden up from its roots, tearing her soul free. Sound and color filled my senses, all the pieces the seeress was made of rushing past me, the last remnants of her visions drifting around me like shed petals caught in a cyclone. In each one, I saw a face, melting. Dying. Hundreds of faces, of deaths, brushing against me.

I let go and fell to the floor.

The seeress's eyes were still open, but there was a measure of peace in her features. It was a merciful death, if there truly was such a thing.

Her curse died with her—this time, I would remember her. I would remember everything.

Above me, someone moved in the passageway. I had to get out.

I ducked out of the cell, locked it, returned the keys to their peg. There was a door on the other side of the dungeon, and I pushed through it just as someone came down the stairs.

The door opened on another passageway, this one winding around, back to Draki's dusty library. I hurried through it, into the hallway on the other side that passed my bedroom, then up the ladder that stretched to the landing and the rooftop balcony, where I would make my grand entrance.

Music flowed through the balcony doors, coming from outside. I cracked a door open and peered at the crowds below, people milling about in the space between the fortress and the lava field, dressed in their finery. I recognized the emissary to Glasnith, laughing with a group of warriors. Servants flitted between the guests, carrying trays of food and wine and ale, setting up a feast on the many tables that had been arranged. Musicians played near the tables, flutes and lyres and fiddles, and harps that made me ache for Hilde. There were Dragonmen everywhere, more than I'd ever seen—of the hundreds of attendants, over half of them were Draki's soldiers.

A hand touched my back, and I jumped.

"It is time," Draki said.

When I turned, he stared at me, his expression stony. The gentleness he'd shown earlier was gone, replaced with impatience. And something more, something worse. Disdain. "You know," I choked out.

He'd been in the dungeons. He saw what I did to the seeress.

"I always know. There is nothing you can hide from me, no escape from the consequences of your actions. Your punishment awaits." He ran his fingertips along the skin of my throat. "For now, you will wait here until I announce you. Do not fail me in this. Remember what is at stake, all those who will suffer if you deny me."

He left me there, though his touch lingered, phantom hands around my neck. I crossed my arms over my chest, standing out of sight beneath the bone archway, the skulls of Draki's victims grinning at me. Minutes later, I heard him call out my name.

Jarl Lira of Drakin. Consort of the Dragon.

I wanted to run, but there was nowhere to go. The tunnels were locked up tight and heavily guarded. There was no other way out except to leap from another cliff, and I didn't expect I'd survive such a feat again. Besides, Draki held all the cards now—the fate of Glasnith and everyone on it, including my brother; the lives of the children of Vaknavangur.

And Reyker. Always Reyker.

I threw open the doors and marched onto the balcony, a warrior preparing to fight a different sort of battle, one that would test the strength of my mind and soul. The sun had taken its leave not long ago, and the air was cold against my skin—I wore no coat, no cloak, only the gown that matched Draki's tattooed flesh, and my own warrior-mark of thorns. The staircase was three stories tall and wound in the center like a corkscrew, the perfect platform for Draki to display me to all his guests. I could feel them staring, judging me in the glittery wash of moonlight and torchlight. Head high, I descended the first step.

My gaze was fixed ahead, but I couldn't help glancing down. There was Draki, standing to the side of the stairs, watching me. There was his sea of followers—Dragonmen and servants, commanders and emissaries, lords and ladies. Anyone influential in Iseneld. Anyone whose power the Dragon could bend to his will and use to fortify his throne.

They were all going to die.

These were the faces I'd seen in the seeress's final vision, melting in floating petals as her soul slipped away. The noise of the gala faded, replaced by a buzzing in my ears, the rubbing of insect wings—death, preparing to swarm.

I'd only made it a handful of steps. My foot froze in midair.

At the bottom of the staircase, one face stood out from all the others. He was dressed formally in shades of gray and blue that matched his irises, and thin braids had been woven into his golden hair. His lips formed the syllables of my name, brows raised like he wasn't certain it still fit the girl he was gazing at.

The buzz grew louder until it consumed me. The world faded, until all I could see was the seeress's vision of Reyker's bloody face, all I could feel was his soul being ripped away.

My gifts rose up, unbidden. Unbound.

The pitchers on the tables shook as the water inside them spewed up like fountains. A howling wind knocked over glasses, blew out candles, sent guests stumbling. The staircase began to shake. The nails holding it together tore free from the wood, shooting out into the air and raining over the guests like a thousand bits of metal confetti. Gasps and shouts rang out.

The wood gave way under my feet.

CHAPTER 43

LIRA

I pulled as much wind to me as I could, forcing some of the planks to crash into the fortress instead of on the guests below, but I couldn't divert all of them. Everything was happening too fast—the staircase and balcony were falling, I was falling. I pushed another wave of wood into the fortress wall, but stray pieces landed on the people below.

Reyker caught me before I hit the ground, the force knocking him flat with me sprawled on top of him. Wooden planks tumbled around us, deflected by my shield of wind, and we lay in the middle of the debris. We both coughed and wheezed, trying to get back the breath that had been punched from our lungs by the impact. "What in bloody fates are you doing here?" I asked.

"I was invited."

"What?" I rolled off him and sat up. "You have to go, Reyker."

Where was Draki? I didn't see him. The gala was a cataclysm, with guests and Dragonmen searching beneath piles of wood, pulling out survivors. And corpses.

Reyker rose to his knees beside me. "I'm not leaving without you."

I drew back and looked at him. My hands slid up his arms, over his shoulders, ensuring he was real. "You came for me."

"Did you think I wouldn't?" He tilted his head, searching my face. His fingers grazed my warrior-mark, showing me it changed nothing. "As long as there is life left in me, I will always come for you."

"Brother." Draki was suddenly there, looming over us, an effigy carved from ice. "Thank you for protecting my consort, but I will take over from here."

Guests and servants and Dragonmen idled in the background, waiting to see what would happen. I was the Dragon's chosen consort, and I was kneeling in front of him, surrounded by the balcony I'd destroyed, embracing his brother.

"Come to me, Lira."

"Don't." Reyker tensed, reaching for his sword out of habit, but the guests had been forced to disarm before entering the gala. Only the Dragonmen carried weapons. "Not again, Lira. Stay with me."

Little warrior, Draki said, speaking inside my mind. *You will do as I say, or I will be forced to punish him for your disobedience.*

"I have to," I whispered. "I'm sorry." I let go of Reyker and went to the Dragon.

Draki wrapped his arm around my waist. Reyker and I were separated by only a few paces, yet it was like we were back on different ships, drifting farther apart.

"I am grateful my brother could be here on this eventful evening, as I name Jarl Lira of Drakin my consort. You have seen her display a fraction of the power she possesses. She will combine her powers with my own, and together we will ensure the dominance of Iseneld, seat of the Empire of the Dragon, center of the conquered world."

Despite the wrecked balcony, and a handful of injured and dead guests, the ceremony commenced. There were scattered cheers and whistles in the crowd, as if nothing strange had happened. Servants brought goblets to those not holding one already. I felt the stem of a glass slipped between my fingers. The wine sloshed in my trembling hand.

This was life with Draki—violence and death were an ordinary occurrence.

"Lira."

Speak the words.

I'd come this far. There was no turning back.

The speech Draki made me memorize filled my head, spilling from my mouth like vomit: "In front of these witnesses, these esteemed guests, I make my pronouncement. I, Jarl Lira, declare myself your consort, Emperor Dragon. I commit myself to you. All my earthly possessions are yours. My power is yours. I am a weapon to be wielded for the glory of Iseneld."

I'd avoided Reyker's gaze as long as I could, but I looked at him now. He was stunned, a wild animal caught in a hunter's snare.

This was why Draki invited Reyker tonight. To taunt and torment and humiliate him, in front of anyone who might consider allying with the Dragon's brother. A show of force, to convince Reyker and the rest of them who was truly in control of Iseneld. And I was helping him do it.

Say the last line, or I will break him.

I wanted to live. I wanted Reyker to live. I did not want to belong to the Dragon.

I could not have all three of these things.

"I give myself wholly and willingly," I said. "My heart, my soul, and my body belong only to you, Emperor Dragon."

One of Draki's commanders whooped with glee, raising his goblet in a toast, and others followed suit, drinking to our union. My goblet slipped from my fingers and crashed to the ground, a maroon puddle spreading across the dirt. Draki tipped my chin up, his mouth descending on mine to seal the promise I'd made.

"Lies!" Reyker dove at the nearest Dragonman, stealing his sword before anyone could stop him. "Jarl Lira is an illusion. She is Lira of Glasnith, and she is no one's possession. She speaks your words under duress. You hold her homeland and her brother hostage, you use the love she and I share to control us."

A hundred Dragonmen circled closer, weapons raised, but Draki waved them off. He glanced at me, and asked somberly, "Is this true, Lira?"

Deny him, or I will chain him to the floor of our bedchamber and make him watch you consummate your pledge.

"No!" I shook so violently, only Draki's arm around my waist kept me on my feet. "He is mistaken. I feel nothing for Reyker Lagorsson. He means nothing to me."

"Defy him, Lira!" Reyker stalked back and forth, sword at the ready. A sword that would turn to dust as soon as it struck Draki. "I won't let him hurt us anymore, I promise you."

"He means—"

Say it to him, *Lira. Look at him. Make him believe it, or I will make him suffer.*
Draki filled my head with images of all he would do.

"I don't love you, Reyker." I spoke through stiff jaws that fought against
every word. "I never did. I tricked you. My heart has always belonged to
the Dragon. He is the one I love. You are just a weak, foolish little lordling,
a puppet controlled by a better man. How could I love someone with a
soul as tainted as yours?"

Reyker's steps faltered.

Doubting me, as I had doubted him. Barely. Briefly. But enough to
cut deep.

Enough to make the Dragon smile. "Whatever you think passed between
you is over, brother. Lira will rule at my side. She will share my bed this night,
and every night after. She will bear me magiska daughters and sons, jarls and
queens and future emperors. Everything she is, every part of her, is mine."

Reyker's breaths rattled through him, his pupils widening into black
holes. His battle-madness—Sjaf's gift—was a beast inside him, threatening to rip free.

"Now, my loyal Sword of the Dragon, you will channel that rage and
do as I command. Ride to the Fjordlands. End the pathetic scourge of the
Fjull Uprorsmund. Bring me the head of their leader, Solvei Snorrisdottir."

"If I don't?"

Draki's grip on me tightened. When he spoke inside my mind this
time, I knew Reyker heard him too. *Then I will take what I need from this
consort, dispose of her, and find myself another.*

Because if Draki could not have me, no one would.

Reyker laughed, turning to the crowd. "Behold, your fearless sovereign
who uses his consort as a shield because he is too cowardly to face his kin."
He pointed his sword at Draki's chest. "What's the matter, *brother*? Are
you frightened that I've finally uncovered the secret to making you bleed?"

The Dragon flinched.

It was barely perceptible, but it was there—Draki, who feared nothing,
was worried Reyker would figure out how to kill him. And that meant
there *was* a way.

I wasn't the only one who saw it. Murmurs traveled through the ranks of Draki's guests.

"Fear is a mortal weakness, and I am no mortal." Draki let go of me and drew his sword. "Shall we take this fight to the Blood Ring?"

"I prefer to fight in the open, where men and gods can bear witness."

Reyker lunged, and Draki met him, their swords ringing like bells as they clashed. People scrambled out of the way of the chaos of blades, the brothers swinging and stabbing and parrying with unearthly speed.

It quickly became clear who was the better swordsman. They were both fast, but Reyker was more agile, his strikes precise and graceful, his body flowing like a stream in contrast to Draki's brutal, godlike strength. Reyker swung again, a blow that could have sliced Draki's face in half if he were mortal, but Reyker stopped the blade just before it met flesh.

Reyker grinned.

Draki kicked him, and Reyker flew backward, landing in the wrecked pile of wood that had been the balcony.

My gifts thrummed to life. I lifted the balcony's nails from where they lay scattered on the ground, sent a cloud of broken stairs flying on a gust of wind, aiming them all at Draki. Metal and wood slammed into him, exploding into splinters and dust.

Draki's gaze scraped over me. He spread his arms wide and addressed his guests. "Now my consort will show you more of what she can do, and prove the Dragon's might." He jerked his head at me. "Again."

That was nothing, little warrior. You disappoint me.

I didn't care that I was helping his performance, that he'd stoked my rage on purpose to incite my war gift. The power in my blood bubbled up, demanding release. I whispered to the earth under Dragon's Lair, and the ground shook. Cracks formed in the dirt, opening wide enough to swallow the tables of decadent food and expensive casks of wine, and pockets of guests who weren't fast enough to escape the spreading fissures. A hole opened beneath Draki, but he didn't fall. He seemed to hover an instant, and then he was standing on solid ground a few paces away without so much as shifting a muscle.

More, I had to use more. There had to be a way to hurt him.

I looked up to the clouds speckling the sky above the fortress. Reaching out, I sent one into a spin, drawing down a narrow column from the cloud's center. Dropping it on Draki's head. The swirling funnel sucked up broken stairs and dishes and dirt, spiraling around the Dragon. He stuck a single finger into the whirlwind and it recoiled, dissipating.

A strangled howl leaked from my lips. More, I could do more.

Reyker called my name.

"Put my brother in chains," Draki said to his Dragonmen.

Unless you can stop them.

Clenching my fists, I beckoned the horses. All of them. There hadn't been room in the stables for those the guests had ridden here, so most were tied up around the buildings. They reared and shrieked, jerking free from their ropes, and stampeded toward Draki and his men. Like he was a boulder in a river, the horses parted around Draki in two waves crashing to either side, straight into the crowd.

Screams shattered the air. The stomp of hooves, the crunch of bones.

"Lira! Stop!" Reyker's voice floated to me from far away. He ran toward me, but Dragonmen surrounded him, and he was forced to fight.

Draki locked eyes with me.

Are we flirting or feuding? Do you want to fight me, or do you want to fuck me? I doubt you even know. But soon, we will have plenty of time for both.

I tasted blood in the air, the reek of death. My senses were inflamed, spanning out across the distance in search of a weapon.

There—water. Not the sea, which was too far below. But up, high above, was moisture I could wield. It was heavy. It resisted.

If you can knock me down, I might let you have one last night with my brother before I send him off to kill my enemies. Maybe I will send him after your brother. Do you think he would ever forgive himself? Could you still love him if he put a blade through Garreth's back?

I pulled hard, commanding the water to come to me. My blood was boiling in my veins. I felt trickles of it drip from my nose, my ears, my mouth. Tears of blood streaked down my cheeks. I threw my head back and screamed.

The water came.

CHAPTER 44

LIRA

It started with a creak. Followed by a rumble. Then a roar.

It was a tidal wave of snow, careening down from the summit of the nearest mountain, flattening trees, sweeping across the northern side of the lava field. Screams rang out as the white wave crashed over half of Dragon's Lair. Buildings broke apart. People turned and ran, but they were sucked beneath the barrage of snow.

I didn't see it take Draki. One moment he was in its path, the next he had vanished.

Reyker appeared beside me, grabbing my hand, startling me out of my stupor. We ran for the fortress, but we'd never make it. With what little power I had left, I managed to push some of the snow back, enough to keep it from drowning us. Snow surged around our legs, burying us up to our chests.

The war gift droned within me. I closed my eyes and shivered. *What have I done?*

"Lira?" Reyker wiped away the blood on my face.

"I'm all right." I opened my eyes and saw a pearlescent plain where a crowd had stood. "I killed them. All of them."

I made the seeress's vision come true.

"Most of them deserved to die," he said. He shifted as much as he could, loosening the packed snow, and then he began to dig us out.

"How many?" On the other side of Dragon's Lair were clusters of people who had scaled the fortress or the cliffs in time—a fraction of the Dragonmen and guests who'd attended. In my mind, I saw the various faces of servants who'd brought me food and filled my bath, the young women who'd helped me into my gown and fixed my hair only hours ago. "Two hundred souls? Were none redeemable? You lived here once, and your mother. Hilde, Andrithur—"

"Stop." Reyker paused his digging to cup my cheeks with icy hands. "What you're feeling now, I've felt it myself, many times. When this is over, I will mourn with you. I will rage and scream and weep with you. But first, we have to get out alive."

"He's not dead, is he?" I searched the shroud of white coating the land, as if I could see beneath it.

"No." Reyker pulled himself free and hauled me out after him. He looked toward the far side of the lava field, the section that hadn't been buried by the avalanche, where a small army stood in formation. The Mountain Renegades.

With them were four massive creatures, furry as wolves, their heads crowned with ram-like horns. Ice demons. Skrikflaks.

One of those things had brought Stalwart Bay to ruin. One had cracked a glacier. What could four of them do?

"Hurry," Reyker said, and then we were running toward that army, sinking up to our knees every few steps, pulling each other out again.

The surviving Dragonmen shouted and drew their weapons, trekking across the snow toward the Renegades. Their contingent was small, but vicious—they would die fighting for Draki, taking as many of his enemies with them as they could, loyal to their master until the end.

In the distance, the skrikflaks lifted their heads, arched their necks, and began to shriek, a cacophonous chorus that shook the earth. What was left of the lava field shattered. Reyker and I pressed our hands to our ears as the block of sound rolled across the snow, over us, past us. Slamming into the fortress.

The walls of Dragon's Lair groaned and snapped like brittle bones. The whole structure, every building from one side of the cliffs to the other, came down in an eruption of smoke and debris.

There was a pause, like a held breath, and then the ground trembled. The cracks I'd made with my earth gift spread, widening into crevasses, and the land could no longer hold itself aloft. With a thunderous *boom*, the cliffs themselves crumbled, swallowing the rubble, dropping every trace of the fortress into the sea.

It didn't stop. The ground kept falling, and the land behind us caved in. The end of the earth chased us, growing closer, so close I felt dirt and snow give way beneath my heel. We ran, lungs burning, legs straining, until the skrikflaks' shrieks fell silent and the shaking ceased.

Reyker and I slowed to catch our breaths, and a mad laugh escaped me, seeing how close the drop-off was, how close we'd come to falling.

Dark laughter joined mine.

Poised on the cliff's ragged edge, a hundred paces away, halos of dust and dirt swirling around him but never touching him, was the Dragon. Lips twisted into a snarl. Eyes gleaming. His followers were dead, his kingdom gone.

Because of us.

"The secret to killing him is in my soul, in one of my buried memories," Reyker said. "How quickly could you find it?"

The Dragon stalked toward us with the slow, sleek motions of a predator craving blood. With the fixation of a god, seeking retribution.

"Not fast enough," I said.

Reyker nodded, as if this was the answer he'd expected. "Then you have to run."

The Renegade army advanced across the snow, cavalry and infantry marching for the furious Dragonmen, but they traveled over broken chunks of lava rock and snowdrifts so deep the horses and warriors had to wade through them. They were too far to come to our aid, and my gifts were too depleted to clear a path. I'd never reach their lines before Draki stopped me. "He won't let me go, Reyker. He won't let either of us go. I'm staying with you."

"Lira—"

"I lied." I wrapped my arms around his neck, filling my vision with him so I wouldn't have to see what was coming for us. "Everything I said before. I didn't mean it. I only wanted to save you."

"I know." He leaned his forehead against mine. "I wish we'd made it onto that ship. I would have run with you to the edge of the world and beyond."

I kissed him with the force of my fear, our chests pressed together, our hearts beating the same fierce rhythm. We held each other tight, and I promised myself I wouldn't let go. If Draki took Reyker, I would follow; if Draki killed him, I would die by his side.

But when the Dragon came, he tore us apart, throwing me in one direction and Reyker in the other. I hit the snow so hard I sank. Digging, clawing, I had to crawl my way out, until I was lying on top of the snowbank.

The Renegade army was closer—I could see Solvei leading them, riding atop one of those horned ice demons—but still not close enough.

Draki and Reyker were fighting not far from me. Blood and furrowed snow marred the space, a map of violence painted across the white canvas.

Reyker's knuckles were swollen, his clothes torn. Punches and kicks that would have leveled a mortal man did nothing to Draki. The best Reyker could do was dodge Draki's attacks, but some of the Dragon's strikes still landed, and each one sent Reyker sprawling. They shouted and cursed at each other, hurling insults as if this were an ordinary brawl between brothers.

"You wreck my home, steal my consort, and bring an army of traitors to my door, after all I have done for you? I left you your precious Vaknavangur. I could have destroyed it, but I kept it safe, waiting for the day you join me. I spared all but one of its children. I allowed you a final night with Lira to say your goodbyes. All of this I did for *you*, Reyker, you ungrateful little prig. But you do not deserve my mercy. You do not deserve to call me brother."

Draki swung his fist.

Reyker ducked. "Have you finally grown the balls to kill me, Draki? Do it then!"

"I will send you to join our father in the Mist, where Ildja and her Destroyers feast on the flesh of cowards."

With a growl, Reyker barreled into Draki, the two of them falling, wrestling in the snowbank. Reyker kept punching his brother in vain as they rolled, until Draki was on top, one hand around Reyker's throat, the other curled into a fist. Reyker shifted his head out of the way just before Draki's punch slammed down into the snow hard enough to have split his skull in half.

I clambered to my feet, throwing myself at Draki, wrapping my hands around the fist hovering over Reyker's head. "Draki, stop!"

Draki's lips curved. "Finish what you started, little warrior, or I will. Make Reyker believe that your love was a lie."

Reyker hissed. "I would never believe—"

"Not with words," Draki said, looking from Reyker to me. "With your gifts. I have seen what Eyvor allows you to do. Not just read a soul, but shred it. You can twist his memories, his emotions. You can make him believe that everything you shared was a ploy, and I am the one you truly love."

It was the same thing Veronis threatened to do to me if I didn't obey him—to take everything Reyker and I had shared and poison it.

Reyker struggled against Draki's grip. "Lira, don't you dare! I would rather die."

"Of course you would, you noble fool." Draki slapped Reyker's cheek. "Do as I ask, Lira. Or I will do worse."

"You won't kill him," I said with more conviction than I felt. "I've seen into your soul. He's your family, and you don't want him to die."

With a twirl of his fingers, Draki produced a small, delicate blade—the stiletto he used to carve his mark into the magiskas he collected. "I do not wish to deprive myself of the lively diversions Reyker provides. But death is not the only solution." He tapped the stiletto against the black flames tattooed over Reyker's right eyelid. "I'm afraid the warrior-mark I gave you is too subtle. We can do better. A Star of the Dragon where it cannot be missed. A constant reminder of who owns you."

I had to close my eyes to steady myself.

Reyker has no skoldar.

How could he? There were no magiskas left in Iseneld, none on Glasnith willing to give him one besides me—and I couldn't, because I'd already marked Eathalin.

"I gave you so many chances, Reyker," Draki was saying. "I did everything I could to strengthen you, to bring you to my side, but I've grown tired of waiting. Your power will be mine to wield, as it was always meant to be."

Across the backs of my eyelids, I envisioned Reyker's future: his gaze unfocused, his will stolen. His sword no longer mine, but Draki's once more. A life Reyker hated and feared, a nightmare he would never wake from.

A choice that was not a choice.

I opened my eyes and found Reyker watching me, shaking his head. "The Dragon can steal my mind, my body. But if you let him break my soul, I am nothing. You might as well kill me yourself."

On the field of snow, the two armies reached one another, and a song of swords played on the wind. Two horses broke off from the rest to come to us. Two warriors? Even if the entire Renegade force came, it would not be enough.

"Your indecision bores me." Draki sat on Reyker's chest and slid the stiletto through Reyker's right brow, opening the skin, leaving a jagged trail of red as the blade sliced down his cheek to his jaw. "To complete the mark, this eye will have to go," Draki said, forcing Reyker's eyelid open, touching the blade's tip to the black circle of Reyker's pupil.

Reyker's face was bloody, as it was in the vision of his death the seeress showed me. Panic, sharp and maddening, took hold. The world slowed, and a single thought flared in my mind: *I will not be Aillira.*

A woman who had everything torn from her and still ended up a slave to a vengeful god.

I'd watched my home burn, lost my brother, my father, my dearest friend, and promised myself to someone I loathed. Reyker wouldn't stop fighting for me, and Draki would kill Reyker before he'd let us be together. But I had the power to stop it. I could buy him safe passage out of the Dragon's reach. I could buy him time to remember how to kill his brother.

All it cost was our love.

I grabbed Draki's wrist. "If I do as you ask, you will let him go. Not just for today. For good. Exile him if you must, but you will not touch him again."

The Dragon nodded. "So long as he doesn't set foot in Iseneld, I will not harm him. On the blessed life of my goddess-mother, you have my word."

It was the word of a madman, a monster, yet there was weight to his pledge. He would honor it, because even a monster like Draki had to live by a code, otherwise he could never have garnered such loyalty.

"Then we have a deal."

Draki pinned Reyker to the ground. Blood slipped down his cheek. He writhed and kicked, but Draki's grip was unshakable. "Gods-damn you, Lira. You cannot do this to me. I will never forgive you!"

I offered him a final smile, his face blurring as tears welled in the crevices of my eyes. "You aren't supposed to, my love. That is the point."

I pressed my palm to his chest.

The black river of flames roiled around me. Somewhere in its depths was the secret to executing the Dragon, but I sensed so many memories beneath the surface, things Reyker had buried to keep his sanity. Too many for me to sort through in what little time I had.

He would find a way to reach it without me. He had to.

High in the canyon walls of Reyker's soul, jewels of memory glistened, dripping with love and longing, passion and anguish. Every moment we'd spent together, the sweet and the bitter, the pleasure and pain we'd suffered to keep each other alive.

This was another one of those moments.

It was instinctual, what must be done, born of all the hours I had spent here. I ran my fingertip over each memory, changing nothing, simply pushing a tendril of doubt into the way he viewed them—suspicion that I was not what I seemed. It spread like an infection, casting shadows where there had been only sunlight, fear where there had been unshakable faith.

The only one I changed was today. I plucked the memory from its place and circled my finger over it, weaving a different story, one where the balcony did not collapse. Where the lies I told Reyker became truths— that I loved the Dragon, not him, and always had. In this version, I smiled as I promised myself to Draki, kissed him with the fervor of the last kiss Reyker and I shared.

A memory I erased.

The black river splashed and tugged at me as I worked. Even now, Reyker fought me. He would not give up so easily; it was not in his nature. It was why I loved him.

As long as there is life left in me, I will always come for you.

To keep him alive, I would have to change his nature.

"Sleep, Reyker," I whispered, waving my hand over the water. "Shut down your mind."

The river went still.

"When you wake, you will leave Iseneld's shores. You will stay far away from the Dragon." I thought of the seeress's curse, and added, "You will forget me. You will forget *us*."

A shudder rocked the canyon. Fractures spiderwebbed across the cliff face, and the jewels studding it broke free, raining down around me, sinking into the black river. Everything we'd been to each other, every moment we'd shared. Buried. Gone.

A breeze whistled through the chasm, followed by a sigh that sounded like my name. Then, silence.

My wolf, I thought, but did not let him hear.

I'm sorry.

CHAPTER 45

REYKER

His eyes opened to a bleak gray sky.

A young woman bent over him, her hair the deep burgundy of wine, her eyes the bright green of spring. "I only wanted to save you," she said.

He loved this woman.

And he hated her.

He couldn't even remember her name. When he reached for her, she broke into pieces and vanished like a startled flock of birds.

A blade swung into view, aimed at his head.

Reyker rolled out of the way. He was unarmed and half blind, one eye filled with blood. The Dragonman's axe was on him again.

Let me out, a familiar voice whispered.

He welcomed the black river into his muscles and veins, into his mind, more open to it than he'd ever been before.

He ducked beneath the falling axe and punched the Dragonman in the throat, crushing his windpipe. When a second Dragonman came for him, Reyker shifted away from the sword, slipping inside the warrior's guard, slamming his palm into the man's face. Nasal bones crunched as they were forced upward, piercing the Dragonman's brain.

Pure ecstasy sang through his blood, heady and sharp, and he gasped. He smiled.

More, the black river cried.

Two riders were nearing him—Brokk and Alane. The magiska rode atop Vengeance, and Reyker lifted her from the saddle when she was close enough.

"Oh, Reyker," Alane exclaimed, taking in his bleeding face. "You need a healer."

"Where did they go?" Brokk was searching the ruins of Dragon's Lair. "They were just here. Did that bastard take her?"

Reyker didn't know who Brokk meant, nor did he care. There was a battle happening, and he had to be part of it. He snatched the axe from the Dragonman he'd killed, then mounted his horse and kicked her flanks. Vengeance snorted and bucked, as if the beast did not recognize him. Reyker kicked again, and this time the horse obliged, racing toward where the Renegades and Dragonmen fought. Brokk and Alane shouted after him, but their voices faded quickly under the clang of weapons, the pound of his heart beneath his ribs.

It should have taken longer to cross the snow, but Vengeance had once belonged to a seeress, had lived in a decaying land touched by mad gods—the mare had as much magic in her as Reyker did, and soon he was wading into the clash of bodies. The black river flowed through him, down the arm wielding the axe, and the blade fed his gnawing hunger, splitting flesh, cleaving skulls, spraying blood.

The remaining Dragonmen surrounded him, all of them wanting to be the one to kill the Sword of the Dragon.

None of them landed a single blow.

When it was over, he dismounted and prowled among the bodies, kicking them to see who cried out, finding those who still clung to life. He brought his boot down on their backs, cracking their spines. The feel of these men breaking beneath his foot made him shiver with bliss.

"Enough, Lagorsson. They are dead. They belong to the soul-eater now."

Reyker looked up at Jarl Solvei. She rode on the back of her skrikflak, dressed in armor and a horned helm. She wasn't what most people would call beautiful, but she was like that beast she rode—fierce, intimidating, a force worth bowing to. For the first time, he wondered what it would be like to take her to bed, this woman who was as big and strong as he was, who commanded such loyalty and respect.

Her brows furrowed. "Stop eyeing me that way, lordling, you are not my type. Where is your woman?"

"Who?"

She grunted in disgust and turned to address her waiting warriors. "Dragon's Lair has fallen. Its soldiers are dead. The Dragon has fled with his tail between his legs." Renegades cheered. Solvei raised a hand to silence them. "But Draki has many tricks he has yet to play. He will return. We must be ready when he does."

"We must leave Iseneld." Reyker spoke without thinking, but once the words were out, they seemed right. "Draki will search for us in the Fjordlands. We cannot stay there."

"Leave the country we are fighting to reclaim?" Solvei's sharp gaze narrowed on him. "What sort of idiot does that?"

"The one who lives to fight another day. The one who lives long enough to discover the secret to killing the Dragon."

The Renegades glanced at one another, then at their leader.

"All right, Lagorsson," Solvei said. "Your last plan was a success, so I will grant you the benefit of the doubt. Indulge us. Where should we go?"

Reyker's smile was a gruesome thing, his skin coated in blood—his own, and the many he'd killed this day. "Somewhere unholy. The only place the Dragon fears to tread. The Haunted Isles."

⁑

The caravel's sails caught the wind and launched it far ahead of the other longships as they eased out of the fjord, into open sea, where fog hung over the surface like damp cobwebs. Beads of water clung to Reyker's hair and misted his skin. He stood at the gunwale, a bandage wrapped around one eye, distorting his vision. The slice on his face and the abrasion on his eye were already healing, another useful aspect of his gift that was stronger in his homeland. A weapon of the gods was no good if it could not mend quickly from the damage it accrued.

The ship passed over Eyvor, and the serpent remained on the ocean floor, not bothering herself with those leaving Iseneld. The sea unfurled before the bow, an endless ribbon of blue-gray frothed with white. Their destination wasn't far.

Steeped in mystery and superstition, the Haunted Isles were an archipelago a few leagues off Iseneld's coast. It took a fleet to move an army there, which meant they would see Draki coming.

And he would come for them. Of that, Reyker was certain.

"We grew up telling stories of how the Haunted Isles are cursed," Brokk said, leaning against the gunwale beside him. "Giant trolls. Man-eating fish who've grown legs to walk upon the land. Murdered witches who return to their fleshly bodies every full moon and brew mead from the blood of unfaithful husbands."

"Then it is good you have no wife."

"Hmm." Brokk glanced across the deck to Alane.

Reyker grinned knowingly at his friend. "Draki's soldiers have heard these same stories. We can use the isles' reputation to keep the Dragonmen away, and to run them off when they attack. Even the Dragon avoids the isles, wary of the spirits of the *volvur* he massacred there."

"So you say, and Solvei agrees. Though she's not happy about leaving Skrim behind."

There wasn't room on the isles for the skrikflaks to roam, so they'd been released into the mountains of the Fjordlands, where they belonged. The Renegades couldn't take their horses, either, so he'd left Vengeance with a family Solvei trusted, hoping to return for the mare. Someday. If he lived to see the end of this war.

Brokk cleared his throat. "You still haven't mentioned what happened in Dragon's Lair. You haven't spoken of her at all."

"Who?"

"*Who?*" Brokk glared at him. "Lira! The woman you claim to love, the one you risked all our lives to save."

"Lira." The foreign name tasted caustic on his tongue. Pain resonated through his temples as memories stirred, fuzzy and dim, as if from ages ago. He'd loved a woman by that name once, and it had cost him much. She'd made him weak. She'd played him for a fool. "Lira made her choice. She chose the Dragon. She's of no concern to me anymore." The words felt perfunctory, like they belonged to someone else, a written script rather than a natural thought.

"She did not choose the Dragon. He took her from you. Alane saw it. She saw—"

"I do not care what she saw!" The black river slid into Reyker's arm, took hold of his fingers, closed them around Brokk's throat. "Speak of the woman again and I will kill you!"

Brokk blinked at him. Alane cried out. Renegades reached for their weapons.

Reyker wrenched his hand back. "Brokk. I'm sorry. I didn't mean—"

"Save it, lordling." Brokk turned and stomped to the other side of the caravel, as far from Reyker as he could get. The Renegades sheathed their swords and axes, but eyed Reyker warily, whispering to one another.

Reyker stared at his hands. He'd never lost control so quickly, so completely. Never attacked someone he cared for on purpose. The black river inside him hungered, and it didn't care whose blood it was fed. It took effort to leash it.

He'd grown tired of leashing it.

He stood alone in the stern as the Haunted Isles came into view, stretched along the sea like floating corpses. A cursed place, befitting a cursed man.

Something cold touched his chest, and he reached for it, finding a circle of silver. A medallion, carved with Glasnithian words and symbols.

I only wanted to save you, a ghost murmured in his mind.

"I cannot be saved." He ripped the medallion from his neck, hurling it as far as he could, watching it sink below the waves. And then he forgot who he had spoken to, and why, yet he said it again because it was true. "I cannot be saved."

CHAPTER 46

LIRA

The tunnels beneath the lava field went farther than I ever imagined. Draki didn't bother with a torch. Those serpent eyes of his must have been able to pierce the darkness, but I could see nothing. I tripped and stumbled into the walls, following the irritated sound of his footsteps, which could only be for my benefit, since the Dragon could move silently. It was one of many things that made it clear he wasn't human.

His stamina was another. We walked for hours, maybe days. My feet blistered. My legs felt boneless, and I slowed to a crawl. Eventually, my knees gave out and dropped me to the tunnel floor.

As I struggled to stand, Draki sighed. He lifted me into his arms, exuding annoyance, and I was too weary to protest. This close, I could just make out the shape of his face, a shadow deeper than the darkness surrounding it. "Why did you make me do that to him?" I finally asked. "Why do you take such pleasure in hurting him?"

I didn't expect an answer. The quiet stretched out long enough that I'd begun to nod off when he spoke. "Because he had everything given to him from the day he was born. A mother and father who cared for him, a birthright he had not earned, the respect and adoration of the villagers. He never had to fight for anything. It would have made him a terrible warrior and a terrible lord."

"Don't ask for my pity, Draki. You won't get it."

"This is not about pity. I do not regret the hardships I faced, only that the world is built to favor those who are born lucky. I was given nothing. I honed my strength, raised an army, led them and fought beside them. I took what I wanted with my own hands. I earned everything I have through might and bloodshed, and I have turned Iseneld into a nation of warriors instead of a nation of lords, as I will do for the rest of the countries I conquer. I forced Reyker to be the kind of man who could survive in this new world I created." Though I could not see them, I felt his eyes cut to me, my nerves prickling beneath his gaze. "Love makes him weak. His affection for you will get him killed, but losing you will harden him. It will strengthen him."

"You were born half god. You don't find that to be a lucky advantage?"

His laughter rustled my hair, brushed across my neck. "I have paid a heavy price for immortality. Any gifted mortal willing to pay could become as I am."

"What price?" This time he said nothing, and I thought of that sword in Draki's wardrobe, their father's sword, with Reyker's flames etched into the blade. I thought of Vaknavangur, how Draki had finished rebuilding it instead of tearing it down—*waiting for the day you join me*, Draki told Reyker. In the silent space, understanding took shape. "You think if Reyker suffers enough, he'll become like you. That he'll lose all hope and be willing to pay some awful price to be part god, and the two of you will conquer the world side by side."

"Such a clever creature you are, my pet."

"You were never going to mark Reyker with your Dragon Star. You tricked me." I shifted in Draki's arms, trying in vain to keep his skin from touching mine. "But you're wrong about him. He won't be like you. Ever."

"No? I suspect he is broken beyond repair now. When he comes to me, I will have you to thank."

The air had grown stifling and sweat trickled along my spine. *Dear gods, what have I done to you, my wolf? What have I done to us?*

"Rest, little warrior. You will need it."

My head fell against his shoulder, suddenly too heavy to lift. "Are you going to kill me?"

"Do you want me to?"

"No." Unlike before, the answer came instantly. Maybe I deserved to die, in payment for all those who'd lost their lives because of me, but it would not bring them back. The only honorable choice was to keep fighting, foiling Draki at every turn, giving my life only if it served to stop him.

In the dark, I couldn't tell the difference between when my eyes were open and when they were closed. I wasn't aware I had slept until I realized I had woken.

There was light here, torches flickering in sconces. The bed beneath me was piled with furs, the ceiling and walls around me carved of ice. This was where I'd first discovered Draki's invincibility. He'd brought me back to the glacier.

There was nowhere to run, no way to escape, so I rose and walked across the frosted floor, through halls of ice, to where I knew Draki waited. In the Mountain of Fire, the scalding, pulsing heart of the Frozen Sun.

Heat poured from the crater, and the hollow space was bathed in red light. Draki turned when I entered, his expression grim. A woman stood beside him on the rocky ledge. She was unlike anyone I'd ever seen, her beauty unsettling. Her very presence shook me to my core. There was a living ice serpent wrapped around her throat like a torque, one decorating each of her wrists, all of them the same silvery-white hue as Eyvor. Her eyes were burning embers of black and gold. Her hair was a lava flow, the liquid fire dripping from her scalp, over her shoulders and down her back.

A goddess.

"Ildja," I whispered.

Draki's mother, the serpent-goddess, the eater of souls. The one who started the Gods' War by convincing her brother, the god of death, to seduce Aillira and destroy Veronis.

Ildja didn't seem to move, yet she was abruptly in front of me, circling, assessing. "You chose well, my son." Her voice was the music of crackling flames and boiling magma. "The Fallen Ones' vessel will prove quite useful in the war to come."

Something gleamed in her fist. A dagger made of ice.

It hadn't fallen into her fire.

Veronis's warning from when he first told me to go to Iseneld came back to me: *DO NOT LET HER TAKE THE KEY FROM YOU, OR ALL WILL BE LOST.*

My journey here. The trek across the wilderness. Quinlan's death. It hadn't been for nothing—it was much worse than that. Every struggle, every sacrifice, had resulted in my delivering this weapon of destruction right into Ildja's hands. The Fallen Ones had gambled on me, and I had failed.

"That's mine," I said, pointing at the dagger. The war gift swelled beneath my rib cage until my heart was a drum.

The goddess's gaze seared me. My eyes burned and watered, and I had to look away. "The key to the Fallen Ones' prison has always belonged to me," Ildja said. "It was misplaced after I gifted it to my son's father, a boon that bestowed him with immortality. The fool betrayed me, trading it for a healing potion."

"For his wife, who you poisoned." I'd overheard this in my vision from Aillira's Temple—Reyker's mother had been stricken, and his father had given the ice dagger to the Daughters of Aillira, in exchange for an elixir to save her.

"I offered him the world," Ildja said, "and he chose to remain a mortal and share his life with a mortal woman. I offered him a god to be his heir, and he chose his mortal son instead. You have done the same, choosing your mortal lover over the god who could give you everything."

"I chose the man I love."

"Love is fleeting. Mortals die. The strength of a god is forever."

"Forever is meaningless if you must spend it without the one you love." Which was exactly what I had done to Reyker—stolen his love to keep him safe and alive. My love for him had made me as selfish as the soul-eater.

"Meaningless?" Ildja cocked her head. "You sound like Veronis."

Draki observed us, crouched at the edge of the crater. Waiting for something. "They're here," he said.

A cloud of skeletal shadows with black-veined wings emerged from the crater and swarmed around us. Hundreds of creatures with emptiness where their faces should have been, with multiple heads and tails, and too many twitching limbs to count. The swish of their wings sounded like the rasp of parchment being rent in half, the rattle of bones in a jar.

Ildja smiled at them. "Your mortal Dragonmen failed you, Draki, but my soldiers will build you a new kingdom, even greater than your last one. An unstoppable army of Destroyers to dispatch your remaining enemies, secure your holdings, and conquer the countries beyond."

Destroyers. Demons of the nether-realms that dragged the souls of the damned into the Mist and tortured them. Ildja was releasing these monsters into the world. My world.

"You will not send those demons to Glasnith." The wind gusting over the glacier was strong, and I drew it to me, unleashing it on the goddess.

She caught it and slammed it back into me, hurtling me through the air. I collided with a wall of ice and slid down it. The impact jolted things inside me, but I made myself stand. I could feel the moisture running through the glacier, the vein-like rivers and streams. I tugged, and the whole glacier shuddered.

I could bring it down on our heads. If I could get the dagger away from Ildja, I could stab myself and tear the floor from beneath us, sending us all into the fire. Freeing Veronis. *This* was something worth dying for.

Ildja waved a dismissive hand at me. "Do not be ridiculous, Daughter of Aillira. I cannot be harmed within my own home, not even by your war gift." The goddess addressed her son. "As you warned, she is strong but far too spirited. I shall have to make some adjustments."

Draki's eyes grazed me with more sentiment than I thought him capable of. Reluctance. Resignation. He nodded, and Ildja's hand wrapped around my wrist, tight as a vise. Ildja's skin shifted from pale cream to the burnt-orange of a fire iron.

A scream burst from my lungs as my flesh burned, as the acrid scent of seared meat filled my nose and I realized what she was doing—burning away my *skoldar,* the mark of protection Reyker had given me to keep Draki from ensnaring my mind. Beneath the pain in my wrist was something deeper, a ripping that traveled through my chest. Threads tearing loose in my soul. Ildja was sundering the connection the *skoldar* had forged between myself and Reyker, and it felt like every inch of my body was filled with thorns, shredding me from the inside out.

This was how Reyker's mother had died.

Ildja removed her hand, and I collapsed in a heap, staring at my wrist. The skin was gone, leaving only charred muscle and bone. Through the fog of pain, I saw Destroyers drifting high above me, faceless phantoms crowding the space, waiting for me to die so they could snatch my soul and deliver it to the darkness. I watched Ildja give the dagger to Draki, and he kneeled next to me, brushing my hair aside. My mouth wouldn't do more than groan. I couldn't beg him to stop, though he read the plea in my eyes.

"This will not kill you, little warrior. The Fallen Ones' blood heals you too quickly. It also weakens my influence over you, so I must carve my mark into you again with Ildja's key. When it is done, your war gift will be stable. Your guilt and sorrow will be vanquished." His voice was gentle. He thought he was helping me.

I want them, I tried to cry. *My guilt, my sorrow—they make me human.*

With a final burst of strength, I snatched the dagger from his hand and stabbed beneath his collarbone. The blade did not shatter, but neither did it break the skin. It hit Draki with a leaden *thump* and skidded harmlessly down his chest. He shook his head at me. "How like my brother you are," he said. "We will fix that. I will fix you."

A gods' weapon was useless against the Dragon. What hope did Reyker or I have of stopping him?

Defeated, my arm fell limp at my side, and Draki peeled the dagger from my fingers. The blade slid behind my ear.

Reyker will kill you for this, I thought. But no, Reyker no longer remembered me. I was alone. No one was coming to save me.

As the dagger traced the lines of my scar, blood trickling down my neck, another flood of pain swelled within me, not a tearing this time, but a joining, like welding together two antithetical elements. A union of enemies. With this mark, I wasn't just Draki's possession, I was his tool. His thrall.

Something was seeping out of me—my will, my emotions? No, something deeper—the spark of life in my soul, the forces that drove me, the fire that made me *Lira.* It guttered.

Stop, stop, stop, I howled in my mind. *Sto*—

The fire. It died.

As was death's wont, there were no blurred lines, no detectable shifts. I was one girl, and then I was another—awakening inside that other girl's skin, with no care for who she'd been. Where that fire once lived there was only ash. I could think, but what point was there in thinking? I could speak, but had no use for words. My body ached, but that's what bodies did when things were broken. Pain was a temporary condition that could be ignored.

"Rise, Lira of Drakin."

Yes. That was my name.

The wound behind my ear tingled. My arms and legs obeyed.

"How do you feel?"

Such an odd question. "Alive," I answered. "Awake. Cold. In pain. Shall I list more sensations?"

"No. What do you feel for Reyker?"

My lips twitched. Strange. "Reyker Lagorsson of Iseneld. He is a man. Your brother. A warrior. Strong. Healthy. Blond hair, blue eyes. He sides with your enemies, Jarl Solvei Snorrisdottir and the Mountain Renegades. I feel nothing for him."

"Would you be willing to harm him? To kill him?"

"If you asked it of me, yes. I—" For some reason, I stammered. "I would kill Reyker Lagorsson."

The citrine-eyed half god glanced at the goddess made of fire. Both seemed pleased, though I wasn't certain why. "Do you know what it is I want you to do, Lira? What I once showed you would happen, just before you leaped from the cliffs on Glasnith?"

I sorted through memories, located the one he spoke of. "Yes."

"Do it, little warrior. Show me your devotion."

Devotion. Was that what drove me to kneel, to bow? He wished for me to worship him, and every shred of my being knew this was what I'd been created for, the only thing that mattered. So I did.

"You are my savior, my master," I told the Dragon. "You are my god."

ACKNOWLEDGMENTS

First, I have to thank Rick Bleiweiss for his support of this series, and for sending me an email after reading a draft of this book that read simply, "You are a very good writer." There's no higher form of praise than that, and it means so much to me.

To the people who helped this book be the best it could be: My editor, Madeline Hopkins, who always has the coolest ideas for how to make my manuscript better; my copyeditor, Ember Hood—formatting and grammar extraordinaire—who catches all my sloppy mistakes; managing editor Ananda Finwall, who makes sure my book goes out into the world dressed to the nines.

To the designers and artists who get my book noticed: Kurt Jones, who has probably sold more copies of this book than anyone with his gorgeous cover designs; Sean Thomas, for his amazing book trailers; Alana Kerr Collins and Tim Campbell, whose narrations of these audiobooks bring Lira and Reyker to life (I could listen to you both read the dictionary for hours).

To the people who promote my book and keep it from fading into obscurity: Mandy Earles, who always has some good news ready for me to share on social media, and is a blast to hang out with at book festivals;

Lauren Maturo and Jeff Yamaguchi, for all your hard work, but also for early morning donuts and expensive wine in cheap plastic cups; Greg Boguslawski and Roger Cox—who I'm dubbing honorary Southerners—for getting this series into bookstores.

A quick thank you to the rest of the Blackstone team not mentioned above: Craig and Michelle Black, Josh Stanton, Josie Woodbridge (who is always kind and patient when I send her things because I don't know where I'm supposed to send them), Stephanie Hall (my favorite cat lady librarian), Rob Erdmann, Bryan Green, Stephanie Stanton, Jesse Bickford, Amy Craig, Tom Williamson, Kathryn English, and Keith McFarland.

To Juliet Marillier, Erin Beaty, and Jessica Leake, who wrote beautiful blurbs for the first book—I will always be grateful. To my fellow writers I've met on this journey: Cadwell Turnbull, who is quite humble for someone so talented; Lani Forbes and Coco Ma, my YA fantasy Blackstone debut sisters; Catherine Ryan Howard and Nick Sansbury Smith, who let me talk their ears off about writing and assured me it gets easier; fellow debuts Alex Messenger and Robert Haller, who had no qualms admitting they were as clueless as I was (shh, don't tell anyone).

To all the bloggers, booksellers, and librarians who have recommended this series and helped spread the word—you are fantastic, and I can never thank you enough! To Jonathan Ley of LeyPhotography.com, whose photos and blog about hiking across the Icelandic highlands helped in the writing of this book. Also, to Genevieve Gagne-Hawkes and Beth Miller of Writers House, for being awesome.

To Katla, who is powerful and destructive and beautiful, just like her namesake. To Brock, who keeps me sane and happy and fed, and reminds me that it's okay to relax and join the real world now and then. Without you, none of this would be possible. (Also, for designing the badass Glasnith and Iseneld maps.)

And finally, to every reader who gives these books a chance. It's an honor to have you reading my words and sharing in Lira and Reyker's journey!